IN THE DESPERATE CLUTCH OF LOVE

At the mention of Satanta's name, Suzette's eyes widened. She knew what Kaytano was going to tell her. Hadn't she always known? From the first time she'd looked into Kaytano's black, beautiful eyes, it was as if she knew him. She started to speak, but Kaytano put his fingers to his lips, motioning her to remain silent.

Kaytano spoke. "The proud Satanta saw the pretty blonde child and fell in love with her. He was a respected young chief. Brave and daring. The girl w̲___ ___n to him and he immediately took her for his w___ ___ ___w months she was carrying his child. The g___ ___ ___nta, but she never got over her love f___ ___ ___een taken from. In June of 1853 ___

Suzette looked ___ ___es, Suzette, I'm Satanta's s___

"But Kayta___ ___ She fell silent. She was in love wit___ ___e who had killed Luke Barnes and the o___ ___wallowed and studied the handsome face she ___ ___uch.

was given
turned. In a
didn't hate Sali
for the sweetheart she'd once
the girl bore Sahmin a son.
at him, Kaytano nodded. "You
no."
no, he was . . . Sahmin
all the son of the savage
village. Sahmin and
loved so much

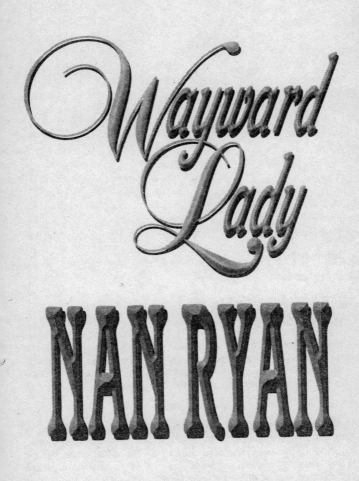

Wayward Lady

NAN RYAN

LOVE SPELL BOOKS NEW YORK CITY

LOVE SPELL®

February 1999

Published by

Dorchester Publishing Co., Inc.
276 Fifth Avenue
New York, NY 10001

ISBN 0-505-52298-5

The name "Love Spell" and its logo are trademarks of Dorchester Publishing Co., Inc.

Printed in the United States of America.

In memory of
My daddy
Glenn Howard Henderson
March 31, 1913 – May 18, 1984
A lifelong resident of Bryson, Jack County, Texas
and for
My mother
Roxy Bost Henderson
His faithful wife for fifty-one years.

Wayward Lady

1

Suzette Foxworth awoke with the first light of day. She smiled, stretched, and pushed back the bedcovers. In one fluid movement, she swung her long, slender legs over the edge of the bed and sat up. Padding barefoot across the room to her desk, Suzette lit the lamp and took her velvet-covered diary from the top drawer. Lifting the ribbon marking the last place she had written, Suzette sat down and began to write:

Today is May 17, 1871. My sixteenth birthday! Life could not be more perfect. Of all the places in the vast land, my home is on the glorious plains of North Texas, where wildflowers abound and blue stem grass as tall as my waist stretches as far as the eye can see. It is here, and only here, that I wish to spend all the rest of my life, and I am forever grateful that my mother and daddy chose to leave their home in Louisiana and come to Texas while I was still a child. If they had not, would I have met the only true love of my life?

I think not! Only in this wild, free, beautiful land could a man such as Luke Barnes be able to breathe. Luke! My handsome Luke of the curly red hair. Luke of the big green eyes that sparkle with excitement when he sees me. Luke of the wide shoulders and broad chest, long legs and trim hips. Luke! Luke! Luke!

Too excited to write more, Suzette slammed the book shut and put it back into the desk drawer. She dashed across the room to the tall bureau. Folded neatly on its scarred top was a bright red silk bandanna which made her smile. She picked up the soft scarf and proudly fingered the bold, blue "L" embroidered at one corner. She had worked painstakingly on the scarf for weeks, pushing the sharp, long needle through the embroidery hoops with an eagerness she usually didn't feel for such feminine chores.

It was a labor of love. Suzette didn't mind the pricked fingers or the frustration of getting the initial crooked twice and having to tear out the stitching. The bandanna was for Luke and she wanted it to be perfect. She was stubbornly intent on having the blue "L" stand out prominently on the red silk. She finally got the effect she was looking for and declared the bandanna finished and ready for presentation.

Suzette placed the colorful square on the bureau. She would give it to Luke at the party tonight. The two of them would slip away from the crowd and when they were all alone she would hand it to him. He would be very pleased and proud of her and he probably would insist on kissing her. The thought of his kiss made Suzette's cheeks grow warm and she closed her eyes and thought of her handsome sweetheart. Shivers ran up her spine. She opened her eyes, giggled, and pulled the long white nightgown over her head. Then she ran to the washstand and began splashing cold water over her face. Sputtering, she hastily patted her face dry and went to dress. Five minutes later she was tiptoeing down the long hall, her boots making little sound on the polished wooden floors. She sashayed into the big dining room and through the swinging door to the kitchen. There she stopped, her hand still on the door.

Her father, Jack County's only physician, sat quietly at the table, a steaming cup of coffee in front of him.

"Daddy." Suzette's voice was soft. Blake Foxworth turned his head. Seeing her, he smiled. Suzette, quickly noting the coat flung over the back of his chair, returned his smile and hurried to him. Forgetting momentarily that she was a grown woman, she dropped into her father's lap and put her arms around his neck. "Did you just get home?" she asked.

His arm, slender and tanned, encircled her narrow waist. "A child out on the Dillingham prairie came down with a high fever. Her mother was afraid of typhus." Blake pushed a thick lock of blond hair behind Suzette's left ear. "Luckily it was just a slight infection. The little girl's already much better."

"You need a partner, Daddy. I worry about you. You look so tired. Have you been having your headaches lately?" She cupped his beard-stubbled chin in her hand.

"No, no. Really. Let's forget about me. What are you doing up so early today?"

"Don't you know what day this is?"

"Hmm, let's see... it's May 17." He pretended to be puzzled. "No, I can't think of anything special about today."

"You're teasing me." She giggled and hugged his neck. "Can you believe it, Daddy? Sixteen years old! I'm a woman."

"I can't believe it, sweetheart. It seems like only a few days ago that I got my very first look at your little pink face. You were pretty from the beginning. Now you're beautiful."

"You think so? Honest?" Her big blue eyes were on his.

"I know so. You are lovely."

"You don't think I'm too tall and skinny? I mean, Mother's so little and dainty. I'm not very delicate, am I?"

Blake chuckled at her foolish anxiety. "My dear, lovely daughter, you are a tall, slender woman. I suppose you take your height from me. Frankly, I think it gives you a regal look that enhances your blond beauty."

"You mean it?"

"I do." He smiled warmly and touched the tip of her turned-up nose. "However, for one so regal and grown up, I would almost swear she forgot to brush her hair." He narrowed his eyes in mock disgust. In truth, nothing Suzette did displeased Blake Foxworth. He adored his only child and found it charmingly sweet that one day she was the mature seductress, flirting prettily with the young men; the next she was the tomboy, caring not at all how she looked, only how fast she could ride her beloved horse across the rolling plains. This morning was definitely one of the times she chose to ignore her appearance. In a pair of worn buckskin breeches and a cotton blouse that she was rapidly outgrowing, its bodice straining across her chest, she was obviously dressed for a horseback ride.

"Daddy, I didn't have time to fool with my hair. I'll wash it this afternoon before the party." Suzette jumped from his lap and poured herself a cup of coffee. Dropping down into a chair beside him, she said, "This is going to be the most wonderful party Jack County has ever seen, and I can't wait. Aren't you excited?"

"Of course I am, dear. And I hope that I can be here in..."

"Daddy! Don't you dare miss my party. I will never, ever forgive you. I don't care who picks tonight to have a baby or fall off a horse. I want you right here!"

"I'll be here for at least the last part, darling. Surely you remember I told you that General William T. Sherman has been sent by Washington to make a tour of the frontier forts. He will be at Fort Richardson this evening, and I've promised I'd help make up a delegation to meet with him."

Suzette made a face. "Why would you want to see him? He was a destructive Yankee in the War Between the States, wasn't he?"

Shaking his blond head, Blake said, "You've spent too much time with old Nate. Darling, the war has been over for six years. Don't you think it's time we forget about it?"

She touched a long scar at the side of her father's head, pushing back his thick hair to examine it. "Those Yankees left you with a scarred head and you tell me you can forget about it?"

Blake brushed her probing fingers aside. "Yes, I can. And

the meeting with General Sherman is most important. We've got to impress on him that something must be done about the Indians soon."

"Who's afraid of the Indians?" Suzette shrugged slender shoulders. "Nate says we've been as mean to them as they've been to us, and I'll just bet he's right. After all, they were here first, weren't they? Anyhow, I don't care about the Indians or the Yankees or your patients. This is the most important birthday of my whole life, and it's also important for another reason." Suzette folded her hands on the table and looked at her father, an impish grin lifting the corners of her mouth.

"Is that my cue to ask you what else is important about this day?" His voice was warm and teasing.

"You know me too well. The reason it is doubly important is that I've every reason to believe that on this historic May night, a certain Mr. Luke Barnes — who, by the way, agrees with you that I'm not too tall — will ask me to be his wife!"

The smile Blake Foxworth had worn throughout the conversation faded a little. "Suzette, I had no idea it was that serious between you two. Are you sure... I mean, dear, do you think you're in love with Luke?"

"How can you ask such a foolish question, Daddy? Of course I'm in love with Luke. Good Lord! How could I not be in love with Luke Barnes? He's only the handsomest, strongest, bravest, dreamiest, tallest... "

"Darling, I'm sure Luke is all of those things, but as your father, I'm more concerned with unimportant things, like: Can he support a wife? Will he take good care of you? Will he treat you right? Will he make you a good husband?"

"I think he will be the most wonderful husband in all the world and I just know our life together will be wonderful! Daddy, Luke kissed me on the lips at the church picnic last month and I knew right then that we were meant for each other. I think I'd like to be a June bride." She wore a dreamy expression.

"Suzette, I think Luke is a nice young man, but marriage is more than kissing at picnics. I have no idea what Austin

Brand pays Luke, but I'm not sure it would be enough to provide you with a home. Where would you live if you and Luke married? What would you do when Luke had to be gone on cattle drives for months at a time? What if you should become pregnant?"

Suzette impatiently pushed her chair back, the wooden legs scraping the polished floor. She stood up and laid her hand lightly on her father's shoulder. Leaning down, she kissed his left cheek and said, "Daddy, you worry too much about unimportant things. I'm off now. See you this evening. And you'd better be here!" Whirling, she bolted from the room and collided with her sleepy-eyed mother in the kitchen doorway. "Oops! Sorry, Mother. You're so little I almost didn't see you!" Suzette laughed at the startled expression on Lydia Foxworth's pretty face and gave her a quick hug before stepping around her and hurrying out.

"What is Suzette doing up?" Lydia put a hand in Blake's thick blond hair and gave him a quick kiss on the mouth. Blake grinned at his sleepy wife and pulled her down onto the lap his daughter had recently vacated.

Nuzzling her warm neck, he said, "She's going for an early morning ride, Lydia. Why are you up?"

"Blake, you shouldn't let Suzette go off by herself, especially at this hour. Sweetheart, you know Suzette. If she came upon a band of savage Indians, she'd try to become their friend." Lydia shook her dark head and pushed her hair from her eyes.

Rubbing his wife's back through her soft silk wrapper, he laughed. "You're so right, she probably would. Don't worry. I told Nate that any time our unpredictable daughter rides, he is to follow her if she refuses to let him ride with her."

"Poor good-natured Nate. I'll bet she leads him on a merry chase." Lydia sighed and yawned. "I do wish Suzette would try being more of a lady. I've told her time and again that it doesn't look nice for her to be wearing trousers and riding astride that big beast she so adores."

"Well, dear, I don't know about her being a lady, but it

appears she is becoming a woman. She tells me she is in love with young Luke Barnes and is expecting a proposal very soon, perhaps even tonight at her party."

"Such nonsense." Lydia dismissed it with a wave. "She's much too young; she has no idea what love is. Why are you looking at me like that, Blake?"

Smiling fondly, he kissed her soft cheek. "Darling, are you forgetting that you were barely seventeen when we got married?"

"That's entirely different. I was very grown up for my age. I knew exactly what I was doing."

Blake chuckled softly. "Lydia, you were a naive child when I married you. A beautiful, dark, irresistible child-woman. And you know what else? You still are." He kissed her ear and let his lips move back to the warmth of her neck.

"Blake," she giggled, "your behavior is not suited to the kitchen."

"You are so right. Let's go to our room."

A mild flutter of excitement started somewhere in Lydia's stomach. She whispered softly, "Darling, you've been up all night. Aren't you tired? Don't you want to go to bed?"

"Umm, bed is exactly where I want to go, but I want you in it with me." He lifted his head and looked into her dark eyes.

Her fingertips began to make circles on the white shirt covering her husband's slender chest and he knew she was rapidly weakening. Still she mildly protested, "Blake, the sun's coming up and I have so much to do to get ready for Suzette's party. I really should..."

His mouth covered hers in mid-sentence. He kissed her persuasively, lips warm and demanding. Melting against him, Lydia sighed and kissed him back. When the ardent kiss ended, Blake grinned and whispered, "Suzette can have her party tonight. Let's have ours now."

With that he rose, holding his wife in his arms, and walked from the kitchen. Lydia clung to his neck and covered his lean face with sweet, moist kisses. "Blake, you look so exhausted. Have you been having your headaches again?"

"My dear," he whispered against her dark hair, "there's only one part of my anatomy that is aching, and you alone can take away the pain."

Once in their big bedroom, Blake tiredly sat down on the edge of the unmade bed. While Lydia knelt on the floor and tugged off his high boots, Blake unbuttoned his shirt and removed it. His wife rose and took off her long silk wrapper, smiling at him. When she started around to the other side of the bed, Blake put out his hand, "Wait, don't get into bed yet, Lydia."

Puzzled, she said, "What is it, Blake?"

He pulled her small hand up to his lips and kissed her wrist. "Take off your nightgown." He released her hand and sat watching her.

"Whatever you say. You're the doctor," she teased as she pulled the soft nightgown over her head. "Satisfied?" she asked timidly, standing naked in front of him.

"Come here."

She took a step closer and Blake pulled her between his knees. His hands encircled her slim waist and he smiled up at her. "Satisfied?" he echoed. "You have no idea." His blue eyes filled with passion and he buried his face in the valley between her full, soft breasts. "You're thirty-five years old, yet you're more beautiful than ever. How could it be possible?"

Hugging his blond head to her, she kissed his hair and said affectionately, "Perhaps it's because you're an old man of forty-two and your eyesight is beginning to fail."

He kissed the undercurve of her left breast, then slowly pulled her down across the bed, moving with her. "Never in my life have I been able to see things so clearly," he whispered hoarsely. "I'm a very fortunate man, the most fortunate man I know. I love you, Lydia. I love you more today than when I married you." His lips covered hers and he kissed deeply while his long arms bound her to him.

Lydia gladly yielded to his heated kisses and clung to him. Through slitted eyes she could see the sun streaming in the tall open windows over Blake's shoulder. In minutes it would be day and she had a million things to do to prepare for Suzette's party. She closed her eyes, shutting out the sun and willing her cares away. "Blake," she whispered against his ear.

"Yes, my love?" He lifted his head to look down at her.

Her dark hair had fanned out around her small, lovely face, and her dark, expressive eyes were smoldering now. Her heavy, bare breasts were rising and falling with her rapid breathing. She smiled and murmured, "If you love me so much, please take off your trousers and show me."

They laughed together as two pairs of eager hands went to the waistband of his black trousers. It was more than an hour later when Lydia kissed her sleeping husband's mouth and stole from their bed, her face still flushed, her lips swollen from his kisses, her legs weak with satisfaction.

Suzette whistled as she swung her saddle down from the wall of the tackroom. Her mother constantly chastised her about this habit, saying that young ladies were not supposed to whistle, that it was a distinctly masculine trait. The first time her mother mentioned it, Suzette had frowned down at Lydia and shrugged her slender shoulders. "Mother, I'm beginning to think that everything in this world of ours is meant only for men to enjoy. It's not fair and I won't have it. When I'm happy, I like to whistle. I'm getting better at it all the time, and it just doesn't make sense that I shouldn't be allowed to do something that is so much fun and completely harmless."

Lydia had sighed and said, "I know, dear. It does seem foolish, but we have to live in the world the way it is. Young ladies are not supposed to... "

"Shoot! I'm sick and tired of hearing about what young ladies are not supposed to do."

"Please, Suzette, do not say *shoot*." Lydia's brow wrinkled.

"You see?" Her daughter threw up her hands. "Everything I do is wrong to you. Mother, I love you, but I'm very much afraid that you're still clinging to the days when you were a

Southern belle in Louisiana. All you did all day long was drink lemonade under the shade of the magnolia trees while the darkies pulled cotton and serenaded you. But this is Texas! It's a land of relentless sun and wind and sometimes it's hard to find any kind of shade, much less an old magnolia. This is a prairie so vast Daddy has to ride sometimes thirty and forty miles to tend a sick child. This is a frontier so wild the Indians still roam at will, the women right alongside the men, and you can bet your mint julep they don't ride side-saddle. My Lord! Wild longhorn cattle and mustangs still cross my path when I ride a few miles from the house. Everywhere I look there's grand adventure, and yet I'm not supposed to partake of it!" Suzette put her hands on her hips, took a deep breath, and continued. "Don't you know if I had my way I'd be going on the cow hunts and trail drives? Can you imagine how cheated I feel at being left out simply because I'm a woman? Why, if I could, I'd... "

"Suzette. Suzette, please," Lydia interrupted. "All I asked was that you stop whistling. I'm sorry I mentioned it. Perhaps you're right. I expect you to behave the way my friends and I behaved. You do live in a completely different time. She took her daughter's hand and smiled at her. "I'm sorry you feel cheated. It never occurred to me that you would want to go on trail drives. I can think of nothing more unpleasant than riding hard all day behind hundreds of bawling, stubborn long-horns while the wind and dirt blow and dust gets in your nose and mouth, to say nothing of your hair and your clothes. I would think it far from enjoyable to sleep out on the hard ground in hot and cold weather and bathe in cold rivers and streams. Take a look at Nate and some of the other old drovers, darling. Their tired, weathered faces should give you some idea of what their occupation does to them. Would you want to look like that?"

Frowning, Suzette reluctantly shook her head.

"I'm sure you wouldn't," her mother continued. "You're so pretty, Suzette. Let's leave the cow hunts and drives to the men. Believe it or not, in time you will find that being a woman can be quite rewarding. You're much too young now, but in time the young men will start to court you, and when they do, you'll be very glad you're a woman. A well-mannered, pretty, soft, dainty lady."

Unconvinced, Suzette mumbled, "I suppose so, but..."

"But what, dear?"

"Can't I please just whistle until the young men start calling on me, Mother?"

Dissolving into laughter, Lydia pulled Suzette to her and hugged her tightly. "If it means so much to you, I guess so. But, please, darling, don't let it become too much of a habit. Bad habits are often very difficult to break."

That had been over a year ago and her mother was right. Sometimes she didn't even realize that she was doing it. Like this morning, when Nate, the only hired hand on the Foxworth ranch, stuck his head in the door of the tackroom and grinned at her. "You're getting mighty good at your whistling, Miss Suzette."

Suzette smiled at the grizzled old cowboy. "How are you this morning, Nate?"

Pushing his battered Stetson to the back of his graying head, he took the saddle from her, carried it outside, and slung it onto the back of the waiting mare. "Tolerable, I guess," he called over his shoulder. "Just tolerable. My rheumatism is acting up this morning."

Following close on his heels, Suzette said, "Shoot! Nate, I'll tell you what. I know Daddy makes you trail me every time I go riding. He's sound asleep by now and he'll never know the difference. Why don't you go on back to bed?" She gave him a winning smile.

Pale, watery eyes squinted at her from a sun-creased face. "You know I can't do that, Miss Suzette."

Sighing, she nodded. "No, I guess not. In that case, why don't you ride along with me? I'll teach you to whistle the new song Luke taught me. It's very pretty, but it's real sad. It's called 'Oh Bury Me Not on the Lone Prairie.' Nate, it's a true story about a drover that died on the trail to Abilene. He knew he was dying and he begged his fellow drovers not to leave him out there on the desolate prairie. He died and his friends had no choice; they couldn't bring him back home. They buried him out there miles from anywhere, but they felt so bad about it, they wrote the song and dedicated it to the cowboy's memory. Don't you think that is the most romantic, beautiful, saddest story you've ever heard in all your life?" She clasped her hand to her breasts, momentarily lost in the sad drama of the song.

She looked at Nate. Tears shone in the tired old eyes and he sniffed. "If you're gonna tell any more tales that sad, I'm not gonna ride with you, Miss Suzette. I'll just stay back and trail you."

"Oh, Nate." Suzette leaned close and kissed his wrinkled cheek. "I'm sorry. Saddle your horse. I'll tell you some funny stories Luke told me." With a laugh and a toss of her blond head, she mounted Glory, her big palomino mare.

Finding it impossible to understand how her mood could change so rapidly, Nate scratched his chin and went for his horse. Minutes later he was spurring his chestnut gelding to catch up with the beautiful young girl galloping ahead of him, her whistling piercing the quiet of the gently rolling prairie.

2

Suzette swept into the parlor that evening at half-past seven. Magically transformed from the tall coltish figure in worn buckskins, she was now the essence of femininity in her new blue cotton dress. Delicate white shoulders and high rounded breasts were accentuated by the low bodice of the gown. A long, tight waist gave way to ruffles that began at the hips and tumbled seductively to the floor. On her feet, soft kid shoes laced with ribbon peeked from under the long dress when she walked.

Her thick blond hair had been swept atop her head; her mother told her the style would be attractive, that it would showcase her long, swanlike neck and lovely throat. Tiny sprigs of bridal breath had been added to the silky blond curls arranged attractively at her crown. Suzette knew she was pretty. She felt pretty; she felt grown up. Still, she wanted to hear it.

Blake stood at the cold fireplace, feet apart, hands clasped behind his back. He turned as she entered. "Suzette... I... Suzette... " He stopped trying to talk and looked at her as she smiled brilliantly and turned around for his perusal.

"Well?" she demanded.

"You take my breath away, Suzette. Surely you must be the most beautiful young lady in all of Texas."

Pleased with his compliment, she went to him and kissed his cheek, then put her arm through his. "Thank you, Daddy. Most of all, thanks for being here for my party."

"I'm glad I didn't have to miss it, sweetheart. The meeting with General Sherman was postponed until tomorrow night since the general won't be arriving until tomorrow afternoon."

"My thanks to the Yankee general." She grinned and hugged his arm.

"Darling, he's not a Yankee general. He's a respected general in the Army of the United States, of which even the great state of Texas is a part."

"Maybe so, but I've heard you say more than once that Washington knows little about what goes on down here and cares even less."

"Suzette, dear, sometimes I say foolish things; I wish you wouldn't concern yourself with them. Young ladies shouldn't... "

Releasing his arm, she stepped away from him. "You

sound just like Mother. I'm disappointed. Do you want me to be some simpering female only interested in learning how to make lye soap or crochet or beat rugs? That's boring, Daddy, admit it. Would you want to spend your time thinking about such dreary things?" Her hands were on her hips.

"You've got me, I'm afraid. But, darling, you're being unfair. Those pursuits have taken up very little of your time. Seems to me most of your days are spent on Glory's back or writing in that journal of yours or poking around in my library — that is, when you aren't in my office watching me stitch up cuts or dig bullets out of cowboys." He paused. "In fact, honey, you've spent so much time assisting me, you could almost be my partner."

"It's fascinating! I love to watch you work. Aren't you proud of me? Not once have I ever gotten sick. I'm real tough, aren't I, Daddy?"

Blake laughed aloud. "Darling, let's say you're strong. That sounds better." He reached into his breast pocket and took out a small box. "Now, before the guests arrive, I want to give you your present." He held it out to her.

"Oh, Daddy, thank you!" Her eyes danced as she opened the black velvet box and looked at the tiny gold locket resting on a bed of white satin. In the center of the gold locket, a tiny sapphire sparkled. Throwing her arms around her father's neck, Suzette clutched the necklace in her palm and shouted, "I love it! I shall wear it forever. I'll never, ever take it off. When they come to bury me, I'll still be wearing my beautiful gold locket!"

Chuckling, Blake patted her slim waist. "Sweetheart, you're being just a bit dramatic, don't you think? You don't have to wear it forever. Your mother and I just thought it was pretty and wanted you to have it. Happy sixteenth birthday, sweet Suzette."

"And happy birthday from me, too, darling." Lydia came into the room, looking almost as lovely as her young daughter, in a dress of deep rose. She smiled at Suzette and gave her a warm hug. "I believe it's time, Suzette. The Brands' carriage just pulled up. Would you like to go out and invite them in?"

Suzette fairly flew from the room. As the front door slammed loudly, Blake and Lydia looked at each other and smiled. "Think she'll ever grow up, Blake?"

Pulling his wife close to his side, he grinned down at her. "I hope not, darling. I'd like to keep her just as she is forever. A sweet, beautiful child who's never been touched by any heartache or tragedy."

Straightening Blake's narrow string tie, Lydia looked up into his soft warm eyes. "You're a sweet man, Blake Foxworth. Maybe our Suzette will be lucky and have a life as good as ours."

Blake smiled and kissed her lightly on the lips. Before he could speak, a high, shrill scream came from the front porch. Blake and Lydia hurried outside.

Suzette was on her knees, mindless of her new party dress, examining a beautiful hand-tooled leather saddle. Austin Brand, his arm around his wife, Beth, stood looking down at Suzette, smiling broadly. Little Jenny Brand held her father's hand and giggled. The expensive saddle was the Brands' birthday present to Suzette.

Suzette's screams finally ceased and she leaned over the shiny new saddle and kissed its smooth surface.

"I think she likes it." Lydia smiled at the tall, handsome Austin Brand.

"It's hard to tell." He grinned and shook Blake's hand. Lydia put her arm about Beth's slim waist and drew her toward the door.

"I'll carry the saddle out back for you, Suzette," Austin offered as he helped her to her feet.

She clasped Austin's big right hand in both of hers. "Thank you so much, Mr. Brand. You're too kind."

"You're very welcome." He touched a blond curl at her cheek. "And, by the way, you look very pretty and quite grown up. Play your cards right and you might get that curly-headed cowboy that works for me to dance with you."

"Oh, you!" She blushed and pushed him away. Then she turned and squealed loudly, "Anna!" She jerked up her skirts and ran lightly across the yard to greet her best friend.

Pretty Anna Norris, her dark, shiny curls bobbing, bolted out of the carriage driven by a household servant and embraced the radiant Suzette before thrusting a present at her.

"Is your Luke coming?" Anna inquired.

"He should arrive any minute!" Suzette said excitedly. "Come on inside. I'll open my present."

Looking as if he had scrubbed his boyishly handsome face to a permanent pink, Luke Barnes clutched his broad-brimmed Stetson as he stepped onto the porch. Suzette answered the door and suddenly felt very shy and tongue-tied. He was so good-looking. His emerald eyes sparkled, and his curly red hair was so clean it glistened in the last rays of the setting sun. He wore a starched, snow-white shirt open a couple of buttons at his throat. His dark trousers were snug over his long, muscular legs, and his boots were highly polished. A silver belt buckle gleamed at his waist.

Suzette was certain there could be no other twenty-one-year-old cowboy in Texas quite so handsome. Her eyes went to Luke's mouth, which was curved into a wide grin. Butterflies took flight inside her. Before the evening was ended, she would feel those warm, full lips on hers. Those long, powerful arms would hold her tightly in the moonlight, and that curly red hair would be hers for the touching. Suzette loved everything about this tall, smiling man, but his beautiful hair was her big weakness. Even now, shyly looking up at him while her family stood behind her in the hall, she could hardly keep from reaching up to feel its pleasing texture. She longed to wind the curls around her fingers. Never had she seen such beautiful hair on a man.

"Luke, if Suzette's not going to ask you in, I will." Blake Foxworth stepped up beside his daughter while she stood admiring the tall youth.

"Thank you, Dr. Foxworth." Luke shook hands with Blake and grinned.

The party was a success. By nine o'clock, the rug had been rolled up and many pairs of booted feet and dainty slippers tapped rhythmically on the wooden floors. The three best fiddlers in Jack County kept the music lively, to the delight of the breathless dancers.

Baked hams, fried chicken, potato salad, roastin' ears, cornbread, and a half dozen other dishes filled the sideboard in the dining room. On a pedestal table not far away, the big birthday cake sat amidst a dazzling arrangement of Texas wildflowers.

Suzette's face was flushed with excitement as she spun around the room in Luke's arms. When the tune came to an end and everyone clapped for more, Suzette, her hand to her throat, looked up at her tall partner, who was also gasping for breath. Wordlessly, Luke took her hand in his and they made their way through the couples and out into the hall. Seeing Suzette's father engaged in conversation with his employer, Austin Brand, Luke's face reddened and he hastily explained to both men, "Mr. Foxworth, sir, Mr. Brand. Suzette, well, she's a little overheated, what with all the dancing. I thought we'd just step outside for a breath of air."

"A wise decision." Blake Foxworth smiled at the young couple, and Austin Brand nodded.

The two watched Suzette and Luke slip onto the porch and hurry down the front steps into the night. "He's a fine boy, isn't he, Austin?"

"One of the best," the big rancher agreed. "Luke's smart, too. For a kid of twenty-one, he's one of the best hands I've ever had work for me. I'm fifteen years older than Luke, and I swear at times I feel he could teach me things about raising cattle and running a ranch. That boy'll have something one of these days, mark my words."

"I hope so, Austin. Suzette tells me she's in love with him."

"Little Suzette? Why, she's a baby. I hope they'll wait a few years. If not, looks like I'll have to see about building some kind of living quarters over on my place. I know she — "

Austin was interrupted by his five-year-old daughter pulling on his trousers leg. "Daddy, Mommy said to tell you to get me a plate of food. I'm hungry."

Blake and Austin smiled at the small girl with long, dark curls. "Come with me, Jenny." Blake put out his hand. "Let me fix you a plate." He picked her up and Jenny put her arms around his neck, looking over his shoulder at her father. "I'll bet you like strawberries and cream, don't you?" Blake headed for the dining room.

"Uh-huh. And chicken and biscuits and cake and milk." Jenny's dark curls danced as she nodded her head, naming all her favorite foods.

"That's good, because I think Mrs. Foxworth prepared enough food to feed all the troops at Fort Richardson."

Austin Brand looked on fondly, a drink in his big hand, as the slender doctor bore Jenny away. If not for Doc Foxworth, he reflected, the pretty little girl might not be at Suzette's birthday party. She might not be alive.

Austin's wife, Beth, had gone into labor with Jenny too early. Beth, in great pain, had clutched at Austin's big hands. "Austin, help me, please." Her lips were blue, and perspiration poured from her pale, drawn face.

Austin had soothed her, then shouted for Kate, the housekeeper, to summon Tom Capps. In minutes, the cowboy was riding fast across the prairie to waken Dr. Foxworth. Pausing only long enough to pull on his trousers and grab the saddlebags with his medicines and instruments, Blake was up on the horse behind Austin's ranch foreman and on his way to aid the suffering Beth within minutes.

When he saw the frail woman whose agony was so great, Blake smiled calmly at her and at Austin. "Don't you worry, Beth." He smoothed a dark lock of hair from her cheek. "It's a little early, but that's no cause for alarm." Turning to Austin, he said evenly, "Why don't you go have a drink? If Beth and I need you, we'll call." He patted Austin's broad back and, reluctantly, Austin released his wife's cold hand and went to the door. There he turned and smiled at Beth.

"Doc, you take care of her. She's very precious to me."

The sun was peeking through the tall windows of the library. Austin, his white shirt unbuttoned halfway down his massive chest, long sleeves rolled up over muscular forearms, was still waiting. His beard had begun to make a shadow on the lower half of his square-jawed handsome face. His eyes were red-rimmed with fatigue. He ran a shaky hand through his disheveled blond hair, then rubbed his eyes.

Austin had walked the floor all night. Half a dozen times he had gone up the stairs. Each time he'd begged to be allowed inside, and each time the housekeeper, a kind, stout woman with thin gray hair and pale blue eyes, had come out and told him gently that it wouldn't be too much longer, that he should just be patient.

His patience gone, his fear escalating with each hour that passed, Austin could stand it no longer. His jaw set, he bounded back up the stairs. Halfway up, he heard it. Faint, almost inaudible. Austin clutched the polished banister to keep from falling. Straining every muscle of his tired body, he didn't dare breathe. Then he heard it again.

An infant's cry. From the room at the end of the hall, a baby was crying. His baby. Relief and happiness flooded through him. When he reached the door, it opened and Kate came out, beaming happily. She caught Austin's arm and said, "A girl, Mr. Brand. You have a beautiful baby daughter."

Austin squeezed the woman's hand and looked over her head to see Blake turn and smile. "Yes, Austin, come on in. We're all ready for you."

Austin never knew when the doctor left the room to give him some time alone with his wife, because his wide eyes never lifted from the pair in the bed. Beth, hollow-eyed and pale, smiled up at him and held out her frail hand. On her breasts, a tiny little girl with hair as dark as her mother's was sleeping soundly.

Tenderly clasping his wife's hand, Austin slowly sank to

his knees beside the bed. "Beth, dear," he whispered and kissed her fingers, "she's beautiful. Beautiful."

"Austin," Beth spoke through her tears, "she's so little. Much too little. I'm so afraid she won't... "

"Sweetheart" — he choked and put his hand to her cheek — "she will live. Dr. Foxworth brought her into this world and he will see to it she survives. Now, don't you worry about her for one minute. She's going to make it."

Later, when an exhausted Beth was asleep and the tiny baby slumbered peacefully in the satin-trimmed crib nearby, Austin stole out of the room and down the stairs. He found the weary doctor in the kitchen drinking coffee.

"Dr. Foxworth, you have to make that child live, do you hear me? Beth couldn't stand it if she lost that baby. I know the infant's too small to have much chance, but you have to promise me she'll live." Austin's gray eyes were fierce.

Blake calmly sipped his coffee and motioned for the big man to take a seat across from him. "Austin, your daughter is the very first baby that I've delivered since coming to Texas. I'm not saying that should make her special to me, but it does all the same. I have no intention of losing her. For the next two months, you'll see more of me than you want, and you'll follow my instructions to the letter regarding her care. Starting tonight. You are not to pick her up unless I'm in the room with you. Find yourself another bedroom for a while. Mother and daughter will be sleeping in yours, but you won't." Seeing the frown on the younger man's face, Blake chuckled softly. "You're a daddy now, Austin. Congratulations."

True to his word, Blake Foxworth had spent a lot of time at the Brand ranch until baby Jenny was strong and healthy and completely out of danger. More than one close call with the delicate infant had terrified Beth and Austin, but Blake was there to clear her congested little lungs so Jenny could breathe. He was there to apply cold packs that made Jenny's dangerously high fever recede. He was there to walk the floor with the tiny girl until her crying subsided and she was able to sleep. Blake Foxworth had literally willed the child to hang on, just as her parents had done, and Austin and Beth would never forget his kindness, skill, and care. They owed him a debt of gratitude that could never be repaid. The healthy five-year-old the doctor carried into the dining room was a strong bond between Blake and the Brands.

"If there is ever anything at all I can do for you, Blake, please name it," Austin Brand had told him more than once.

"Your friendship is payment enough," Blake assured him. "You, Beth, and Jenny are like kinfolk."

Smiling, Austin agreed. "We feel the same way about you and your family."

For reasons that Austin Brand could not fathom, Blake's smile had faded and he had put a hand on the younger man's arm. "Austin, if anything should ever happen to me, will you look out for Lydia and Suzette?" His eyes held a sad, resigned look that unsettled Austin.

"Doctor, you know I will. You're not... that is... "

"No, no." The smile was back on Blake's lean face. "I'm planning on a long life. I just meant should the unforeseen ever happen."

"Depend on me, my friend."

The music from the fiddles grew fainter. Voices were now indistinct, barely audible. Still Suzette and Luke continued walking, under the tall cottonwoods, past the dozens of empty buggies, Suzette clinging to Luke's hand. When they had gone far enough to be certain they could not be seen by anyone on the porch or in the yard, Luke grinned and drew her to his side, sliding his arm around her narrow waist.

"Suzette, honey, I've been waiting all evening long to get you alone." His warm lips brushed across her temple.

Eyes sparkling with happiness, she nestled her head in the crook of his shoulder and sighed, "Luke, I feel the same way."

"Do you, honey? Will you let me kiss you, Suzette?" He had stopped walking.

Blushing under the light of the pale spring moon, Suzette

smiled up at the tall, handsome boy and nodded her blond head. "If you'll promise that you'll only kiss me once, Luke," she answered demurely.

Excitement caused his heart to pound, and Luke looked hastily around them. Never loosening his hold on her waist, he inclined his curly head southward. "This way, sweetheart."

Suzette daintily picked up her long skirt and let Luke guide her off the road and into the underbrush. Moonlight filtered through the tall oaks and elms and dappled their path into a small clearing. Drawing her to the trunk of a stately water oak, Luke turned and leaned against the tree's rough trunk, then gently pulled Suzette close to his tall, hard frame. She was looking up at him, her soft lips parted in anticipation. When her slender arms stole up around his neck, she smiled.

"You're so pretty," Luke whispered and lowered his lips to hers. He kissed her softly, his mouth warm and gentle on hers. Suzette closed her eyes and gloried in the feel of his lips tasting hers. It was an innocent, brief kiss. Two bashful pairs of lips meeting, touching, retreating.

Lifting his curly head, Luke said quietly, "Suzette, honey, I've been hired to escort Warren's wagon train to Fort Griffin tomorrow. They're bringing corn and supplies from Weatherford for the troops at Fort Griffin, and they need an extra man to ride shotgun across Salt Creek Prairie. Luckily, it's a few days before I leave on the cow hunt, and Mr. Brand said it would be all right with him if I want to pick up some extra money." Luke stopped talking and looked at her.

"Luke, please don't do it." She touched his cheek. "I want you to spend your time with me until you leave on the cow hunt. After all," she dropped her eyes to his sunburned throat, "you'll be gone for weeks on the hunt. Then as soon as you get back, you'll be leaving on the drive to Abilene. When will I ever get to be with you?" When she raised her face again, she was frowning.

"Honey" — he squeezed her and grinned — "one of the reasons I've hired out to escort the wagon train is so I can save enough money for us. Suzette, I love you, honey. I want you to be my wife."

"Luke, you... you're asking me to marry you?"

"Yes, sweetheart. Yes, oh yes. I want you to be Mrs. Luke Barnes, and just as soon as possible. You love me, don't you?" It suddenly occurred to him she might turn him down.

"Oh, Luke." She pressed closer to him and buried her face in his warm throat. "Yes, I do. I love you and I want to be your wife."

"Suzette." He sighed as he gently pulled back to look at her. Then his mouth came down on hers again and his arms wrapped around her, pulling her firmly against him. Suzette gasped when his lips opened on hers and his tall frame was crushed against her. She could feel the fierce pounding of his heart through his cotton shirt. Just when she felt she would surely swoon from his searing kiss, Luke's mouth moved from her lips to her ear. "We'd better go back now, honey. Your daddy will be wondering where we are."

Her hands clinging to the fabric covering his chest, she fought for breath and murmured, "Yes, I know, I know." She whispered, "Luke, I have something to give you." Shyly, she pulled from his arms and turned her back. From inside the bodice of her party dress, she took the new red bandanna. Smoothing it into a nice folded square with the hand-embroidered "L" at the corner, she turned back to him and proudly thrust it up to his face.

"Say, now, what's this?" Luke grinned and took the shiny bandanna. "Why, Suzette, there's a big 'L' on it."

"I know," she whispered. "I put it there, Luke. Do you like it?"

"Like it? Honey, it's beautiful. I'll never be without it." While Suzette beamed, Luke tied the red scarf about his throat, fingering the initial, his green eyes flashing in the moonlight. "How do I look?"

"Handsome." She grinned. "Luke, are you sure it's safe for you to go across Salt Creek Prairie? You know it wasn't too long ago that those four men were killed and scalped out there."

"Suzette, don't worry. I'll hang on to my scalp. We'll be crossing the prairie in broad daylight, so don't spend your time worrying your pretty blond head about me. They're paying me real good and I'll be wanting to buy you a ring. If it suits you, I thought we'd get married as soon as I get back from Abilene next autumn." He looked to her for an answer.

"Yes, as soon as you return from Abilene. Mrs. Luke Barnes!" She sighed. "I'm going to be a good wife to you, Luke. I swear I will. I'm not much of a cook, but I'll learn for you."

"You don't have to, Suzette. We'll live on love."

"Umm," she murmured. "In that case, you may kiss me again, Luke."

His lips were once again on hers and Suzette kissed Luke with growing enthusiasm as her hands stole up to rake through the thick red curly locks she so admired.

3

It was noon on May 18, 1871. General William T. Sherman, Commander in Chief of the United States Army, riding with his escort of fifteen troopers under Lieutenant Mason Carter, 4th United States Cavalry, reached Salt Creek Prairie in Young County. The portly general and his protectors were en route from Fort Belknap, in Young County, to Fort Richardson, in Jacksboro.

When the small contingent of men started across the prairie, the sky was a deep, cloudless blue, the air still and sweet — a beautiful spring day in North Texas. There were only seventeen miles more to travel; by suppertime, the general would be at his quarters at Fort Richardson. General Sherman, skeptical about the complaints coming from the frontier regarding the reservation Indians, looked at the young lieutenant riding with him and smiled, his merry eyes disappearing into the laugh lines in his fleshy face.

"Lieutenant Carter, it appears just as I had presumed. Mountains have been made of molehills. This land seems as safe and tranquil as it must have been on the very day our Creator made it. I see no traces of all the 'savage Indians' I keep hearing so much about from these good, but unnecessarily nervous, settlers."

"Begging your pardon, General, but I have to disagree. I was in this part of the country before the war, and at that time the population was denser than it is now. I put that down solely to fear and flight from the savages." The lieutenant's steely eyes raked the horizon as he spoke.

"That may well be true, Lieutenant. Nonetheless, I feel much of that fear is unfounded. We are, at this very hour, crossing what is supposedly one of the most dangerous stretches of prairie in all Texas. I don't know about you, but I feel as safe as if I were taking lunch in the great dining hall of the White House in Washington City." His hand came up to hide a yawn.

Yet, as the confident general spoke, he was silently observed by one hundred fifty pairs of dark eyes. On a conical hill overlooking the barren prairie the slow-moving caravan now traversed, eager Kiowa and Comanche warriors sat on their war ponies, their lances adorned with human scalps, impatiently awaiting word from their great medicine man, Dehate, to attack. As they strained to rein their horses in, corded muscles rippled across their powerful naked backs. The warriors were thirsty for blood, anxious to thunder down the hill and hurtle themselves on the unsuspecting white men, to yell and shout and count coup, to do the only thing they were born and bred to do — make war.

But they must wait a while longer. Dehate had sung his medicine song on the previous night. He had heard the hoot owl's cry and was pleased. At dawn he had gathered the eager warriors and told them he had seen the sign of a successful attack.

"Tomorrow two parties will pass this way," the medicine man had announced with authority. "The first party will be small and we could easily overcome it, but it must not be attacked. The medicine forbids! Another party will come by later and we will attack. The attack will be successful."

So it was that the relaxed general and his escort passed safely by and disappeared around Cox Mountain and into the timber country. The general dozed atop his seat in the horse-drawn ambulance as it bumped along under the clouds rapidly gathering overhead.

Not three hours later, Warren's wagon train rounded Cox Mountain, heading west. Riding at the front of the slow-moving caravan, Luke Barnes, his green eyes scanning the terrain for any possible danger, his new red silk bandanna tied proudly about his throat, exhaled and breathed a little easier. As far as the eye could see, nothing moved.

Cleverly hidden from young Luke's view, Dehate, along with the mighty war chiefs Satank, Satanta, Big Tree, Fast Bear, and Eagle Heart, prepared to teach the eager young warriors how to make war. At the signal from Dehate, Satanta, his handsome face painted red, regally raised his brass trumpet to his lips and blew the charge. The warriors swept down the mountainside to surround the unsuspecting white men, war chants bursting from their throats.

"God in heaven!" Luke murmured, then reined his horse in a tight turn and signaled for the others to move quickly into a circle. While Suzette's words fleetingly rang in Luke's ears — *Please, Luke, don't go across Salt Creek Prairie, it's not safe* — the mountain came ablaze with painted, screaming Indians, riding fast, armed with long-range guns, revolvers, and carbines.

James Long, the wagon master, was shouting commands as the terrified men hastily made a circle with the mules at its center. Luke dismounted to help build a protective breastworks from sacks of grain.

But there wasn't enough time. The speed and surprise of the attack left the white men vulnerable as one hundred fifty shouting warriors rode around the wagons in an ever-decreasing circle, firing with frightening accuracy. Wagon master Long was killed immediately. Within minutes, four more men were dead. Knowing it was futile to remain inside the wagons, Luke shouted to be heard above the bloodcurdling melee, "It's no use! We'll have to make a run for it!"

Running frantically for the safety of the trees two miles east of the wagons, the men fired as they retreated through the circling, mounted warriors.

Luke Barnes never felt the shot that shattered his backbone, that rendered his long legs useless. He did hear the hoofbeats of a war pony as a young, grinning warrior jumped from his blowing, snorting horse and came toward him. Just before the mahogany face bent over Luke, a cloud passed directly over the sun. In that instant, Luke Barnes knew he would never see the sun again.

A cruel, savage face was above his, a half-naked body astride his chest. When the warrior reached into his breech cloth for his sharp hunting knife, Luke fought valiantly with the upper part of his body. Strong arms forced the furious brave over onto the ground and restrained the hand wielding the knife. Fighting desperately for his life, Luke never saw the tomahawk that entered his broad back. His hands were still subduing his first attacker when he began to choke on his own blood. As the life seeped from his body, he was slammed to his back by two smiling, triumphant braves.

Luke never saw their happy faces. Before his eyes danced the vision of a lovely young girl, her blond, silky hair framing her sweet face, her blue eyes flashing with happiness. She was calling Luke's name softly.

"Suzette," he murmured and clutched at the red silk bandanna with a sunburned hand that his two attackers were in the process of chopping from his arm.

"May I offer you a cigar, General Sherman?" Austin Brand smiled engagingly at the stocky man across the table from him. It was late evening and General Sherman was tired from his long day's journey. He and his troops had arrived at Fort Richardson at the dinner hour and he'd hardly had time to eat his meal before a contingent of frustrated Jacksboro citizens rode into the fort, determined to meet with the visiting general.

Austin Brand, Blake Foxworth, and several other concerned men of the community told the weary general that the reservation Indians roamed at will, killing and stealing horses, terrorizing the gentlefolk with their atrocities.

General Sherman took the offered cigar, bit off the tip, and struck a sulphur match, puffing the smoke to life. Rolling the cigar between his thumb and forefinger, he nodded his approval to Austin.

"Dammit, General!" Blake Foxworth slammed a slender hand on the table. "Unless the army does something about the Indian situation, North Texas will soon have no population at all. It is not safe to live here. The Indians know they can raid at will and then ride to the safety of the reservation, where they can't be followed! It makes little sense! What good are the soldiers manning this fort if they can't touch the marauders once they cross the Red River?"

Glancing at the doctor, a benevolent smile lifting his lips, the general drew on his cigar and spoke. "Gentlemen, I can see that you good people of Jacksboro are fearful, but I think a lot of that fear is ungrounded. I'm sure there have been some scattered incidents of the Indians driving away some of your horses, but I don't see — "

Austin Brand, his full mouth thinned into a tight line, rose abruptly from his chair. "We are getting damned tired of having Washington look on us as nothing more than a nuisance, General Sherman! We're here to tell you that it is not safe to live in this part of the country. The savages raid right in sight of this fort. That should give you some idea of the kind of respect they have for these well-meaning but woefully ineffective troops. It's been said that the soldiers have succeeded in tracking many a smoldering campfire left by the Indians, but never managed to catch up with a redskin. Were I a cynical man, I'd have to question whether or not they actually want to catch up with the fleeing savages."

"Now, see here, Mr. Brand, I — " The general's face was growing red.

"No, General Sherman, *you* see here. It's been less than two months since four Negro soldiers were killed and scalped on the very road you traveled today. It's dangerous out there, truly perilous. You're not addressing a bunch of nervous spinster ladies, afraid of their own shadow. No, sir, General, we're here to speak of death and torture and thievery, and we damned well want something done about it!" His face colored and he put a hand up to the tight collar of his shirt and jerked it open.

The general studied the man who was so passionately pleading his case. "Mr. Brand, it's quite late and I really must get some rest, but I assure you that when I get up to Fort Sill in the Indian Territory, I will investigate your charges that the reservation Indians are receiving arms and ammunition at the post. I find it hard to believe, but I'll sure check it out."

Snorting derisively, one of the delegation got up and pushed his chair back. "We might as well go. We're getting nowhere." He looked at the general and said coldly, "Those Indians are better armed than we are, General, and they are taking *our* stolen stock back to their camp. Investigate that while you're at it!"

The unhappy delegation departed, feeling they'd accomplished very little. The clouds that had been gathering since noon had finally boiled into a spring storm. When Austin and Blake stepped out onto the porch of the general's quarters, it was raining heavily. Dreading the ride home in the rain, they stood on the long gallery and talked, hoping the deluge might soon slacken. They were still talking quietly when an agitated young captain hurried up the steps to summon General Sherman to the fort hospital.

Even the noise of the raindrops pelting the porch's roof didn't muffle the conversation that took place when the general's door was thrown open.

"General Sherman, sir," the youthful captain spoke excitedly, "my commanding officer has sent me to dispatch you at once to the hospital."

"What is it, Captain? It's quite late. Has something happened?" The tired general rubbed an eye.

"Yes, sir. A wounded man has just walked into the fort. He was attacked, along with twelve other men of Warren's wagon train. 'Twas the Indians, General Sherman. They've struck again."

Blake Foxworth looked at Austin Brand. Although uninvited, both men followed the general across the muddy parade ground to the post hospital. Inside, Thomas Brazeale, in severe pain from a gunshot wound and an arrow in his foot, lay pale from loss of blood while the fort surgeon worked to ease his suffering. Fully conscious, Brazeale repeated to the horrified general the story he had told the officers gathered around.

Blake offered to help with the man's wounds, and he listened intently to his terrifying tale. When the injured man said that he was not sure if any of the others had escaped with their lives, Blake, his stomach tightening with fear, assured himself silently that there was a good chance Luke Barnes had gotten away. He was young and strong; if Brazeale could manage to slip from the savages with a wounded foot, surely young Luke had eluded them.

Throughout the night, torrential rains continued to pour from the heavens. General Sherman, appalled at the tale of horror the injured Brazeale had told, called out Colonel Ranald S. Mackenzie — the man the Indians called Chief No-Index-Finger and a man they fearfully respected — to take a force from the 4th U.S. Cavalry and ride west to the scene of the massacre.

The parade ground stood in puddles of water when Colonel Mackenzie mustered his men at dawn for the journey to Salt

Creek Prairie. Soldiers longing for a few more minutes in their bunks sleepily mounted in the falling rain, unready to depart on the unpleasant mission that would take them to the theater of one of life's bloody dramas, then on to Fort Sill in the Indian territory in pursuit of the tragedy's villains, the hated savages.

In tones that brooked no argument, Blake Foxworth and Austin Brand had informed General Sherman that they intended to ride to Salt Creek Prairie with Colonel Mackenzie's command.

The general looked up at both men with an apologetic expression on his full face. "I'm certain Colonel Mackenzie will be glad to have you accompany him, gentlemen. You are more than welcome to ride along with the detachment. Go as far as Fort Sill if you choose. There I shall rendezvous with Colonel Mackenzie and see that this unforgivable and unwarranted attack be fully investigated and the perpetrators duly punished."

When Colonel Mackenzie's command moved out into the gray dawn, their slickers pulled up around their ears, water dripping from the brims of their hats, Blake and Austin brought up the rear. Both had gone home quickly to change clothes and inform their wives of their intentions. Blake had spoken to Lydia in low tones while Suzette slept peacefully through the exchange, never knowing that her father had returned home.

Dressed and ready to return to the fort, Blake looked at his distraught wife. "Darling, please try not to worry. There's every chance that Luke escaped. Brazeale said he has no idea who got away and who was killed. We must keep up our hopes. Luke may show up in town or at the fort before morning. Go back to bed, dear, and try to sleep. Say nothing to Suzette. She's not expecting Luke back until sometime tomorrow, so let's wait until we know for certain."

Clinging to her husband, Lydia nodded and pressed her cheek to his shoulder. Fighting back her tears, she whispered softly, "Blake, I'm so frightened. Must you go with them?"

Cradling her head in his hand, he said, "I'll wake Nate and tell him to keep watch over you and Suzette. I have to go, Lydia. If there are survivors, I may be able to assist Dr. Patzki, the regimental surgeon."

"Of course," she said quietly. "Maybe you can save a life. Go, darling. I'll say a prayer."

Blake kissed her and was gone. He rode into the fort while the troops were assembling on the muddy parade ground. Austin Brand, mounted on an iron-gray gelding he called Confederate, rode in five minutes after the doctor.

It had been exactly twenty-four hours since the attack. When Colonel Mackenzie's men reached the sight of the massacre, the rain had stopped, the sun was out, and the Texas sky was a brilliant blue. It was a glorious spring day on the prairie, but a grizzly sight greeted the horrified command.

Jaw set, nerves steeled for the worst, Blake Foxworth dismounted and went about his unpleasant task. At his side, Austin Brand fell into step, idly exclaiming under his breath, "Damn them to hell! Damn them all to eternal hell! The murdering, bloodthirsty red-skinned bastards!"

Stooping down in the mud, Blake touched the first poor soul. Stripped and mutilated, the man's stomach had been slashed open, his intestines scooped out, and in their place were coals, the fire long since doused by the falling of the rain. The second victim they came upon had suffered similar torture. His fingers, toes, and genitals had been cut off and stuffed into his mouth. He was lying on his back in two inches of water and was horribly bloated. Identification was impossible.

Blake, crouching beside the body, shook his head in disbelief. He'd seen a lot of suffering and horror in his profession and in the war, but never had he seen anything to match the hideous scene surrounding him. When he heard a loud retching near him, he raised his head and saw his friend Austin Brand clutching his churning stomach. Austin Brand, a man who had spent four years in the Confederate Army and had seen some of the bloodiest battles of the entire campaign. Austin Brand, a man huge in stature and seemingly fearless. Austin Brand, a frontiersman who'd spent his boyhood in the wilds of Texas, fighting wild beasts and wilder men just to survive. Austin Brand, a man Blake Foxworth always regarded as larger than life, was on his knees vomiting, tears streaming down his sun-bronzed cheeks.

Rising, Blake moved on to other victims, hoping against hope that he would find someone alive, yet knowing instinctively that all were dead — including Luke Barnes.

The next man the doctor saw had obviously put up a valiant effort to the end. For his daring, he had suffered even more than his companions. The poor wretch, firing from inside one of the wagons, had been wounded. He was then chained between two wagon wheels. A fire had been built, and the chained man had been slowly roasted alive. Blake knew the man was still alive when his torture began; his blackened limbs were drawn up, contracted.

The gruesome inspection continued. Among the spilled grain sacks, corn floated in the puddles, and arrows lay everywhere. Dr. Foxworth and Austin Brand continued the search for bodies with Colonel Mackenzie and his troops, making their way through a mass of dead mules, hats, bits of clothing, and other rain-soaked debris from the furious struggle. More bodies were located, arrows jutting from rain-swollen corpses. Any one of them could have been Luke Barnes; it was impossible to make positive identification. Still, Blake felt he hadn't yet found the boy.

He massaged his tense neck muscles, his sad eyes sweeping across the scene of destruction. Fifty yards from where he stood, a red bandanna fluttered in the breeze.

Without a word, Blake Foxworth made his way to the body, his heart hammering. He reached Luke and slowly knelt beside him. The wet red bandanna was the only thing left on his body. His tormentors had tried to take that too; it was pulled tightly around his throat, as though in desperation they had finally given up on the tricky knot. Sadly, Blake fingered the red silk. When he saw the neatly embroidered "L," the shock of recognition brought a groan of despair from his pain-tightened lips.

Luke had been shot several times. One hand was missing. His tongue had been cut from his throat. His once-sparkling green eyes were staring in fixed horror. His beautiful red curly hair was gone.

4

They buried the fallen men on the prairie where they had died, and the two civilians turned back for home, while Colonel Mackenzie and his men headed north to the Red River and the Fort Sill Indian reservation.

The tired, bedraggled troops reached the fort on June 4. General Sherman had been there and departed, but had left specific orders for Colonel Mackenzie to take the three chiefs responsible for the senseless slaughter back to Texas to be tried for murder.

The prisoners were turned over to the colonel on June 8. Handcuffed and in leg irons, the three chiefs were put into wagons for the journey to Jacksboro. Satank, the oldest chief of the Kiowas, a man the Quaker Indian agent referred to as "the meanest Indian on the reservation," refused to climb into the wagon, stating he'd never be taken to Texas alive. A formidable figure of a man even at seventy years of age, Satank wore a thick moustache and beard. He was leader of the Principal Dogs, the highest military order of the Kiowa tribe; each member of the respected order swore to "return from every battle with honor, or die trying."

Satank was tossed into the wagon by four soldiers. Two guards crawled in beside him. Satanta and Big Tree were placed in a wagon together, guards beside each one. As the wagon train rolled out, over the clatter of the horses' hooves and the creaking of the wagons, an eerie sound was heard. Satank had begun his death chant. He pulled his colorful blanket about his shoulders and head, mindless of the heat of the still June day. The two young corporals seated on the floor near Satank, their backs against the wagon bed, carbines between their legs, looked intently at the strange old savage. The hair on the backs of their necks stood up and the fingers on the triggers of their guns began to sweat.

Crouching in the folds of his blanket, Satank coolly, methodically gnawed the flesh from both his wrists, working doggedly with sharp teeth. As the train neared Cache Creek, the old chief slipped his bloody wrists free of the handcuffs, gave a piercing yell, stood, and dove at a corporal with a scalping knife he'd concealed in his leggings.

As the old chief swung into action, so did the two young corporals, somersaulting right out of the wagon, but leaving their carbines behind. Joyously, Satank grabbed a gun, leveling it at the nearest guard. The gun misfired.

A bullet ripped into Satank's naked chest, felling him. He struggled up and tried once again to fire the carbine. A second shot went through his chest and exited his back.

Satank was dead. His body was taken from the wagon and placed beside the road. His people were allowed to take him back to the reservation for burial.

The crafty old chief had carried out his plan. At the start of the journey, he'd summoned George Washington, chief of the Caddos, who was riding near the wagon. To the Caddo scout, Satank had said somberly, "Tell my people I died beside the road. My bones will be found there. Tell my people to gather them up and carry them home. Tell the Kiowas to bring back the mules and don't raid anymore. Do as the agent tells them." The old chief's lips had then turned up into a devilish smile, and he added, "You may have my scalp."

No sooner had Satank's body been taken from the wagon than the contingent moved on, extra guards now riding with

Satanta and Big Tree. Throughout the one-hundred-twenty-five-mile journey to Jacksboro, both chiefs were closely guarded by wary young soldiers. At night the Indians were placed on the ground, spread-eagle, rawhide strips securely binding each foot and hand.

On the last night before reaching Fort Richardson, the chiefs lay on their backs on the ground, their rawhide restraints in place. Young Big Tree was asleep. Satanta's black eyes searched the sky as he wondered if this were to be the last night he would sleep under a blanket of stars, the last time he would breathe fresh air, hear the call of the coyote, smell the smoke from the campfire. Would the white eyes hang him, or worse, cage him like some animal? Put him into their prison to rot away while his skin grew pale and his body weak? Was he never again to taste the meat of roasted buffalo, make love to a woman, lead warriors into battle?

A lone tear made a salty path down his mahogany cheek, but he couldn't lift his hand to wipe it away.

Blake, Lydia, and Austin and Beth Brand sat on the broad porch in the twilight, the men smoking their after-dinner cigars, the ladies sipping coffee. On the lawn in front of the modest Foxworth house, Jenny Brand chased fireflies with great enthusiasm, her squeals of delight piercing the stillness each time she captured a new twinkling bug.

In her bedroom, Suzette Foxworth stood at the tall, open window, looking out at the gathering darkness of the June evening. June was the prettiest month in North Texas. The fertile prairie was splashed with vivid color, from the orange, red, and black of the wild Indian blankets to the butter-yellow of the sunflowers to the distinct hue of the bluebonnets. Morning glories and trumpet vines climbed the back walls of the house. Purple honeysuckle near Suzette's bedroom window filled the air with sweetness. Startlingly pink crepe myrtles battled for glory with the lilac bushes along the front gallery of the house.

Birds sang sweetly each morning, their small throats opening wide in a melodic salute to the season. Colorful butterflies flitted majestically from bush to bush, drunk from an abundance of sweet pollen. Mustangs, their winter coats long since shed, glistened sleekly in the bright summer sun. Proud stallions romped in the meadows with spirited mares. In other pastures, spindly-legged colts followed close behind their mothers.

Suzette had always loved June in Texas, but this year it held no pleasure for her. It never would again. Her sweetheart had been brutally murdered. Gone forever were those sparkling green eyes, that curly red hair. No more sweet kisses in the moonlight. Never again would she be held in his long arms.

Luke had been dead for almost a month. Suzette's tears had ceased. After the first outpouring of grief, she'd become strangely calm. Suzette felt that something in herself died with Luke. She would never be quite so carefree and happy again. She would go on living; she had no choice. In time she would even laugh again, care again about the events taking place around her. Not yet. It was too soon, and although Suzette hated to see her dear parents look so worried, she couldn't shrug off her gloom and attend parties or go on picnics as though the terrible tragedy had not happened.

Since she'd met Luke, she had known exactly how her life would be spent. They would marry and raise a family and build a good solid life together, working side by side to become prosperous ranchers with a place of their own, a place that would be their pride, a legacy to leave their children.

Her dreams had been snatched from her in the blink of an eye. She wouldn't be a wife, mother, partner. If she couldn't be married to Luke Barnes, she wanted never to be married at all. That was the only thing Suzette was completely certain of on that June evening.

Suzette's room was growing stuffy and too warm. Silently, she stepped out onto the side porch and inhaled deeply. Subdued voices floated to her from the front of the house. There were only male voices, as Lydia, Beth, and Jenny, who was carrying her treasure of fireflies, had gone into the house to get fresh strawberries and cream. Suzette couldn't help overhearing.

"Austin, I'm worried about her," her father said. "I need to get her interested in something and I'm not having any success. Last week I suggested she go to Fort Worth this autumn and enroll in college. She just shook her head and left the room."

"Doctor, I'm sorry to hear that," Austin's deep voice rumbled. "Poor little Suzette. Such a terrible thing to happen to her. But she's young; she'll heal."

"Of course she will," Blake responded, "but it's such a tragedy to waste any of her precious youth. When you get to be my age, Austin, you begin to realize just how quickly it all goes by."

"I know." They sat in silence for a few minutes and then Austin lowered his voice to a whisper. "They're bringing them in tomorrow, you know."

"Yes." Blake bit out the word. "That is all my patients have been talking about. I think the entire community is going to turn out to see the chiefs."

"I'll be there," Austin admitted. "When Satank, Satanta, and Big Tree are brought in to be tried for murder, I want to be there. I've been hearing stories of Satank's cruelty and Satanta's intelligence all my life. My editor tells me he's been deluged with inquiries from the eastern newspaper people about the upcoming trial. Says the Wichita Hotel is full of reporters."

"I'm not surprised. I may attend the trial, but I won't be in town tomorrow. I have to ride over to Mount Hecla station to see if Ben Taylor's crushed leg is improving. He's lucky he didn't lose it."

June fifteenth dawned clear and warm. Suzette rose early and dressed in a simple blue-and-white-checked calico dress. She fastened her heavy blond hair into a chignon and grabbed a sunbonnet from a bedpost. Knowing her father would have gone to Mount Hecla by the time she went to breakfast, Suzette felt sure she would have no trouble convincing her mother that she was going to Anna's to spend the day. Smoothing the folds of her dress nervously, Suzette took a deep breath and walked into the kitchen to join her mother at the breakfast table.

Lydia looked up at her daughter and smiled happily when she saw Suzette had dressed, brushed her hair, and had a little color in her cheeks.

"Darling" — Lydia took her hand — "it's so good to see you at the breakfast table again. Shall I fix you some buckwheat cakes or some bacon and eggs?"

"I'm not hungry, Mother, and I haven't time."

"Haven't time... Dear, where are you going? Why are you..."

Suzette's words tumbled out in a rush. "I'm going to Anna's to spend the day, Mother. She's learning how to sew and she has a new bolt of organza in the loveliest shade of green."

Relieved to see her unhappy daughter showing some signs of recovery, Lydia said, "Darling, that sounds wonderful. I'm glad you're wanting to learn to sew. We'll go shopping one day next week and pick out several pieces of fabric. I'll help you get started on a new Sunday dress if you like."

"Thank you, Mother, that would be nice. Now, if you don't mind, I think I'll leave before it gets too hot." Suzette turned to go.

"Suzette," her mother chided.

"Yes?" Suzette knew what was coming.

"Dear, you know your father took the buggy this morning. You'll have to ride your horse to Anna's."

"I know. That's fine." Suzette slipped out the door.

Following, her mother asked, "Then why are you dressed up? You've always worn your trousers when you ride. Suzette, why do you have on your Sunday dress?"

Suzette turned. "You're always wanting me to act more like a lady; I thought I'd please you and wear a dress. I'll have

Nate put that old sidesaddle on Glory. Now, I really must be going." She kissed her mother's cheek.

Lydia's arms went around her daughter's narrow waist and she held her for a minute. "I'm so glad you're feeling a little better, darling. I love you so much."

"I know, Mother. I'll be fine." She twisted from Lydia's embrace and hurried to the stables.

"Close the door," Suzette said conspiratorially as she and Anna went into the big upstairs bedroom in the Norris home.

Complying, Anna closed the heavy oak door and stood with her back to it, looking expectantly at her best friend. "Suzette, what is it? Has something else happened?" Anna went to Suzette, taking her hand. "Tell me."

"Anna, did you know that they are bringing in the Indian chiefs that murdered Luke? They are to arrive this very day!" Suzette's blue eyes flashed.

Dropping her chin, Anna slowly nodded her head. "Yes, I know." She lifted her head and looked at Suzette. "I couldn't tell you, Suz. I promised I'd not tell you anything that might upset you. We've all been so worried about you, I was afraid that... "

"Never mind." Suzette pulled her friend down onto the bed. She clung to Anna's hand, eagerly telling the wide-eyed girl of her plan. "Anna, you and I are going to ride into town. I'm going to get a look at the murderous savages that killed my Luke."

Jerking her hand from Suzette's tight grip, Anna began protesting, "Oh, Suzette, no, no. We can't do that! It wouldn't be good for you. Why pour salt into a wound? Spend the day here and we'll have the cook pack us a lunch and we'll ride down — "

"Anna Norris, I am going to town to see those chiefs with or without you. I want their faces stamped upon my memory so that I'll never forget. I didn't hate Indians before, and I used to think perhaps they were human beings, too, but they are not. They are despicable vermin and I shall hate every member of their race for as long as I live! I want Luke's murder avenged and I won't be satisfied until the chiefs are hanged for their deeds. I shall take great pleasure looking at them in shackles, knowing that they will soon be swinging from the gallows!"

"Suzette! Suzette!" cried her worried friend. "You are frightening me. I've never heard you speak like this. You aren't yourself. Why don't you lie down? I'll get you a drink of water."

Suzette's eyes softened a little. "Anna, don't worry. I didn't mean to alarm you, but I feel so strongly about what happened. Please, say you'll go into town with me."

"Do your mother and father know you plan to do this?" Anna's dark brows raised a little.

"No, they do not. Daddy left early this morning and won't return until night. Is your father here?"

"He left yesterday for Fort Worth." Anna was beginning to weaken. "I suppose I could tell Mother that I'm going to spend the day with you. If we do go, we could stay well back from the crowd. No one need ever know we were there."

The sun was high overhead and the day was growing uncomfortably warm. Suzette and Anna, their horses tethered to a gnarled oak tree behind the officers' quarters, walked close to the Fort Richardson parade ground, weaving in and out of the parked carts, wagons, and buggies. The area was alive with people. The residents of the small community had turned out for glimpses of the war chiefs, and a holiday atmosphere prevailed. Ladies with dainty parasols over their heads sat in buggies, gossiping with friends and neighbors. Children shouted and chased one another. Men stood in groups and talked animatedly about the bloody red men who would soon get their just reward. More than one man checked his pocket watch, eager for the minutes to pass, anxious for the awaited arrival.

On the parade ground, federal troops stood at attention in the hot June sun. The regimental band, instruments in hand,

.wore stern expressions, belying the excitement underneath. Every man, woman, and child assembled at the fort had heard of the daring Satanta. His reputation for unspeakable deeds was legendary. The mention of his name could strike terror in the heart of the boldest of white men. No wonder a huge crowd would gather to see the formidable chief, now a prisoner of war, subdued and defanged, shackled and humiliated. They longed to see the look of fear and shame they were certain the captured savage would be wearing.

"I want to get up closer." Suzette pulled at Anna's sleeve and started inching her way through the crowd.

Rushing to catch up, Anna said under her breath, "Suzette Foxworth! We're not supposed to be here, remember? The whole town is going to see us."

Suzette continued to press forward. "I don't care. I am going to get as close to those savages as I can. I want to be able to reach out and touch them!"

"Slow down, will you!" Anna was exasperated. "We should never have come. We should..."

Anna stopped talking. A low buzz went through the crowd, its volume quickly rising. Suzette, pushing past a large man in her path, turned and stood on tiptoes. The tired command of the 4th Cavalry rode into Fort Richardson. Their bronzed faces dusty and sweaty, their blue uniforms soiled, they rode regally nonetheless. They had been on a long and torturous mission and they had returned with their prisoners. Satanta and Big Tree rode in the middle of the column, Satanta more regal than the troopers escorting him.

Every eye was on him, and those who had longed to see a pitiful, repentant, frightened redskin were disappointed. Satanta, an Indian so intelligent he'd earned the name Orator of the Plains, was in his prime at age forty. He was stark naked save for his breechcloth and beaded moccasins. His thick raven hair hung long and loose, and his scalp lock was adorned with one eagle feather. His gleaming body was nothing short of beautiful. A tall man well over six feet, his shoulders were immense, his chest deep, his hips slim, his glistening thighs powerful. He sat astride his pony like a statue, the only movement a rippling of muscles, made more evident by the sheen of perspiration covering his smooth mahogany skin.

But for the occasional blinking of his black eyes, Satanta could have been made of stone. His face was proud and handsome, and he wore a fixed expression of disgust. Disgust with the curiosity of the white race, the race he hated with every fiber of his powerful body. Without uttering a sound or making a move, the savage chief left no doubt in anyone's mind how he felt about the stares and gazes sweeping eagerly over him.

Satanta was handcuffed; his feet were tied underneath his pony. He was completely helpless. But the proud blood that ran through his noble veins still surged. If the big man was afraid, it didn't show. The set of his jaw, the rigid back, and the cold black eyes bespoke nothing but bored indifference.

Suzette, clutching her sunbonnet in her perspiring hands, stood at the very edge of the crowd. She and Anna had managed to work their way to the front, and it was there they stood when the command halted. The two Indians were no more than twenty-five feet from the girls. Big Tree, the younger Indian, was not impressive. One quick look at the smaller man revealed regular features, lighter color, and a nervous manner. Suzette swung her gaze back to Satanta. The band began to play; Big Tree gazed at the bustle and excitement and looked as if he were about to smile. Not so Satanta. He sat staring straight ahead.

Suzette couldn't take her eyes off the impressive figure. She hated him with every fiber of her body. Was it he who took the life of her precious Luke? Did those cold black eyes look down into Luke's green ones as he sliced away the scalp? Did this magnificent-looking animal wear his cold, uncaring expression while he stole the very life from Luke's body?

Suzette could feel the blood pounding in her temples as her hands balled into fists and her stomach churned. She could feel her nausea rise, and perspiration trickled between her heaving breasts and behind her knees. Her gaze was locked on the naked chief, and in her mind's eye she could see his powerful body astride Luke's immobile frame, a long scalping knife raised high. The hand was dropping lower and lower and Suzette could feel the fever in her blood raging out of control.

At that instant, Satanta slowly turned his head. The black, glittery eyes were on her. She opened her mouth to scream and started to run toward him, revenge her intent. But darkness washed over her and she could feel her legs giving way. A strong pair of hands gripped her as Suzette screamed.

"She'll be all right, Anna. Stop worrying." Suzette heard a deep, resonant voice close to her. She emerged from the fog to see Austin Brand's face near hers. She was seated in his covered carriage, her head back against the fine, soft leather. Austin was seated beside her, pressing a dampened handkerchief to her brow. The bodice of her checkered dress had been loosened down to the swell of her bosom. Anna, a worried expression on her face, stood beside the carriage, fanning Suzette with her sunbonnet.

Smiling kindly, Austin said softly, "Are you feeling better, dear?"

Struggling to rise, Suzette, who was uncertain of what had happened, looked at his smooth, bronzed face.

"No, Suzette, don't try to get up yet." Austin eased her back against the seat and pressed the cool handkerchief to her throat. "Dear, you fainted. It's the heat, I'm sure. You should have left your sunbonnet on your head. Luckily, I was standing nearby and saw you falling."

"You just keeled over, Suzette," Anna said excitedly. "You opened your mouth like you were fixing to say something, and then you just collapsed. Are you okay?"

Embarrassed, Suzette murmured, "I'm perfectly all right. I'm so sorry. I've never fainted in my life, and I've always poked fun at females who did." She pushed Austin's big hand from her throat. "Thank you, Mr. Brand."

"There's no shame in fainting, Suzette. As I said, the sun's much too hot for you girls to be bareheaded." Austin looked from the pale Suzette to Anna. "Besides, it's difficult for me to believe that your parents let you two come to town alone." He raised his thick eyebrows. "Hmm?"

Ducking her head, Anna shuffled her feet. Suzette looked straight into his gray eyes and said, "They didn't know. Now they will. Everyone in town saw us, and I suppose the majority saw me pass out." She made a face.

Austin smiled. "I can't say that I blame you for wanting to see the chiefs. However, now that all the excitement is over and the savages have been placed in the guardhouse, I think you should be going home."

"I agree." Anna nodded. "Come on, Suz, let's go get our horses."

Suzette started to move across the leather seat, but once again Austin Brand put a hand on her arm to stop her. "No, dear, I don't think you should ride your horse home after you've just fainted. Stay where you are. I'll get Glory and tie her to the back of the carriage. I'm driving you home."

"Oh, Mr. Brand, that isn't necessary, really." Suzette was shaking her head. "I'm feeling just — "

"I'm taking you home, Suzette. That's final." He turned to Anna. "I'll be more than happy to take you, too, Anna. Why don't you get in and I'll go get the horses."

"Thanks all the same, Mr. Brand, but I don't have that far to go and I'm not ill. I'll ride my horse home."

Climbing out of the carriage, the big man took Anna's arm. "Then let's go to where you left your horses. Suzette, I'll be back with Glory in a few minutes."

"Yes, sir." Suzette sighed and watched him walk away with her friend. Pressing the damp cloth to her face once again, Suzette felt almost glad Austin Brand was there to take her home. She was drained and tired after the experience of the morning. She recalled the black piercing eyes of Satanta turning on her and she shivered. Hate for him and his entire race welled up in her and she laid her head back, muttering, "I hate you! I hate you and all your bloodthirsty brothers! I wish I could personally kill each and every one of you!"

When Austin Brand got into the carriage beside her, Suzette put a hand on his arm and said softly, "Mr. Brand, I'm sorry to be of trouble to you. You have no idea how much I despise those savages. My hatred is so intense, it makes me ill." She looked at him, her eyes narrowed.

His lips a thin line, he responded. "You couldn't hate Satanta any more than I do!"

Suzette had never seen such a look of venom on anyone's face, much less Austin Brand's. Alarmed, she said, "Mr. Brand, are you upset?"

Composing himself immediately, Austin said, "Sweetheart, I'm sorry. Let's try to forget. Sit back and relax."

On the ride home, Austin Brand used his abundant charm to try lifting the girl's spirits. Suzette hardly listened; her thoughts were still on Satanta. She tried to reply to his questions, but found it hard to listen attentively.

"Suzette?" He was looking down at her and she knew he must be waiting for her to respond. She looked at his strong, handsome face. His gray eyes were soft and kind, his full mouth was turned up in a warm smile, and his thick chestnut hair gleamed in the bright sunshine. As always, Austin Brand looked as though he had just stepped from his bath. His expensive custom-made clothes looked fresh and clean, though he'd been standing out in the hot June sun for hours. His silky shirt was as soft and snowy-white as the puffy clouds high above them. Austin was a massive man, his chest broad and powerful. He stood well over six feet, four inches, and he was not slenderly built. His thighs and legs were muscular, as were his long, bronzed arms. He took pride in looking his best and he was sure enough of his manhood not to be bothered when some of the local cowhands and saloon crowd kidded him about being a dandy. Austin Brand could easily whip any man in Jack County with one big hand tied behind him, so it was easy for him to laugh away remarks that would cause a less confident man to take offense.

"Suzette," he repeated. "What is it? You are staring at me."

"I… I'm sorry," she stammered a little and lowered her eyes. "I was just thinking that you are wearing a suit coat, yet you don't look too warm. I'm in a cool dress and I passed out from the heat. It doesn't make sense."

Austin grinned at her. "I had a couple of drinks of strong whiskey before I went down to the fort. Nothing to keep you nice and cool like a good hot drink." He winked at her.

"You are teasing me, Mr. Brand." She smiled.

"Yes, I am, sweetheart, because I want to see that sweet smile back on your lovely face."

Suzette looked at her hands in her lap. "I know I've been… well, Mother and Daddy are worried, I'm sure. I hate it, but I… I… "

Austin reached out and gently patted her folded hands. "Suzette, I know it's been very hard on you. Luke was a fine boy and he would have made you a good husband. Such a terrible tragedy. I'm so very sorry, dear."

"I know you are, Mr. Brand."

"Suzette, it's much too soon to say this, but you will find someone else someday and… "

"No!" She looked into his eyes steadily. "No. I don't want to find someone else. I don't want to love anyone else ever again. Never!"

Austin sighed. "I understand. Your father tells me you're not interested in attending college in Fort Worth."

"No, I'm not."

"How would you feel about a trip to Europe on a big ship?"

"Mr. Brand, my parents certainly don't have the kind of money… "

"I thought it could be Beth's and my gift to you for completing your school studies. You know how we feel about you and your parents. My little Jenny is a happy, healthy little girl because of your father. We're all like family, Suzette. I'd be happy to give you the money."

"Mr. Brand, I would never take money from you. Neither would my family." Suzette saw the look on his face and reached out to touch his arm. "You're very kind, and I appreciate it. But, honestly, I don't care anything about seeing Europe."

"There must be something I could do. I've got an idea, Suzette." His gray eyes sparkled. "How would you like to work for me at the newspaper? Blake says you've always kept a journal. Perhaps you could write a nice article to interest the lady readers. Let's see, you could give them new recipes, and tell them about the latest fashions, and —"

"Austin!" Suzette surprised herself at the familiarity, but her hand tightened on his arm. "Austin! Yes, yes! I'd like to write for your newspaper!"

Suzette's face had taken on some color and her blue eyes were shining. Her perfect mouth was turned up into a smile and the hand clasping Austin's arm was holding him in a tight, excited grip. Delighted to see the transformation, Austin carefully removed her fingers from his arm, then slipped the arm around her waist, pulling her to his side.

"Sweetheart, I'm so glad you're interested. It will be good for you to be busy. I'll talk to your father about it. Tonight you can see if your mother has any special recipes to print, and I'll speak to Beth at dinner. She'll help you, I'm sure." He squeezed her slim waist, then released her.

Blue eyes narrowing just a little, she touched his shoulder and said in an even voice, "You've got it wrong, Austin. I'm not going to write a ladies' column. I'm going to be a reporter. I'm going to write news, real news!"

Austin shook his head. "No, Suzette, I'm afraid that's impossible. Reporting is a man's job, and I just can't allow you to do it. I don't think you understand what... "

"I most certainly do understand! You think me an empty-headed young girl who doesn't know... "

"Now just a moment, Suzette," he interrupted. "That's not what I think at all. I know very well that you are an intelligent and capable young woman."

"Then, please, Austin, let me be a reporter. I want to cover the trial of the Indian chiefs."

"No, dear, I just can't. Frankly, I don't think you should even attend the trial. Have you already forgotten about fainting this morning?"

"Austin Brand, that was from the heat!"

"Was it, dear?" His expression was knowing. "We're alone, Suzette, so be honest with me. You were ill with rage against those savages. That's what made you faint."

"That's not true!" She was shocked that he could read her thoughts so accurately.

"Yes, Suzette, it is true. But I understand, and I'll tell no one. Listen to me, I'm your friend. Take the position I'm offering you at the paper. Write a nice column. Lord knows you always look lovely, and let's face it, most of the dear ladies of Jacksboro could use some tips on how to dress. Don't you agree?" He smiled at her with an easy warmth that made it impossible not to smile back. "That's much better. I know you're smart, Suzette. If you don't enjoy it, you can resign and I promise I won't be upset with you."

Suzette was silent for several minutes. He was adamant that she not be a reporter; kind though he was, there was no changing him on the subject. Suzette looked up at him and smiled her most charming smile. "Mr. Brand, thank you for offering me a position at the *Echo*. Perhaps you're right. I could write some nice articles on fashion and cooking. I accept."

Delighted she'd come to her senses, Austin touched her cheek. "The position is yours, Suzette. We'll speak to the editor of my paper tomorrow and tell him you're coming on board."

Suzette, her mind racing, impulsively kissed him on the cheek and said sweetly, "Mr. Brand, with the exception of Luke and Daddy, you're the nicest man I've ever known."

Grinning at her, he responded, "My dear, with the exception of Beth and Jenny, you're the sweetest young lady I've ever known."

5

Suzette set herself on a campaign to convince her worried mother and father that she was putting her grief behind her. She proudly announced that Austin Brand had generously offered her a position at his newspaper, *The Prairie Echo*, and that with their permission, she would like to pursue what seemed to her an interesting and honest profession.

"Sweetheart," her father said as he put an arm about her slender shoulders, "your mother and I are delighted you are feeling better, but are you certain you want to work at Austin's paper? Most young ladies wouldn't be interested in a man's position."

"I'm not most young ladies, Daddy, and it isn't a man's position. I'm very grateful to Mr. Brand for this opportunity. Please say it meets with your approval. I so need something to interest me!"

Looking from Suzette's hopeful young face to Lydia's, then back again, he smiled and nodded. "If it will make you happy, Suzette, you have our approval and permission. However, you will ride into town each morning with me. When I'm unavailable, Nate is to accompany you. You're much too young to be riding alone, especially with all the soldiers from the fort constantly milling about on the sidewalks near the newspaper office."

"Your father's right, Suzette. If you insist on working at that paper, then we won't stop you. But you are never to go into town alone, no matter what," her mother added.

It had been easier than she'd hoped. The very next morning, she rose early, dressed sedately, and rode into town with her father, who was bound for Ross Valley, where he would inoculate settlers against smallpox. Austin Brand, immaculately turned out and smiling warmly, was awaiting her at the *Echo* office on the north side of the town square.

As soon as Blake left, Austin introduced Suzette to his editor, a slight man with greenish eyes, a sallow complexion, a tuft of thin gray hair circling his head, and a smile so bright it transformed his appearance. He clasped Suzette's hand and pumped with amazing strength. "Miss Foxworth, welcome, welcome. Mr. Brand tells me you're to be the new fashion editor for *The Prairie Echo*."

"I... yes, sir, Mr. Keach. I will work real hard and I know I can learn a lot from you."

Ben Keach beamed. "I'm sure you're an intelligent young lady and that you will learn rapidly." He gave her a small bow, nodded to Austin Brand, and backed away.

Austin's hand went under her elbow as he propelled her past the noisy machinery to the back of the room, then pushed open a door to reveal a nicely furnished office. He motioned her inside and closed the door behind them.

"There," he said and pulled out a chair for her. "It's a little quieter back here." After she had seated herself in a straight-backed chair in front of a big mahogany desk, he stepped behind the desk and lowered himself into the padded swivel chair facing her. "Suzette, this is my office, but you're to feel free to use it any time you like. It's not locked, so when you desire privacy, just lock it from the inside. Be very careful around the machinery. Catch a petticoat in it and no telling what damage it might do — to you, I mean, not the machinery. I can't caution you too much, dear. Oh, yes, there are soldiers loitering about outside most of the time, and often as not, they have been drinking. You must be very careful. You're so pretty and I'm afraid... "

"Please, Mr. Brand." Suzette raised her hand. "You sound exactly like my daddy."

He grinned sheepishly. "I'm sorry, sweetheart. I suppose I do. But, then, I'm old enough to be your father, so I feel very protective of you."

Suzette smiled broadly. "Mr. Brand, thirty-six may be quite old for a woman, but not for a man. I don't think you are at all old. Why, my friends talk about what a handsome man you are. I assure you, they don't consider you the fatherly type."

"I'm flattered," he said with no embarrassment. He was aware of his attractiveness, but he had no intention of telling Suzette that on more than one occasion the very young ladies she spoke of had openly flirted with him, making it known that advances from him would not be repelled. He had never considered satisfying their curiosity. To him they were children and he a married man with a lovely daughter. He ignored advances made by hopeful females of any age, a fact that made him even more desirable. They were puzzled that a man so good-looking could be content with Beth Brand, a woman who, although sweet and intelligent, was no beauty. Tall and much too thin, Beth had a pleasant but rather plain face. Her eyes, hazel and very expressive, were her best feature; they lit up when she met a friend, and held a look of joy when they rested on her daughter, Jenny. When she looked at her big, handsome husband, pure adoration radiated from them.

"I must be going now. I'll give you no more lectures, but should you ever need me to slay a dragon for you, be assured I'll be your knight." Austin stood up and walked around the desk to her.

When he put out his hand, she took it and rose. "Mr. Brand, you'll never know how much I appreciate this opportunity. I won't let you down, I promise."

"You'll do fine. I'm not the least bit worried about you." He led her out into the noisy outer room where black machinery printed, stamped, batched, clamped, and spewed out the newspaper.

That night Suzette sat cross-legged on her bed and picked up her journal from the night table. She opened the worn velvet book and began to write:

June 16, 1871

It has been almost a full month since my darling

Luke was killed by the heartless savages. Oh, how I long to slip unseen into the guardhouse at Fort Richardson and kill the murderous chiefs! I could sleep like an innocent infant with their blood on my hands! I live only to hear the sentence passed down in court that they will be hanged for their crimes.

I am grateful to our family friend, Austin Brand. I have accepted a position at his newspaper and I fully intend to cover the trial without his permission. It's the only reason I accepted. I can think of nothing duller than writing a foolish column about clothes and hairstyles. How could such frivolous things matter when Luke is dead and the animal responsible is at this minute lying down to sleep right here in Jacksboro. Ladies' fashion, indeed! The trial of the despicable Satanta is the only thing on earth that matters to me.

When Suzette arrived at the newspaper office the next morning, she carried under her arm several fashion books. "'Morning, Mr. Keach." She removed her bonnet and pushed back her long blond curls.

"Miss Foxworth." He bobbed his head and his eyes twinkled. "I thought you might like to learn a little about how all this complicated machinery operates." He swept his arm out in a wide arc. Proud of the latest equipment Austin Brand had bought for the *Echo*, he was like a parent eager to show off his new baby.

Suzette stepped closer and nodded eagerly. There were two reasons for her enthusiasm. She had an inquiring mind and was always anxious to learn new things; and she saw immediately how much Ben Keach wanted her to appreciate the clanking machinery that so fascinated him. Suzette gladly gave him the quick response he wanted.

And there was another reason, a strictly selfish one. She intended to make the editor aware from the beginning that she was intelligent, dependable, curious, and competent — and the only person to cover the impending trial. She would make him respect her; he would become a friend. She might even be able to make him forget she was a female. Austin Brand need know nothing of her plans. Anyway, Austin refused to see her as anything other than the pretty young daughter of his good friends. She'd make him change his mind in time!

Long before eight-thirty A.M. on July 5, 1871, when the trial of the Kiowa Indian chiefs was scheduled to begin inside the sandstone courthouse on the square, the small community of Jacksboro bustled with excitement. From all over Jack and Young counties came people intent on witnessing the big event. Never before in the history of the United States had Indian chiefs been tried for their crimes in a white man's court.

Carts, wagons, buggies, and cow ponies crowded each side of the square. The dry goods store, blacksmith shop, Wichita Hotel, and saloons swarmed with settlers, farmers, and cowboys. Blue-coated soldiers from the fort mingled with gun-toting cowhands; and churchgoing ladies rubbed elbows with ladies of the evening. Eastern newspaper gentlemen, their fashions and their accents drawing amused snickers from the Texans, made their way to the back room of the dry goods store. There they could help themselves from the upturned barrels of whiskey or brandy, a custom of the frontier they most heartily approved.

They didn't much care for the rowdy saloons, which the tough elements of Jacksboro, that unsavory class of men that even the local townspeople feared, preferred. The saloons were a second home to the local troublemakers, men like the Taylor brothers. Bold thieves, they were mean and ruthless, and decent folk made it a rule to avoid them.

Suzette Foxworth sat rigidly in the back of the family buggy, her hands clutched tightly in her lap. The broad-brimmed bonnet she wore shaded her delicate skin from the harsh rays of the July sun. Fresh and pretty in a pink organza dress trimmed with white lace, her appearance belied the excitement she felt. Knowing that to display her true feelings would be just cause for her parents to keep her home from the trial, she had played her part perfectly. Only the kindly Mr. Keach knew what she was intending.

Suzette's position at the newspaper afforded her access to a coveted front-row seat in the crowded courthouse on this memorable day. Hastily explaining to her parents that Mr. Keach had told her she could sit in the press section, she left them to their bewilderment and quickly made her way to the front of the room. She took her seat proudly in the all-male press section, stepping confidently past overdressed men from eastern newspapers, most of whom were already perspiring in the withering Texas heat.

The small room was packed. The crowd swelled from the courthouse and overflowed outside. Spectators blocked every window, preventing any possibility of a cooling breeze reaching those inside.

Suzette sat between two tall strangers, her tablet in her lap, pencil in hand, and scanned the noisy, overcrowded room. Her mother and father sat near the back on the left side of the aisle. Anna Norris, who sat between her parents, was waving wildly, trying to get Suzette's attention. It was then that she caught sight of Austin Brand, hat in hand, dapper in a summer suit of linen, standing against the far wall. He was looking at her, his expression puzzled. Suzette bent her head. He'd understand her presence in the press section soon enough.

A commotion pulled Suzette's attention to its source. The two Kiowa chiefs, guarded by twenty armed men, burst through the doors of the courtroom. Satanta and Big Tree were wearing blankets and their chains clanked loudly. Accompanied by an interpreter from Fort Sill and their counsel, they marched to the front of the room.

The jury had been impaneled; the district attorney rubbed his hands together in eager anticipation. Every man on the jury wore a gun. While the charges were read, Suzette, her heart in her throat, watched the Indians. Satanta, his cruel, handsome face expressionless, listened to the interpreter plead "not guilty."

The counsel for the defense, Tom Ball, opened the proceedings with an eloquent speech on behalf of the accused, claiming "the noble red men" had suffered, had been "cheated and cheated and despoiled of their lands, driven westward, westward, until it seemed as though there was no limit to the greed of their white brothers." Mr. Ball threw off his suitcoat and continued his impassioned speech, finally urging that the great chiefs be allowed to "fly away free and unhampered."

Suzette Foxworth, her heart threatening to pound out of her chest, bit the soft inside of her lip until she tasted blood. When, to her surprise, she locked eyes with Satanta, she saw a faint flicker of approval in his. She quickly looked away. Her eyes swept to Austin Brand. He, too, was looking at Satanta, but in his gray eyes was pure hate. Never had she seen Austin Brand look so frightening; it was as if he longed to snap the Indian's neck with his bare hands.

Satanta was allowed to speak in his own behalf. At the sound of the deep, resonant voice, the hush in the crowded courtroom was palpable. All eyes were on the handsome chief, who looked unblinking at his armed jury as he spoke: "I have never been so near the Texans before. I look around and see your braves, squaws, and papooses, and I have said in my heart, 'If I ever go back to my people, I will never make war on you again.'

"I am a big chief among my people and have great influence among the warriors of my tribe. They know my voice and will hear my word. If you let me go back to my people, I will withdraw my warriors from Texas. I will make them cross the Red River and that shall be the line between us and the palefaces. I will wash out the spots of blood and make it a white land and there shall be peace. The Texans may plow and drive their oxen to the banks of the river."

Satanta paused, his black eyes roving over the crowd. A slight smile lifted his full lips. "But if you kill me, it will be like a spark on the prairie. Make big fire! Burn heap!"

Suzette had never heard anyone lie so convincingly. A natural actor, an eloquent speaker, a magnetic figure, the chief held his audience spellbound. Suzette started to think the unthinkable. Would the jury, knowing he was lying, be afraid of his bold threats of war and let him go free?

Witnesses took the stand. General Mackenzie, the Fort Sill interpreter, and Brazeale, the man who had survived the massacre, told what they knew. Suzette wrote rapidly. After the last one had left the box, S. W. Lanham, the district attorney, rose grandly from his chair. An able attorney, he convincingly reminded the jury, as well as the packed courthouse, that the bloody chiefs murdered the unsuspecting victims in cold blood, butchering and torturing them for no reason, leaving them to die of their wounds; and, yes, even slowly roasting one poor soul chained helplessly to a wagon wheel.

Suzette studied the jury, who now rose and retired to a corner of the building. They were back in their seats within minutes, and Suzette knew what the verdict was even before she heard the words.

"Has the jury agreed upon a verdict?" Judge Soward's voice was calm.

"We have," said the foreman.

"What say you, Mr. Foreman? Are these Indian chiefs, Satanta and Big Tree, guilty, or not guilty, of murder?"

The foreman, shouting loud enough to be heard on the square, proclaimed, "They are! We figger 'em guilty!"

Suzette exhaled. Smiling, she looked at Satanta, whose black eyes flickered briefly when the judge sentenced the chiefs to death by hanging on September 1. The proud and handsome face showed no emotion at all.

As Satanta and Big Tree were led from the room, Suzette, light-headed now, scrambled from her place, anxious to get across the street to the newspaper office. Ignoring Anna's summons and Austin Brand's black looks, she pushed through the throngs of people jamming the sidewalks. Rushing to her small desk, she jerked a fresh tablet from the middle drawer and, with a trembling hand, wrote her headlines:

The Prairie Echo

July 5, 1871
Jacksboro, Texas

INDIAN CHIEFS FOUND GUILTY OF MURDER!
HANGING SEPTEMBER 1!

Justice prevailed on this memorable day! Satanta and Big Tree, Kiowa chiefs who led the senseless attack known as the Warren Wagon Train Massacre, were found guilty of murder by a jury too brave to be frightened by threats of retaliation from the eloquent, bloodthirsty savage they call Satanta.

Satanta, his days numbered, failed to bluff and bully his way out of a date with the hangman's noose. On September 1, the redskin known as the Orator of the Plains will be hanged by the neck until dead! Big Tree will follow the older chief to the gallows for his date with destiny.

Suzette, her pencil flying, wrote as rapidly as she could. When finally she finished the long, vivid account, she dashed out to Mr. Keach and handed him her notes. "Please, please, Mr. Keach. Before you say no, just read what I've written. It's good, I swear it is."

Ben Keach blinked and began to read. After what seemed an eternity to Suzette, he looked up. "Miss Foxworth, you've a real talent. Let's get this set in type!"

Suzette hugged the skinny little man, much to his embarrassed pleasure.

Promptly at nine the next morning, Austin Brand appeared at the newspaper office. Nodding a greeting to his editor, he made his way to Suzette's desk. Under his arm he carried a copy of *The Prairie Echo*. She didn't hear him approach — the room was much too noisy — but sat thumbing through a fashion book until he leaned over the desk and called her name.

Startled, she jumped, looking up at him. "M — Mr.

Brand," she stammered and rose from her chair. "I didn't see you come in."

Austin smiled devilishly. "Too interested in your fashion column, I imagine." His left eyebrow lifted.

"Why, yes, I was... I..." She laughed and slammed the book shut. "No! You know very well I'm not. What did you think? Did you read it? Was it good? Can I continue to do real reporting?"

Austin Brand dropped the newspaper on her desk and threw up his hands in surrender. "Please, please. For such a slip of a girl, you're most intimidating. I read it, dear, and much as I hate to admit it, you're really very talented. No man could have done a better job. I'd be lying if I pretended otherwise."

Her blue eyes sparkling, she ran around the desk and grabbed his arm. "You mean it, Austin? You really think it was good?"

Patting her hand, he nodded. "It was great, Suzette. I underestimated you and I apologize for that."

"That's all right." She was happy to forgive him. "Now you'll let me be a real reporter. That's all that matters."

Austin sighed. "I suppose I've no choice, have I, pretty girl?"

"Absolutely none," she assured him happily. "Now, if you'll excuse me, Austin, I've work to do. Seems a dark, handsome renegade not more than eighteen years old has pulled off a daring daytime robbery in Fort Worth. Got away clean with more than twelve thousand dollars!"

6

Less than a month after the famous trial, the death sentence for the two murderous chiefs was reduced to life in prison. Pressured by the Superintendent of Indian Affairs, President Grant, fearing an all-out war if the chiefs were executed, sent down a federal request to the governor of Texas to commute the sentences. Upon hearing the news, Suzette asked Ben Keach if she might be excused for a moment.

Nodding his assent, he watched her turn and make her way to the back of the building, where she let herself into Austin Brand's private office. She stood with her back pressed against the heavy door frame, fighting a fury she'd never known before. Her temples throbbed, and she clumsily loosened the hooks of her high-necked dress and commanded her knees to stop shaking. Making her way to Austin's big oak desk, she grabbed at the smooth edge and clung to it. She closed her eyes tightly and saw again the proud, handsome chief, his black eyes on her.

"If they won't kill him, I will," Suzette muttered and moved behind Austin's desk. She jerked open the middle drawer and felt around until her fingers touched the small pearl-handled revolver she knew he kept there.

When she asked Mr. Keach about the revolver, he'd responded matter-of-factly. "It belongs to Mr. Brand," he said, as though he had always known it was there. "It's not loaded, though there are bullets in the drawer. It's not much of a weapon, a lady's gun really. Mr. Brand said he bought it for his wife but she was horrified and refused to take it. He brought it here and it's been here in the desk ever since."

Suzette pulled the gun from its resting place and fished around for the ammunition, then painstakingly loaded the small handsome gun. She'd never seen one quite like it, but she knew something about firearms and was not afraid of them. It was then that she realized she didn't have her small handbag with her. Laying the gun on the desk in front of her, she turned the big swivel chair around and pulled her dress and petticoat up over her knees. Smiling wickedly, she reached for the loaded gun and shoved it into the pale pink garter she wore on her left thigh. The revolver's cold steel felt good against her warm skin; with a self-congratulatory "Well done," she lowered her skirts just as there was a knock on the office door.

"Suzette, may I come in?" It was Austin Brand.

"I... yes, yes, of course, come in, Mr. Brand."

His face was grim as he closed the door behind him. "My dear, I just heard the news. I know how you feel." His voice was low, concerned.

Her own voice much too shrill, she asked, "How? Austin, how could it be? It's not fair, not at all fair! They killed my Luke and the others! Why aren't they going to pay with their lives?" Her blue eyes flashed fire, her pale cheeks showed high spots of color.

Austin stepped past her, nodding in understanding. He went behind his desk, pulled out the right bottom drawer, and brought up a half-full bottle of whiskey. "Suzette, sit down, please." She dropped into the chair facing him and watched as he took two glasses from a shelf behind him. He splashed a small portion of the whiskey into each glass and handed one to her. "If it's any consolation, dear, I think a man like Satanta would much rather be put to death than spend his life in prison. Can you imagine a man who has roamed the plains all his life being confined to a tiny cell, never to be set free?" He motioned for her to drink.

"But, Austin, I can't... I've never had liquor in my life." She thought he was teasing her.

"I know," he said evenly, "but I want you to drink it, Suzette." He watched as she put the glass to her lips. She took a sip and made a face. She coughed and looked at him. "Take the rest of it," he instructed.

"But, I... "

"Drink it."

She obeyed and drained the contents of the glass. She fanned at the air in front of her burning lips and looked at Austin. He tossed his down in one swallow and rose from his chair. "That's good. Feel a little better? More relaxed?"

"Yes, I do," she admitted and leaned back in her chair, some of the blinding rage ebbing.

"I'm glad." He smiled and walked around the desk. He stood directly in front of her chair and lounged back against the desk. "Now, Suzette, give me the gun."

"What? I... I don't know what you're talking about... I never —"

Austin leaned over her, placing his big hands on the chair arms, trapping her. "I want the gun, my dear."

"I have no idea what you are speaking of, Austin," she said indignantly. His gray eyes made her lower her head.

One of his hands left the chair and went to her chin. Gently he raised her face, forcing her to look at him. "Suzette, I think you know exactly what I'm talking about. If you don't do it, I will have to take it from you." He released her chin and sat back, then moved away from her.

Suzette bolted for the door. Moving with incredible quickness for a man of his size, Austin blocked her way. Noticing her frustration, he pleaded softly, "Please, Suzette, give me the gun and I'll let you go."

"No!" she shouted. "I won't! I'm going to kill Satanta! Do you hear me? I intend to kill the animal that murdered Luke. You can't stop me; no one can stop me. I want him dead. Dead! Now, get out of my way!"

Sighing, Austin took her arm and pulled her to him. Ignoring her protests, he let his hand glide lightly over her right hip and thigh, then the left. Through her skirts, he could feel the small gun riding high on the inside of her left thigh. He shook his head and said, "Suzette, I'm going to release you. When I do, you're to turn away from me and take the gun from under your skirt."

"I won't do it! You can't make me, and I'm not going to do it. I'm going to kill the savages!" He frightened her; she sensed he meant what he was saying, though she couldn't imagine a gentleman like Austin Brand would actually...

"Very well." His voice was calm. He turned her away from him, then pulled her back against him. He wrapped a long arm around her small waist, then moved his hand to her long skirts.

"Stop!" she begged, horrified. "I... I'll give you the gun. Just let me go, Austin."

"No," he said evenly. "You're not getting away from me until that gun is in my hand." The arm encircling her waist tightened and she could feel his powerful chest pressing her back and shoulders.

"But... but... the gun is under my petticoats. I'll have to —"

"I know. You'll have to raise your dress to retrieve it. Do it. I'm standing behind you; I won't see anything. I'm losing patience; I want the gun."

Suzette knew he meant what he said. She pulled up her skirts. The man behind her smiled to himself at her youthful embarrassment.

"Close your eyes, Austin," she commanded feebly as she struggled with the heavy folds of muslin until her fingers touched the small gun. She snatched it from its resting place and jerked her skirts down once again.

His hand closed over hers as he took the gun from her and put it in the waistband of his trousers at the small of his back. Suzette, trembling slightly, let her head fall back against the broad expanse of his chest.

Softly Austin said into her ear, "Sweetheart, I just want you to know that I understand. If I could, I'd kill that filthy savage for you... for me. I hate him, too, believe me. But neither of us would be allowed to get close enough to kill him. They guard him night and day. They'll be transporting him to the state penitentiary in Houston any day. You must try to put him from your mind."

"Austin," she said tiredly and relaxed against him, not yet realizing that he had released her, that his hands were at his sides, not touching her. She could have stepped away from him. "You won't tell my parents about this, will you?"

"Tell them what?" He smiled.

Suzette smiled too and slowly turned to face him. "Thank you, Austin."

"I must be going, Suzette. You'll be all right now, won't you?"

"Thanks to you, yes. However, if you don't mind, and if Mr. Keach has no objection, I think I'll leave early this afternoon."

"Of course you may leave. Need a ride home?"

"No, thanks. I'll go down to Daddy's office and ride home with him."

"Good enough." He put his hand on the doorknob.

"Austin."

"Yes?"

"Do you think it's disrespectful for me to call you Austin?"

"I think it's flattering. Makes me feel a little less like a decrepit old man." A dazzling smile lit up his handsome face, and his gray eyes twinkled with mischief.

It was impossible not to smile back at him.

Ten minutes later, Suzette stepped into the quiet reception room of her father's office. An elderly lady sat by the front window, but didn't lift her head at Suzette's entry. There were no other patients waiting, Suzette was relieved to note. She was hot and tired and longed to go home.

She took a seat across from the woman and loosened the ribbons of her bonnet, then pulled it off and shook the long blond hair about her shoulders. Longing to yank it up off her neck, she reined in the impulse and endured the discomfort. When she heard a door opening from the back office, she snapped her head around. Her father's voice was kind. "You're not to worry, Mr. Mason. I know you're an honest man. I don't mind waiting until you are able to pay. We all come up a little short at times. Think no more of it."

Suzette shook her head. Her softhearted father was once again letting a patient go away without paying for his services. It was nothing new; half the community owed him money. At times Suzette wondered if he made any money at all caring for the sick of Jacksboro. Who but her father would spend every waking hour tending the sick and afflicted for miles around, going where he was needed at any hour of the day or night, often getting nothing for it but several frying chickens or perhaps a pig? Suzette smiled. Maybe that was one of the reasons she loved him so much. He was good, as good a man as God ever created.

Blake's eyes lit up when he saw his daughter. She smiled at him, and was relieved to see the elderly man take the arm of the woman by the window. The old couple made their way out of the hot room and Suzette rose and went to her father. "You look tired, Daddy. Through for the day?"

"That I am. You, too?"

She nodded and went with him to the back room to put away his instruments and tidy up. While she spread a clean white sheet on the hard, oblong table at the room's center, Blake cleared off his desk. Suzette watched her father. He looked more tired than usual and very pale. Unaware of her eyes on him, he clutched the desk as though he were afraid of falling.

"Daddy, what is it?" She was at his side in an instant, her heart beginning to pound.

"Nothing... nothing, darling. I just had a little pain in my head. It's passed already." He smiled at her, but she was standing near enough to see the perspiration on his upper lip and brow.

"Sit down, Daddy." She helped him to his chair. Dropping to her knees beside him, she held his hand and continued to fuss over him. "You're ill, Daddy. Something's wrong!"

He patted her cheek. "Darling, it's nothing. Please don't look so stricken. If it'll make you feel better, I'll see a physician when I go to Fort Worth next month for that meeting on communicable diseases. How does that sound?"

"Promise me you'll do it, Daddy?" Her eyes clouded with worry.

"On one condition." He grinned at her, feeling a little better. "You won't tell your mother about this."

"I promise, Daddy." She smiled back at him and helped him to his feet.

Blake Foxworth didn't tell his daughter that he was in almost constant pain, or that he feared the worst. With great effort he managed to eat supper that night, although his suffering had intensified with the setting sun and he longed only for the blessed relief of sleep. While his wife and daughter cleared away the dishes, Blake went onto the porch and raised both hands to his pounding head.

From inside his vest pocket came a tiny pill. It was only the smallest of doses, but the morphine would make it possible for him to rest. He'd long since passed the time when sleep would come unaided. Already he dreaded the time when the pill was not enough and he would require a hypo. It would be difficult to administer an injection at home without being seen by his wife and daughter.

An hour later, feeling somewhat better, Blake lay in bed watching his pretty wife brush her long, dark hair. She was worried about their daughter and wanted reassurance from her husband.

"Blake, do you think it proper for Suzette to be a reporter? There she was at that trial of those horrid savages, sitting up there with the eastern press, all of whom were men. And it's not just that she's a girl; she's so young! I'm disappointed in Austin. He should never have let her cover the trial. He should have consulted us..."

"Darling," Blake interrupted, "Austin didn't let Suzette do anything. You know what a headstrong girl she is. Don't go blaming Austin. I suspect that when Suzette accepted his offer, she had something else in mind." He smiled, knowing how his clever daughter's mind worked.

"Perhaps you're right, but I don't like it. Austin meant well when he offered her —"

"Lydia, Austin is a good man and a good friend. He was

trying to be helpful. And our daughter *is* better. She can't grieve for Luke when she is busy, so I'm grateful to Austin. You should be, too. He's concerned about Suzette, just as we are."

Lydia sighed and laid her brush down. "You're right, Blake. She is better now, and that's the important thing." Lydia put out the lamp on her vanity table and walked to the double bed. She sat down and put her hand on her husband's shoulder. Tears gathering in her dark eyes, she said, "I'd give anything to see her really happy again."

"Darling, I know." Blake pulled his wife into his arms. Gently he stroked her back and whispered soothingly, "Suzette will be fine, Lydia. Don't cry anymore. She's very young and very beautiful; life is all ahead of her. She'll be all right."

Clinging to him, Lydia pressed her cheek to his bare shoulder and nodded. "I know, I... it's just I want her to be happy all the time. I want her to know a love like ours, to have —"

"Shh," he breathed against her temple. "Suzette is a vibrant young woman, Lydia. She's had a tragic loss, but she will overcome it and be triumphant. She's warm and loving and, I assure you, in time she will fall in love and make some man an excellent wife. After all, she's our daughter, isn't she?" He smoothed the dark curtain of her hair back from her damp face and looked at her.

"Oh, Blake." She looped her arms around his neck. "You always know how to make me feel better. What would I ever do without you, my darling?" She hugged him tightly and kissed his ear.

His arms around her, Blake held her close, fighting the fear he must keep hidden from her. "You would survive, my love."

"Never!" she declared passionately and buried her face in his neck.

It was a sweltering day near the first of September when Suzette, flanked by Anna Norris and Anna's father, stood waving good-bye as the Butterfield stagecoach pulled away from the wooden sidewalk on the Jacksboro town square. Blake Foxworth had kept his promise to Suzette. He was going to see a physician in Fort Worth, and Lydia had agreed to go along for the week in the city. She knew nothing of her husband's plan to see a doctor. He'd told her only that he wanted to attend the physicians' convention and he thought she'd enjoy accompanying him.

Suzette, watching the clattering stage pull out of sight, knew her father's intentions. Beside her, Anna, her dark hair lying limp on her neck, complained, "They're gone. Let's get home. I want something cold to drink. I don't remember ever being so hot in my life!"

But Suzette was mesmerized by the slowly settling spirals of dust left by the departing coach. When Anna touched her arm, she jumped. Noting Anna's flushed, hot face, Suzette wondered why she herself had gooseflesh on her arms and why her hands suddenly felt so cold. And she wondered why she felt the need to run after the stage. Shuddering, she turned and said, "It is miserable here in the sun. Let's go."

It was still terribly hot two days later when Blake Foxworth climbed the stairs to the second-story office of young Dr. Perry C. Woods at the corner of Tenth and Commerce in Fort Worth. Dr. Woods, not yet twenty-five, a slim, nice-looking man with lively green eyes and an engaging smile, shook hands with the older doctor and invited him into the clinic. Dr. Woods, already noted throughout the west for his brilliance and candor, gave his patient the most extensive examination he had ever endured.

Flat on his back on a long, draped table, perspiring though he wore only his underwear, Blake Foxworth studied the intense features of the preoccupied young man as he poked and pried. "Dr. Woods, are you about finished? I'm to take my wife to lunch, and it's getting close to the noon hour."

Five minutes passed with no reply from the young doctor

standing over him. Finally, Woods, his face somber, said evenly, "Sit up, Dr. Foxworth, I'm all through." The young doctor went to a basin to scrub his hands. From over his shoulder, he said, "Get dressed and come into my office. We'll talk a bit." With that he toweled his hands dry and left the room.

When Blake, dressed and smiling, took a chair across from the young doctor, he saw his mortality in the green eyes fastened on him. "Dr. Foxworth, I'll not waste precious time, yours or mine. I'm terribly sorry, there's nothing I can do for you. Your fears are well founded. Apparently, the wounds you suffered in the War Between the States have caused permanent damage. You have a tumor on the brain, most likely caused by minute pieces of shrapnel lodged there. I wish I could tell you that we can operate and correct the problem. We can't. My guess is there is more than one piece of metal, perhaps several. It's much too late, Doctor. The tumor has been growing steadily and its location makes an operation impossible." Woods leaned back in his chair and studied the older man. "I'm sorry, Dr. Foxworth, truly sorry."

"Dr. Woods, it doesn't come as a great shock. For some time now I've suspected as much." He looked at the other man and smiled weakly. "Looks like the Yankees got me after all."

Dr. Woods said, "I'm from Boston, Dr. Foxworth. I've been in Forth Worth for only a couple of years. I don't suppose I could persuade you and your wife to come to the home of a Yankee for dinner."

Rising, Blake put out his hand. "We'd be delighted to dine in your home." They shook hands and walked to the office door. Shaking his head, Blake mused, "You know, Dr. Woods, I must find a doctor to take over my practice. Will you help me?"

"I know several young doctors who would jump at the opportunity, Dr. Foxworth. In fact, I might be interested myself."

"You? Why, Dr. Woods, you've a thriving practice here. Besides, are you sure your wife would want to move from the city?"

"I haven't a wife, Doctor. Are there any pretty girls in Jacksboro?"

"Well, it so happens I have a beautiful daughter, but I guess she'd be a little young for you. She's only sixteen."

Woods smiled. "I'm not yet twenty-five, Doctor. Is your lovely daughter in Forth Worth with you?"

Blake shook his head. "Afraid not. Truth is, Suzette's brokenhearted over the loss of her beau. She was planning to marry a young cowhand, but the lad was murdered by the Kiowa Indians last spring."

"I recall reading about the tragedy. Sorry to hear it touched your family so closely." Pausing, Woods looked up at Blake. "And I'm very sorry I had to give you such bad news today."

"How long, Doctor?"

"A year at the most, though I'm afraid... " He shrugged.

"I see. Don't speak of this in front of my wife, Doctor. She doesn't know."

"Sir, I'll say nothing, but you should prepare her, don't you think?"

"When the time is right, I'll tell her. Now, good day, Dr. Woods. I've taken up too much of your time."

"Nonsense, Doctor. Shall we set dinner for tomorrow evening at eight o'clock?"

"That would be very nice."

"Good. I'll call at your hotel at half-past seven."

When autumn winds began to whip the barren prairie, Blake Foxworth knew it would be the last time he went down to the creek bed with his daughter to pick up pecans from under the tall old trees that spilled their bounty onto the dying undergrowth. Suzette didn't see the look of sadness in her father's eyes when he surveyed the sprawling hills ablaze with fall's colors. The water oak by the back gate had turned a glorious shade of purple, as it did each year, its brilliance dueling with the oranges and yellows surrounding it. The air was crisp, clear, and invigorating. It was one of those rare, beautiful days in North Texas that made one glad to be alive. Indian summer.

"Look, Daddy!" Suzette shouted, running ahead of him. "There's more pecans this year than ever before. Mother will have us shelling them from now till Christmas!"

Christmas came with amazing speed that year. Blake sat in his favorite chair in the living room. A crackling fire burned in the grate, its flames lighting the lovely features of the two women seated on the floor near its warmth. Suzette and Lydia Foxworth, attired in their warm winter robes and slippers, their hair brushed and gleaming about their shoulders, giggled as they wrapped Christmas gifts. Blake, holding in his hand a steaming cup of coffee laced with brandy, watched affectionately as his two women decorated their Christmas packages with hair ribbon, colorful yarn, and sprigs of cedar sprinkled with flour. He looked from one pretty face to the other, from his blond daughter with her blue eyes shining and her ivory face glowing to his dark, beautiful wife, her brown eyes flashing, her olive skin flawless. Lydia was laughing at something Suzette had said. Unaware of her husband's intense perusal, she looked as young as their daughter and as vulnerable. His chest ached dully at the thought of leaving her. He'd taken care of the lovely Lydia since she was fifteen years old. He'd decided soon after they met that she would belong to him and he'd told her as much. Tossing her long, dark curls, she had smiled saucily and retorted, "Then you'd best come around often. There are other young men in New Orleans who want to call on me."

"I shall be here every night," he told her. "If you weren't so young, I'd marry you now. We'll have to wait, but no other man will get near you."

He'd kept his word; he spent each evening with the beautiful young girl until he thought he would surely be consumed with his passion for her. As soon as she turned seventeen, he made her his wife and was overjoyed that he was the only man who had ever so much as kissed the dark beauty. She looked now as she did on that first night ... beautiful and desirable. And young. So young he didn't have the heart to tell her the truth about his condition. He'd tell her soon, but not now, not at Christmas. He'd tell her in the spring. Surely he had that much time.

The spring of 1872 was breathtakingly lovely. Mother Nature outdid herself, as though trying to give Dr. Foxworth one last, glorious glimpse of her splendor before he departed. While honeysuckle climbed the window of his bedroom, filling the chamber with its sweet fragrance, Blake stood at the mirror, the bottom half of his lean face lathered with shaving soap. Across the room, his wife purred and stretched, smiling wickedly. Her ardent husband had made love to her in the sweet, still April morning and she lay watching him shave, content and lazy.

"Blake" — she smiled and smoothed the bedcovers — "it's still early. Dr. Woods won't be here for hours yet. Why not come back to bed and sleep a while longer."

Grinning at her in the mirror, he declined. "Darling, I can think of nothing I'd like better, but I promised Suzette I'd go for an early morning ride with her. She'll be knocking on the door any —"

"Hello in there! You planning to sleep all day?" Suzette's voice came through the closed bedroom door. "Daddy, if you're not in the kitchen in fifteen minutes, I'm going without you."

Lydia Foxworth laughed. "Blake, don't you think Suzette is getting more like her old self every day? Why, it wouldn't surprise me to hear her whistling soon."

Toweling his freshly shaven face, Blake Foxworth hoped his wife was right.

Suzette spurred her mount and bolted across the rolling

plains, thick rich carpets of green grass growing so rapidly that one could almost see it shoot up. Blake Foxworth trailed her, feeling somehow younger and more vital than he had in years. Savoring the feel of fine horseflesh beneath him, Blake gave the creature his head and the big bay galloped with surefooted speed and determination.

Miles were eaten up in minutes, and when the doctor saw Suzette pull up abruptly on her reins, he slowed his gelding. Suzette dismounted, dropping her reins to trail on the ground. Puzzled, Blake swung down and went to her. She walked away and he fell into step beside her. Sunflowers slapped their legs, and in the distance a robin's sweet song filled the morning air. Both were silent for a time. Then suddenly Suzette stopped.

"What is it, honey?"

When she raised her head to look at him, he saw the tears in her big blue eyes. "Daddy, why is Dr. Woods coming to Jacksboro today?"

"Well, darling, he's going to be my partner, you know that."

"So you've told me. Why do you want a partner?"

"Suzette, you're the one who suggested it. Remember, you said —"

"Daddy," she said sadly, and raised a hand to his arm. "Don't."

His hand covered hers and he swallowed. "You're too wise for your own good, dear. Walk with me and we'll talk about it."

Her father explained that the doctor had confirmed what he'd suspected for a long time. Biting her lip, Suzette listened to her father's calm voice.

"*Daddy.*" She stopped walking abruptly and threw her arms about his neck. "I won't let you go. I can't."

"Sweetheart" — he embraced her gently — "I'm depending on you to be strong. Your mother will need you."

Her head buried in his shoulder, she sobbed and said, "No! I can't! I can't! We'll find another doctor, we'll borrow some money from Austin Brand and go back east. They have doctors performing miracles in those fine hospitals. We'll... "

"Listen to me, Suzette." He held her from him and looked down at her. "Nothing can be done. Dr. Woods *is* an eastern doctor; he's been in Forth Worth for only two years. We must face what can't be changed." He raised a hand to wipe the tears from her cheeks. "Now, promise me you'll be my big girl and look after your mother when the time comes. I know it isn't fair to ask this of you, but in some ways you are stronger than your mother." He smiled and confided, "I've always prided myself that you're a lot like me. You and I can take what life hands us. Some people cannot. When young Luke was killed, you pressed on, and you'll continue to do so. I'm very proud of you, young lady. Now, give me a smile and tell me that you'll help to keep this from your mother."

Suzette gulped for air but nodded. When she could speak, she said bravely, "I'll take care of mother when you're gone, Daddy."

"Thank you, darling. Let's get back. It's time for us both to go into town."

When young Dr. Woods came to dinner that night at the Foxworth home, Blake hoped to see some electricity between the intelligent doctor and Suzette, but there was none. The two young people liked each other immediately, but that was as far as it went. After supper, Lydia obligingly asked her husband if he would dry the dishes for her. He knew what she was doing and agreed hastily. Although Suzette invited Dr. Woods onto the porch for his after-dinner drink, and the doctor quickly accepted, there was no magic between them. Snatches of their conversation drifted into the kitchen, and it consisted mostly of medicine, horses, and books.

"I was hoping Suzette and the young doctor might... " Lydia's voice trailed off and she sighed.

Smiling, Blake carefully dried a plate. "Me too. Do you think perhaps in time?"

"No, I don't think so." His wife smiled up at him and

handed him another slippery dish. "It's a shame. There are so few eligible young men in Jacksboro. Suzette may not be interested, but the rest of the girls in town will be after Dr. Woods. He's nice-looking and so likable."

A week later Blake and Lydia threw a small party to introduce the new doctor to their friends. It was a warm, lovely evening, and Lydia and Suzette set up a long picnic table in back of the house beneath the tall cottonwoods by the creek. Austin and Beth Brand and their daughter, Jenny, were the first arrivals. Austin carried a bottle of fine brandy in one hand for Dr. Foxworth, a big box of assorted chocolates for Lydia in the other. Soon families from all the surrounding ranches and farms arrived as friends and neighbors eagerly came to enjoy the hospitality of the Foxworths and to meet Dr. Perry Woods.

Suzette, standing beside Perry Woods, saw Anna coming around the house and called to her. "There's my best friend, Dr. Woods. She's Anna Norris. I'll introduce you."

The doctor didn't reply, but concentrated on the dark girl approaching. Suzette shrugged and looked at Anna. When she reached them, she said nothing to Suzette but stood directly in front of the doctor and looked at him as though she knew he had been waiting there just for her. Suzette's gaze flickered back to the doctor. His green eyes were riveted to Anna's, carefully drinking in her fresh beauty.

"Dr. Perry Woods, may I present my friend, Anna Norris." Suzette wondered if either of them heard her. "Anna, this is Dr. Perry Woods, and he's —"

"Anna," Dr. Woods said in a soft, honeyed voice, and raised his hand to her. Anna shyly placed her hand in his.

"Perry?" she murmured, her lips parted in a smile.

Dr. Woods smiled back and tucked her small hand around his arm. They walked away from Suzette, looking into each other's eyes. Suzette stared after them, then began to smile. The slender doctor was leading the dark-haired Anna down to the creek, away from the crowd.

"Suzette." Blake stepped up to his daughter. "Where is Perry? We're about ready to eat."

"Daddy, I've a feeling Dr. Woods is not hungry tonight."

Suzette was not surprised when, less than a month later, Anna Norris and Perry Woods proudly announced they would be married. Suzette was happy for them; never had she seen two people more in love. Plans were hastily made for the wedding and the young doctor asked Blake to be his best man. Blake Foxworth gladly agreed, but he didn't live to keep his promise.

The day after Suzette turned seventeen, Blake Foxworth was dead, exactly a year to the day after Luke Barnes was killed by the Indians.

May 20, 1872

We buried my beloved daddy today. I had told him that we would take him back to Louisiana if that was his wish, but he assured me that to him this land is his home. He said he belonged in Texas, just as I do.

I shall try to be very strong, just as I promised, but even as I write, tears blur my vision and my hand shakes. The Bible says God works in mysterious ways and it must surely be so. If ever a better, kinder man lived than my daddy, I've yet to meet him. I'm much afraid that my mother will never recover from her loss. He was the sun in her universe and no one can survive long in total darkness.

7

Almost a year had passed since Blake Foxworth had died. Suzette had squared her shoulders and buried herself in her newspaper work, grateful she had duties to perform, deadlines to meet, and a friend as kind and helpful as Austin Brand.

Austin and Beth went out of their way to help the two Foxworth women face their lonely life on the frontier with no man in the house. Austin had insisted they let him help financially when Suzette had finally admited to him that her father had left little money, only uncollected medical bills. But she resolutely declined. Her salary from the newspaper, along with the little money they made from the cattle, would see them through. It wasn't starving that worried her, anyway; it was her mother.

Lydia Foxworth, though still a young woman, had lost interest in life. She never went anywhere, except to church on Sundays. She was painfully thin and pale and talked little, even to Suzette. More than once Suzette had heard her mother sobbing and had gone to her room to comfort her. Lydia, her eyes red-rimmed and tortured, admitted to Suzette that she was simply lost and very lonely without Blake. She felt life had no meaning for her and often prayed to a merciful God to take her to heaven to join Blake.

Suzette was patient and understanding, but she knew there was little she could do. Frantic for a solution, Suzette called on Beth Brand for help. Beth, a kind, sweet woman, embraced the tearful Suzette and assured her that she and young Jenny would spend more time with Lydia while Suzette was busy at the newspaper office.

The very next day, Beth and Jenny packed a picnic lunch, and they had Bennet Day, Austin's watchman, hitch up the buggy. When they arrived at the house, Lydia, still wearing her nightgown and robe, apologized for her appearance at such a late hour and promptly excused herself to dress.

Beth pretended nothing was amiss. Pulling out a large bolt of pink muslin and some pattern books, she told Lydia they had come to ask for her help. Lydia was once a quality seamstress. Would she please help make Jenny a new Sunday dress? By lunchtime, Lydia was fitting the bodice while Beth filled three plates with fried chicken and potato salad, announcing it was time they all took a breather.

Lydia had to be dragged away from the old sewing machine, saying she was just beginning to get the hang of sewing again. Beth assured her she would get plenty of practice, for Jenny would soon be going to school and would need lots of pretty dresses. Lydia, smiling for the first time in months, looked at the beautiful little girl and told Beth that she would personally see to it that Jenny Brand would have the prettiest frocks in all Jacksboro, thoughtfully adding that she had a lovely spool of Irish lace packed in the chest in her bedroom; it would make a nice trim for the pink dress.

Beth's visit had been a tonic for the frail Lydia Foxworth. Soon she was looking forward to the frequent visits of Beth and Jenny and baked cakes and cookies for the Brands and studied pattern books with interest. Suzette breathed a little easier and told Austin Brand that Beth and Jenny's visits had saved a drowning woman. Austin Brand just smiled broadly.

Austin rose with the sun and slipped out of bed. He was shaving when the slender, sleepy Beth came to him, yawning and pushing her dark hair back from her face. "Austin?" she said softly.

"Beth, it's early. Why don't you sleep a while longer." He smiled and touched her cheek.

"Not on your life." She kissed his hand. "I've no intention of letting you slip away to Fort Worth without so much as a good-bye. We're having breakfast together before you leave."

"Whatever you say, dear." Austin was agreeable. "Beth, you know how I hate to leave you and Jenny, but the gentleman from Scotland is only going to be in the city for a short time. If I'm ever to improve my herd, I must buy some quality cattle to breed with the longhorns. It's high time I begin building for our future. I intend to have the best and the most beef in all Texas within a few years."

"Good for you, Austin." His wife watched his gray eyes flash with excitement. He had visions of building the Brand empire into one of the largest and most successful on the plains, and Beth was just as certain as he that it would be done.

Austin grinned at her. "Beth, I'll not get started on all my grandiose schemes this early in the morning, but I promise you, dear, within the next year, I'll start building you the mansion you deserve. We'll use this house for the ranch hands. I realize I only have a few, but I intend to hire several full-time men. That way, I won't be going on cow hunts or up the trail to Abilene. I'll stay right here with my two favorite ladies. In fact" — he reached out and slid his thumb and forefinger up the soft satin lapel of her robe — "this could well be the last trip I take without you and Jenny. I hate leaving you alone."

"Mr. Brand," Beth smiled up at him, thinking as she always did that he was surely the most handsome man the good Lord had ever created, and said sweetly, "that will be wonderful. We're terribly lonely when you are absent. But, dear, don't be worrying about us. You act as though you'll be gone for ages. It's just going to be for a few days, isn't it?"

Nodding, he replied, "Yes. Tom Capps and I have a definite appointment with the man from Scotland, Mr. Samuel Wellington, on the day after tomorrow. As soon as our business is completed, I'll be coming home."

"Then we'll hardly know you're gone. Jenny and I are going to put up some pear preserves this morning. After lunch, we're going to ride our horses over to visit Lydia. We'll stay and have supper with her and Suzette. Or perhaps they'll come over here for the meal and I'll persuade them to stay the night."

Austin wiped the excess lather from his face. "I like that idea. In fact, if they'll agree, why not have them stay here until I return?"

Beth kissed her husband's chin. "I'll try to get them to, Austin, but you know Suzette, she's so independent, she hates to feel she's imposing. She would never have asked me to help with her mother if she'd not been desperate. You know that."

"Yes, I do. Suzette's like her father. When Blake was alive, I tried more than once to loan him money and he would never hear of it. Suzette is the same way. I know they have to struggle. I'd like to help them out."

"You do help them, darling. You gave Suzette a position at the *Echo*. With what you pay her they are able to get along. Then, too, you are letting Suzette send their cattle up the trail with ours, aren't you?"

"Umm," he mused. "Still, I'd like to do more."

"I know, dear, but you cannot force a stubborn young woman like Suzette. Get dressed now. I'll go down and start our breakfast."

Half an hour later Austin stood on the long porch, ready to depart. In his arms was a beautiful, sleepy little girl who had wrapped her hands around his neck. Her feet were bare and Austin cupped them in his hands.

"Darlin'," he said softly, kissing her velvety cheek, "you be a good girl while I'm gone and I'll bring you and Mommy some nice presents from Fort Worth. Don't be riding your pony unless Bennett is around to watch and don't be sneaking down to the creek to wade; you might fall in and drown. Don't dare — "

"Daddy, Daddy" — Jenny screwed up her pretty face — "don't you ever want me to have a good time?"

"Yes, Sweetheart." He hugged her to him. "I always want you to have a good time. I'm sorry, I'm too much of a worrier, I suppose. Just be careful and mind Mommy."

"I will, Daddy." She put her small hands on either side of his face and kissed him. "See you in a few days."

Austin reluctantly put her down and turned to his wife. Beth stepped into his embrace, wrapping her slender arms about his middle. "Hurry back, my love," she said against his throat.

Kissing her lightly, he smiled. "Take care, Beth. I'll be back as soon as possible." He released her and, winking at his young daughter, bounded down the steps and out to his waiting horse. The iron-gray gelding, Confederate, whinnied and shook his head, tossing his thick mane. Austin mounted, tipped his Stetson to the two admiring women in his life, and galloped away.

"Mommy, will we take some preserves over to Mrs. Foxworth's?" Jenny set three luncheon plates on the table in the kitchen while her mother sliced bread from a big loaf.

"Why, I think that would be nice, don't you?" Beth Brand, pleased with their morning's work, took a seat across from her daughter. "I know Suzette likes pear preserves; I'll bet her mother does, also."

She began dishing up food, filling all three plates. "I wonder what is keeping Bennett. He should have come inside by now. When he's finished with his meal, we'll clear away the dishes and be on our way to the Foxworth ranch." She smiled at Jenny, then fanned the air. "My goodness, it's already warm. I dread the summer this year."

"Me, too, Mommy." Jenny buttered a piece of bread. "I want summer to pass so I can go to school. Do you think I'll learn to read and write?"

"Yes, Jenny, I'm sure you'll do well in school. Dear me." She reached across the table and put her hand to her daughter's sweet face. "I can't believe you're old enough for school. Seems it was just..." Beth's voice trailed off and she turned her head, listening.

"What? What is it, Mommy?"

"I... I'm not sure. I thought I heard Bennett or someone... someone calling or..." She rose, motioning Jenny to stay where she was. She walked to the back door and looked outside. "Oh, dear God in heaven!" Beth slammed the door shut and threw the heavy bolt.

Seeing the look of horror on her mother's face, Jenny was out of her chair, rushing to Beth. "Mommy? What is it? What is it?"

Grabbing Jenny's hand, Beth headed for the parlor, pulling

her daughter along. The little girl could hear loud war cries coming from the yard. Her eyes wide with fright, she looked out the front door just before Beth banged it shut. A band of a dozen painted, whooping Indians were moving close to the yard, their circles growing smaller and smaller, trapping the two helpless females inside.

"Get down!" Beth shouted as she pulled the Winchester from its case and loaded it. Beth fell to her knees and pointed the gun at the melee. The sounds of the loud, bloodthirsty calls split the still April air. "Where is Bennett!" Beth cried. "Why doesn't he help?" Now she was firing blindly into the circle of warriors.

Jenny clung to her mother's skirts but made not a sound. Beth, her eyes narrowed, trying desperately to aim, saw a sight straight from hell. Screaming, naked red men, breech-loading rifles in their hands, were now in the yard, firing into the house. She ducked her head as a china vase on the hutch shattered. She continued to fire wildly into the swarming intruders, doing little damage.

"Oh, God, no!" she moaned and pulled the trigger again. A flaming arrow had come through the window and the lace curtains were ablaze, sending tongues of fire up the wall.

Beth dropped the gun and shouted to Jenny, "Don't move from the floor! Stay down!" She crawled to the kitchen to fetch a bucket of water. By the time she returned, a sheet of fire had spread to all four walls. Beth looked at the fire, then at her daughter, and knew that it was hopeless, that she and Jenny would have to take their chances outdoors. She dropped the bucket of water, picked up the rifle, and took Jenny's arm. By now thick smoke was filling the room and Jenny was coughing and rubbing her eyes.

Beth jerked the little girl to her feet, raised the gun, and threw open the door. She stepped outside, her daughter behind her. Quickly she took aim and pulled the trigger, hitting a young warrior in the chest. Another shot hit one of the horses; it stumbled and went down, tossing the rider over its neck. Unhurt, the brave shouted and started running directly at Beth. She pulled the trigger again, felling the savage just as his moccasined feet touched the front porch. He grabbed his throat and fell.

Beth fired for the last time. She was out of ammunition. In desperation, she reversed the hold on the long rifle and ran into the mass of Indians, swinging wildly at the horsemen. Like a madwoman, she screamed and swung the long gun until it was yanked from her hands by a grinning brave. She whirled immediately to find her daughter, but Jenny was no longer behind her. And then in horror, Beth watched her little girl being lifted up into the saddle in front of a tall, young warrior with black paint streaked across his face and chest.

"Jenny! Jenny!" she screamed and ran toward the horse.

"Mommy, help me!" Jenny strained and squirmed in the grip of the long arms encircling her, before being slammed hard against the Indian's chest as the horse sped away, leaving a distraught Beth running after them.

Beth tore across the pasture, her skirts held high, the undergrowth ripping her silk stockings and scratching her legs. She didn't get far. A pair of strong hands reached down and scooped her from the ground, jerking her up onto the saddle of a big paint horse. The warrior who held her smiled while she screamed and pleaded for her daughter's life.

She could hear Jenny crying ahead of her. The other Indians were close, no longer interested in the ranch house, now engulfed in flames. The two warriors Beth had shot were draped over their ponies, led by a young brave. It was then that Beth saw the lifeless body of Bennett Day. The old cowhand lay on his back, his sightless eyes staring at the brilliant April sun. His thick mane of white hair was gone; his head had been spilt open with a tomahawk. Beth stared in horror as the hooves of the horse she rode caught in a torn shirtsleeve and Bennett's body was dragged several feet before the fabric ripped, releasing him.

"Dear Jesus!" Beth choked and began to kick and claw at the dark arms holding her. The powerfully built brave was not bothered in the least by her attempts to free herself. He merely tightened his arm about her, making it hard for her to breathe.

Beth could still see her daughter's long dark hair and knew in that instant that she must calm herself, that she had to keep Jenny in sight. Now her tears evaporated. She had to keep her wits about her for her daughter's sake and she was going to do it. When the horse she rode closed the gap, Beth called to her daughter, "Darling, I'm with you, don't be afraid. It's going to be all right, Jenny. Mommy's here."

The tall Indian behind Beth grunted and jerked her back against him. "No talk!" he shouted near her ear.

"But my little girl," she begged, "she's just — "

"No talk," he repeated coldly, and a strong brown hand came up to cover her mouth. Choking and stammering, Beth continued to try to call to Jenny, but it was no use. She couldn't make a sound. Finally, she gave up and leaned against the Indian, trying desperately to think of some way to save her precious daughter. She said a prayer and hoped God would answer.

Instead, torture began for Beth Brand.

The band of Indians continued to ride fast to the north, still shouting their war whoops, their lances held high. When they had traveled several miles and were safely away from the settlement of Jacksboro, the horse carrying Jenny stopped abruptly. The others, including the one carrying Beth, thundered on across the prairie. Frantically, Beth tried to twist her head over the tall Indian's arm, but she was pinned so tightly it was impossible.

Suddenly her captor pulled up on the reins and the big paint horse halted. Slowly, the warrior turned the pony and Beth could see her daughter once more. All the horses stopped, save for the ones carrying the fallen braves. The young Indian leading those horses continued homeward, never looking back. Jenny was pushed from the horse. She stood alone in the grass, crying for help. Beth felt the big hand that had been covering her mouth slowly slide away.

"Jenny!" she shouted wildly. The word hadn't died on her

trembling lips when a rifle was raised to the little girl's dark head and the trigger was pulled. Jenny crumpled to the ground like a rag doll. Insane with rage and shock, Beth cast off the strong arms of the brave and slid from the horse. She rushed to the still, lifeless body of her daughter, screaming her name.

She was stopped before she reached Jenny and was flung to the ground roughly. As she struggled to rise, a heavy foot was brought down on her stomach and a stocky brave wearing white war paint grinned at her. Beth clawed at his leg; he grunted and kicked her in the face. Blood spurted from her mouth. Again she scrambled up. Superhuman strength flowed through her slender body and again she tried to reach her little girl.

"Jenny, Jenny," she sobbed, and was again thrown to the ground. This time there was no getting up. Her slim arms were jerked up over her head with enough force to snap them from their sockets. Yet she lifted her head, looking toward her daughter and so didn't see the men moving in on her. Her vision was unobstructed just long enough to see a young brave stand over Jenny and lift her limp head from the ground. With a flash of a sharp knife, its blade gleaming in the sun, he quickly sliced away Jenny Brand's long dark curls and scalp. He rose immediately, laughing gleefully. In his hand, Jenny's scalp, blood dripping, was held up proudly to the cheers of the others.

Beth's head fell back to the ground, the scream inside extinguished. She cried. Four braves squatted on the ground, one at each arm, one at each foot. Beth was unable to move, but it made little difference to her now. Jenny was dead; there was no longer a reason to stay alive.

The braves were laughing and one sank to his knees near Beth's face and touched her long, dark hair. Beth closed her eyes. He was going to scalp her, she was certain of it. She didn't mind, but she wished he would kill her first. For what seemed an eternity, he rubbed and stroked her long, loose hair, grunting throughout. Slowly, Beth opened her eyes. The

Indian smiled down at her and released her hair. His hand went to the buttons of her dress and, in one swift movement, he jerked the bodice away.

Beth was pleading again, but not for her life. She was pleading for an end to her life. It fell on deaf ears. Within seconds, several smiling braves were on her, stripping away her clothes with amazing speed. Beth was left naked but for one shoe and silk stocking. Above her the crazed braves were putting on her torn dress and underwear. She began to think that was what they wanted. They loved colorful clothing; perhaps they would just take her clothes and mercifully kill her.

It was not to be.

A huge, well-built brave, one she'd not noticed before, firmly planted a foot on each side of her. He looked down at her white, slender body, the small breasts, the narrow waist and long legs, then smiled at her. Slowly, his huge hand went to his breechcloth and the bit of leather fell from his body onto Beth's trembling stomach. Now the brave stood above her, tall, menacing, and naked.

Beth felt the heart inside her heaving chest stop completely as he lowered himself to his knees. Roughly forcing her legs apart, he moved inside them. A big, callused hand clasped her right breast and squeezed it painfully. He pounded into her and Beth screamed in agony with his first powerful thrust. Soon he fell away from her, spent, but another took his place, this one more brutal than the first. Not content just to rape her, he tore at her tender flesh with his hand. Finally, he, too, thrust himself into her, grunting and sweating. Beth's eyes closed and she prayed for death.

She lived.

The third savage was hideously ugly and dirty, his pockmarked face leering down at her. And he was cruel, very cruel. Before he dropped his breechcloth, he took out his scalping knife and nonchalantly cut crosses on her left breast. Not deep enough to kill her and end her agony, but deep enough to cause more agonizing pain, deep enough to draw blood that ran down her ribcage and onto her belly. The Indian soon tired of the game, sheathed the bloody knife, grinned at Beth, and put his flattened palm in the bright red blood covering her breast. Chanting, he raised the bloody hand and smeared the bright crimson all over his happy face, popping a blunt finger into his mouth. Gloriously elated then, he dropped his breechcloth and raped her. The others stood watching, laughing and enjoying the playful sport, at the same time arguing over who would be the next to mount the naked white woman.

"Mine," said the young warrior who had murdered and scalped young Jenny. He stepped over Beth. The long, dark hair of her daughter, blood still dripping from the scalp, was tied securely to his breechcloth with a rawhide strip. A stifled scream bubbled from Beth's throat, her eyes closed, and at last she mercifully passed out. Before the young animal could ram into her, Beth could feel the blackness blessedly creeping over her, taking her away from a horror too great to bear any longer. It was peaceful and safe, and from the mist came the glorious vision of her handsome husband and her beautiful little girl. Her very last thought was of them.

The fact that Beth was no longer conscious made little difference to the savages. All had their turn and some of them came back for a second go at her, using her limp, fragile body as a warm receptacle. When all had finally tired of the game, one casually took a bow, raised it directly over Beth's chest, and fired. The deadly arrow went into the top of her shoulder, exiting on the other side, pinning her still body to the ground. The Indian shouted and mounted his war pony.

Not to be outdone, another eager brave took out his knife and squatted down over Beth. Lifting her from the ground by her hair, he stabbed her in the back, just below her right shoulder blade, and watched in fascination as blood spilled from the wound. Retrieving his knife, he wiped it clean on Beth's hair, dropped her back to the ground, and swung up onto the bare back of his prancing, pawing horse.

With jubilant shouting and yelling, the braves mounted and rode away to the north, headed for home. It had been a satisfying afternoon. They had all enjoyed it immensely. They didn't take Beth Brand's scalp. She deserved to keep it. She had been a source of joy to them all.

Old Nate Simmons stepped from the blacksmith's shop a block south of the town square. He meticulously rolled a cigarette, wet it with his tongue, and jammed it into his mouth. Before he could put the match to it, he noticed heavy smoke drifting across the clear April sky. Squinting into the sun, Nate located its origin. He knew immediately whose home was burning.

Letting the unlit cigarette drop, he started running. He was at the square and inside the Longhorn Saloon in a matter of seconds. Puffing for breath, the old cowboy shouted at the top of his lungs, "Austin Brand's home is afire! Let's go!" He whirled and started for his horse. Behind him, a dozen men, having tossed down the last of their whiskey, followed.

By the time the mounted men reached the Brand spread, the ranch house was beyond saving. Arrows and shell casings, along with prints of horses' hooves, told the tale. It was old Nate, riding a short distance from the burning house, who found Bennett Day. Muttering only, "Those damned animals, those filthy savages," Nate dismounted and bent over the old man he'd known since boyhood. Nate's eyes filled with tears and he tenderly picked up a lifeless hand and held it in both of his. "Bennett, Bennett," he whispered sadly, "how I shall miss you."

"The women aren't here!" Nate heard a man shout. "Maybe they're still alive!"

Nate placed his friend's hand on his chest and promised, "I'll be back to see you have a proper burial, Bennett." He rose and mounted, spurring his horse to catch up with the others. Silently they rode north, each man hoping for the best, fearing the worst. The worst was what they found.

"Jesus Christ! The woman's still breathing." A young cowboy was bending over Beth's slender naked frame. A faint but regular heartbeat could be heard when he pressed his ear to her chest. The boy stood and hurriedly stripped off his shirt. Kneeling again, he covered Beth and shook his head in disbelief.

"The little girl's dead," a bearded, stocky cowboy informed the others. "At least she was luckier than the woman. It doesn't appear she suffered." The bearded man looked about for Jenny's scalp, his eyes narrowed in hate and disgust. Knowing full well the dead child's shiny hair now hung from a brave's breechcloth or his lance, the man removed his shirt, draping it tenderly over Jenny's head.

The youth who covered Beth was lifting her onto his horse. He mounted behind her, holding her in his arms like a child. Then he applied big roweled spurs to the sorrel he rode, wondering if speed was the answer. Would it not be better if the poor woman didn't survive? If she lived, would she ever be the same again? Could she ever put her ordeal behind her and live a normal life? He knew she'd suffered more than the cut breast, the arrow through the shoulder, the knife wound to the back. Her bruised, bloody thighs told him of her terrible suffering.

Beth Brand was taken to the Fort Richardson hospital. Little Jenny was taken to the undertaker. The post surgeon did what he could for Beth. Perry Woods, hearing of the tragedy, rushed from his office to be with her. Neither doctor could do much. Her wounds were bathed and bandaged and the arrowhead was cut from her shoulder. Throughout their ministrations, Beth remained unconscious. Both doctors wondered the same thing: Would it not be better if Beth passed away?

Perry Woods stood beside the post surgeon. Both men were washing up after tending to Beth. "You know, I wonder sometimes why we keep trying to live on this land." Perry looked at the tall, blond man beside him.

"My home is in the east. Life there is safe and civilized, even enjoyable. What am I doing down here? Why should I stubbornly insist on staying in a country so wild that my wife is in constant danger? Why don't I pack up and return to Boston, where I belong?"

His colleague sighed wearily. "You're needed here, Doctor. I like to feel I am also. My home is in Philadelphia — at least I was raised and educated there. But I chose the army as a career, and here I am. If this section of the country is ever to be something other than a playground for the savages, men like you and me must stay here, make it our home."

Dr. Woods rolled down his shirtsleeves. "I suppose you're right, but I've a pregnant wife to consider. I see something like this senseless butchering of two helpless females and my blood runs cold. My God, Austin Brand will go insane!"

The blond doctor nodded. "I've never seen a man hate Indians with quite the vehemence of Mr. Brand. Perhaps this isn't the first time they've touched his life."

Perry shrugged. "I don't know, but Austin Brand was with the group that recovered the bodies of the men slaughtered at the Warren Wagon Train Massacre a couple of years ago. Young Luke Barnes, one of the slain, worked for Austin, I understand. Dr. Foxworth told me before his passing that he'd never seen anything like the grisly sight of those poor unfortunates."

"I'm sure that's true. I guess you've heard rumors that Satanta and Big Tree are going to be released from prison."

"I know there's been talk, but I don't believe it. Surely no sane, thinking man, be he governor of Texas or president of the United States, would release those redskins."

"I should hope not," the post surgeon agreed.

Austin Brand was informed of the tragedy upon his arrival in Fort Worth. His face a mask of pain, he climbed back on his horse and headed for Jacksboro. He rode nonstop, spurring his horse like a wild man. Confederate, the big gray gelding, pressed dutifully on, eating up the prairie as though he had wings on his hooves. In less than seven hours, Austin arrived back home, having gone the sixty miles without dismounting.

Austin spoke not a word as he was led into the small lamplit room where Beth lay unconscious. When he saw her pale face, her bandaged shoulder and breasts, he began to shake uncontrollably. Sinking to his knees beside her bed, Austin took her frail, cool hand into his and sobbed, "Beth, Beth, I'm sorry, so sorry. I'll make it up to you one day. I will, I promise. Oh, Beth..."

Austin stood with his big hands clasped in front of him. Under the shade of a stately oak tree, a small mound of fresh dirt marked the newly dug grave. It held the small white coffin of Jenny Brand, the beautiful dark-haired child of Austin and Beth Brand.

"The Lord hath given; the Lord hath taken away," the minister said in a deep, soft voice. Austin, his gray eyes staring straight ahead, stood alone in front of Jenny's grave. Behind him, Suzette Foxworth wept quietly. She knew how much Austin was suffering and she longed to ease his pain, but there was nothing she could do. There was little any of the friends assembled at the Brand ranch on this pretty April afternoon could do to help the heartbroken man in his hour of grief. His wife still lay in her bed at the fort hospital. Beth Brand had regained consciousness, nothing else. She'd not spoken a word since opening her eyes, not even when her husband sat by her bed and talked soothingly. Beth didn't appear to recognize him.

The short memorial service for Jenny was over. When most everyone had quietly moved on to their horses and carriages, Suzette stepped forward. She knew he needed comforting, but when anyone had tried to console him, they'd been met with cold gray eyes and stony silence.

Suzette had almost reached him. She stopped and looked about. Only one or two buggies remained; even the preacher had departed. Soon the gravediggers would start tossing the soft earth over the white coffin. Austin mustn't see that; she would insist he leave with her.

"Austin," she spoke very softly, tentatively putting a hand on his shoulder. Slowly her turned to look down at her. He tried his best to speak, but there was no sound. "Oh, Austin,"

Suzette whispered and put her arms around his neck. Slowly his arms closed around her and he pressed his sad face into her hair. His big body trembled against her and he began to cry, but still he said nothing. He didn't apologize. He simply held the sweet girl and wept. When he could cry no more, he raised his head and whispered, "Thank you."

Handing him a dainty white lace handkerchief, Suzette took his hand and led him up the rolling hill to her buggy. In back of them, the remnants of the Brand ranch house stood like a lonely sentinel in the fading sun. Austin stood for a minute looking at the charred earth and the blackened structure, the home where only days before he'd kissed his wife and child good-bye and promised never to leave them alone again.

"Austin, I'm taking you home with me. You must rest. When you awaken, we'll go to see Beth." Austin nodded and stepped into the buggy with her. Suzette said, "I'm terribly sorry that Mother couldn't be there today. She's... she isn't well. I do hope you'll forgive her."

Austin did not reply and Suzette doubted that he knew or cared that Lydia Foxworth did not attend his daughter's funeral. Upon arriving at the small Foxworth ranch, Suzette, holding Austin's hand, led him into the house and straight through the parlor into her bedroom.

"Now" — she pointed to the soft bed — "why not stretch out on my bed." She smiled up at him, but he continued to stand in the middle of the room, stiffly looking about. Pushing him toward the bed, Suzette got him to sit on its edge before she said, "Excuse me just a minute." She left him and hurried into the kitchen. On the top shelf of the cabinet, a half-full bottle of brandy remained where Dr. Foxworth had placed it two years before. It was fine brandy, a present to the doctor from Austin.

Suzette grabbed two glasses from the shelf, then rushed back to her room and found Austin just as she'd left him. She poured a healthy portion of the brandy into one of the glasses, a much smaller portion into the other. She handed the one with the larger amount to Austin. "Please," she tried, "won't you take a drink, Austin? It will help."

Obeying, Austin tipped the glass and drank the brandy in one swallow. Before she touched her own glass to her lips, his glass was empty and she hurried to refill it. He drank that, too. He set the glass on the small table by her bed and rubbed his eyes. Seeing the gesture, Suzette set her glass aside also and said quietly, "You're very tired, Austin. Will you please take off your suit coat and lie down for a while?"

"Suzette," he mumbled.

"Yes, Austin?"

"I don't think I can go on living." His voice was flat.

Biting her lip, she sat down on the bed beside him and took his hand in both of hers. "Austin, please don't say that. You're so strong and brave, and Beth needs you."

"No. Beth doesn't need me. She doesn't know who I am. And my sweet Jenny... I don't want to live in a world without my little girl." Still the same, flat voice. "I'm tired, Suzette, I'm tired of everything."

"I know," she murmured and rose from the bed. "Please, let me help you." Suzette began to tug at his jacket and he nodded his head and helped. She took the fine coat and draped it over a chair, turning back to him. Leaning close, she removed the narrow tie and unbuttoned his white shirt. She knelt in front of him and removed his black leather shoes. "Now," she said sweetly, pushing gently on his shoulders, "lie down."

"Just for a minute." He eased onto his back, his head on her pillow.

"Put your feet up, Austin," Suzette instructed, and Austin lifted his long, tired legs from the floor, crossing one ankle over the other, his hands on his middle. Suzette leaned over him and whispered softly, "Rest, my friend."

A big, bronzed hand slowly raised to a long blond curl falling from her shoulder. "Suzette, will you wake me in an hour? I must go to Beth."

"Go to sleep," she whispered and kissed his cheek. His eyes closed and he was immediately asleep. It was the first time in seventy-two hours that Austin Brand had slept.

Austin remained by his wife's bedside day after day, though Beth looked at him with a blank expression and never responded.

"I'm sorry, Austin." Dr. Woods stood looking down at the pale woman in the hospital bed. "I wish I could tell you that her condition will change. I can't. Beth may never be the same again. She may never come back to you. I'm sorry."

Summertime arrived, and with it came the cattle drive up the Chisholm trail to Abilene. Austin didn't go. He hired cowhands to escort Tom Capps and his herd of two thousand longhorns and told Suzette Foxworth he'd be glad to have Nate throw in with his group and take the hundred head of Foxworth cattle up the trail with his herd. She was grateful and expressed her thanks as she and Austin sat with Beth one hot afternoon.

"Austin, I hope you won't think I'm prying, but, well, don't you think it might be a good idea if you did go on the drive? You've been so diligent about staying with Beth day and night. If you want to go, I'll look after her for you. It might do you good to get away, work hard, be with other men for a change."

Austin rose from the chair where he'd been sitting since early morning. "You're kind to worry, Suzette, but I'm fine. I can't go. I promised Beth I'd never leave her alone again. I don't intend to do so."

"But, Austin, Beth... she... she'd never know." Her eyes were full of compassion.

Austin shook his head. "But I'd know. I'm staying with her until... until..." He stopped speaking. Suzette sat perfectly still.

Austin walked to the window and pulled back the curtains. He stared at the fort's parade ground and at the enlisted men going about their duties as though all was right with the world. Soon the lone trumpet would play taps, signaling the close of another day. He turned back to look at the pale, drawn face on the pillow, then leaned over Beth and pushed a dark lock of hair from her brow. "Suzette, would you think me terrible if I confessed to you that I have spent many a night praying to a God I never before believed in for this poor, sweet creature to... to die?" He leaned down to Beth and tenderly kissed her cold lips. "Oh, my dear, forgive me. Please forgive me for everything."

"Austin," Suzette said softly, "stop punishing yourself. You were a good husband and father. Beth was a happy woman."

"Yes, but I didn't... " Austin sighed and straightened. "I'm not going up the trail. I don't know how long it will be before the end comes, but when it does, I will be here with Beth."

Summer dragged on painfully and finally the chill of autumn was in the air. On a clear nippy October morning, Suzette rose early and went down to the creek to gather pecans. She went about her task remembering the days she and her father had picked up pecans and her mother had made wonderful pies from them. Those happy days were gone forever; her father was dead and her mother was a shell of her former self, frail and in bad health. Winter had not yet come and already Lydia was coughing and weak. The Brand tragedy had been too much for her. Suzette was unable to bring her around.

Suzette made the pecan pies on this autumn day; Lydia didn't feel like baking. "Mother, I'm going over to see Beth this afternoon. Will you come with me?" Suzette knew the answer before she asked.

Her mother sat in the parlor and stared wistfully out at the falling leaves, saying, "I'm sorry, dear. I'm tired. I can't go today. Perhaps tomorrow."

"You don't mind if I go for a while, do you?"

"No, of course not. Poor little Beth. Poor girl." Lydia lowered her head, lost in thought. Determined not to let her mother's melancholy mood get her down, Suzette made lunch for the two of them, baked the pies, took a bath, put on her best dress, hitched up the team, and drove to the fort, a big pecan pie on the seat under a dishcloth.

At the fort, she found Austin alone on the long, wooden gallery of the hospital. He didn't look up when she approached him. "Austin?"

He lifted his head and she saw the stormy, flintlike eyes and knew something was wrong. Her heart raced and she whispered, "Is it... did Beth... ?"

"No," He took her arm and propelled her down the steps, across the parade ground to the shade of an oak tree. He released her and said thinly, "Satanta is a free man."

"No! It can't be true!" Suzette swayed and Austin reached out to steady her. "How could anyone let that animal out of prison? Don't they know that as soon as he's free he'll be riding with the beastly Comanches that killed little Jenny and raped..." She paused and looked at Austin's tortured face. "Oh, Austin, I'm sorry."

"It's so outrageous even General Sherman was appalled by the governor's decision to release him. I'm told he wrote Governor Davis and said that if Satanta took scalps after his release, he hoped Davis's was the first one taken." Austin laughed hollowly.

Suzette stayed only a short time at the hospital. When she left, she went directly to the *Echo* office to write up the story of the chiefs' release.

The Prairie Echo

October 8, 1873
Jacksboro, Texas

SATANTA AND BIG TREE FREE

In the opinion of this newspaper reporter, the double-dealing of your government is appalling. What the president of the United States was traded by our illustrious governor of Texas is anyone's guess, but there's little doubt a bargain was struck for the release of the savages from their prison cells, where they served a brief two and a half years for murdering innocent, helpless men on that blood-drenched day in the spring of 1871. Two and a half years!

Perhaps the governor should have tapped their wrists at that time and asked them to stop their playfulness!

8

On a bleak, drizzly morning in mid-October, Austin Brand ducked into the *Echo* office. Shaking beads of water from his long coat, he headed for his small office at the back of the building. Suzette, who was helping Mr. Keach set up the front page of the morning paper, looked up when Austin swept in the door.

"Suzette." He nodded to them. "May I see you for a minute?"

"Certainly, Austin." She rose from her chair and went to join him.

"I won't keep her long, Mr. Keach."

"We're just about finished, Mr. Brand. It's no interruption." The editor waved a bony hand in the air.

Inside his office, Austin took off his coat and indicated that Suzette was to have a seat. He took the chair behind his desk. "I'm sure you are well aware by now that the stock market in New York has been closed for days."

"Of course, Austin. We wrote it up for the newspaper."

"So you did." He drummed nervously on the desk. "Well, Suzette, you're an intelligent young lady, so I'm certain you must realize what that has done to the price of cattle."

It had not occurred to Suzette that the sale of the cattle

would be affected by what the *Fort Worth Democrat* was referring to as the "Panic of '73." Now, she felt terribly foolish for not realizing how far-reaching would be the results of Wall Street's dilemma. "Austin, are you saying that —"

"Suzette, there is no market whatsoever for the cattle we sent to Abilene. Some of the boys are selling their herds for what little they'll bring for tallow and hides. I intend to hold on to mine, let my hands stay up there through the winter, graze the cattle on land I'll lease, then see if things have improved come spring. Were I you, I'd do the same thing with your hundred head. But, it's your decision. Let me warn you, dear, that there's no guarantee that spring will bring a market."

Suzette sat looking at Austin. She was not sure she and Lydia could survive until spring without the extra cattle money. She'd been counting on the profits from the sale of the cattle to pay Nate's wages, buy seeds for the spring garden, food for the winter, and warm clothes for her and her mother. How could she tell this man who had so many problems of his own that she had no money, save the salary he paid her? She must have looked disturbed, because Austin rose from his chair and came around the desk.

"Listen, Suzette, why don't I buy your herd right now? I'll pay you a fair price. Then I'll keep them with mine and sell all of them in the spring."

"No, Austin, I wouldn't hear of it. You're much too kind, but I'm not about to thrust a hundred worthless longhorns on a man who already has two thousand. I won't do it. When you wire Tom Capps, tell Nate to stay in Abilene until spring with your men. I'll wait with you until the price goes back up."

"You're the boss," Austin said. After pausing, he lowered this voice. "Suzette, I'm sure you were counting on the money from the cattle sale. Suppose I make you a small loan, just until spring. There must be some —"

Standing up quickly, she shook her head. "No. You pay me a fair salary, and Mother and I can make it. I'll get back to work now. How's Beth today?"

"No better, no worse. I'm on my way back over there right now. She had an easy night so I'm grateful for that."

Austin returned to the Fort Richardson hospital in the early afternoon. While the rain dripped from the steep roof and an afternoon quiet fell over the fort, Beth Applegate Brand peacefully passed away while her husband held her hand. Just before the end, she opened her eyes and looked at him. A faint smile curved her thin lips and she looked as though she recognized him. Her frail hand tightened on his for an instant.

Then she was gone.

The panic of '73 was long and widespread. Across the country businesses were devastated. Ranchers in Jack County, their only source of income that of the profits from the sale of their cattle, were desperate for money to feed their families. Unable to hold on until spring, they took anything they could get for their cattle. They put their ranches up for sale, but the land was as worthless as the beef. There was simply no cash.

Only one man in Jack County would flourish and profit from the depression. Austin Brand was now one of the wealthiest men in all Texas. With Beth's death, he was sole heir to a huge eastern banking fortune that had been amassed by Beth's grandfather and passed on to her. A wealthy man in his own right, he was now extremely rich.

Austin felt for his suffering neighbors and he *was* a businessman. He intended to build his empire into one of the largest ranches in the vast state, and there was no better time than the present. He personally met with every man in the area who wanted to sell land, offering them all a decent price for their acreage, along with a job on his ranch. To a man, they were overjoyed with his offer and quickly signed the papers releasing the worthless land into his capable hands. With wives and children to feed and clothe, the worried ranchers were grateful and happy when Austin told them that they were more than welcome to remain in their homes. Although the homes would now be a part of the Brand ranch, they could live there if they chose, provided they were at the Brand headquarters early every morning. For those single men who wished, Austin was building a large bunkhouse and kitchen on the site of his old home. Less than six weeks after Austin began negotiations for the first piece of land, he owned thousands of acres of prime grassland. There was one ranch however, that was not for sale, the small tract owned by Suzette Foxworth. It was her home, the place her father had worked with such diligence, and she would not let it go. She did decide to get out of the cattle business. The decision made, she asked that Austin give old Nate a job on his ranch.

"I'll do better than that, dear," Austin smiled at her one spring day in April 1874. "I'll leave him in place right on your ranch. He can do the chores for you and your mother and be there to watch out for you."

Suzette Foxworth stamped her foot and her blue eyes flashed fire. "No! My mother and I are not charity cases that need you to pay our help. If you can't use Nate, then for heaven's sake, say so, but don't you dare think I'll allow you to meet my obligations!"

"I need Nate! Please, please, don't get excited."

Suzette began to smile. "Austin, I'm sorry. I suppose my pride makes me behave abominably at times. I know you're trying to be kind and I appreciate it. I speak before I think."

"My dear" — he smiled back — "it's the most charming thing about you. Don't ever change. When Nate returns from Abilene, I'll help him move over to the big bunkhouse. By the way, the carpenters are hard at work on the new building. Care to ride out there with me and take a look?"

"Sorry, Austin. I'm tired and I want to get home to Mother. Perhaps one day next week."

"I look forward to it," he said and left.

May came and it was more enchanting than ever. Lilac bushes, trumpet vines, and Virginia creepers made the broad porch of the Foxworth home a fragrant, pleasing place to sit and take the breeze. On Suzette's nineteenth birthday, Perry

Woods, his wife, Anna, who was uncomfortably pregnant, and one-year-old Josh arrived with a huge white cake. Taken by surprise, Suzette, who was wearing an everyday dress of checked gingham and had her hair pulled on top of her head, her feet bare, rose from her rocker and ran out to meet the trio, her appearance the furthest thing from her mind.

"I'm so glad to see you," she chirped, hugging Anna carefully. She turned and kissed Perry's cheek before smiling into the little face of the child in his arms. "Come here to me, Josh," she cooed to the adorable little boy, taking him from his father.

"I see you weren't expecting company," Anna teased, looking at Suzette's bare feet. "Perry, honey, will you get the cake from the back seat of the buggy?"

Paying her friend no attention, Suzette crossed to the porch, looking at the smiling face of the healthy, handsome little boy in her arms. "You know, he looks more like Perry every day, don't you think, Anna?"

"Shh!" Anna hushed her. "Don't let Perry hear you say that. He'll get a big head. He asks me every day if I think Josh isn't the spittin' image of him."

"Anna, you are mean. He looks just like Perry, and you should be happy he does."

"I am." Anna grinned. "I just don't want Perry getting too vain." Anna eased into a chair. "Tell me, Suzette, when are you going to start acting like a woman and hunt yourself a husband? You could have children of your own." Suzette glared at her friend. "Sorry, not another word, I promise." Anna laughed good-naturedly. "How's your mother, Suz?"

Suzette's eyes clouded slightly. "The same. She hardly leaves her bed. Perhaps she'll join us tonight."

Perry, cake in one hand, a bottle of wine in the other, joined the women, saying, "I'll put this in the kitchen and look in on Mrs. Foxworth."

"Thanks, Perry." Suzette smiled. "Try to get her to come out and join us for a while. Maybe she'll listen to you."

Ten minutes later, Perry led Lydia Foxworth onto the

porch. She stayed only long enough to see the baby and say hello to Anna. Pleading fatigue, she returned to her room while Suzette sighed and watched her go.

"Perry, tell me what to do for her," Suzette said in low tones.

"There's nothing you can do, Suzette. It's up to her. We've done all we can."

Suzette turned her attention back to the little boy, while Anna slipped into the kitchen to cut the birthday cake. As twilight fell, a lone horseman rode over the rise.

Austin Brand, casual in a pair of denim trousers, a pullover shirt of gray, a yellow bandanna at his throat, and cowboy boots, dismounted from a big bay. Slapping his Stetson against his thigh, he strode into the yard, his sun-tipped hair gleaming in the half light. In his big hand, he carried a small package tied with a pink bow.

"How's everybody?" he drawled, stepping onto the porch.

"Austin, you're just in time for birthday cake." Anna was cordial, slicing him a big piece. Austin shoved the box into his breast pocket and shook hands with the doctor before nodding to Suzette.

"Look, Austin." Suzette smiled up at him. "Have you ever seen anything sweeter in your life than this little boy?"

Austin took a seat beside her, reaching out to clasp the tiny fingers of the baby she held. "He's a mighty fine boy."

He sat, politely eating the cake, telling Anna how delicious it was.

Pouring wine for the four of them, Perry said, "Austin, I thought you and your men were off on the cow hunt."

"We are — that is, they are. I was, too. Then I remembered it was Suzette's birthday."

Suzette's blond head snapped around. "Austin, you mean you came in off the cow hunt just because it's my birthday? That wasn't necessary."

Unruffled, Austin said, "Very few things we do are really necessary. It isn't necessary that I go on the cow hunt with my men, or up the trail to Abilene, but I intend to do both."

Suzette looked from him to the Woodses. "Austin seems to think I'm his helpless ward and he must constantly look out for me." There was a hint of irritation in her voice.

"That isn't it, my dear. I think of you as one of my dearest friends and count it a pleasure to be able to celebrate your nineteenth birthday with you, just like the Woodses."

"In that case, I'm very glad you came, Austin." She softened. "And, had I known to expect you, I'd have tried to look more presentable."

"You look cute." He smiled with wry amusement and stared pointedly at her bare feet.

"You should try it sometime," she said haughtily, then turned her attention back to the baby.

It was a lazy, pleasant evening and all too soon Anna was taking Josh and telling Perry it was past time for bed.

Suzette, still barefoot, padded out to the buggy to say good-night. Austin stood behind her, waving to the departing couple.

"Shall I carry you back to the porch?" he kidded her after the Woodses were out of sight.

"Certainly not." She tilted her head.

"In that case" — he reached out and took her elbow — "I'd better be going." He brought the small box from his shirt pocket and held it out to her. She stood with her hands at her sides. "Well, aren't you going to take it?" He grinned while she looked at him warily.

Slowly she reached out and took the gift. The pink bow and white paper were rapidly stripped away and thrust into Austin's upturned palm. Suzette looked at the shiny gold hair clasp and sighed. The prettiest one she'd ever seen, it had her initials in blue enamel on its edge.

"Austin." She looked up shyly. "It's lovely, but I can't take it. It's too... too expensive, too much." Her eyes went back to the clasp and she rubbed its smooth surface.

"You most certainly are going to keep it, Suzette Foxworth. I got it especially for your nineteenth birthday. Don't hurt my feelings by refusing it."

"Oh, Austin, it isn't that I don't want it. Why, any woman would, but I just don't think it would be proper for me to accept it."

Austin chuckled and put a finger under her chin, raising her face. "I'm disappointed in you."

"Why?" she asked innocently.

"Because I thought you were much too wise and willful to care about what is and is not proper." He smiled impishly, challenging her.

Laughing softly, she unpinned her hair and tossed her head about, sending the long, golden locks cascading down around her face and shoulders. She thrust the clasp into the thick curtain of her hair on the left side, pulling it firmly back and fastening the shiny adornment. She put her hands on her rounded hips and lifted her chin, the moonlight catching her brilliant blue eyes. "Of course I don't care if it's proper! The clasp is exquisite. I want it, and that's that!"

"That's the Suzette I like best," he said and took her hand. "Walk me to my horse. I've got to get back. I won't be coming home until the hunt is over, since we'll be moving farther out now." He paused for a second. "So... take care of yourself, give my best to your dear mother, and promise you'll let me buy you dinner at the hotel when I come back."

"I promise, Austin." They were next to his horse. "Austin?"

He untied the reins and turned back to her. "Yes?"

"I don't mean to pry, but ... well, don't you ever intend to rebuild your home? I mean, are you going to live at the Wichita Hotel for the rest of your life?"

Austin hung his Stetson on the saddlehorn. "I don't know if I'll rebuild, Suzette. I haven't thought about it. I moved to the hotel after the tragedy and I'm comfortable enough there. Besides, the bunkhouse is completed now. I can spend the night there if I choose." He fell silent, absently patting the horse's sleek neck. "Perhaps someday there'll be a reason to build a home." He looked thoughtful, the lightness of his mood gone, his gray eyes wintry.

Suzette was sorry she'd brought it up and said, "Thank you

for visiting on my birthday. I love the hair clasp, Austin." She touched the shiny gold and smiled.

Austin put a hand on her arm, then said in a voice that was barely above a whisper, "It's only the beginning."

Suzette frowned and leaned toward him. "What? I didn't hear you."

Austin laughed and bent to kiss her cheek. "I said, 'I'm pleased you like the present.'"

9

Two days after Suzette's nineteenth birthday, Lydia Foxworth died. Suzette was shocked and saddened; she thought that since her mother had made it through the winter, she'd improve and get well with summer's approach. Feeling strangely cold under the warm May sun, Suzette said goodbye to her beautiful mother and wondered why she longed for Austin Brand to be there with her.

But Austin was away on the cow hunt; she knew he wouldn't be back until month's end. It seemed a lifetime. Of all her friends, including Anna and Perry, who insisted Suzette come stay with them for a time, Suzette wished for Austin's company and comfort. She felt frightened and alone without him and realized for the first time how important he was in her life. Always she'd taken his presence for granted; she'd never even considered what life would be like without him.

As she lay in the strange bed in Anna's house on the night of her mother's funeral, Suzette cried softly into the pillow. "Austin, Austin," she sobbed, "help me."

Austin Brand was on the prairie unaware of Suzette's suffering. He sat smoking while the campfire died and the other cowboys slept. The quiet of the prairie night was interrupted only by the occasional snorting and whinnying of the horses in the remuda and the crickets' call.

Austin drew on his cigar and let his thoughts drift. To his dismay, they kept coming to rest on Suzette Foxworth. Her pretty, fresh face. The way she looked on her birthday with her hair pulled up and her feet bare. The smile she'd given him when she fastened the gold clasp into her hair.

Austin shook his head and berated himself. *Suzette Foxworth is a child; I'm old enough to be her father. Besides, it's been less than a year since I was widowed. Add to that the fact that Suzette's father was one of my best friends. He'd turn over in his grave if he knew I would consider behaving in less than a fatherly fashion toward his daughter.*

Perhaps I need a woman. I'm a healthy, normal man and it's been too long. There's nothing more to it; I'll slip away to Fort Worth for a couple of days. No one will know and then I'll quit having these impure thoughts.

Austin tossed his cigar into the dying fire and went to his bedroll. Utterly exhausted from the long, hard day of riding herd on the dangerous longhorns, he soon dozed, then dreamed. He awoke with a start and sat up. From the depths of his dream, Suzette Foxworth was calling to him, her sweet voice desperate, her eyes wide with fear. Austin ran a hand through his thick blond hair and got up.

Quietly pulling on his boots, he made his way to the pallet where his trail boss, Tom Capps, was snoring. "Tom." Austin spoke urgently.

Tom's eyes opened. "Trouble?"

"No, everything's fine. I'm leaving camp for a couple of days. I'll meet you over at the Squaw Mountain corral on Friday. Go back to sleep."

"My God, man! Can't you wait till morning?"

"No, I can't."

He arrived in Jacksboro as the sun was rising. Feeling more

than a little foolish, he debated whether he should ride out to the Foxworth ranch or go directly to the Wichita Hotel and sleep. He was still arguing with himself when he reached the Foxworth ranch house. Seeing no lights inside, he figured Suzette was still asleep. He dismounted, then lit a cigar and waited, leaning his big frame against a tall elm. Time passed and still no one stirred inside the house. Austin strolled across the yard and onto the porch. He knocked loudly. Nothing. He knocked again and this time he called her name. "Suzette, it's Austin. Honey, open the door. Suzette?"

His heart thumping, he pounded on the door and shouted her name again and again. Finally, he pushed in the door and rushed inside. He went from room to room but saw no trace of Suzette or her mother. Alarmed, her hurried back to his horse. Spurring his tired mount all the way to town, he went directly to the *Echo* office. It was dark and locked.

Fishing a key from his pocket, he let himself in and went straight to his office. Knowing he should remain calm and rational, he nevertheless wanted a drink. From the bottom drawer of his desk he pulled a bottle of Kentucky bourbon and poured himself a glass, then downed it in one gulp. He was wiping his mouth on the back of his hand when he noticed Suzette, looking fragile and tired, standing in the doorway.

"Sweetheart." He sighed with relief and went to her, gathering her into his arms. To his intense surprise and pleasure, she did not pull away but buried her face on his broad chest and clung to him.

"Austin," she whispered, "thank God you're here. Oh, Austin, how did you know?"

He pulled back to look down at her. "Know what? What is it, sweetheart?"

"Austin, Mother died. I lost my mother."

Austin tenderly pressed her face against his chest. "My darling, I'm so terribly sorry." His arms tightened around her. "I didn't know, Suzette, but I'm here and I'll help you."

"Austin, I prayed you'd come. Did you know that? I wanted you to be here with me. I'm not as frightened when you're here."

"Suzette, I'll be here for you always. You're not alone, dearest. I'm with you. I'll take care of you." Austin Brand continued to hold her in his warm embrace, and Suzette had no idea how elated he was to be the one she wanted in her time of trouble.

Four days after her mother's funeral, Suzette kissed Anna good-bye and moved back to the ranch. "Suz, please stay here a while longer," Anna pleaded. "You can't live alone, it isn't safe. Why must you be so stubborn? Lord knows you're welcome to stay here with Perry and me for as long as you like."

"You and Perry are very kind, Anna, but I'm going home where I belong. Really. I've no intention of arguing."

"Very well. You won't listen to me, but I'll bet Austin Brand will have something to say about this."

Suzette looked at her friend. "And what is *that* supposed to mean?"

"It means that he will most assuredly not allow you to live alone at the ranch. You know how protective he is of you. Do you honestly think he'll hold still for you living way out there by yourself?"

"Anna, listen to me. Austin Brand is a kind and dear friend. He's been very good to me and I appreciate it, just as I appreciate your help. Where I live is none of his concern, and he is not going to be consulted about it."

Anna smiled at her obstinate friend. "Do I wish I could be there to see his face when you tell him about it!"

"Absolutely not! I won't hear of it! Have you lost your mind?" Austin waved his arms around, his gray eyes like stormclouds.

"Will you kindly calm down, Austin?" Suzette said irritably.

"Calm down?" Austin grabbed her elbow. "You tell me you're going to live alone, miles from the nearest neighbor, and you want me to calm down! Dammit, girl, you can't be serious!"

"I'm very serious, Austin. The ranch is my home, and that is where I'm going to live."

"I won't allow it, Suzette. It's foolish and out of the question. I refuse to argue about it." Austin's eyes narrowed.

Her temper flaring, Suzette wrenched out of his grasp. "Just who do you think you are, Austin Brand! What gives you the right to tell me what I can and cannot do? I'm a grown woman, Austin, nineteen years old."

Austin couldn't help smiling. He took her arm. "Nineteen. Sweetheart, that's hardly a woman. You're still a little girl and..."

Suzette pushed on his chest and spun away from him. "I am *not* a little girl! I'm a woman, a full-grown, independent woman, and I'll thank you to treat me like one! Now, I don't want to hear one more word about it. Starting tonight I'll be living at the ranch, and if you don't like it, you can ... you can..." She flounced to the door of his office. "I'm going to work. I'm sure poor Mr. Keach must be wondering what's going on in here. Austin, why don't you just go back to your cow hunt!"

Sighing, Austin shook his head. "I am. I'm leaving this afternoon."

"So soon?" she asked, softening. "I... Austin, thanks for giving me a shoulder to cry on. I promise I'll never need it again. I'm going to manage, you know. I intend to be strong and resilient. From this day forward, you are looking at a new Suzette Foxworth."

"I saw nothing wrong with the old one," he said quietly.

"Good-bye, Austin. Take care of yourself." She slammed the door behind her.

"Bye, darlin'," he mumbled to the closed door.

Austin left town that afternoon and by nightfall found his

men and his herd at the camp near Squaw Mountain. He'd no sooner dismounted than he called one of his hands aside and offered a cigar to the lean, leathery man who was an expert marksman. "Dale." Austin clamped the man's slim shoulder. "I'm giving you a raise."

Half grinning, the cowboy eyed him. "Yeah? What's the catch?"

"I want you to return to Jacksboro at once. Ride directly to the Foxworth ranch. You choose the spot, but you're to guard the young lady who lives there. She's not to know, so be extremely careful. You're to go there each evening at dark and remain awake and alert throughout the night. At sunup, you return to my ranch to sleep. Will you do it?"

"Are you serious about a raise?"

"You'll get double what I'm paying you now. Your only duty will be to see that Suzette Foxworth is safe in her home."

"I'm your man, boss." The lean cowboy smiled. "I'm already tired of these stinking, stupid longhorns."

"Then go get your horse. Time's wasting. I want her to sleep safely tonight, so you'd best be on your way."

"I'm as good as there, boss."

"One last thing, Dale," Austin called after him. "If I ever catch you sleeping on the job, be prepared to leave Jack county."

Dale Jackson tipped his Stetson and saluted.

Austin returned to Jacksboro the first week in June, riding into town ahead of his men. They had taken the large herd to the holding pens on the Brand ranch to rest for a couple of weeks before beginning the long ride up the Chisholm trail to Abilene.

Austin, dirty, disheveled, and unshaven, tethered his horse and hurried into the Wichita Hotel, but not before casting a longing glance across the street at the *Echo* office. He wanted to see Suzette, but it would have to wait. He wasn't about to let her see him looking less than his best. When he finally sank into a big tub of hot water, he sighed and closed his eyes.

Would she be overjoyed to see him? Would she be thin and pale? After all, she was only a child. Would she weep and cling to him when she greeted him?

Half an hour later, dressed impeccably, his thick blond hair trimmed and brushed, his face clean-shaven, Austin Brand strode across the street. Suddenly as nervous as a young boy, he stepped into the newspaper office, squinting from the glare of the noonday sun.

Suzette, looking fresh and radiant, was bent over her writing pad, working furiously. He watched her for a long minute. She was not the pale, distraught girl he'd expected to find, but instead looked rested, vibrant, the picture of good health — and very, very beautiful.

"Suzette," he said softly.

The blond head flew up and their eyes locked. The smile she gave him dispelled any doubts, and she jumped up from her chair. "Austin!" she squealed and stood on tiptoes to kiss his cheek, then pulled back. "Let me look at you! It's so good to see you, Austin. When did you get in?"

"An hour ago." He beamed. "How are you, dear?"

"Busy!" she exclaimed happily. "You must come look at the lead story for today's paper." She took him by the hand and proudly presented him with her pad. "Read this! Can you believe it? Isn't it too exciting for words?"

Austin smiled indulgently and read.

The Prairie Echo

June 8, 1874
Fort Worth, Texas

A dark young bandit, known only as Kaytano, led a band of desperadoes in a successful holdup of the First National Bank yesterday. Eyewitnesses say the fearless half-breed was wounded in the getaway, but those reports are unconfirmed, as the young renegade and his gang once again slipped through the fingers of the pursuing Rangers. It is said Kaytano...

Austin's smile had gone cold. "What *is* it, Austin?" Suzette was puzzled. "I thought you'd be pleased. The holdup took place yesterday afternoon and will be reported in today's paper."

Austin handed her the pad. "Perhaps if the world is lucky, the man will die of his wounds. Come, let me take you to lunch."

"But, Austin, I'm not finished writing my story."

"Let Mr. Keach finish for you. Get your bonnet."

She frowned but took her bonnet from its hook. "No, I'll do it when I get back. I can only stay at lunch for half an hour."

"We'll see." Austin was grinning again as he took her elbow.

10

June eleventh had dawned, a warm, perfect day. Austin Brand mounted his horse for the long, hard ride up the Chisholm trail. An even dozen of his best cowmen were awaiting the signal to start the drive. Tom Capps, the trail boss, astride a big dun-colored horse, drew up alongside Austin. It was Tom, the capable, weathered native Texan, who would raise a gloved hand for all to see. When his hand came down, the drovers would move out.

The best and most experienced riders would set the pace. Tom Capps had chosen Randy Lancaster and Randy's best friend, Bob Coleman, for his point men. Both were in excellent physical condition and expert cattlemen. Seasoned veterans, Randy and Bob had known each other since childhood; they bickered like an old married couple, but they were fierce and rugged, in their prime at forty years of age. Two other skilled herders, young Red Wilson, a drover who'd drifted to Jack County from Montana, and tough old Zeke Worth, a Confederate veteran from Alabama, rode near the middle of the bawling herd.

Four other cowhands, Freddy Black, Monty Hudspeth, Slim Hester, and old Nate, were positioned along the sides. Their job was to keep the strays in line. The two youngsters, eighteen-year-old Clyde Bonner and seventeen-year-old Jimmy Davis, would spend the next six weeks eating dirt and complaining bitterly about it. However, even Clyde and Jimmy felt superior to the horse wrangler, a tall, skinny youth whose sole duty was to oversee the large remuda. Young Denis Sanders took ribbing good-naturedly from his saddle pals. Denis liked horses more than he liked people, and he was as talented a horseman as ever cared for a remuda of saddle ponies. Rarely did Denis need help; though there were at least five mounts for each man on the drive. Denis's job was to keep them fed, watered, brushed, and ready to ride.

Brand's chuck wagon, groaning under its load of flour, bacon, dried beef, beans, cornmeal, sugar, cooking supplies, and pots and pans, was already rolling ahead of the herd, with Big Al MacRae holding the reins. He would drive the chuck and cook, but he could also be coaxed into cleaning clothes, treating wounds or snakebites, and even fixing bedrolls each night.

Big Al loved the drives, loved to cook, and was as excited as a child at Christmas. He felt most alive when he was seated on the plank seat of the covered chuck, bumping across the open prairie, the sound of bellowing longhorns and shouting cowboys music to his ears. He could think of nothing more rewarding than standing at the back end of the chuck come sundown, the smell of his prize biscuits filling the air, dishing up bubbling beans and juicy steaks to the tired, grateful drovers. He was as proud of his fried pies as the ablest of housewives, and a wise cowhand was sure to get seconds if he praised the old cook's culinary talents.

Austin sat tensed, ready for the drop of Tom Capps' gloved hand. He felt a shiver of excitement run down his broad back as he always did at the beginning of a trail drive. Like many a man who went up the trail, Austin would be complaining before they reached Abilene. He'd be weary, bored, overworked, restless, homesick, tired of his fellow cowhands, longing for a woman, and downright sick of the whole way of living long before the first of the longhorns were pushed close to the holding pens in the boisterous Kansas town. But right now he felt young and strong and ready. Ready to wrestle the headstrong longhorns over the prairies, across swollen ravines and raging rivers, into the Indian nation, and on into Kansas. This was a man's work and just what he needed.

His saddle creaked when he shifted and the big gray mount he rode tossed its head in anticipation. Tom Capps squinted in the morning sun. In front of him, a sea of multicolored steers, their long horns clacking, their hooves kicking up dust, snorted and bellowed. It was a pleasing sight to the experienced cowman. His gaze swung slowly to Austin. Softly, in a voice so gentle it belied his fierce, rugged nature, Tom said, "Hell, let's go to Abilene." Austin nodded and smiled, pulled his Stetson down over his forehead, and tightened his hold on the reins. Tom Capps's hand lowered. "Move 'em out!"

Shouting their approval, the eager cowmen wore identical smiles as they dug big-roweled spurs into their horses and began the journey north.

Austin's steed pranced in the morning sun, its thick mane flowing, the hand-tooled saddle trimmed in silver glittering brightly. Austin, debonair even when cowboying, wore a gray silk shirt the exact color of his eyes. His trousers were snug, custom-tailored, and his soft boots of fine black leather were polished to a high gleam. At his throat, a colorful bandanna was knotted loosely. His well-creased Stetson was pulled low on his forehead, and bits of metal on his gunbelt and his silver spurs glinted in the bright sun. He held the reins easily in one large hand. His eyes were sweeping the horizon, coming to rest on the approximate location of the Foxworth ranch.

He couldn't really see it, but he pictured it — and the lovely girl who lived there. He wondered if Suzette was up yet. Was she dressing now, or was she still asleep, her sweet warm body peaceful in slumber? Would she miss him? When he'd told her he'd be gone for as long as three months, he'd watched closely for her reaction. There had been none. She'd said only that she hoped it was a safe trip.

Austin sighed. She didn't give a damn that he was leaving. He'd come home for a week from the cow hunt, and in that time he'd only been allowed the pleasure of her company on two occasions; lunch at the Wichita Hotel, and dinner last night. But, then, why should she care? *Why should a young beauty like Suzette be mine for the taking?*

He shook his head. *To hell with Suzette Foxworth! She's a sweet young kid, nothing more. This drive is what I need. A couple of days out, and I'll forget about her.*

While Austin argued with himself, Suzette, riding side-saddle on her mare Glory, reined her horse in on a hillock nearby and observed the milling herd. Well out of harm's way, she watched fascinated as the cowboys calmly moved the big herd out, pushing them slowly across the meadows. Shading her eyes, she scanned the men for a glimpse of Austin. He was easy to pick out. Taller in the saddle and much broader of chest than the others, he sat his horse regally.

Suzette smiled. Austin was unquestionably the picture of the handsome, rich cattle baron. Now, while he was unaware of her scrutiny, she could feast her eyes upon his impressive physique. While her gaze took in the powerful chest and bulging muscles of his arms, Austin turned in his saddle. Abruptly he pulled up on the reins of the big gray, and Suzette knew he'd seen her. As he turned his horse, he said something to Tom Capps. Suzette's breath caught: Austin was riding to meet her. Now there could be no pretending; when he neared her, she smiled disarmingly.

Austin was smiling too, and when he brought his mount alongside hers, he tipped his hat and winked at her. "Honey, I guess you're just about the prettiest sight I've ever seen," he said.

"You're quite the dashing figure yourself, Austin."

"My dear, you make it mighty hard for a man to discharge his duties when you say things like that." He held out a gloved hand to her. She laid her hand in his and Austin immediately brought it to his lips. Kissing the warm palm, he murmured, "Say the word, darlin', and I won't go."

Suzette snatched her hand away. "Austin Brand, don't speak such foolishness! What's gotten into you?"

His eyes registered the rebuff for only a second. Then he smiled at her. "Sorry, Suzette. Forgive me, I was behaving foolishly."

Now it was her turn to be sorry. "Austin, I didn't mean... that is, I..." Suzette stammered.

"My dear, I know exactly what you mean. I must be going. Please take care. I'll see you in three months." Without further adieu, he spurred his horse and galloped off to rejoin the drive.

"Wait, Austin... you took it the wrong way... Austin..." Suzette called as she nervously twisted the gold chain at her throat. He was too far away to hear her.

Austin was grateful to Suzette. She'd made it clear that she wanted no undue attention from him. And she was right. He was glad she spoke her mind; it would make it easier. She'd be the daughter of his dead friend, that was all. Certainly he cared for her, but like a daughter. He'd watch after her, take care of her, for Blake Foxworth's sake and for no other reason.

The drive was hard, dangerous work, and Austin worked alongside his men. He stayed in the saddle all day long, and his back ached, his head hurt, and his eyes burned from the ever-present dust kicked up by thousands of hooves.

Stragglers had to be forced from the underbrush; danger of stampede was constant. A gunshot or even a clap of thunder could push the skittish mass out of control. And at night, Austin did his part, singing in a low, soothing baritone, lulling the big beasts to sleep.

The drovers grew more weary with each passing week. Austin was weary, too, but not enough to push Suzette Foxworth from his thoughts. He thought about her while he rode in the hot sun, while he lay in his bedroll, his eyes on the starry heavens, and he even dreamed about her golden hair, her brilliant blue eyes, and the lovely figure of this girl he'd known for so long. Try as he might, he couldn't get her out of his mind. Surprised, even alarmed at the hold she had on him, Austin decided to handle the situation in the same way he'd always taken care of things. He'd stay in Abilene, a redhot town with numerous bars, brothels, dance halls, theaters, and gambling houses where a man could entertain himself and perhaps forget about a girl back home.

It was late July when Austin and his men pushed the longhorns into the corrals outside Abilene. It had been a successful drive with few mishaps. The final tally pleased Austin to no end; losses had been minimal, and the herd was healthy and fatter than when they left Jack County.

Austin contracted for the sale, met with the buyers, and oversaw the exchange. Shouts of relief rose from the dirty, tired cowhands when the last big longhorn clamored into the railroad car.

Austin Brand smiled when he paid his hands for a job well done. To a man, the cowboys headed into town, eager for a bath, a shave, a good time. Austin and Tom Capps watched them depart, shouting and whistling, a couple of the younger ones waving their six-shooters high.

"What are we waiting for?" Tom Capps rolled a cigarette, wetting it with his tongue. "Let's go raise a little hell, Austin."

"An excellent suggestion," Austin responded. "The first thing I want is a shave. This damned beard is itching more every day."

"That's not all that's itching." Tom Capps grinned and took a drag on his cigarette.

Within the hour, Austin lowered his big, tired body into a wooden tub of hot soapy water. With a glass of whiskey in one hand and a fat Cuban cigar in the other, Austin sighed with pleasure and let the steaming water soothe his tired muscles and cleanse his sunburned skin.

At dusk, Austin headed out for an after-dinner stroll and made his way toward the Alamo Saloon, sidestepping more than a few swaggering, drunken cowhands. Three glazed double doors at the west entrance to the Alamo stood wide open. Austin stepped inside and went directly to the long bar. Large mirrors behind the bar reflected row upon row of liquor bottles. Austin ordered bourbon straight up from the mustachioed bartender and turned slowly to look at the paintings of nudes adorning the walls. A small band of musicians in the corner of the big saloon competed with shouts, laughter, clinking glasses, and jangling spurs.

Three drinks later, Austin picked up the half-empty bottle and made his way to one of the many green felt-covered tables. Nodding to the faro dealer, he took a seat. An hour later Austin was bored with gambling and his eyes were drifting around the smoke-filled room. Soon they were met by a pair of vivid green ones as a curvaceous, milky-skinned woman edged close to his chair. A pretty redhead, she smiled seductively at Austin, her pert mouth curving into a brazen invitation. Austin returned the smile.

Her green satin dress shimmered as the woman wordlessly sat on Austin's left knee, exposing shapely legs sheathed in silk stockings. As she put a slender arm around his neck and leaned close, the soft green feather of her hat tickled his neck. She touched his face lightly and said sweetly, "Buy me a drink, cowboy?"

"Sure, darlin'." Austin wrapped an arm around her. He

continued to gamble and drink, the redhead perched on his lap, clinging to him while he dropped silver coins down the bodice of her dress each time she gave him a kiss.

Austin cashed in and left the game, the friendly redhead holding his arm and chattering ceaselessly. Although Austin had been drinking heavily all evening, the alcohol affected him not at all. Nor did the pretty woman on his arm.

He sighed and reached into his pocket. Stuffing a generous amount of money down her dress, he kissed her cheek and apologized. "Honey, forgive me, I'm tired. Perhaps tomorrow night. Right now, all I want is some sleep."

"Well, sure, sugar," the redhead trilled and kissed his mouth. "You get some shut-eye and when you wake up we'll have us a time. I'm Shirley and I promise you a night to remember. You won't forget me, will you, handsome?"

Austin shook his head and unwrapped her long fingers from his arm. "No, ma'am."

But he did.

Back in his hotel room he stripped and fell into the soft bed. He closed his eyes, certain sleep would follow instantly. Instead, Suzette Foxworth's lovely face floated before him. He couldn't remember what Shirley looked like, but he could vividly recall every feature of Suzette's beautiful face. It was for her he yearned and no other.

It irritated him and it worried him. He needed to change his plans again. He would stay away from Jacksboro for a long time, but not here, not in Abilene; here he'd never get her off his mind. He would go to New York, spend the winter season with the city's café society. New York's most beautiful and sophisticated ladies would surely make him forget his little country girl.

Austin yawned and turned over. Certain his little problem was solved, he went to sleep instantly. The next day he made arrangements to take the train to New York City.

11

In Jacksboro Anna Woods needed her friend Suzette. Her parents had moved to Fort Worth, and although they promised to return in time for the birth of their next grandchild, Anna went into labor early. On a sweltering night in late July, Anna gave birth to a tiny girl. Suzette moved in to help take care of mother and child.

Perry Woods insisted they call the infant Sunny. Anna kissed her husband and said Sunny would be a perfect name for their beautiful daughter. Fourteen-month-old Josh gently stroked his new sister's silky hair and squeezed her delicate hand. Only a little jealous of all the attention the new baby was receiving from callers, Josh followed Suzette about the house, certain she still liked him as much as she liked the baby.

It was a wonderful week for Suzette and therefore very lonely for her when she finally went home. Sitting alone on the porch at twilight, she compared her life to Anna's and felt an ache in her breast. She was woman enough to long for a husband, a home, and children, but she feared it was never to be. She'd not thought about love and marriage since Luke Barnes's death. She'd not accepted any invitations from young men, though lieutenants from the fort frequently attended church and smiled at her, asking if they could come to call. Cowboys from the surrounding ranches invited her to box suppers and dances, but somehow she never cared to accept their invitations.

She shrugged her slender shoulders and, as so frequently happened, thought of Austin Brand. She missed him; she'd be glad when he came back from Abilene. She smiled, remembering how he'd looked on that last morning. So big and handsome and rugged. Yes, she'd be very glad when Austin got home.

Suzette tucked her long hair under her sunbonnet and pulled on her short white gloves. Stepping from the door of the *Echo* office, she blinked in the hot September sun, then turned as she heard her name called. From the direction of the Longhorn Saloon, a drover hurried toward her.

"Nate!" she exclaimed, her face lighting up with a smile.

"Miz Suzette." The old hand swept the soiled hat from his head and came to meet her. "How are you? My, you look pretty."

"Oh, Nate, it's so good to see you." Suzette embarrassed the old man by kissing his weathered cheek. "When did you get back?"

"Why, we just rode in an hour ago. Haven't been out to the ranch to clean up yet. Pardon my appearance." He looked down at his dusty denims and sweat-soaked shirt.

"Never mind about that." Suzette waved her hand. "Did everything go all right? Was the market good? How long did you stay in Abilene? Where's Austin? Is he in the Longhorn?" She felt mild excitement begin inside her.

"Everything went just fine. I tell you, Mr. Brand's got the best crew I ever worked with, and he works as hard as his men. I had a great time, felt like a young man again. Why, when we hit Abilene, I —"

"Nate, please," Suzette interrupted. "Where's Austin? Will you go in the saloon and get him? I'm anxious to see him."

Still smiling, Nate said, "He's not there, miss. No, sir, that Austin, he didn't stay in Abilene but a couple of days. Now, the rest of us, we —"

"A couple of days? You mean Austin came back before the rest of you? He's been here in Jacksboro and didn't —"

"No. He didn't stay in Abilene; he caught a train and went all the way up to New York City!"

Suzette's smile disappeared. "New York? Austin's in New York? But why? For how long? I don't understand."

She was more disappointed than she cared to admit.

"Yes'm, that's what he said. Are you all right Miz Suzette? You look pale."

"Of course I'm all right." Suzette forced a smile. "I think it's grand that he went to New York. He has friends there, and after his tragedy he needs to enjoy himself."

"That he does. He's a mighty nice man, and I just hope he'll find himself a nice lady someday soon and remarry. Yes, sir, I hope —"

"Yes, yes, Nate, I do, too. Come over to the house soon for supper. It's good to have you back."

"It's good to be home," He grinned.

The next morning Suzette received a short letter post-marked New York City. She recognized Austin's scrawl immediately.

Dear Suzette,

I am in residence at the Stonely Hotel in New York City. Should you need anything, speak to my foreman, Tom Capps. I've instructed him to be of service to you in any way that would be of help. If you need money, see Tom.

I trust you have had a nice summer. I've no idea when I'll be coming home; as you know, I've many old friends up here.

Take care.

Warmly,
Austin

Suzette folded the letter and put it back in the envelope. She was hurt and angry. She'd thought Austin would be anxious to return home.

She tore the letter in two and dropped it into a trash can. She'd been foolish to depend on him. She didn't care how long he stayed away; she could certainly take care of herself.

Autumn came early and with it blue northers and cold, biting winds. The ranch house was never warm enough, and when Suzette was at home, she sat directly in front of the fireplace, a heavy quilt draped over her lap. The days grew short, the nights too long. Suzette was lonely, desperately lonely, and there was a time or two when she strongly considered Anna's offer to live with the Woodses.

The Christmas holidays came and Perry, Anna, Josh, and baby Sunny were off to Fort Worth to spend the season with Anna's parents. Anna and Perry begged Suzette to accompany them, but she declined. Alone, she walked into the woods and chopped down a cedar tree, decorating it with popcorn and cranberries. On Christmas Eve she sat staring at the tree. On the table by the worn couch, a letter from Austin Brand remained where she'd tossed it. He had wished her a Merry Christmas and said he doubted he'd be home before spring. Picturing the exciting time he was having in New York, Suzette gritted her teeth and tried not to pity herself.

It didn't work. Hot tears welled up and overflowed. It was a miserable Christmas, the worst she'd ever had. She twisted her gold locket while the tears slid down her cheeks. She missed her mother and father. She missed Perry and Anna. Josh and Sunny. She missed ... she missed Austin Brand. Slowly her shaking hand came up to her face and she sobbed like a heartbroken child.

"Oh, Austin, I need you, I need you so much! How could you leave me all alone like this?"

But by New Year's her spunk had returned and she was determined never to need Austin Brand or anyone else again. She had her position at the *Echo*, she had her home, she had friends; she needed nothing more.

Spring swept over the plains in all its glory, and Suzette, wearing an old pair of buckskin pants, a cotton blouse, her hair caught at the back of her neck with the gold clasp, her feet bare, stood bent over a hoe in the newly spaded earth behind her house. Proud of her blossoming garden, she worked tirelessly, chopping away the weeds choking the tender green tomato vines. A sheen of perspiration covered her face and throat and made her shirt stick to her back. The setting sun was a large fiery ball behind her, turning her tangled hair to flame.

Austin Brand dismounted in front of the house. He started to call to Suzette, but then caught sight of her. He started toward her. Still she hadn't seen him and still he didn't call to her. She paused for a moment, the hoe in the crook of her left shoulder, and raised the tail of her shirt to wipe her face.

Austin Brand wasn't completely certain if he'd been in love with Suzette before. He knew he had felt very protective toward her. And he'd been unmistakably attracted by her beauty. He knew she'd filled his thoughts much too often, that he'd missed her terribly in all the long months he'd been away. He also knew he desired her. But on this warm May evening, watching her silhouetted against the spectacular sunset, he knew. He knew for sure that he loved her. He would always love her.

"Suzette," he called softly.

She whirled and saw him. She smiled, dropped the hoe, and started toward him, and his heart sank. There was no love or affection in the brilliant blue eyes looking at him. She hadn't missed him as he'd hoped. He'd spent every day missing her. Now she was walking casually to him as though he'd never been gone. He knew then, just as he knew that he loved her, that he would have to wait, perhaps a long time. She did not love him, of that he was sure. So he watched her walk across the furrows to him and held himself in check, refusing to yield to the burning temptation to run and sweep her into his aching arms. He was older and wiser than Suzette. He could make her his if he played his hand correctly. She was worth the wait. She'd come around in time, and when she did, he'd be there waiting to make her his own. Until then, he'd be as patient as Job.

Austin smiled. "My dear Suzette, how nice to see you again." She couldn't know that his heart was drumming loudly against his ribs, or that he was solemnly vowing that one day she would belong to him.

"Austin," she greeted him warmly, "I'm delighted you're home. You must tell me all about your visit to New York."

Austin didn't see Suzette as often as she would have liked. Occasionally he took her to dinner at the Wichita Hotel, and now and then he called at the ranch. For the most part she saw him only at the *Echo* office. He was, as he had always been, a real friend, and she knew, should she need anything at all, Austin would see to it. He was also witty and charming and his hilarious tales made her laugh and blush.

Suzette didn't understand Austin's behavior. After a day in the *Echo* office, a day of helping out as though he were the employee, a day of closeness and shared interests and laughter, he'd pull on his fine frock coat and say good evening; she might not see him again for a week. Even stranger were the times he'd spend at his desk, saying nothing, a wistful look on his handsome face. Each time she looked up, he was staring at her. It flustered her and made her uneasy. She wondered what was going through his mind.

And then it was time for him to leave again for Abilene. When Suzette told him good-bye, she ventured, "I suppose you'll be going to New York again this year?"

Austin grinned. "Will you miss me if I do?"

"No," she answered flippantly.

"In that case, I don't believe I'll go this year. Take care, Suzette. I'll see you this fall."

"Suit yourself," she said and flounced away.

It was an unusually dry summer; by September the prairie was scorched. On a night so hot that Suzette lay covered with a film of perspiration, she awoke and blinked. Her bedroom was lit up. Then she could hear the roar. Prairie fire! Terror gripping her, she jumped from her bed and ran to the open window. Sheets of flame were sweeping up the hillside, heading straight toward the house.

By the time Suzette got to the front door, there were men in the yard. The red glare illuminated the faces of ranchers and friends. Stunned, Suzette watched them fill buckets from the creek and fight the blaze; she looked on as others with wet rags tied to sticks and hoes battled the raging fire. Still others grabbed grain sacks from the barn and beat at the roaring, advancing monster.

Finally moved to act, Suzette headed for the barn and her mare, Glory. By the time she got there, a man was leading the terrified horses from their stalls just ahead of the crackling inferno. Clouds of heavy smoke choked them and the intense heat made their eyes water and sting. Suzette, her tangled hair sticking to her face, struck at the flames with a dampened sack, her chest aching, her face smarting. She raised an arm high, then staggered as the sack was caught from behind. She uttered a cry of protest and whirled, then released the sack gratefully.

Austin Brand tossed the sack aside, picked her up and carried her across the yard into the house. It was not until he sat her down gently on the worn settee that Suzette realized she hadn't put her shoes on. Her feet were bruised and scratched.

"Darlin', the fire's about out. The house and barn are no longer in danger. Don't you move." He left her looking after him, fighting back the tears. When he returned, he carried a pan of water and went about the task of bathing her feet. He crouched down in front of her, tenderly sponging away the blood and dirt while he spoke quietly. "Sweetheart, I got back late last night. I couldn't sleep so I went for a walk around the square. I saw the glow on the horizon. By the time I'd reached the livery stables and saddled up, the others were headed out here. Thank God we made it in time. Are you all right, Suzette?"

"Yes, Austin, you don't need to... here, let me finish with this." She tried to pull her foot from his knee.

He clasped her slender ankle firmly. "Don't, Suzette. Stop squirming."

The sun was up when the last fires had been extinguished. Suzette thanked the men and offered to cook breakfast for them. Declining her invitation, they assured her they were happy to help out and departed. Only Austin remained. He drank coffee as he straddled a straight-backed chair in the kitchen.

"Honey," he drawled, "why don't you stay home today? Your feet are tender, I'm sure. I'll tell Mr. Keach you're taking the day off."

"You'll do no such thing," she said. "I'm going to the *Echo* office today."

Austin set his coffee cup aside and stood up. "Fine." He scratched his cheek. "Me, I'm going to stretch out on your couch and go to sleep." He started for the parlor.

"No, Austin, you can't do that." Suzette frowned.

Austin sat down and pulled off his tall black boots. "Be kind to me, Suzette, I've not been to bed yet." He yawned and stretched out on his back, hands under his head. "Wake me when you get home this afternoon." His eyes closed.

Suzette shook her head, pulled a coverlet from the closet, and draped it over his large frame. "Austin," she whispered, leaning close.

"Hmm?"

"I'm glad you're back."

Austin smiled without opening his eyes. "Me too."

Throughout the day the thought that Austin Brand was asleep at her home brought a faint smile to her lips. At day's end she hurriedly put away her things, said a hasty goodnight to Mr. Keach, and went to the stables for her horse. Excitement made her stomach churn as she galloped homeward, planning what she would cook for Austin's supper. But her excitement was quickly replaced with disappointment. Austin wasn't there when she arrived. On the table was a note:

Thanks for the use of the settee. Forgive me for imposing.
Austin.

Austin didn't remain in Jacksboro. By the first frost, he'd headed east once again. Suzette missed him more than she had the year before, just as Austin planned. When he returned in the spring, he didn't come directly to her ranch, nor did he drop by the *Echo* office. In fact, he made no attempt to see her, and she was hurt and confused, though she had no intention of letting him know it.

More than ten days had passed since his return. Suzette lay wide awake in her moonlight-streaked bedroom and wondered why a man who professed to be her best friend didn't bother to call on her after being away for six months. Sighing, she turned onto her stomach.

She was dozing off when she heard a noise. She lifted her head from her pillow and heard it again.

Whatever it was, it was very faint. Like little bells ringing. Suzette froze. It could be only one thing. The Comanches wore moccasins with bells sewn on to the ties.

Quickly, she got out of bed and tiptoed to the window. Just as quickly she jerked her head back and flattened herself against the wall, her breath coming in shallow gulps. Immediately beyond the yard, three half-naked Indians were dismounting.

When her heart finally slowed a little, she moved across the room. She could hear nothing but the little bells as she edged toward the parlor. Once inside the larger room she dropped to the floor, afraid she would be seen. She crawled to the guncase, fumbled with the lock, and somehow got the Winchester out. Then she realized she had no ammunition. Stifling a cry, she stood with the gun in her hand and watched helplessly as the three lithe braves stole into the barn and out again, leading her beloved Glory. The other two horses she owned whinnied and followed the big mare. A slender warrior remounted his paint horse and led the others.

The two remaining braves spoke to each other briefly, then one mounted up and the other started toward the house. Suzette's hand flew to her mouth and she bit her knuckles, drawing blood. He was in the yard, his mahogany body gleaming in the bright moonlight. The other brave watched. The first would be at the back door in seconds. Suzette raised the empty gun and prayed.

A single shot pierced the still night air and Suzette

screamed. She saw the tall brave running away, out of the yard. He was on his horse in one swift leap and the two were racing away. Baffled, she looked at the rifle she held. She hadn't fired. She heard other shots as the Comanches thundered away.

She stood rooted to the spot, trembling, the gun clutched tightly. From out of the shadows she saw a man approaching, a rifle in his hand. She didn't know whether to throw open the door and embrace him or run.

"Miss Foxworth," the man called in a soft drawl, "it's Dale Jackson, ma'am. I work for Austin Brand. Are you all right?"

Sobbing with relief, Suzette flew to the door and unlatched it.

Dale Jackson took the heavy gun from Suzette gently and leaned it against the door. Then took her elbow carefully and led her to the table.

"Mr. Jackson, I... I was so..." Suzette stammered, relief mingling with the terror she still felt.

"Ma'am, you're safe now. You just sit there and I'll make us some coffee."

"But... I don't understand. What are you doing here? How did you know?"

Dale Jackson sighed. "Miss Foxworth, Austin Brand hired me to guard you at night. You weren't supposed to know about it. He's going to be powerful mad at me. In fact, I imagine I'll be on my way out of Jack County come sunup."

"You mean you've been watching my ranch *every* night?"

"Yes, ma'am. I let Austin down tonight. I must have dozed. I didn't know the savages were on the place until it was too late. I'm awful sorry about the horses."

"Mr. Jackson, I'm very grateful to you. You've no reason to apologize. You saved my life and I shall tell Mr. Brand as much."

When morning came, Suzette rode into town with Dale Jackson. Austin Brand, dapper in a custom-made suit, lounged outside the *Echo* office. When he saw the mounted pair, his sun-bronzed face lost some color.

"I'm in for it," Dale Jackson muttered. He reined in his mount as Austin stepped off the sidewalk. Scowling darkly, Austin reached for Suzette.

Suzette put her hands on Austin's broad shoulders as he lifted her from the horse, then smiled prettily at him. "Austin, how nice to see you. I heard you were back in town."

Austin held her arm and pushed her in front of him. "Get down from your horse," he said coldly to Dale Jackson.

"Yes, sir," mumbled the cowboy.

"Austin Brand." Suzette grabbed his lapels. "Before you make a spectacle of yourself and me, let me explain."

"I want Dale to explain," Austin said roughly.

"For heaven's sake, people are staring!" Suzette hissed.

"To hell with 'em!" Austin shouted.

Suzette managed to get both men into the newspaper office, where explanations were given. Austin calmed down quickly when he realized the cowboy was responsible for saving Suzette's life.

"Dale," Austin finally smiled, "no need to leave Jack County. I'll hire another man to keep you company at night. That way you won't get so sleepy."

"Thanks, Mr. Brand." The cowboy twisted his hat brim in his hands. "If I may be excused now, sir."

"Yes, go on home." Austin waved him away, then turned to Suzette.

"Austin Brand," Suzette said, her eyes flashing as he led her into his office, "what makes you think you can have hired men watch my house? Why, you have no right to..."

"I'm glad to see you, too, darlin'," Austin smiled and touched her soft cheek with the back of his hand.

Austin was growing more and more anxious to have Suzette. He felt precious years were being wasted. Though he stayed as busy as possible and fought the overwhelming desire to sweep her into his arms and tell her that he could wait no longer, he wanted her for his own and he intended to have her. He knew in his heart she'd eventually turn to him, that it was best to wait, but the fever in his blood made the waiting agony for the big rancher, who desired no other woman but the pretty, strong-willed Suzette Foxworth.

Austin bought more land and more prized cattle. He went on the trail drive again, and again he visited New York. In February 1877 he met with Oliver Loving and other ranchers in Graham, Texas, and helped organize the Cattle Raisers' Association of North West Texas.

He was becoming more rich and powerful each year, and though Suzette would never know it, a great deal of his success was the direct result of his love for her. Because he was determined not to rush her, he buried himself in his work. If Suzette were his already, he'd probably have spent less time in the pursuit of business, more on taking pleasure with her. At times Austin convinced himself he was actually lucky she'd not yet come around; it made it possible for him to build an empire for their future.

Suzette struggled on. She refused a gift horse from Austin, insisting that she pay him a little each month for the big, gentle chestnut mare she chose from his large remuda. She paid no attention to the twitching of his full lips when she told him she would not accept charity from him.

The summer of '77 brought with it a bountiful garden for Suzette. Tomatoes hung heavy from the vines, and black-eyed peas, okra, potatoes, onions, and snap beans abounded. In the fruit orchard, juicy pears, peaches, apples, and plums filled the air with their sweet fragrances, while blackberries grew just in sight of the grape arbor.

Suzette smiled happily as she walked to the house with a pan of ripe peaches. It was a hot Sunday afternoon, a lazy, peaceful day. Yawning, she set the peaches on a cabinet and took off her sunbonnet. Debating whether to make a peach cobbler or take a nap, she soon opted for the nap; the heat was making her drowsy.

She awoke to a sound unlike any she'd ever heard. It was a deafening roar. Bright sunlight no longer streamed in the window by her bed. As in Indian summer, the sun was veiled and a haze hung in the air. Suzette jumped up and ran for the front door.

Swarms of grasshoppers obscured the summer sky. They swooped down on Suzette's glorious garden. Screaming, she grabbed a dishrag and ran across the yard, swatting and stomping as she went. "No, I will not let you have my garden!" she shouted desperately.

By nightfall there was nothing left. The grasshoppers were energetically digging into the fertile earth for the potatoes and turnips now. Suzette dropped to her knees and sobbed. All her hard work had been for nought.

The worst was yet to come. The bugs moved from the garden to the fruit orchard, quickly devouring all the fruit, even the green leaves. Suzette could do nothing but watch in helpless frustration. When the orchard had been stripped, the grasshoppers invaded her home, eating the linen curtains from the windows and the clothes in her closet. As they crawled onto her bed, she fought them with brooms. She beat on a tin pan to drive them away. She tried poison. Nothing helped. They stayed until everything was gone. Then they departed.

Suzette sat on her front porch and wondered if it might not be wise to leave Texas, as some of her neighbors had chosen to do. They'd given up living in this wild, untamable frontier. Perhaps she should, too. Maybe she should sell her ranch to Austin Brand and with the money go to New Orleans. She had cousins there. Perhaps she could report for a city newspaper.

For a long while Suzette rocked back and forth and considered leaving. Then she shook her head, dismissing the notion.

She would stay.

12

It was mid-afternoon on a day in the bitter January of 1878 when a very pale, apologetic Mr. Keach came to Suzette's desk and cleared his throat. Suzette looked up and knew immediately that he was feeling worse. He'd been ill all morning, and now he looked as if he might have a bit of fever.

"Good heavens, Mr. Keach, you must go home at once — or, better yet, to Dr. Woods's office." She hurried around her desk and pressed her palm to his forehead.

"Now, Miss Foxworth, I'm not sick enough to see the doctor, but I was wondering if you'd mind too much if I left early." The thin man's teeth were chattering.

"Mind?" Suzette pulled him along to the coat rack. "I insist you go home! You're going to have pneumonia — if you don't already." She was grabbing his heavy coat and holding it out for him.

"Please don't fuss so, Miss Foxworth. I'll be fine if I just go home and lie down for a while." With shaky fingers he tried to button his coat.

Brushing his hands away, Suzette did it for him. "Shall I step out and see if any of the men in town are in carriages? Perhaps one could give you a ride home. Dear me, any other time Austin would be around. He's in Graham today, and we don't expect him back until tomorrow."

"Please." The editor tried to smile. "It's not that far to my home. I'll be there in a matter of minutes."

"Then be off, Mr. Keach. When you get home, you get right to bed and have Mrs. Keach fix you a hot lemonade mixed with whiskey. That'll set you straight."

"I will." He shoved his hat down on his head and went out into the cold wind. Suzette stood on the wooden sidewalk and hugged herself. The sky was bleak and leaden with that dismal wintry look that made one long for one's own hearth and a hot drink.

"Brrr!" she said to no one in particular. She watched until Ben Keach had disappeared around the corner and then went back inside. She was still there hours later when the heavy sky turned to black velvet. Suzette didn't realize it had grown so dark until she stood to stretch her legs and rub her tired eyes. The room was shadowy, the lamp on her desk the only illumination. She turned to glance at the clock behind her and grimaced. It was after seven P.M.

"I should have left hours ago," she moaned. Dreading the cold ride home and the empty house waiting for her, Suzette slowly began to gather up her things. She put the half dozen wooden pencils back into a box and neatly sorted and stacked papers. She took her woolen gloves from the middle drawer, along with her small handbag. From the coat rack came the only coat she owned. It was warm and that was about all. But tonight the plain brown wool looked good to Suzette. As she pulled it on, she looked about for her bonnet and stamped her foot when she remembered she'd not worn one. Of all the nights to be out without her head covered! The wind seemed to be whistling louder as if to remind her. "Oh, well," she said aloud, "at least it isn't raining or snowing."

When she stepped outside, a blast of frigid air took her breath away. The town square was almost deserted. Only the Longhorn Saloon, two doors down, showed any life.

Austin had warned Suzette about being on the streets after dark. He'd told her it wasn't safe for a lady, especially a young and pretty one, to go about unescorted. She thought he was exaggerating, but now she saw what he meant. Cold though it was, the good-time drinkers were spilling out of the saloon onto the sidewalks. Several drunks loitered around the swinging doors.

Shivering, Suzette remained at the door of the newspaper office. She would have to walk past the saloon to get to the livery stables. But it wasn't getting any warmer, so she raised her chin and started down the street. Before she reached the

saloon entrance, the men standing outside saw her coming.
There were four of them, soldiers all. They wore the blue uniforms with the bright yellow trim and shiny brass buttons.

"Evening, miss," the four said simultaneously. Suzette
hurried past, but their loud laughter indicated the kind of
remarks they were making about her. Still, she figured they
were harmless enough. After all, it was payday and they were
in town for fun.

When the laughter grew louder, Suzette quickened her
pace and tried not to give in to fear. Were they following her?
She had reached the alley. As she hurried down the steps and
turned the corner, she took the opportunity to glance back at
the soldiers. Her breath caught. Two of the men *were* behind
her. But there were no other saloons at this end of the street
and no other businesses open. There could be no good reason
for the two drunken soldiers to be coming this way.

Suzette debated whether she should return to the sidewalk.
Quickly dismissing the idea, she told herself there was no
cause for alarm. She would walk the length of the alley to the
back of the buildings, then across to the livery stable, just as
she did every day. No one was going to hurt her. Soon she'd be
on the chestnut mare and on her way home. Even as she tried
to reassure herself, she knew without looking back that the
two soldiers had turned into the alley and were pursuing her.

She hated the thought of having to scream to save herself
from two drunk soldiers. Every tongue would wag for weeks
and Austin would be livid. Nevertheless...

It was too late. A dirty hand clamped on her mouth. She
was whirled about by a tall, grinning, young corporal. His
companion, shorter and very stocky, was wiping his mouth
on his uniform sleeve as though he intended to kiss her.

Suzette's eyes were wide with fright and disgust. The men
lifted and pushed her down the alley until they were in back of
the buildings. Here there was only the sound of the wind and
an occasional horse. No one would hear her if she screamed.

Suzette felt her head rock on her shoulders as she was slammed up against a building.

"Don't try nothin' foolish, missy," the tall man said. "We ain't gonna hurt you." With that he lowered his head, and his mouth took the place of his hand. He was kissing her, and though she screamed her outrage, it was swallowed up in his plundering, punishing mouth. His hand went to her throat, and as the kiss ended he pulled back and said coldly, "Make one sound and I'll choke the life out of you. Understand?" Unable to speak, Suzette violently shook her head up and down. "Good." He smirked wickedly. "Now you just hold still for a minute till we get your coat off."

It was not until then that Suzette realized the shorter man's plump hands were pulling furiously at her heavy coat. He stripped it from her in seconds and was reaching for the buttons going down the middle of her wool dress. She began to kick and fight, but was easily subdued by the tall man. He laughed at her pitiful attempts to free herself, his breath hot and smelling of whiskey. He forced her arms behind her and held them there in one hand. Then his lips came back to hers.

Feeling she would vomit from the horrible kisses, tears of disgust and fear stung her eyes. His lips were roaming over her face and she felt nausea grow in the pit of her stomach as the private's groping hands touched bare flesh and cold air rushed into her open dress. Suzette closed her eyes and prayed.

The stocky man yanked the cotton chemise down over her breasts and Suzette felt his hands squeezing her roughly while the tall corporal continued to wet her face with his sloppy kisses. Longing for the earth to open and swallow her up, Suzette moaned when the tall man said heatedly, "Move, dammit! I'm first."

His head was moving down to her breasts and Suzette braced herself. But before his lips could capture a cold, creamy breast, the corporal was lifted off his feet and thrown with such force that he hit the side of the building and crumpled. The short, stocky private followed, landing on top of his companion. It happened so fast Suzette could only blink, dumbstruck.

A familiar voice said softly, "You're okay, darlin'," and Austin Brand smiled as he covered her with her coat.

Before the two stunned soldiers could stumble to their feet and flee, Austin lifted them both and held them by their lapels, one in each massive hand. They were as helpless as trapped butterflies against the superior strength of the big man.

"Listen to me, you bastards. If you ever again so much as look at this woman, I'll kill you. It won't be a pretty death, either. I'll cut off what you're obviously so proud of and feed it to you!"

By now Suzette had come to her senses and was at his elbow. "Austin, please, let them go. Don't kill them, they aren't worth it. Austin, please."

He didn't look at her. To the men, he said, "You've been lucky this time. You'll never be so fortunate again." He promptly knocked their heads together and released them. Both slumped to the ground.

As though he'd done nothing more than ruffle their hair, he turned and gently took Suzette's arm, his gray eyes immediately soft and warm. "Sweetheart, are you all right?" He swept her up into his arms and carried her back through the alley.

"Yes, Austin, thanks to you." She clung to his neck.

Austin lifted her into his open carriage and got in beside her. When she protested that her horse was at the stables, he said, "Don't worry about it; don't worry about anything. Just slide over here close to me and I'll have you home in no time."

She complied, then nodded her thanks when he tucked a lap robe securely about her. They were silent on the ride home. When they arrived at the Foxworth ranch, Austin dismissed her attempts to walk to the house. "Don't be foolish," he said and picked her up.

Inside he lit the lamps and built a fire in the grate after he'd placed Suzette on the long settee, telling her to stay where she was. When the fire was burning to his satisfaction, Austin left her and went into the kitchen to put on the kettle. While the water was heating, he stepped to the door and asked, "Sweetheart, do you have any liquor?"

"There might still be some brandy on the top shelf of the cabinet. There's not much in it, but perhaps enough for you to have a drink." He turned without responding and a moment later came to her carrying the brandy and one glass. "Dear, it's for you." He handed her the glass. "Drink up." She did as she was told, and when he poured another, she drank it. "That'll help take the chill from your bones," he said, smiling down at her. He extended his hand and she took it and rose. "Suzette, I've heated water. I'll pour it into a basin and bring it in here by the fire. You can wash yourself while I make coffee."

"Austin." Suzette held her coat together. "My dress is torn."

"I'll go with you to get another," he said quietly and led her into her bedroom. She picked the first winter dress she saw.

While she stripped off the torn dress and underclothes and sat on her knees in front of the fire bathing away the kisses of the drunken soldiers from her face, neck, and breasts, she could hear Austin humming in the kitchen. It was a wonderful sound, a safe sound, a welcome sound.

She rinsed the soapsuds from her gleaming breasts, cleaning herself leisurely. She knew Austin and she trusted him. She didn't have to hurry to cover herself. Austin would never take advantage of her. She felt no uneasiness about being in a state of undress with him just inside the kitchen, the door wide open. He was a good man, a dependable man. He'd never harm her.

Dressed and feeling much better, she called to Austin. He quickly joined her, a cup of coffee in his hand. "You know, sweetheart," he said softly, "maybe I should spend the night here. You've had a terrible experience. I know you're shaky from your ordeal."

"No, Austin, thanks. Really, I'm fine." She smiled and took the coffee.

Austin didn't push it. He waited while she drank her coffee, making pleasant conversation, not daring to scold her for being out alone at night, though he longed to turn her over his knee and spank her.

After an hour, he rose. "It's getting late, Suzette. I'll say good-night now." He started for the door, hoping she'd change her mind. She said nothing. "Sweetheart, you get some rest."

"I will, Austin. Thank you. Austin... I... I..."

"What, darlin'?"

"Nothing. Nothing at all. Good night."

13

Suzette watched him walk to the door. Soon he would be in his buggy, gone down the hill, and she would be alone. Alone, always alone. Night after night, year after year, alone. Could she stand one more long frightening night by herself?

Wondering what was wrong with her that she should be behaving this way, Suzette told herself she should be ashamed, that tonight was not the first time she'd lived through a hardship. Nor would it be the last. She would get hold of herself just as she always had.

But she couldn't summon the strength on this cold winter night to square her shoulders and press on as she had always done. Tears stung her eyes, and although she swallowed several times, the lump refused to go away. She was tired, so tired of fighting, so tired of being afraid, of being alone.

Suddenly she wanted to shout at Austin to stay, to come back to her, to never, ever leave her. She needed his warmth, his strength. Why couldn't he see it? Why did he continue to walk away from her when she needed him so badly?

Please, Austin. Please don't leave me.

Austin turned. He looked at her for what seemed an eternity. His hand was on the doorknob, and the front door was open. Still he stood looking at her. She could hold back no longer; she opened her mouth to beg him to stay, but she couldn't speak. A muffled sob was all she managed.

Austin quietly closed the door. He walked over to her and put a gentle hand to her face. That's all it took. All the loneliness, all the pain, all the fears, so long bottled up inside the proud girl, surfaced. Suzette began to cry with the sort of release she'd never allowed herself.

Very calmly Austin lifted the distraught girl in his arms and walked into the sitting room. He took a seat on the worn sofa, carefully balancing her on his lap. Lightly resting his left hand across her knees, with his other he firmly gripped the worn fabric of the couch. Suzette covered her eyes and sobbed. Finally, her shoulders heaving, she lowered her hands from her face and looked at him, her vision blurring. "I... I'm sorry... I — "

"My dear, don't be sorry. Never be sorry. I'm here, my precious girl. Will you let me hold you close and take away the pain? That's why I'm here, Suzette. Let me comfort you, darling."

"I... I... can't, I'll get you all... all wet," she protested, but even as she spoke, she looked at him and thought how wonderful it would be to feel those strong arms around her. She longed to snuggle close to him, to bury her face in his expensive shirt, to cling to him until she was no longer shaking.

As tenderly as one would handle an infant, Austin's big hand moved up to the nape of her neck. Gently he pulled her down on him. Suzette felt unbelievable warmth radiate from him. Her wet cheek was pressed to his massive chest; his white silk shirt felt wonderful, and the clean masculine smell of him was pleasing, intoxicating. His hand had remained at the back of her neck under her hair and he was gently kneading the knotted muscles. His other hand was under the swell of her breasts, tightly holding her to him. She felt safe for the first time in years. She shyly slipped her arms around him, letting her cold hands run up and down the warm wool fabric of his jacket.

And she talked. His kindness at long last opened the door to her heart and she couldn't wait to confide in him. "Austin, Austin," she sobbed, her lips pressing his chest, her tears wetting the white silk shirt, "I've been so unhappy, so miserable. I don't think I can stand any more."

"My sweet baby," he soothed and slid his hand comfortingly over her trembling back.

"I loved Luke and he was killed. I loved my mother and daddy and they're dead. I'm alone, so alone. I have no one."

"You have me, darlin', I'm here."

"Oh, Austin." She hugged him tighter. "You won't leave me, will you? Please don't leave me, I'm so frightened."

"I'll never leave you, sweetheart. Never."

"I... I've tried so hard, but I can't make it. I'm a coward, Austin, a terrible coward. You've been through terrible tragedies and here I am crying to you. I'm not —"

"Listen to me, Suzette." His voice was soft and kind. "You are not a coward. You're one of the bravest women I've ever known, but you've been through too much. Let me make it up to you. Let me take care of you." He drew a snowy-white handkerchief from his breast pocket and gave it to her.

She took it, then slowly raised her head. "I did get you wet, Austin. I ruined your fine shirt." She began to dab at her eyes.

He smiled. "Forget the shirt, I have dozens. Listen to me. I never want you to spend another night alone. I'm going to stay here with you tonight. From this day forward, I'm taking care of you. I'm a wealthy man, Suzette, and nothing would make me happier than giving you anything you might want. You're to quit your job at the newspaper. You are tired and too thin. I want you to take care of yourself, get plenty of rest and eat good foods. Sweetheart, you like me, don't you?" He smoothed a damp lock of blond hair from her cheek.

"Austin, what a foolish question. You're my best friend. Of course I like you." Suzette blew her nose and tried to smile.

"Honey, I want to marry you. It's really the only way I can look after you properly. I can't have you living with me if we aren't man and wife; this town would never accept it. Marriage is the only answer. I hope you see that."

Her swollen eyes grew wide and she stared down at him. "Austin, you want to marry me?"

"If you'll have me. We'll be married right away. You can move into the hotel with me until I can get a home built for you. We'll travel. I'll take you to New York or New Orleans or anywhere you'd like to go. It might be a good idea to go to the seashore, let the sun put some color back into your cheeks. I'm going to pamper you, Suzette. You won't be sorry you married me, I assure you."

"Austin, I don't know. I never thought about the two of us..."

"Suzette, I know you think of me as an old man because I'm twenty years older than you, but, my darling, I'll indulge you as only a man my age can. You'll have a good life — I'll see to it. No demands will be made of you, none of any kind. Do you understand what I'm saying?"

She looked into the warm gray eyes. It wasn't hard to say yes to Austin. He was handsome, kind, knowing. He was exactly the man she needed and wanted. "Austin," she said softly and with her fingers touched the gray streaks at his temples, "I will be your wife if you want me. I'll do my best to make you happy, but I'm afraid you're getting the short end of the bargain. I have nothing to offer you."

Austin Brand smiled and pulled her back down onto his chest. Kissing her soft blond hair, he said happily, "You've everything to give me, and in time you will. There's no rush; we've the rest of our lives."

She snuggled closer and relaxed completely. His big arms were wrapped around her, shutting out the cold and the fear. Within minutes Suzette was sleeping peacefully, trusting completely the big, kind man who held her close against him and tenderly kissed her parted lips so lightly she didn't wake up.

Suzette awoke to find herself stretched out on the long couch in her clothes, a warm coverlet over her. Her slippers had been removed and were peeping out from under the couch. The smell of coffee permeated the air, and from the kitchen a deep baritone voice sang a mellow love song.

Suzette was confused for only a second. The memory of the preceding evening flooded over her and she knew that Austin was with her. Austin would be with her forever. He was going to marry her on this very day. She smiled and fingered the delicate gold chain at her throat. She touched the tiny heart with the sapphire in the center and thought of her mother and father. Silently she told them she was going to be all right, that their trusted friend was going to take her for his wife, to provide for and protect her until death.

She was smiling sleepily when Austin came into the room carrying a tray with coffee and orange juice. His jacket was off, his white shirtsleeves were rolled up over muscular forearms, his thick sun-tipped hair was slightly disheveled, and a faint stubble covered his cheeks. Other than that, he looked fresh and rested. And handsome.

"Do you always wake up smiling?" he teased and placed the tray on a square table in front of the settee. Suzette, suddenly embarrassed and afraid he would ask why she was smiling, sat up and tucked her feet under her.

"Not always," she admitted, then tried vainly to rake the tangles from her long, loose hair with her fingers.

Austin took a seat beside her after lifting the coverlet from her, folding it, and draping it across a chair. He made a big show of pouring coffee from a silver pot, lifting the heavy container high into the air away from the cups and miraculously hitting the tiny china cup with the scalding stream. When both cups were filled, he looked around at her for approval.

"Very impressive." She laughed.

"That's why I did it," he said. "I'm going to spend the rest of my life trying to impress you." With that he leaned close and kissed the tip of her pert nose. Immediately he turned back to pick up a cup of coffee and handed it to her.

"That isn't necessary, Austin. I've always been impressed with you." She took a sip of the hot coffee and felt it warm her throat.

"You're flattering me, but I like it. Now drink up, love. Then I'll cook you a nice hot breakfast. After we've eaten, you'll pack your things and we'll go into town. This afternoon we'll step over to the courthouse and become man and wife. Perhaps tomorrow we'll go on down to Fort Worth and hop on the private railroad car and take ourselves a honeymoon." He took a sip of coffee and set his cup aside, then leaned back beside her and waited for her to speak.

She looked at him and said bluntly, "Austin Brand, you have your own railroad car?"

Delighted with her reaction, he draped a long arm around her shoulders and pulled her close. Kissing the tangled blond hair, he said, "No darlin', *we* have our own railroad car. It belongs to you. Anytime you tire of life on the prairie, just say the word and it's there to sweep you across this big land. I told you, I'm going to pamper you, and I can hardly wait to begin. But, first things first." He released her and rose. "And first I'm going to feed you. I want to put some meat on your bones. Let's have breakfast." He took her coffee cup and set it aside.

"Breakfast it is." She smiled and reached for her shoes. Before she could locate them, he bent and swung her up into his arms.

"Austin!" she squealed as he pulled her to his powerful chest.

"My dear, you look so cute barefoot, I insist you leave your slippers behind. I shall carry you." With that he strode out of the parlor and into the kitchen. Suzette was well aware that he was treating her more like a child than a bride-to-be, but didn't care. If he took pleasure in coddling her, she found it to her satisfaction. It had been a long time since she'd been catered to and fussed over. It felt good and she intended to enjoy it. There would be plenty of time after the marriage for her to fit into the role of woman, wife and mother. For now it was fun to be a child again and have a great big adoring man spoil her.

It was nearing noon when Austin and Suzette climbed into his carriage for the ride into town. The weak sun that had risen earlier was nowhere in sight. Ominous black clouds filled the winter sky and sleet peppered their faces. Suzette pulled her wrap tighter and clung to Austin's arm. He carried her small valise. She'd spent a painfully long time packing. She knew she had to choose a dress suitable to be married in; since it was a cold day she finally decided on a high-necked blue velvet with white lace collar and cuffs. It wasn't new, nor was it the latest fashion, but it was one of the best she owned.

Not until she pulled out the middle drawer of her bureau to look for stockings did it occur to her that she would need to pack a nightgown. Her cheeks flushed when she pulled one of her long-sleeved cotton gowns from its resting place. Her fingers shook slightly when she held up the gown. It was the first time she had let herself think about the fact that she would be sleeping in a bed with Austin Brand.

Suddenly feeling faint, she went to sit for a minute on her bed, the gown clutched tightly in her hands. She bit her bottom lip and pictured herself wearing nothing but her nightie in his presence. The gown was modest — as all her gowns were — and not particularly pretty. She'd heard girls talk about the fancy, revealing gowns they planned to wear on their wedding night. Suzette frowned. This one would have to do; she had no money to buy a new one.

"Suzette," Austin called from the other room, "are you about finished? The weather's turning rapidly. I'd like us to get into town as soon as possible. I'm afraid it's going to get real bad and I don't want you catching cold. I don't have the covered carriage."

"Almost ready," she replied and flew from the bed to finish her packing. Folding the gown neatly, she tucked it into the flat valise and slammed the lid shut.

New she sat huddled by Austin inside the carriage, a lap robe over her knees. Her wool bonnet deflected the biting drops of sleet, but still she felt cold. Austin's arm came around her and she was drawn to his warmth. Her head rested against his shoulder, and she smiled up at him and knew she would never be cold again, no matter how bad the weather ahead.

Shortly after one o'clock, they pulled up in front of the Wichita Hotel. It was stuffy in the small crowded lobby and Suzette could feel every pair of eyes on her. She could hardly suppress a grin as she stood at Austin's elbow and listened to him tell the skinny, bespectacled room clerk that he would be needing the large room connecting with his for an indefinite period of time.

The slight man looked from Austin to Suzette, his expression leaving no doubt in her mind that he found the situation quite shocking and he would lose little time in telling everyone that a certain Miss Suzette Foxworth had checked into the hotel with Mr. Austin Brand and that she was going to be staying in the room that connected to his.

"Is something wrong?" Austin asked the man.

"I... uh, no, sir, Mr. Brand. Not a thing. No, sir," The man quickly busied himself with finding the key to the room next to Austin's.

"Good," Austin said evenly. "Miss Foxworth will be occupying the larger room where I've been staying. She'll be requiring two baths. Have one prepared for her within the hour. The other should be ready at approximately eight-thirty this evening. Can you manage that?" Austin took the key the man offered.

"Two baths on the same day, sir? And in the winter?" The clerk was incredulous.

Austin chuckled. "Please have someone lay a fire so she won't freeze. And I'll be needing a bath in the other room in an hour. Can you arrange it?"

The desk clerk nodded. "Yes, Mr. Brand. It will be done."

"Good." Austin took Suzette's elbow and escorted her

through the men loitering in the lobby, turning to nod and speak as he passed. When he and Suzette reached the stairway, they could hear the twitter behind them and knew exactly what the men were talking about. "Looks like I'll have to marry you, Miss Foxworth. If I don't, you'll be a scarlet woman in the eyes of the good people of Jack County." He patted the hand clinging to his arm.

"You know, it's rather exciting being the object of gossip. Let's forget about being married." She turned her smiling face up to his and she looked so fresh, so young, so very lovely that Austin Brand felt his heart race.

"Sorry, but you'll have to find other forms of excitement. I'm going to make you my wife before the day draws to a close." He was alarmed to realize that her teasing frightened him. He wanted her, he'd wanted her for longer than she would ever know. And he wanted her in a way that would shock and scare her if she ever knew, because although he cared a great deal for her, and she'd been like family for years and he wanted to take care of her, the truth was he had fantasized about holding her in his arms. So many times he'd tossed in his bed, wishing he had her there beside him. He'd wondered a lot how it would be to make love to her.

Now she was climbing the hotel stairs beside him. By nightfall she would be his wife. Would he hold her in his arms this very night? Would she give herself to him and let him love her? He'd told her that nothing would be required of her, and he had meant it. Was that why she agreed to become his wife? Would they spend a lifetime together without consummating the marriage vows? Would he be required to have her constantly near him, yet never be allowed to possess her?

"Austin." Her sweet voice shook him from his reveries. "Is something wrong? You're frowning." They were in the upstairs hall.

"I'm sorry, I was just deep in thought. I have many things to do. I want to get you a ring, then see about having the judge perform the ceremony." They were at the door of his room and he unlocked it and handed her inside. "You're to make yourself at home here. I'll have my clothes moved into the other room." He drew the heavy curtains while she stood looking around the spacious room.

"Austin, I don't need a ring." She let him help her out of her heavy wrap. He shook out the wool coat and hung it up on the tree beside the door.

Turning back to her, he smiled and asked, "Don't you want a ring?"

"Yes, I do," she admitted happily.

"Then you shall have one. A solid gold one for today. A diamond to go with it when we get to a big city where we can shop." He walked to her and took her hand in both of his. "I'll leave you now, dear. I want you to rest this afternoon. I'll arrange the ceremony and wire our people in Fort Worth that we'll be traveling soon." Then he lifted her hand up to his mouth, turned it over, and kissed the soft palm, letting his lips slide up to the inside of her delicate wrist.

Austin Brand softly kissed the faintly throbbing pulse there. It speeded not at all. His did. His heart hammered in his broad chest. He lifted his head and smiled down at her. And he promised himself he'd eventually make her pulse race just as his was doing.

He could hardly wait.

As the weather continued to worsen that cold winter afternoon, Suzette sat before the fire in her hot tub and smiled at the sound of the sleet tapping the tall windows. She felt giddy and almost naughty. For the first time in ages, she was not busy at some task. It was the middle of the day and she was taking a leisurely bath that someone else had drawn for her. After a good soaking, she would be allowed to stretch out on a soft bed and rest for the remainder of the afternoon. Suzette sank farther down into the soapy water. She hummed to herself and looked forward to the years ahead — the years she would spend as Mrs. Austin Brand.

It was growing dark outside when Austin and Suzette stood

in front of the judge at precisely five P.M. His chambers were drafty and Suzette shivered; her feet were cold, her nose red, and she was quite certain she was not a beautiful bride.

Austin Brand put an arm around her and held her close. He could feel the tremors in the slender body pressed to his. He looked at her and saw her perfect white teeth chatter slightly. Her nose was pink. His chest constricted painfully; never in his life had he seen a woman more beautiful and appealing.

While he smiled down at her the old judge said brusquely, "Suzette Foxworth, will you take this man to be your lawful wedded husband?"

She looked up at Austin and said softly, "Yes, I will."

"Then I now pronounce you man and wife. You may kiss the bride." The judge shook Austin's hand, nodded to Suzette, and left the room.

Austin kissed her cold cheek and said, "Let's get back to the hotel where it's warm. I know you're freezing."

In the small dining room of the Wichita Hotel, the newly married couple sat at a table by the wall. Though Austin ordered the finest food the hotel had to offer, his new wife ate little. Suzette felt the food expanded the longer she chewed, and though she tried bravely to eat the meal before her, swallowing was difficult. She'd hardly had anything to eat all day, but for some reason her appetite was missing.

Austin, who had devoured his large portion of rare roast beef, saw Suzette picking at her food and knew the reason. He was well aware the innocent girl across from him was uneasy about the coming night. To his knowledge, she'd never even spent time with a young man since Luke Barnes's death. Suzette was undoubtedly ignorant of a man.

"Sweetheart," he said warmly, "If you aren't hungry, perhaps you'd like to go on up."

"I... I... yes, Austin, I don't think I can eat any more." She said this apologetically as she placed her fork and knife on her untouched plate.

"Doesn't matter," he assured her and dropped his napkin on the table. He rose and helped her to her feet. They made their way through the crowded room and Suzette's apprehension increased when she saw the looks of amusement following her. Men whispered behind their hands and she was aware that by now all of Jacksboro knew that she and Austin had been married today; she was sure they were making crude jokes. Her face flushing, she nevertheless raised her determined chin, lifted her skirts, and preceded her big, burly husband from the room.

Upstairs, Austin helped her out of her wrap and urged, "Warm yourself by the fire, Suzette. I'll go back down and have my cigar and brandy while you take your bath." Suzette noticed the big tub pulled up close to the fire's warmth. Steam rose from the hot water. She turned and looked at Austin. Smiling, he explained, "I had the staff prepare your tub while we dined. I wanted to have it waiting for you."

"Thank you, Austin," she said stiffly and wondered if he intended to remain while she disrobed.

"You're very welcome, sweetheart." He walked to the door. Pausing there, he asked, "Can you manage alone?"

"Yes!" She almost shouted the word. "I... yes, Austin, I need no help."

"Good girl. Then I'll go down. I'll see you in approximately half an hour. Is that satisfactory?"

"Half an hour will be fine," she assured him with a confidence she didn't feel. As soon as he was gone, the smile she had been wearing disappeared. She closed her eyes and was dizzy. When she opened them, she resolutely began to undress. She slipped into the hot water and wondered why all the pleasure had gone out of bathing. This afternoon it had been so delightful; now she joylessly cleansed herself, rushing to be finished with it so that she might cover her nakedness with her modest nightgown.

Precisely one-half hour had passed when Suzette, standing beside the bed, her white nightgown buttoned up to her chin, her long blond hair fanned out loosely over her shoulders, her feet bare, heard a sure knock on the door connecting the two rooms. She took a deep breath and tried to smile. "Come in,

Austin," she said in a voice that sounded strange even to herself.

He entered the dimly lit room, leaving the door ajar. He smiled easily and started toward her. His fine coat had been discarded and his clean white shirt was open to his waist. Suzette looked at him and suddenly he appeared gigantic. Terror filled her as he loomed nearer, his shoulders wide, his broad chest covered with thick curly hair. She felt small and defenseless. He was bearing down on her and she felt panicky, trapped; he was so huge; he was enormous, awesome. Her heart thumped against her ribs and the soft material of her gown rose and fell. She'd never felt so intimidated and uneasy. She longed to scream at him not to come one step closer. Fleetingly, she wondered why on earth she had agreed to marry this man who was old enough to be her father. What lunacy had possessed her to become his lawful wife and be subjected to the fearful things he would surely do to her.

"Suzette." His voice didn't fit his alarming stature. It was soft and soothing. "Why don't you get into the bed? I'm afraid you'll catch a cold." He turned back the covers and put out a hand to her. Biting her bottom lip, she automatically took his hand. He helped her into the middle of the soft bed and she cringed, knowing that within seconds he would be in the bed with her.

He was fluffing up the fat pillows behind her back and then he pulled the bedcovers up over her, tucking them in around her waist. "How's that, dear?" he asked, making no move to undress or get in bed.

Breathing just a little easier, she nodded and managed to say, "It's fine, Austin. Thank you."

Nervously, she watched as he turned and walked to the fireplace. He poked at the smoldering logs and added two new ones to build the fire up. The dry wood caught and snapped, shooting sparks up the brick chimney. He came back to her, pulling up a chair close to the bed. Smiling, he folded his large frame down into it and, resting his elbows on his bent knees, he leaned close and began to talk, telling her of the plans he'd made for them.

He spoke quietly, gently, and Suzette listened fascinated as he told her of the trip they would take, the sights he would show her, the good life they would have. She began to relax and soon she was clinging to his big hand, her eyes roaming his handsome face and his broad chest. Close up, he looked less frightening, and Suzette decided it might not be so terrible to sleep in the bed with him.

Austin continued to talk. Suzette, who found herself relaxing completely, loved the sound of his deep, warm voice. When at last he fell silent and released her hand, she looked up at him to protest. He merely smiled and walked to the window, then closed the heavy drapes and came back to the bed. He stood above her, gazing at her. When he finally bent over her, he carefully placed her hands under the covers and pulled the sheet up to her chin. She snuggled deeper into the bed's softness, hardly able to keep her eyes open.

Austin whispered softly, "Sleep now, sweetheart. I'll be in the next room if you should need me. I'll leave the door open." He kissed her cheek. "Thank you for becoming my wife, Suzette. You've made me happier than you will ever know." His knuckles moved lightly over her soft cheek.

"Austin," she whispered, her eyelids drooping, "I'm happy, too."

"I'm glad, darlin'," he murmured and kissed her tenderly on the lips.

But the new Mrs. Brand was fast asleep.

When the newly married couple arrived in Fort Worth, some forty-eight hours later, it was mid-morning. Exhausted and stiff from the arduous sixty-mile journey, Suzette felt as though her back would break. Her understanding bridegroom was solicitous and eager to get her aboard the railroad car, where she could rest.

Tired as she was, her eyes grew big when she saw the sleek, green hotel-on-wheels parked on the side spur at the train terminal. On the car's shiny side, the word ALPHA was painted in gold lettering near the door. Suzette laid a gloved hand on the lettering and turned to question her husband about the name.

"I'll tell you about the name and everything else later, dear. Right now, I insist you sleep." He handed her up the steps into the impressive car, where they were met by a tall, middle-aged woman. She wore a black uniform trimmed in snowy organza. Her gray hair was pulled tightly into a knot on top of her head, but the primness was relieved by her friendly, open face and engaging smile. "Suzette, darlin', this is Madge." Austin nodded over Suzette's head to the older woman. "Madge is here to help you. She'll be traveling in the car ahead of us."

"Hello, Madge." Suzette offered her hand and the other woman clasped it.

"Mrs. Brand." She smiled. "I'm so happy to meet you. I hope you know you've just married the finest man in all Texas. Why, I've known Austin Brand since he wore —"

"Now, now, Madge," Austin cut in. "Mrs. Brand is exhausted. I want you to get her into bed." He took Suzette's shoulders and gently turned her to face him. "Suzette, I've got some business to attend to. You're to get into that bed immediately. I'll see you when you wake."

"But, Austin, I want to look around, I haven't —"

"Later," he said firmly and kissed her temple. "She's all yours, Madge."

Much too tired to argue with either of them, Suzette let Madge undress her as soon as Austin left. She looked around sleepily at the room. Small but well arranged, the room had satinwood panelling and rosewood furniture. As she crawled gratefully into the bed, Suzette fleetingly wondered how she and her big husband could both fit in it. It was her last thought before sleep overtook her.

When Suzette opened her eyes, she saw Madge moving quietly about the room. She pushed herself up on one elbow drowsily, then yawned and asked hoarsely, "Madge, what time is it?"

Madge looked up from the large box she was opening and said cheerfully, "Mrs. Brand, it's almost eight. Are you feeling better?"

"Eight at night?" Suzette bounded from the bed and rushed to the window. She jerked back the drapes and peered out the ice-crusted windows. It was pitch-black, though a few lights twinkled from afar. For the first time it occurred to Suzette that the room was in motion. She whirled. "Are we leaving Fort Worth now, Madge?"

"No, dear," the woman replied, "we left Fort Worth this morning. Now, come, your husband is waiting. I'll help you with your bath."

Suzette looked around, but saw no tub. "Come," the woman beckoned, and Suzette followed her into an adjoining room where a huge, square bathtub of fine Carrara marble was filled with steaming soapy water. More hot water ran from a gold faucet. Suzette squealed like a happy child and lifted her nightgown over her head. Immersing herself up to her chin, she studied the bottles of sweet scented oils arranged on a gold shelf above the faucets, then extended a soapy arm to put in a dash of this, a drop of that, until the water smelled of glorious spring, while outside her private fairyland the cold prairie winds howled with a vengeance and the temperature dropped with each passing minute.

When Suzette stepped dripping from the marble tub, Madge wrapped her shimmering body in a big white towel. She followed her back into the bedroom, asking, "Madge, where did you hang my dress?" And then she gasped. A beautiful eggshell satin gown and robe and dainty satin slippers, the most feminine ones she'd ever seen, lay before her on the bed. "Oh, Madge," she said in wonderment, fingering the rich fabric, "wherever did these come from?"

"Mr. Brand bought them for you today. He said that he would like you to join him for dinner."

"Dinner? How? I can't go out in a satin nightgown!" she exclaimed.

"No, Mrs. Brand." Madge laughed merrily. "You will dine here in your quarters. Now, let's get you ready. Austin's waiting!"

Suzette loved the feel of the lush satin against her clean, naked skin, but she blushed when she saw that the lovely gown's bodice was cut very low and composed entirely of a very sheer white lace. It fit snugly across her full breasts, exposing them as though she were uncovered, and ended in a deep V below her waist. The long, soft skirt clung seductively to her hips and thighs and fell in soft folds at her feet. Suzette looked at her reflection in the French mirror and was embarrassed. The older woman seemed to sense this and held out the satin robe for her. It had but one tiny button at its high-banded neck. Suzette hastily pushed the satin button through the lace loop and looked at herself again.

She felt better. Long, full sleeves, trimmed in white lace, reached to her knuckles. She was covered from throat to feet in the thick, luxuriant satin. She smiled and stepped into the slippers while Madge nodded her gray head in approval.

"Your husband has excellent taste."

"Yes, he does." Suzette ran her hands over the fabric. "It really is lovely, isn't it?"

"I was referring to you, Mrs. Brand. Now, come, you can't keep Mr. Brand waiting any longer."

"Well, I'm ready. Tell him to come in, please."

Madge smiled and said, "No dear. He is waiting for you. Come."

Suzette followed Madge, who indicated a closed door, then whispered, "He's inside. I'll wish you good-night now, dear. When you need me in the morning, ring the bell." Madge disappeared, and Suzette turned back to the door. She knocked lightly, and Austin's deep voice invited her to come in.

Suzette pulled the door open and stepped inside, then

stared in amazement. The compartment was at least twice as long as her room and twice as grand. It had the same satinwood paneling and ornate carved ceilings, and it was filled with fine, heavy furniture. Sofas upholstered in brocade faced each other across a square marble table. Thick, rich carpet — a veritable blur of jewel tones — covered the floor. The tall ornate French mirrors in the sitting area reflected the big bed facing them. The bed could only have been designed for the huge man who owned it. Its soft expanse was covered with satin bedclothes the exact color of Suzette's ensemble. Small marble tables flanked each side and held gold illumination lamps, which cast a soft, pale glow. The room fairly shimmered, and Suzette was entranced.

"Do you approve, darlin'?" Austin's deep voice drew her attention back to him. She whirled to see him standing, massive and magnificent, in a velvet robe of deep burgundy, its lapels a shiny satin of the same hue. At his throat, a burgundy foulard hid the virile chest. His dark blond hair was trimmed and brushed, his face smoothly shaved. He was grand, she thought happily, and very, very handsome.

He stood behind a square table covered with a cloth of white linen that reached the floor. A silver candelabra stood majestically at one corner. At its center, a silver bowl held freshly cut white orchids. A bottle of champagne stood chilling in a silver bucket filled with crushed ice. Long-stemmed glasses of sparkling crystal sat beside fine porcelain plates rimmed in gold.

Suzette Foxworth Brand had never seen anything so splendid in all her life. Her husband took her hand and offered her a chair across from him. Suzette still hadn't convinced herself she wasn't dreaming. Here she was, seated at a table with her handsome new husband, eating lobster and quaffing champagne. She giggled with unabashed joy.

The man looking at her laughed, too. Austin, accustomed to riches and grandeur, had lived a life of comfort and grace for more than twenty years. It had been pleasant, to be sure, but never had it been as rewarding as it was at this moment.

The look of wonder and happiness on the beautiful face across the table made Austin as light-headed as the wine was making Suzette. She was everything he'd ever envisioned in a woman. She was truly beautiful. She was bright, she was spirited, and she was impressionable, though intelligent. To have her here with him in this fairyland, her lovely young body draped in the seductive nightclothes he'd picked for her, to hear her laughter as she drank the champagne he'd poured for her, to know that before the winter night was over he would carry her to that big bed and make love to her — this was to him the end of the rainbow.

When the sumptuous meal was finished, Austin pulled a gold cord that hung near the bed and a white-jacketed Oriental servant suddenly appeared. His eyes averted discreetly, he quickly rolled the dinner table out of the room, though he left the candelabra, orchids, and champagne behind. Then Austin extinguished the lamps on each side of the bed, leaving only the candles to light to room.

He walked slowly to where Suzette stood watching him. He looked at her so intently as he neared her that she felt the smooth wine catch in her throat. She had to swallow a second time. Austin smiled and moved closer. She coughed nervously when he took the glass from her shaking hand and set it aside.

His hand went slowly to her hair. He touched it gently, holding a long strand, studying it with interest. He lifted it to his mouth and kissed it, inhaling its fresh fragrance. "Suzette, you're the most beautiful woman I've ever seen," he said hoarsely.

She gave no reply. Her heart was pounding now and she could hear it drumming loudly in her ears. She stood completely still, looking at the handsome head bent over her hair, grateful she didn't have to meet his gaze. Her arms hung at her sides, but her fingers worked nervously at the satin of her robe.

Slowly Austin raised his head and released the strand of golden hair. His fingers moved to the tiny button at her throat.

He unfastened it and pulled the robe slowly over her shoulders, letting it slide to the floor. Wearing only the gown with its revealing lace bodice, Suzette watched as fire leaped into his gray eyes, while her rapid breathing made her breasts swell and strain against the tight lace.

"Darlin'," he murmured as his mouth covered her trembling lips and he pulled her up into his arms. Her arms still hung limply at her sides, the palms of her hands moist. He kissed her gently, expertly, pushing her head back as he pulled her closer to him. His warm, sensual mouth moved from her lips to her throat. He kissed her there just as tenderly, and Suzette's apprehension began to melt away. Her arms came around his neck and she molded herself to him. She could feel his muscular solidity against her as his strong arms lifted her into his embrace and he cradled her head in his hand.

She whimpered softly as his lips slid down, down, until finally they were pressing against the soft lace covering her heart. Austin kept kissing her there until Suzette felt she could not breathe. At last he raised his head and his lips covered hers once again. She was responding to the gentle kiss when she felt herself being lifted from the floor. She was no longer afraid. She closed her eyes and clung to his neck and soon the softness underneath her told her she was on the big bed, Austin's full weight beside her. She opened her eyes and looked at the handsome face so close to her own.

"Let me love you, Suzette," he murmured, his gray eyes smoldering. His mouth again took hers and she was glad that the faint flickering of the candles was the only light in the room, the crimson of her flushed face mercifully hidden in their soft glow.

His mouth, hot and moist, moved very softly on hers. He kissed her slowly, persuasively. It felt very good and Suzette relaxed and let his mouth tease and tempt her while she slipped deeper and deeper into the vortex of consuming desire.

Never did she bother to question whether it was Austin's expert kisses, or the effects of the champagne, or the provocative touch of all that satin that made her body feel so hot, so sensitive. She only knew she'd been foolish ever to have been frightened of this big, handsome man. He was tender and gentle and she loved his warm lips moving on hers, his hands sweeping over her satin-covered body, tenderly touching and caressing.

So lost was she in her newly awakened sensuality, and so experienced and gentle was her handsome husband, that Suzette hardly knew when the nightgown somehow slipped away from her body. She hardly realized that Austin's robe had disappeared. She only knew that his mouth was still pressing hers and that his hands, moving slowly over her body, felt more wonderful now that both were naked. And when his heated body nestled against hers, a flame ignited deep within her.

As her excitement grew, inhibitions tumbled and Suzette gloried in the feel of his crinkly hair against her naked breasts as Austin crushed her to his broad, heaving chest. Her hands explored his shoulders and back, playing over the smooth skin as they moved up into his hair. When his lips left hers and went to her neck, Suzette sighed and pressed her head back against the pillow. Her tiny gold locket rested in the hollow of her throat, where Austin kissed it, and then with his teeth he moved the locket out of his way.

"My beautiful wife," he murmured as his hot mouth pressed fiery kisses into the sensitive hollow of her throat.

Suzette had never had her throat kissed, and she marveled at how wonderful it felt. She didn't hesitate to let him know it. "Austin," she breathed and clutched his back, "that feels good to me. So good."

"Umm," he murmured and gently probed with his tongue. "I want to make you feel good, my love." His mouth continued to awaken her, sliding around to the side of her neck to the gentle pulse. He touched it with his tongue and lifted his head to look at her.

Her blue eyes held a look he'd thought he wouldn't see there for months, perhaps years — a look of unmasked hunger. Seeing it made his blood pound, and his passion soared.

"Suzette, my sweet," he breathed, sliding a big hand into her hair. His mouth came down hard on hers, open and questing. He moaned when her sweet tongue touched his eagerly. His kiss inflamed her, and his caressing hands fanned the fire. By the time his hand sought the warmth between her silky thighs, Suzette was whispering her husband's name in wild abandon and her soft, pliant body was craving the glorious release his hard, male body promised.

"Suzette, my Suzette." He continued to whisper her name as every sensation became acutely heightened for her. She heard distinctly the ding, ding, ding of the train's bell as they passed through a station; the clickety-clack of the wheels on the track dueled with the rhythm of her pounding heart. Everything in the room took on a vivid clarity in the soft candlelight. On Austin's face, just above her own, she could see the tiny pores of his smooth bronzed skin and the dark pupils and pinpricks of light in his gray eyes. Her flesh was extraordinarily sensitive to the stroking hand whose fingertips spread incredible heat wherever they touched her. Her husband's kisses tasted sweet, while his shoulders and throat were mildly salty to her tongue and mouth. When she ran her hands over his broad shoulders and smooth back, she could feel every muscle, every bone, the hot skin.

"Austin," she breathed into his open mouth, "please... please."

The pain was brief and bearable, her soft sobs muffled by his bare shoulder, as he thrust into her. Austin lay completely still within her until he felt her slender, sweet body begin to relax beneath him. Only then did he begin the slow, sensual movements of loving. And as he moved he quietly spoke to her of love, confessing that he'd wanted her for years, that he loved her as he'd never loved a woman, that to hold her this way in his arms was heaven. He punctuated each sentence with tender kisses to her open lips, her flushed cheeks, her shell-like ears, and her swelling breasts.

Suzette was wrapped in a warm, wonderful dream. A beautiful dream. New things were happening to her and she was torn between the wish to be held and loved by Austin all night long and the aching need to have this throbbing cease. She wanted both, and her sweet confusion made her cling to her husband and plead, "Austin, Austin, I... I..."

"Yes, my love," he whispered and changed the pace of his lovemaking. He was moving more rhythmically now and she clung to him as the first involuntary spasms of her climax claimed her. Her blue eyes widened as the ecstasy became so intense she thought she would surely be torn apart by the violence rippling through her. She was aware of Austin's face just above her own. Then his mouth dipped to hers as something shook her with alarming intensity. She cried out and strained to hold her husband to her until the rapture subsided.

He lifted his head to gaze down at her. He looked pleased, and she wondered if it was because he'd felt the same explosions inside that had rocked her. She decided that he had, because his powerful chest was heaving, perspiration dotted his hairline, and his smoothly shaven face was flushed. Like her, he was breathing heavily, and he was calling her name.

"Suzette, my love, my beautiful wife. Suzette, Suzette," he groaned and scattered kisses over her face and bare shoulders.

"Austin?" she whispered, her eyes still wide.

"Yes, darlin'?" His mouth was near her ear. "What, my love?"

"Austin, I want to tell you something."

He lifted his head to look at her. "Darlin', you can tell me anything, anything at all."

She smiled and let her fingers roam over his strong jawline. "I just wanted to say that I loved the way you made me feel, and I wonder if you felt the same way. I mean, did you feel like you might just actually die if you didn't stop, and yet it was much too good to do so?"

Austin Brand moved to her side and rolled over onto his back, chuckling as he pulled her into his embrace. His laughter rumbled deep in his chest and his spent body shook with it. He laughed until his stomach hurt and tears rolled down his cheeks. Calming a little, he took her sweet, bewildered face between his palms and said, "Darlin', that is exactly the way I felt. I couldn't have expressed it any better." He pulled her mouth to his and kissed her lips. "My God, life with you is going to be paradise. You are something, Mrs. Brand. You are beautiful, intelligent, sweet, sensual, and above all, honest." He kissed her again.

Already completely at ease with her new husband, Suzette turned on her stomach and looked into his smiling face. She spread a hand on his chest and curled the thick, blond hair around her fingers.

"Austin, do you really think I'm all those things?"

"Indeed I do." He beamed and raised a hand to her hair.

"Austin."

"Hmm?"

"Where do you suppose we are right now?"

"Darlin', we're somewhere in western Louisiana."

"Oh, shoot!" she said, tickling his chest.

"What?" His smile faded slightly. "What's wrong, Suzette?"

Giggling, she said, "Nothing, really. It's just... well, Austin, I wanted to make love to you in Texas the first time."

Laughter again shook Austin Brand. "Honey," he drawled contentedly, "you did make love to me in Texas. It just extended into Louisiana." She grinned and kissed him. "Tell you something else." He sighed happily. "You're going to be making love to me in Mississippi, Alabama, Georgia, the Carolinas, Virginia, and —"

"Stop, stop!" She laughed and covered his mouth with her hand. "Before I make love to you in all those states, there's something else I want."

"Name it, sweetheart."

She buried her face on his chest and mumbled, "I'm hungry." She raised her head. "How long is it till breakfast, Austin? I'm starving!"

Austin took one of her small hands and placed it on the gold tasseled pull by the bed. "You see this, darlin'?"

"Uh-huh."

"You've only to pull it. You can have something to eat anytime you've an appetite."

"Even in the middle of the night, Austin?" Her fingers played with the tassels.

"Yes, sweetheart." He smiled and ran a hand over her soft, bare bottom. "I told you, I intend to put some meat on your bones. Now pull on that cord, Mrs. Brand. Then kiss me and tell me you like being married."

Suzette did as she was told, then leaned over her husband's face and kissed him wildly. "I love being married to you, Austin Brand. May I please have ham and eggs and buckwheat cakes?"

Wrapping her in his big arms, Austin Brand laughed as he nodded his head. Burying his face in her warm, sweet neck, he murmured huskily, "Yes, yes... oh, God, yes!"

14

The remainder of the trip to New York passed rapidly for the honeymooners in the private railroad car known as Alpha. The ardent bridegroom, feeling much younger that his forty-two years, revelled in the role of lover to his luscious twenty-two-year-old bride. Entranced by Suzette's beauty, Austin never tired of holding her in his arms while the train sped across the frozen countryside.

Suzette, though not in love with Austin, found him extremely appealing and welcomed his lovemaking eagerly. Never in her life had she felt so adored. She knew she was fortunate that such a kind, rich, and handsome man had wanted her for his wife when she was positive he could have had his pick of the society ladies of Dallas and Fort Worth, and perhaps even New York City. It was still a mystery to her that Austin had chosen her over women who were much better educated, more sophisticated, and nearer his age.

On that first romantic night aboard the train, Suzette fell asleep in her husband's arms, full from the huge breakfast they shared at three in the morning. Austin remained awake long after she curled up against him. He was tired, but he was much too happy for sleep. Suzette lay with her arm across his chest, her face pressed into his neck and shoulder. Her soft, naked body touched his, its warmth and silkiness a constant sensual delight to him. He'd had many women in his life. Beautiful women. Experienced women. Women so in love with him they were anxious to please. But never before had he made love to a woman and found the ecstasy his innocent young bride had given him.

He trembled as he lay beside her in the darkness. He loved her too much and it frightened him. He worshipped her already and this was only their first night together. What if he should lose her the way he lost Beth and Jenny? Austin's big arm automatically tightened around the slender body next to him. His happiness was tinged with fear — and guilt. He knew that, should he lose Suzette, it would hurt him much more than losing Beth had. It would hurt him more than losing his darling little Jenny. It would kill him.

Kissing the silky blond hair that fell about her bare shoulders, Austin vowed silently never to let her out of his sight. He would be at her side always. No one would take this precious creature from him as long as he had breath in his body. Never would he allow her to be alone and vulnerable. No man would ever harm one hair on her golden head. Suzette Foxworth Brand was his and his alone. No one had ever touched her but him, and any man who dared try to touch her would pay with his life!

Suzette moaned faintly in her sleep and Austin whispered, "Darlin', I'm sorry," and eased the tight grip he had on her.

She never opened her eyes, but turned over and backed up against him. Smiling, Austin kissed her shoulder and turned with her so as to curl around her. Soon the hypnotic lull of the wheels on the track bed pulled him into a deep slumber.

When Suzette awoke the next day, Austin was not in the bed. Brushing her hair from her eyes, she pushed herself onto an elbow, holding the sheet with one hand to cover herself. As if by magic, Madge appeared.

"Your bath is ready, Mrs. Brand." The woman smiled as she held out a large white towel.

Suzette reached for the towel. "Where is my husband?"

"Right now he's in the car ahead where the chef is preparing your meal. When your bath is finished, breakfast will be waiting, and so will Austin."

Suzette blushed as thoughts of the preceding night came back to her. She almost dreaded seeing Austin in the stark light of day. Her stomach aflutter, she drew the towel about her body and rose from the bed.

Inside the bathing chamber, she sighed when she stepped into the huge marble tub of hot sudsy water. She laid her head back against the tub's rim and let the soothing water work its magic. When her soak was finished, Madge held out a robe. It was not the eggshell satin from last night but a rich, luxuriant midnight-blue velvet with long tight sleeves and an empire waistline. The square neckline was daringly low; it would barely conceal the swell of her bosom!

Suzette looked about for a gown or underclothes and saw none. She put on the robe and pulled the ribbon sash tight under her breasts. She slipped her bare feet into the blue velvet slippers Madge indicated and patiently let her brush the tangles from her long hair.

"There," Madge said, satisfied. "You look very pretty this morning."

"Thank you, Madge." Suzette pulled at the neckline of her robe and stood stiffly, waiting for the woman to leave.

"I'll be going now, dear. Mr. Brand is back in your stateroom."

Suzette nodded and went to join him. When she stepped inside the door, Austin rose from the table and smiled at her. "Darlin'," he said softly, his eyes feasting on her beauty, "you look lovely."

Wishing the neckline of her velvet robe covered more and that she were not completely naked underneath the heavy robe, she started toward her husband shyly. From the corner of her eye, she noted that the big bed had been remade. The eggshell satin sheets had disappeared, as had the satin nightgown. Sky-blue sheets of soft silk now stretched tightly across the expanse of the huge bed; a heavy coverlet of blue velvet was folded at the foot.

"Good morning, Austin." She let her eyes slide over him. He wore tight gray cashmere trousers and a white shirt open down his chest. He stood with his arms out to her.

"My wife," he breathed against her temple as he pulled her up into his embrace. Cradling her head in his big hand, he bent and tenderly kissed her lips. "How do you feel, sweetheart?" He nuzzled her mouth. "Are you... uncomfortable?"

"I'm wonderful," she assured him saucily, "except I'm hungry."

Austin laughed. "I personally went to the galley to oversee the preparation of your breakfast. Shall we?" He extended a long arm to the table behind them.

Suzette's place setting was across from his. As soon as his hands dropped from her, she started to step around the table. "No," he said, and pulled her back. "Please, sweetheart, that's too far away from me." With that he sat down and pulled her onto his lap. "Indulge me for a bit, Suzette. I like to hold you close; it's still such a new delight. I can't bear to have you away from me."

His candor was appealing. She giggled and kissed his bronzed jaw. "Austin, you may hold me whenever you like, but don't you think it will be difficult to eat with me on your lap?"

"I only want coffee. The sight of you made me lose my appetite for food." His eyes gleamed devilishly. "But I shall be delighted to feed you! We'll begin with fresh orange juice mixed with champagne." He picked up a stemmed crystal glass and held it to her lips. Suzette took a small sip, swished it around in her mouth, and sighed.

"This is good, Austin. I insist you have a drink."

He took a drink to please her, then set the glass aside. He buttered a blueberry muffin and held it up to her. Suzette laughed and let her husband feed her poached eggs, crisp, thick-sliced bacon, honey, assorted pastries, and fresh fruits. While he lifted the silver fork back and forth to her waiting mouth, Suzette playfully entwined her fingers in his thick hair and sprinkled kisses over his smoothly shaven face. Her arm around his neck, her hand in his hair, she unwittingly offered her husband a tempting view of her breasts. As she moved the rich material fell away to give him glimpses of the soft rounded mounds of creamy flesh, their pale pink crests clearly visible.

With great patience Austin fed his hungry wife, all the while fighting the blinding desire to toss the fork to the table and bury his face between her soft breasts and kiss them until she sighed his name in ecstasy. He longed to yank the long robe up over her legs and thighs, to push it high up around her waist so that her bare buttocks were deliciously pressed against his aroused body, straining now against the tightness of his trousers. God, how sweet it would be to unbutton his pants hastily and immerse himself in her sweet warmth while she sat on his lap. To feel that velvety bottom squirming against his thighs while she offered her tempting breasts up to him for his further enjoyment!

Austin bit his lip and tried to compose himself. He knew that he must be very careful with his new wife. He loved her as much as he lusted after her, and he would rather suffer than do anything that might shock or disgust her. With super-human effort, he continued to feed her until finally she pushed the fork away, rubbed her full stomach through the velvet robe, and sighed contentedly. "No more, Austin. I'm so full I may pop." With that she bounded from her husband's lap and rushed to the window, pulling open the drapes. "Austin, come look, it's snowing! Isn't it beautiful!" The frozen countryside rolled gently by. Huge snowflakes, coming from the northwest, hit the warmth of the train window, melted, and slowly trickled down the shiny panes. Her eyes wide, a dazzling smile on her face, Suzette turned to look at her husband. He remained where she had left him. "Austin," she pleaded, holding out a hand to him, "come look, please. It's so lovely."

His face grew pink and he gave her a strained look that puzzled her. Her eyes drifted from his face down over his chest and finally to his lap. Her hand flew to her mouth. "Austin!"

"I'm sorry, darlin'," he said sheepishly. "I suppose I should have let you sit across from me."

Suzette, suddenly wise beyond her years and awakened by his tender loving, smiled and walked slowly to his chair. She fell to her knees beside him and brazenly put a hand on his thigh. "Austin," she whispered in a soft, honeyed voice, "I'm flattered you find me so attractive. Come with me." She rose, touched his cheek affectionately, and turned away from him. She strolled to the bed, untied her robe, and let it slide seductively to the floor. Austin saw only her bare backside as she got into the bed and pulled the blue sheet up around her.

With a shaking hand, he pulled the drapes together, shutting out the falling snow and its brilliant light. He came to the bed and hurriedly undressed in the semidarkness while she watched him, a sensual smile on her face, her eyes now glazed with desire. In seconds he was holding his naked wife in his arms while the blood in his temples pounded and his heated mouth took hers in a kiss of hunger and possession. When his open lips moved to nibble on her neck, Suzette's hands slid up into his thick hair. She closed her eyes as he moved his handsome head down over the swell of her breasts.

They opened for an instant when his mouth tenderly closed over an erect nipple. When finally he shifted, making a place for himself between her silky thighs, Suzette clung to him while she murmured sweetly against his lips, "Austin, my husband."

The entire trip to the big city was one long idyll as the newly married couple did little but eat, sleep, drink champagne, soak in the marble tub, make love, and occasionally play a game of cards or read a book. Their days and nights became mixed and they would sleep throughout the day as the train made its slow steady progress northward across the vast country. At sundown they'd awaken, have a huge meal, take a leisurely bath, and spend the long winter night talking and making love.

On the final night of their long journey, Suzette lay propped on her husband's chest. Austin was telling Suzette that when they arrived in New York he would take her to the dressmaker first of all. She would need many new clothes, as he intended to show her the city and show the city her. Her arms folded over his broad chest, chin resting in her hands, she lay on her stomach and looked at him as he spoke. The large Seth Thomas chimed four A.M. but neither was sleepy. She loved to listen to her knowledgeable husband talk; he seemed to know so much about everything. She was impressed that he'd often visited the magic city and promised her that he knew many people, had lots of friends there.

"Austin" — she raised her head and put an elbow on his chest — "what shall I wear when we arrive at the train station? Will Madge press the dress I got married in? That's really all that I have. I've worn nothing on this trip but gowns and robes. Do you realize I haven't dressed since we left Forth Worth?"

"My love, that's the way I planned it. If I could have my way, you wouldn't even have robes to wear. I'd have had you nude from Fort Worth to New York if I could have managed."

He smiled and brought a hand from under his head to caress her shoulder.

"Austin, I think you've managed pretty well." She giggled and kissed his furry chest. "Answer my question. Will I wear the dress I was married in when we arrive?"

"Darlin', it so happens I purchased a couple for you before we left Fort Worth. One is a brown wool that should be nice and warm and quite appropriate."

"You bought me dresses?" She smiled and sat up. "Where are they, Austin? I want to try them on."

Pulling her back down to him, he said, "Sweetheart, it's the middle of the night. I just got you undressed, and I intend to keep you that way until morning." He lifted his head from the pillow and kissed her throat.

"But, Austin," she protested.

"But, Suzette," he teased and gently pushed her over onto her back. He leaned over her, pinning an arm over her head with his big hand. He kissed her lips softly, over and over, and between each kiss he tried to convince her that this was not the time for a fashion show. "Darlin'," he murmured, "it's so nice and warm here in our bed. Stay here with me, please." He traced her upper lip with his tongue. "Let's play awhile, my love. Let's drink more champagne and let it warm our blood." He teasingly bit her soft bottom lip. "Let's lie here and explore each other." His lips closed more surely on hers and his kiss deepened, his tongue penetrating between her lips. "Please, beautiful girl, let me love you once again." His mouth moved to the side of her neck, located the throbbing pulse, and worried it with his tongue. "You taste so good, sweet, let me feast on you for a time." His mouth came back to hers; it dipped down and teased at hers, leaving her craving for more. "Let's fill our big bathtub with bubbles and sit in it together. I'll take the champagne bucket with us." He released her arm, his big hand sliding down to cup a breast. He heard her gentle sigh.

"Austin," she whispered, smiling, "you've made me forget what it was I wanted to do." Her arms went around him.

15

As though nature itself were at their command, the snow ceased during their last night on the train. By the time the Alpha snaked into the giant city, the skies were clearing and the air was dry, though bitter cold. Austin, natty in a suit of pearl-gray flannel, white shirt, gray silk cravat, and gray kid leather gloves, stood at the window of the slow-moving train, his arm around his excited wife, pointing out landmarks of the old city.

Suzette, her face glowing as her eyes swept the skyline, looked fresh and radiant in the soft brown wool dress Austin had picked for her. Long-sleeved and long-waisted, it was topped by a waist-length matching cape trimmed in red fox. Boots of buttery brown kid kept her small feet warm, and a saucy brown wool hat trimmed in red fox complemented the fur muff covering her gloved hands. A strikingly handsome couple, they were both eager to arrive and together explore the many delights awaiting them.

Suzette had been unusually quiet. Now she pressed her head to her husband's shoulder and sighed. "Sweetheart" — he squeezed her neck — "is something wrong? You haven't said a word for five minutes. That's not like you." His big hand toyed with the fur-trimmed bonnet.

Tossing her muff aside, Suzette turned and put her arms around his waist. "Austin, suddenly I'm not sure we should have come to New York. I'm afraid I'll embarrass you. I've never been anywhere and I don't know —"

His hearty laugh interrupted her. He put a finger underneath her chin and bent to kiss her small nose. "My dear, not only should you be here, but I predict that you will take this jaded old city by storm. You'll be sought after by the handsome sports longing for a smile or a dance, and you'll be the pride of all hostesses eager to have you make their parties the best of the season. Trust me, my love, you belong. Don't be fearful. It is I who should be afraid."

"You afraid, Austin?" she asked incredulously. "Whatever of? I can't imagine you frightened of anything."

His hands on her upper arms, he said seriously, "My only love, you are much too sweet and unspoiled to realize just what power you have over me. I am afraid — afraid of losing you to one of the well-heeled playboys you'll undoubtedly meet while we're here. You see, you're correct, you haven't been anywhere. If you had, you'd know just how desirable men find you. I fear someone handsomer, wealthier, more charming, and, frankly, younger will turn your lovely head and you'll be tempted to leave me." His great gray eyes were somber and Suzette knew her husband was not teasing her; he really was worried.

"Shoot, Austin!" she said and stood on tiptoes, clinging to the lapels of his fine suit. "You've turned my head until I feel quite dizzy." She smiled fetchingly up at him and put her thumb to the thin line of his mouth. "You won't lose me, Austin, so stop your fretting. For heaven's sake, you're the one who wanted to bring me to New York. I've had the most wonderful time of my life traveling up here, just the two of us alone. I would be as happy if we never stepped foot off the train. Why, we could turn right around and go back to Jacksboro and it would suit me fine." The lips she traced were beginning to curve into a smile and the hands on her shoulders went to her waist. "Austin, already I'd be lost without you. I am naive, just as you said. You'll teach me all I need to know, won't you?"

Smiling down at her, he murmured happily, "Why is it I feel it's you who will teach me?" He kissed her lightly. "Yes, love, I'll teach you. In time you'll be as polished as any Fifth Avenue millionaire's wife."

"Good. Then it's settled." She whirled around and drew his arms about her waist. Leaning against him, she said, "Austin, you never told me why the name of your railroad car is Alpha."

The soft fur of her bonnet tickled his chin as Austin inhaled deeply of her sweet perfumed fragrance and said without hesitation, "Suzette, for a long, long time I have wanted you, planned to have you. I knew I couldn't rush it, but I have prayed the time would come when you would turn to me. About a year ago I was in New York, and though I attended many fine parties, I was terribly lonely. The notion came to me then how wonderful it would be to have you with me in New York. I pictured you traveling with me, and the vision was so vivid and pleasant that I wired the Pullman Company and commissioned them to build this car. I called it Alpha, for if I were to travel in it, you would be with me, and it would truly be the beginning."

"Austin, that's romantic and very flattering," Suzette mused. "I had no idea you wanted me that long ago." She paused and plucked at the fingers of his hand. "It's also a little arrogant, don't you think? How did you know I'd consent to be your wife?"

Slowly Austin moved a hand up to the soft curls on her neck. Gently he pushed the gleaming hair aside and bent to press his lips to the curve of her neck, while his free hand moved from her waist to rest lightly on a cape-covered breast. "You're here, aren't you?" His breath was warm, ruffling her hair.

"Yes, I am." She smiled as shivers ran up her spine. "Now, sir, if you don't unhand me, I shall pull the curtains and demand my wifely rights!" She laughed and pulled away from his embrace.

Laughing with her, he shook his head. "You're a lovely little tease, Mrs. Brand, and I shall make you pay when I get you to the hotel."

Suzette clung to her husband's arm as they stepped down from their car at the train station. Swarms of people, more than she'd ever seen in one place, swirled about them in all directions, all seemingly in a great hurry. Suzette was almost frightened by the mass of humanity pressing so close; her eyes were wide as she jerked her head about, taking in the crowd.

"Scary, isn't it?" Austin said above her, sensing her uneasiness.

"Is it this crowded everywhere in New York?"

"No, not quite. You'll be able to breathe again as soon as we get outside." He indicated the tall steamy windows just ahead. "Hang onto me, I'll get you through this."

With one hand gripping his arm, the other holding onto her hat, Suzette put her head down and made her way determinedly through the milling, jostling crowd. Bumped and jolted on all sides, she gave a sigh of relief when finally Austin opened the tall door leading out onto a street and maneuvered her in front of him. The cold, crisp air struck her face and she inhaled deeply, relieved to be out of the oppressive, stuffy terminal.

Within minutes she was seated in the back of a handsome covered brougham whisking them down the busy avenue to their hotel. Austin, tucking the lap robe about her knees, proudly pointed out sights along the route, smiling when she stared in awe at the tall buildings on the horizon.

Suzette said over and over, "I can't believe it. I really can't believe it."

"I know," he said understandingly. "It's impossible to tell someone what New York City is like. They have to see it for themselves."

"Oh, Austin, thank you for bringing me here. Already I love it!"

Happy with her pleasure, he assured her, "Darlin', I promise you a wonderful time in New York."

Austin kept that promise. From the minute the couple checked into their opulent suite at the Hotel Brunswick on Fifth Avenue, Suzette began a glorious romp through a new wonderland and she loved every minute, every hour, every day of her new life. A grand suite of rooms awaited her in the magnificent hotel, and she was not through the lobby before she was asking her husband questions about the elegantly dressed couples she saw there.

"Look," she whispered, longing to point. "I've never seen such beautiful ladies. Look at their clothes. Wherever did they find such stunning dresses?" Handsome couples promenaded about the lobby as gentlemen in tight trousers and custom-made coats and haughty young women in billowing skirts, motioning with their gloved hands, nodded and chatted with one another.

"Looks as though the Coaching Club is having an early meeting," Austin explained. "The Brunswick is their headquarters. When spring comes you're really in for a treat. They put on quite a show."

"Oh, I'd like to see that!"

"We'll still be here when spring comes."

"You mean it?" She looked up in surprise.

"Yes, I do. We're going to stay until it's warm enough to go to Atlantic City and swim in the ocean."

Beaming, she nodded her agreement and lifted her skirts to climb the ornate stairs to their quarters. Inside, she hurried from room to room, admiring the high-ceilinged, well-appointed apartment, while a uniformed porter unloaded their luggage.

When the door closed behind him, Suzette came into her husband's arms and hugged him tightly. "Austin, this is the most beautiful place I've ever seen. It must cost a fortune."

"We can afford it, darlin'." He grinned and swept the small fur-trimmed hat from her head, smoothing the golden hair.

He untied the cape and took it from her. She handed him her gloves. "Now, the first thing we must do is have a wardrobe made for you."

"Austin, may I have some lovely dresses like the ones the pretty ladies downstairs were wearing?"

"Indeed, lovelier. I have some ideas about what would suit you. Shall we get started?"

"Let's do." She rubbed her hands together. "Let me freshen up a bit, and we can be on our way."

She turned to go to the bedroom, but Austin reached out and took her arm. Laughing, he said, "No, sweetheart. There's no need for you to be out in the cold again. The dressmaker will come here. I'll take care of it. But first, why don't I fill a tub for you? While you're soaking I'll have lunch sent up. After we've eaten, you can rest while I engage the services of one of the finer dressmakers and take care of a few other things. By the time you've had a nap, you can start with the fittings. How does that sound?"

"Austin, you are going to have me so spoiled; I'll not be able to do a thing for myself."

"My love," he said, leading her into the large bathroom with its gleaming ivory tub mounted on gold claw feet, "that is exactly my plan."

Not one, but three dressmakers were engaged to make glittering garments for the lovely young woman whose adoring husband wanted his bride to have the very best. Long hours were spent as Suzette stood dutifully still while nimble hands pinned, measured, smoothed, and pulled fabrics around her slender body. Bolt after bolt of the finest silks, satins, woolens, taffetas, velvets, and brocades in myriad luscious colors were brought to the Brand suite at the Hotel Brunswick.

Madame Marie de Corday, the most expensive and talented dressmaker in the city, fussed over designs and patterns and draped soft, colorful materials over Suzette's tired body while snapping commands to the girl. "Mrs. Brand, you must stand straight and proud like a queen!" The woman jerked Suzette's shoulders back and patted the underside of her chin. "Head held high, bosom thrust out. If you are to wear my clothes, you must do so with grace."

"Yes, ma'am," Suzette offered lamely, trying desperately to please the bullying little dark-haired woman.

"*Chérie*, I take this assignment only because your big good-looking husband told me you are part French. *Oui*?"

"Yes. I mean, *oui*. My mother was half French, from Louisiana. My grandfather came to Louisiana from Nova Scotia. I'm very proud of my French ancestry."

"As you should be. Now stand straight and behave like you are French." The woman's dark eyes flashed and she smiled. "Mrs. Brand, I am harsh, but when I am finished, you will be the most desirable lady in all New York." The smile faded before Suzette could respond. Madame snatched a corset from the bed and thrust it at Suzette. "Shame on you for not owning any corsets! Put this on. I shall shape your figure anew, and you will be as curvaceous as the most prized courtesan when you appear in my gorgeous gowns."

When Suzette first appeared in one of the new gowns Madame had fashioned for her, even Austin blinked. As she shyly entered the sitting room of their suite, Austin gaped at the beautifully gowned young woman. She wore a satin dress of ice-blue, its color bringing out the darker blue of her large eyes. The daringly low neckline curved just over her shoulders and came to a deep V between her creamy breasts. Her slender waist was made smaller still by the tight corset Madame insisted she wear. While inches seemed to disappear from her waist, the push-up effect of the tight garment added those inches to her exposed bosom. The high swell of her breasts above the dress gave the impression that any second she might spill completely out and disgrace herself. The swirling skirt was topped by an overskirt of the same material and was pulled to the back with row on row of dainty bows. Satin slippers peeked from under the rustling skirts.

Her long blond hair had been dressed and was pulled up off her neck into a cluster of fat, shiny curls atop her head. Blue sapphire-and-diamond earrings, a gift from her husband, sparkled brilliantly and hung daintily suspended from her shell-like ears almost to her bare shoulders. At her throat she wore only the tiny gold locket with the single sapphire. Austin, knowing how much the delicate necklace meant to her, wisely bought no adornment for her neck. He knew she would take off the locket to wear any bauble he bought for her, but he didn't want her to feel it necessary.

"Your mouth is open, Austin," she teased him, bringing him out of his reverie.

"I'm sure it is." He nodded his head. "I can't believe that you could look any more beautiful than you've always looked, but you do. I'm not sure I want to take you out. You'll turn the head of every man in this city!"

Embarrassed, Suzette looked down at herself. "Austin, I could change if you wish. The dress is a little bold, isn't it?"

"Very bold. That's what makes it so stunning. You have a magnificent bosom, so why not display it? As long as I'm the only man allowed to touch it, I don't mind other men looking." Smiling, he walked to her and bent his head, pressing a quick, warm kiss to her left breast, just above the blue satin. Straightening immediately, he said, "Mrs. Brand, shall we be on our way? We've reservations at Delmonico's at ten."

Turning her back to him, she waited for him to drape her long wrap about her bare shoulders. "I'm starving, but I'm afraid I'll not be able to eat very much in this dreadful corset."

Grinning, he put his lips in her hair. "Perhaps the lady will require a snack later tonight when she's discarded corset, dress, underwear, shoes, and stockings. When you are again bare in our bed, I'll see to it you have a tempting repast to hold you till breakfast."

The crusty snow crunched under their feet as they walked across Fifth Avenue to the entrance of Delmonico's. Assuring her husband she saw no need for a carriage when they were close enough to throw a stone and hit the restaurant, Suzette breathed deeply of the chill air as her cheeks flushed with color, heightening her youthful beauty. They soon joined the swell of finely turned-out couples entering the popular dining place.

Inside, Suzette's eyes swept the huge room. Lined with mirrors and lit with magnificent silver chandeliers, the restaurant was enormous. At the room's center, in the midst of masses of fresh flowers, a beautiful fountain splashed.

Longing to appear sophisticated, Suzette said nothing, but she couldn't refrain from twisting her head to look behind her. Austin, his hand at the small of her back, guided her up the stairs to the second floor. She'd been too preoccupied to notice when her wrap was taken by a bowing man dressed in black.

Another tall, impeccably dressed gentleman led the pair into one of the dining rooms. Suzette couldn't stifle the gasp that escaped her lips. Her eyes were on the splendid walls, covered entirely in rich satin. Seated, she looked across the table at Austin. Handsome in his dark evening clothes; his bronzed face gleamed in the candlelight and his full mouth curved into a pleased smile.

"Austin Brand!" She leaned across the table to whisper excitedly, "Satin walls! Have you ever seen anything so grand?"

"I thought you'd like it, my love." He looked over her head, nodded, and a waiter hurried to their table. "We'll wait a bit to order, but perhaps you could bring us a nice bottle of Cordon Rouge."

Suzette sipped her champagne and pursed her lips. She studied the fancy menu. "I've never heard of so many foods in my life. And they all sound delicious."

"Del's is famous for its fine selection."

"Let's see," she said with conviction, "I believe I shall have the *ragout de tortue*." She laid her menu aside, feeling quite pleased with herself. She looked smugly at her husband and saw the grin curving his mouth. "What?" She glanced about and lowered her voice. "Austin, what is it?"

"Darlin'," he laughed and reached across the table to cover her hand with his, "are you certain you would enjoy stewed terrapin?"

Making a face, she said, "Good Lord, Austin! Do people actually eat such things? The fancy French names all sound so good. Will you order for me, please?"

"I'll be delighted, my love." When the waiter returned to take their order, Austin chose *filet de boeuf*, fresh green beans in butter, fricasseed potatoes, and eggplant with sauce.

Taking a big swallow of champagne, Suzette gave Austin a smile of approval. But when the food was served, she ate little. Tightly laced and corseted, it was impossible to have her fill. Instead, she continued to drink the bubbly champagne while her husband entertained her with humorous stories; the more champagne she drank, the more humorous his stories became. Her laughter, high and tinkling, floated through the room. Eyes turned her way. Austin never noticed, for his eyes were on her too. He was enchanted, as were the other gentlemen casting admiring glances at the lovely young woman.

"Austin," she said, holding his big hand, "I'm afraid I've grown a bit tipsy. I'm sorry. I must be making a spectacle of myself. People are staring."

Austin casually turned his head and looked about. When his gaze swung back to her, he smiled and raised her hand to his lips. "My dear, Madame de Pompadour once said, 'Champagne is the only wine which leaves a woman beautiful after drinking it.' She was so right, you are lovelier than ever, and if people are looking, I don't blame them. Drink up, beautiful girl." He released her hand and filled her glass again.

The cold winter days and cozy winter nights were gay and happy for the couple bent on seeing all the sights and tasting each delight the city offered. Carriage rides in the afternoons, teas at the Fifth Avenue mansions of Austin's friends, dinner parties at those fine homes, gala balls, and wine suppers after midnight at the cafés made life an unending adventure for both. Austin found new pleasure in the city's social life now that he had a beautiful young wife on his arm.

If ever a person took quickly to the high life, it was Suzette Foxworth Brand. She wore her new clothes with flair, she charmed the blue-blooded aristocrats who made up New York society, she drank wine and laughed at ribald stories with the sporting crowd, she attended the theater and met and admired actors and artists, and quickly became the darling of the maître d's of the finest restaurants and eateries in Manhattan.

Hostesses fought with one another for the company of the golden couple, and the season's many parties seemed not quite the success they should be if Suzette and Austin decided to enjoy a private evening alone.

One cold evening Suzette sat on their big bed pulling on her silk stockings as they dressed for the opera, and she said thoughtfully, "Austin, I know you're a very charming, handsome man, but how is it we're invited to every party and ball? Was this once your home? Did your family come from the east?"

Austin, shirtless, sat reading in an easy chair beside the bed. Lowering the *New York Herald* to his lap, he looked at his wife as she pulled the sheer hose up her long, shapely leg. Any other time he would have smiled with pleasure. This time he didn't. Sighing, he said, "No, this is not my home. I thought you knew that Beth came from New York. This was her home. I met her here one summer when I visited a friend from military school."

"Well, go on." She looked up at him.

Austin rose and walked to the window. He slipped his hands in his trouser pockets and stood looking out across Union Square. "What more can I tell you? All the people you've met are friends of mine, but I would never have known them if not for Beth. She came from the aristocratic family, not I. She... she..." His voice trailed off.

Suzette sat very still. Sorry she'd brought up the subject, she mistakenly thought that she'd brought back painful memories for Austin — that he was thinking of the happy times he'd spent with Beth in New York.

Sliding off the bed, she padded across the room, shoeless. She wore only the silky stockings, a chemise of satin trimmed with lace and beading, and her matching drawers with ribbons at the knees. She stood directly behind him and tentatively lifted a hand to his smooth shoulder. "Austin," she said softly, "I... I'm sure you must miss Beth very much. If it's painful for you to be here, where the two of you —"

He whirled around to face her. She took a step backward just as he reached out and clasped her upper arms. "My God, woman, Haven't you listened to one word I've said? Do you honestly think I'm grieving for a wife I never loved one-half as much as I love you?" His fingers were cutting into her arms and his expression was stormy. Suzette dared not interrupt him. "Don't you know what's wrong with me? I feel guilty. Guilty for loving you so damned much! Guilty for enjoying this city in a way I never did before. Guilty because being Beth's husband makes it possible for me to be here with you now; to show you a way of life that would never have been possible but for her. Can't you understand that? It's Beth Applegate's ticket I got in on, dammit!"

Tenderness filled Suzette's heart. Her hands went to Austin's taut middle and she said softly, "Listen to me, Mr. Austin Brand. You have nothing whatever to feel guilty about. You were married to a fine woman from an aristocratic family and you made her a very good husband. I never knew a happier woman than Beth Applegate Brand. She worshipped you. Of course she introduced you to all her friends and they naturally liked you. You're a charming man. Is that so bad? I think not. It's as it should be, Austin, and you're being foolish. Beth loved you. She would want you to be happy, don't you see that? If she had lived, she would be here with you now, not I. But she didn't, so I'm here and I'm your wife and there's no cause for you to feel guilty." Her hands moved up over his chest and went around his neck. "These people are your friends, Austin, and from now on they'll be mine. Does it really matter what made it possible? Should we turn down their invitations because you're not sure they would have ever wanted you if Beth hadn't been your wife?"

Softening, he said tiredly, "Darling, you don't understand. I love you so much and I —"

"I do understand. You're torturing yourself because you feel you love me more than you loved Beth, isn't that it?"

"Yes, it is. I never loved her the way I love you. Never."

"Austin, that's not so terrible. Beth never knew and she was happy. Now I'm happy because you love me. Can't you be happy, too? These parties and friends are not what's important. We don't have to go to the opera tonight if you'd rather not. I don't care, I swear it. What would you really like to do?"

His big hands went to her waist and he murmured, "I'd really like to put you on that bed and take off your stockings and underwear and caress you until I forget there is anyone in this world but the two of us."

Smiling, she leaned close and gently kissed his chest. With her lips still on his flesh, she whispered, "Then why don't you do it?"

Austin shivered. He slowly picked up his wife and carried her to their bed. Gently he laid her across the smooth sheets and bent over her. He began to peel the silky stocking from her right leg as the orange glow from the winter sun disappeared. The stockings discarded, he slowly unhooked the filmy chemise. When he pulled it apart, a muscle jumped in his jaw. A big hand closed over a breast and he looked into her eyes. "Make me forget, Suzette. Take me to paradise, darlin'." He bent to her.

For a long, languid time, Suzette did just that.

By the next day, Austin was himself again and Suzette was relieved. The city was atwitter about a ball the widow Mrs. J. B. Warrington was giving in the ballroom at Delmonico's. Suzette was looking forward to it, and when she went through her many new gowns to pick what she would wear, her husband walked into the room and said, "Suzette, you'll wear the gold taffeta to the Warrington Ball."

"But, Austin" — she turned, holding up a rajah silk of pale lavender — "I haven't worn this, and it's so beautiful, I thought —"

"No, sweetheart, the gold taffeta. I insist." He winked at her and left the room.

Suzette made a face and hung the lovely silk back in the closet. Shrugging her slender shoulders, she mumbled to herself, "I wanted to wear the lavender. Why can't I pick what I'll wear?"

When the night of the ball arrived, Suzette, who'd forgotten that she'd wanted to wear the lilac gown, swept up the steps to the second-floor ballroom on the arm of her beaming husband. In her gold taffeta dress, its décolletage flattering her stunning bustline, its full skirt rustling as she walked, she carried a lone red rose Austin had given her. Her evening bag was of red velvet. Around her slender wrist a gold bracelet studded with rubies matched the earrings she wore — gifts from her husband.

When the Brands stepped into the giant ballroom, every head turned. Austin smiled broadly, took her into his arms, and swept her about the big room while an orchestra played beautiful music and prisms of light from the chandelier high over their heads made pleasing patterns on her shiny gold dress and Austin's golden hair. Aware of the attention they commanded, Suzette was glad she'd worn the dress Austin chose. She looked up at him and said sweetly, "I shall never again question your decisions, Mr. Brand."

"See that you don't, Mrs. Brand," he teased and tightened his embrace.

The glittering ball was a huge success and Suzette Brand was the star. Men of all ages unashamedly watched her with admiration and Austin had no choice but to release her good-naturedly to their eager arms for spins about the floor. He watched her dance by in the arms of a playboy who brazenly flirted with her under the nose of her bridegroom. Austin's easy smile never faltered, but it was with effort that he kept it in place. Never had he seen Suzette look so beautiful, and when handsome young men held her close and ogled her creamy, exposed bosom, Austin's hand tightened on his long-stemmed glass. Ignoring the looks of longing he received from hopeful ladies, his eyes never left his wife. Spirited and friendly, Suzette chatted gaily with each man she danced with and easily charmed them with her wit and beauty. Austin strained to hear what she was saying and cursed himself for his jealousy. Knowing tonight was only the beginning, he took a deep breath and wondered if he'd been too clever in bringing her to New York.

Before he could answer himself, she was back by his side, looking up at him with those luminous blue eyes and dazzling smile. She hugged his arm and said breathlessly, "Austin, could we please escape for a minute and rest?"

Those were the exact words he wanted to hear. He put his hand to the nape of her neck and leaned down to kiss her flushed cheek. "Let's slip downstairs to the café and have a brandy alone at some deserted table."

"Yes, let's," she agreed eagerly, having no idea how happy she'd made him.

16

The gala days and nights of a splendid winter soon gave way to an exceptional spring. Days lengthened rapidly as cold brisk winds became warm gentle breezes. Snowy nights of lovemaking under soft downy coverlets in a firelit room turned into balmy nights of lovemaking atop the silken sheets in the silvery, moonlit room.

Madame Marie de Corday was again summoned to the

Brand suite at the Hotel Brunswick to outfit Suzette, this time for the summer season at Saratoga. Suzette's head-turning woolens, velvets, satins, and silks were packed away and replaced with stunningly stylish gowns of piqué, linen, muslin, and soft silk in an array of pastels.

Before the city became uncomfortable with the heavy heat of summer, Suzette and Austin checked out of the hotel that had been their home since early January. Trunks and valises made their way by separate carriage to the terminal, where the Alpha awaited on a siding. It had arrived from Fort Worth earlier in the week and its staff of servants was aboard and ready to tend the Brands.

"Austin, I'm tempted to cry," Suzette said seriously to her husband as she pinned her pale yellow bonnet atop her shiny curls on their last day in the city.

"Dear, if you must, you ought to wait to put on your hat until you've finished weeping." He watched her, a shoulder against the doorframe, hands in his trouser pockets. "I personally find it hard to cry with a hat on."

"Austin Brand, stop your teasing." She made a face at him. "I'm quite serious. We've been so happy in this room. Don't you think it sad that we're leaving?"

Austin took his hands from his pockets and moved toward his wife. Gently holding her shoulders, he bent and kissed her nose through the wispy veil of her new hat. "My dear, we've been blissfully happy in this room, but the room was not responsible. We were. We'll take our happiness with us. You'll see. You are going to love Saratoga just as you love New York. Now, please, smile prettily for me and let's be on our way."

Suzette wrinkled her nose, then smiled. "You're right, Austin. We'll have times that are just as grand as the ones we've had here, won't we?"

"Madam, I guarantee it. Now, scoot!" He gently turned her toward the door and gave her bottom a playful slap.

The sun was sinking behind the tall, majestic Manhattan buildings when Suzette and Austin arrived at the train station.

An hour later they sat at the dinner table, eating leisurely as the train rolled northward at twenty miles an hour.

"When will we get to Saratoga?" Suzette had no idea where the spa was.

Splashing brandy into a couple of crystal snifters, Austin handed one to his wife and said, "About breakfast time, I imagine."

"That long?" She raised her eyebrows. "I thought we'd be there by bedtime."

He grinned and took a drink. "Sweetheart, although I do my best to give you anything you want, even I can't make a train cover two hundred miles in a couple of hours." Austin pushed back his chair and unfolded the evening edition of the *New York Herald*. Taking the front section, he offered the rest to his wife. "Paper, darlin'?"

Suzette took it from him and opened it, her eyes scanning the first page. She yawned and turned the page, then sat up straight, her eyes wide. Below a picture of a dark, handsome young man was the caption: Prince of Darkness Strikes Again. The dateline was Fort Worth, Texas.

"Austin," Suzette said urgently, "listen to this. Kaytano has done it again. His picture is in the paper. He robbed a mail train east of Dallas and escaped. It says he —"

Hurriedly taking the paper from her, Austin scowled, then said coldly, "Suzette, why are you determined to search out stories about a brutal half-breed bandit! Does this parasite Kaytano hold such fascination for you that you —"

"Just one minute, Austin Brand!" Suzette pushed back her chair and stood up, her hands on her hips, her blue eyes flashing fire. "I do not search out stories about this Indian bandit! It so happens that the eastern press finds this... this... 'Prince of Darkness' so fascinating that it picks up stories about him all the way from Texas and runs them in the New York paper! There must be a lot of people interested in him." Suzette leaned close to her husband's face, her hands gripping the table's edge. "As for fascination or preoccupation with Kaytano, Austin, you're the one who gets overly emotional at the mention of his name. Why? Do you know this Indian? Is there something you aren't telling me?"

His gray eyes were as dark as storm clouds, and his full mouth had become a tight line. Austin glared at Suzette, his big hands clutching the chair arms, his body tense. Finally he spoke. "Suzette, I'm sorry. That was foolish of me."

"Why? Why do you act this way? From the very first time I wrote a story about Kaytano for the Jacksboro newspaper, you've acted strangely. What is it? Tell me why a story about a bank robber upsets you so."

"Darlin', I... it's just that he's an Indian. I thought we both had a reason to despise Indians."

"Austin, I hate them as much as you do, but we can't spend the rest of our lives getting upset every time we read a story or hear someone mention an Indian." She looked down at him and saw the pain in his eyes as his rage subsided. "Austin, love." She knelt beside his chair. Smiling, she laid her head on his arm. "This Kaytano has nothing whatsoever to do with us. He's a cruel half-breed who cares nothing for life. His exploits have made him famous, so I read about him just like everyone else. I'm not made of china, Austin. I won't shatter, nor will I be frightened by anything I read."

Suzette was relieved when she felt his big hand go to her head. Gently he stroked her shiny hair and said softly, "Darlin', say you forgive me my outburst. It's hard to explain, but I love you so much, the thought of anything or anyone bad touching your life upsets me. I'd like to keep you locked away someplace where you'd always be safe and no one and nothing unpleasant could ever come near you. I don't even like you to be aware such people exist!"

Suzette lifted her head and clutched his hand, then pressed a soft kiss into his palm. "Austin, you do keep me safe. Since you married me I haven't been out of your sight for one moment." She smiled. "Don't you think it would be hard for a bandit to harm me as long as I'm with you?"

"Impossible," he agreed, his eyes narrowing.

The sun was shining brilliantly when the Alpha pulled into the Saratoga station. Suzette gasped as she stepped onto the platform, Austin behind her. In the distance, a long chain of mountains rose toward the sun. Nearer, the gentle hills were blanketed in emerald-green. Tall stately trees towered over the enormous white homes, which were remarkable for their gingerbread trim.

Austin had chosen the Grand Union Hotel for their two-month stay at the spa. Elegantly dressed people milled about on the broad veranda of the hotel and in the cavernous lobby. Suzette had thought that she'd seen the most lavish hotels the world had to offer in New York City, but she now knew she'd been mistaken. Surely the Grand Union was the fanciest on earth. From the manicured gardens in front of the hotel, an orchestra played sweet music, though it was only mid-morning. Suzette, clinging to Austin's arm as he spoke to a gentleman at the front desk, let her eyes take in the wonders of the ornate lobby.

"Come, dear," Austin urged, and then they were walking through the lobby to the back of the hotel where a large flower-filled courtyard was criss-crossed with paths for promenading. Suzette whispered excitedly to her husband, "Austin, where is the man taking us?"

"Sweet, the Grand Union has individual cottages for those who desire extra privacy. I thought we'd stay in one."

"Why?"

Chuckling, Austin bent close to her ear. "Because we're still honeymooners and my ardor for you has not yet cooled. Must I explain further?"

Suzette pressed her breasts against her husband's upper arm and flirted. "Explanations are rather chancy, Austin. When we get inside, perhaps you'd better show me what you mean." She ran the tip of her pink tongue around her full bottom lip and lowered her lashes.

Austin Brand felt the familiar tightening of his stomach muscles and was momentarily terrified that the tight trousers he wore would display to all the state of his arousal. When he quickly swept the broad-brimmed hat from his head and carried it nervously in front of him, Suzette bit her lip to keep from laughing.

Suzette loved Saratoga. The resort offered a tranquil, refined life that was the exact opposite of the bustling excitement of New York. Life at the spa consisted mainly of lovely concerts, excellent food, gambling in the Club House Casino, match races between blooded Thoroughbreds at the racetrack, promenading down Broadway in the late evening, and carriage rides about the little city and out to the lake.

It was all wonderful to Suzette, just as it was to Austin, though for him the most precious moments of all were those the two shared alone in the opulent cottage. There he could have his lovely wife all to himself, to hold and caress, to undress and admire, to love and enjoy. On a beautiful summer night when they'd returned from the moonlight ride out to the lake, Suzette lay in his arms, her fingers caressing the thick hair at the back of his head while he feathered kisses over her face and bare shoulders. Pleasantly tipsy from champagne, she smiled lazily up at him and said, "Austin, heads turn wherever we go and many of them are ladies'. I'm envied by beautiful women. I'm a lucky girl! I've the handsomest, most charming husband in the world and I couldn't be more pleased."

"Thank you, sweetheart," he murmured, and wondered if the day would ever come when she would say she loved him. So far it hadn't happened, not even in all the times he'd held her in his arms and made love to her. She was warm, giving and sensual, but she never once said she loved him.

"Honey," he breathed, "I love you so much."

"Hmm." She sighed. "Kiss me, Austin."

17

Austin awoke the next day at mid-morning. Sleepily he reached for Suzette, but the bed beside him was empty. Raising himself on an elbow, Austin ran his hand through his thick, sun-tipped hair and looked about. Across the spacious bedroom, Suzette, wearing a sheer filmy gown, stood pensively staring out the open balcony doors, her arms folded.

"Suzette?" he called, his voice still heavy with sleep.

She turned slowly and looked at him. Her expression was unfamiliar, melancholy. Alarmed, Austin sat up, propping a pillow behind his back. She came flying across the room to him. "Austin," she choked, near tears.

"Sweetheart!" He was immediately awake, throwing back the sheet for her. She climbed gratefully into the bed and threw her arms around him, burying her face in his neck. Austin held her close and caressed her. "What is it, darlin'? Are you ill? Shall I get a doctor?" His heart pounded and his big hands trembled as he stroked her.

"No, I'm not sick and I don't want a doctor." Her voice was muffled against his shoulder.

"Then tell me, Suzette, what is it? Why were you up? Couldn't you sleep? Has something happened?"

She shook her head, but still she clung to him, her slender body pressing close to his warmth. "I'm afraid."

"Afraid?" He was dumbstruck. "Of what, darlin'? Of me? How could you possibly be frightened? I don't understand."

"No, Austin." She lifted her head. Her eyes reflected her anguish. "I'm not afraid of you. It's... it's... did you know today is my birthday?"

"Yes, sweet baby." He pushed her hair from her eyes. "I've a lovely day and night planned for us. Lots of presents and fun and surprises."

"No!"

"No?" What do you mean, no? Don't you want —"

"Please," she cut in, "I don't want parties and presents! I don't want to leave this room." She pressed her face into his neck again.

Completely at a loss, Austin cradled her head and said softly, "Suzette, turning twenty-three is hardly a tragedy. It's really very young."

"It isn't that!" She pulled back to look at him. "Austin, I know you'll think me childish and absurd, but I . . . I . . . I'm always so frightened on my birthday. The worst tragedies of my life happened to me around my birthday. Those horrors come back to haunt me and I always have the terrible feeling that something awful will happen to me. It's the same each year. I'm terrified. It's like . . . like . . . oh, Austin, what if something should happen to you because you married me? What if —"

"Sweetheart," he said, hugging her tightly, "I certainly don't think you are childish and absurd. I can understand your being upset on your birthday. Bless your heart, I should have been thoughtful enough to have guessed. Listen to me, Suzette, nothing is going to happen to me. Nothing. And nothing is going to happen to you. Those tragedies are behind you. There won't be any more. You and I will get all dressed up and then —"

"No! Please, Austin, no!" she pleaded. "Don't make me go out today. I can't. I don't want to spoil your plans, but I just can't."

Austin kissed her temple and smiled. "Relax, there's no need for us to leave the room if you'd rather not."

"You mean it?" she asked relieved. "You don't mind if we don't celebrate?"

Austin drew her closer. "Listen to me very carefully, Suzette. I love you more than you will ever know. There is nothing I would not do to make you happy. You're safe here in my arms and you may stay here for the rest of your life. I told you a long time ago that should you ever need a dragon slayed, I'd be happy to do it." He grinned and kissed her ear. "You could never spoil my plans because every plan I have is for you. If you feel you'd like to remain inside today, let's do it. Just tell me what you want, darlin'. Always tell me what you want. I can get you anything you desire."

"Austin," she murmured, her eyes softening, her hand absently roaming over his chest, "may I really tell you what I want? Will you be shocked if I do?"

"Sweet, it takes a lot to shock me."

"I know, but I'm embarrassed." She let her hand trail down the dark line of hair.

Austin smiled. "Whisper it to me."

Smiling, Suzette leaned close to his ear. "Will you make love to me now, in the middle of the day with the balcony doors wide open?"

"Oh, Jesus!" He groaned and pulled her over on him. Kissing her softly, Austin lifted her to his other side, placing her gently on her back in the middle of the bed. With sure hands, he whisked away her flimsy nightgown while his mouth heated on hers. Suzette's lips parted, her tongue mating with his. She shivered when his big hand spread on her stomach. His touch was feather-light on her quivering flesh, awakening sensitive nerve endings, spreading pleasure with a slow sweep of his hand.

Then his big, powerful body was over hers and Suzette's eyes opened wide as he took her, filling her with warmth, driving out her fears, making her a part of him. A glorious feeling of well-being battled with a sensual feeling of urgency as he moved within her, thrusting deeply, raising her to the heights of erotic pleasure. Her mouth dry, her breath coming in shallow gulps, Suzette's long nails punished his smooth, broad back as the climactic crest came for them at the same time. "Austin, Austin... I... oh... ooooh... yes... yes... Austin!"

Austin's great gray eyes were locked with hers and the sound of her excited voice shrieking out her ecstasy made him groan with satisfaction. After the last small shudders shook them, Austin lay quietly beside Suzette, holding her in his arms, kissing her flushed face. From the courtyard below, soft strains of "The Blue Danube" drifted up through the open balcony doors as the noon concert began. The air inside the bedroom was still and close; the lovers' bodies were damp with perspiration. Suzette, her pulse finally slowing, her head against Austin's shoulder, turned her face to his and whispered softly. "Austin, thank you."

"Thank you, my darlin'," he said against her temple.

By evening Suzette had cast aside her fears, and she and her happy husband were dressing in their finest for dinner at Moon's restaurant on the lake. After their midday loving and short nap, Austin had brought Suzette's birthday presents from their hiding place and dumped them onto the bed with her. Giggling, she had eagerly torn into the gaily wrapped packages. Vowing after each one that it was definitely her favorite, Suzette put each article on as she unwrapped it.

First came a pair of gold and oystershell combs; they immediately went into her hair, sweeping the long, tangled tresses back from her face. Next, a pair of diamond earrings, their unique design making her swoon with pleasure, were fastened to her lobes. A stunning gold bracelet, entirely plain and two inches wide, went directly on her right wrist. A ring of emeralds and diamonds twinkled brightly from its bed of velvet.

"I love it!" Suzette squealed and slipped it on her finger.

There were at least a dozen little gifts: a new journal covered in blue brocade, a gold pen, a Dickens story, a music box that played sweetly while a man danced with his sweetheart on its top. And on and on. When finally Suzette had opened all the gifts and the bed was full of her treasures and the boxes and crumpled paper, she rose to her knees and stretched out her arms to her husband. "Austin, thank you so much. I love everything. Thank you. There's only one gift that I can't use."

"What's that darlin'?"

Suzette handed him the shiny blue brocade journal. "This, Austin. I no longer have to write about life. With you I am living it to the fullest!"

Austin grinned and tossed the journal to the floor. He put a knee on the bed and embraced her. "Happy birthday, Suzette," he said softly, pulling her gently into his arms. "Now, what would you like to do for the rest of the day? Still want to stay in?"

"No. What I'd really like to do is get dressed up, wear some of my beautiful new jewels, and go to dinner. Then . . . I'd like to go to the casino."

"Then that's exactly what we'll do." He lifted her from the bed.

"Are you sure? I mean, I didn't know whether or not ladies are permitted in the casino. If we can't do it, it's fine."

Austin set her on her feet. "I think you'll find that with enough money, one can do just about anything one wants."

Suzette, her new diamond earrings sparkling in the light cast by the chandelier, sat on a velvet stool in a private room in the casino and played faro and roulette while Austin stood above her, motioning the croupier to hand her more chips whenever she ran low. When she won, she happily raked the colored chips into a heap in front of her and looked up at her husband with wide-eyed excitement.

Austin didn't gamble. It didn't interest him. He'd gotten it out of his system in his youth. Now he found it a rather foolish, boring entertainment, but he was perfectly willing to let Suzette play. His fingertips resting lightly on her bare shoulder, he looked down at her with possessive pride. His heart speeded as the vision of her lying in his arms, looking into his eyes, came flooding back. "Thank you, Austin," she had murmured in the afterglow of lovemaking.

Austin's big hand involuntarily tightened on her delicate shoulder as unfounded fear pushed itself in to prick at his happiness. He knew just how Suzette had felt earlier in the day. It was her birthday; bad things happened on her birthday. Would something bad happen? Would they be allowed to be this happy? *Do I deserve such bliss?*

At that minute, Suzette turned around to smile up at him.

."This is the best birthday of my life," she whispered happily. She kissed the big hand resting on her shoulder before turning back to the game. Austin Brand relaxed.

You're damned right we deserve to be this happy! he silently told the fates.

Two thousand miles away, in a lavish hotel room in Fort Worth, Texas, a lean, dark man sat reading the *Fort Worth Democrat*. His cold, black eyes narrowed as he read a society piece on a honeymooning couple. The rotogravure picture accompanying the story showed a young, beautiful woman, dressed elegantly, smiling up at her tall, handsome husband. The man's eyes were on the woman, full of love and adoration.

The dark young man recrossed his long legs and carefully tore the picture from the newspaper. Folding it neatly, he slipped it into the breast pocket of his tight black shirt.

A short, paunchy Mexican walked into the room at that moment, a wide, toothy grin spreading over his fleshy face. "Did you see the latest on the honeymooners?" The dark, handsome man barely nodded, the expression in his eyes never changing. "Well?" the Mexican questioned. "Will it be soon? They will return in a few weeks." His grin broadened and he rubbed his ham-like hands together.

The dark man took a long, brown cigar from a small table beside his elbow. Biting off the tip, he rolled the narrow cigar between his lips before clamping it firmly between even, white teeth. He didn't light it.

Slowly he took it from his mouth, and for the first time he spoke. "There's no hurry, my friend. I may wait years. I want him to be so much in love with his beautiful new plaything, he'll suffer properly. I'll let him be happy for a time. I've the rest of my life."

With a shrug of his shoulders, he placed the cigar back into his mouth and lit it, puffing it slowly to life. He inhaled deeply. In his black, hooded eyes was a look very near to joy.

18

From Saratoga, the Alpha swept its illustrious passengers southward to Atlantic City, New Jersey. Suzette loved the ocean and the strolls down the long boardwalk. The couple stayed at the resort through the end of September, and both agreed it had been the most wonderful trip ever and vowed they would return to their favorite places the next year.

The Alpha pulled into Fort Worth at mid-morning on October 12, 1878. Suzette stood at the window of their stateroom, searching eagerly for familiar landmarks. "Austin," she said, "can you believe we've been away for nine months?"

Smiling, Austin slipped his arms about his wife's waist and kissed the top of her head. "No, angel, I can't believe it. Thank you for the most wonderful time of my life."

"Mine, too, Austin." She leaned back against him. "We're stopping. Shall we get off right away?"

Releasing her, he said, "No, darlin', we'll have lunch on board, then spend the night at a hotel. Tomorrow we'll go home. I'm going to step outside for a few minutes."

"I'll dress for lunch while you're gone." She turned and flashed him a big smile.

Austin returned shortly with the morning paper. As Suzette took the front section of the *Fort Worth Democrat*, her eyes grew wide and she said, "Austin! Listen to this."

HOSTILE PRISONER COMMITS SUICIDE

The last of the great Kiowa war chiefs committed suicide yesterday by throwing himself from a second-story window at the Huntsville prison. The impressive Satanta, who was returned to prison after the outbreak of 1874, jumped to his death yesterday morning, unable to stand the confinement.

Let Satanta's own prophecy, spoken by the rugged warrior years ago, be his epitaph: "When I roam over the prairie, I feel free and happy, but when I sit down, I grow pale and die."

Suzette lowered the newspaper and smiled at Austin. "I couldn't be happier! At last the animal has paid."

"I share your happiness." Austin nodded.

Across town, in a second-story hotel suite at the Mansion, a lean, dark man read the article. Slowly he lowered the newspaper, his eyes narrowed to mere slits.

"I hope the white bastards are happy," he said thinly.

"I am sorry, son," a gray-haired man offered, shaking his head.

The dark man didn't reply. Carefully he tore the article from the paper and folded it neatly, then put it into his breast pocket. Rising from his chair, he sighed heavily as he went to the open window. His cold, black eyes swept over the city. Carriages and buggies and mounted cowboys crowded the unpaved streets below. Music and laughter floated up from the numerous saloons and dance halls. At the edge of the city, train whistles blew as steam engines chugged into town pulling cargo and passengers. Everywhere was noise, shouting, hustle, and bustle.

The dark man released the curtain and said without emotion, "Perhaps Satanta is finally free. The world he knew is no more."

"Austin, may I ask a big favor?" Suzette sat brushing her long hair in their suite at the newly opened Hotel El Paso.

Austin, boots and shirt off, sat sipping bourbon, watching his young wife with unabashed enjoyment. "Darlin', when I see you sitting there in that thin chemise with all that golden hair tumbling down around your shoulders, you could ask for just about anything and get it."

Suzette lowered her hairbrush and turned to look at him. "Remember what fun we had at the casino in Saratoga?" Her big eyes flashed as she spoke.

"I shall never forget, my sweet."

"Well, they have casinos in Fort Worth, don't they?"

Austin chuckled. "Honey, I'm not sure you'd call them casinos, but there's plenty of gambling in Fort Worth. There's gambling in the saloons in Jacksboro."

"Really, Austin? You can gamble in Jacksboro?"

"Sweetheart, wherever there's money, there's gambling. The federal payroll to the troops at Fort Richardson pumps money into town, just as the cattlemen paying their hands brings in money. Why, our little home town is one of the liveliest in all Texas. The famous and beautiful Lottie Deno used to run a faro layout right in Jacksboro."

"Who is Lottie Deno?"

Austin pulled a cigar from a wooden box and lit it. "Lottie is a professional lady gambler. She's cultured and beautiful and highly intelligent. She's had more men in love with her than most women meet in a lifetime. Doc Holiday has been mad about Lottie for years and she won't give him a tumble."

"*The* Doc Holiday? Has he ever been to Jacksboro?"

Drawing on his cigar, Austin grinned. "He followed Lottie to town and he stayed until she left a few months ago."

"Why have you never told me this before, Austin Brand?" Suzette rose from the stool and her hands went to her hips, the hairbrush still in her hand.

Austin laughed. "Why, because you were a proper young lady and I sure didn't think you'd be interested in the adventures of soiled doves and outlaws. Come here." He put out his hand and pulled her onto his lap.

Tossing the loose hair back from her face, Suzette scolded, "You're teasing me, Austin. You know very well I'm dying to know about such things! Did Lottie wear red satin dresses and mesh stockings and... I'm getting off the subject. What I wanted to ask you is" — she began to flirt with her husband, letting her hand run over the curling hair on his broad chest while she smiled at him — "could we please gamble after dinner?"

"I shall have to think it over. Perhaps a sweet kiss would help to persuade me." He grinned and laid his head back against the tall, padded chair.

Suzette giggled and put her hands on the sides of his head, raking her fingers through his hair. Happily, she pressed her lips to his, then pulled back to look at him. "Well?" She raised an eyebrow.

"Still not sure," he kidded.

She immediately leaned to him, kissing him passionately, her parted lips moving intimately on his, the way he'd taught her. Austin's big arms came around her and he held her close and kissed her back with eagerness and fire. When finally she sighed into his mouth and reluctantly lifted her head, her face was warm, her eyes dreamy. "Well?" she asked shakily.

Austin sighed, too, and twisted a long blond curl around his finger. "You may gamble till dawn if you desire."

"Good." She smiled and snuggled close to his warm chest. "Will we gamble when we get home to Jacksboro?"

"Sweetheart, I love you and I'd like always to give you anything you want, but I must forbid you from going into the saloons back home, even in my company. Ladies never go there, and my wife must be the grandest lady in town. Don't fret, I'll take you on enough trips to let you do all the gambling you can handle." He kissed her neck. "Besides, Mrs. Brand, I'm shocked. It's you who never misses church on Sunday. Don't you think the congregation would be surprised to hear you'd been seen turning the cards with a bunch of drunken cowboys?"

"Austin" — she sat up and looked dismayed, — "you won't tell anyone, will you?"

Laughing softly, he raised a hand to her velvety cheek. "Darlin', your secret vice is safe with me. I'm the soul of propriety. Now, get dressed and I'll take you to dinner." She was off his lap like a bolt of lightning, rushing across the room to finish getting ready.

After dinner Suzette held Austin's hand as he led her into the Peers House. His face twitched with amusement when Suzette saw that the waiters were scantily clad females. She gaped at the women and turned to look at him. "Austin, they're..." She saw the mischief in his gray eyes and was determined to undermine his merriment. Knowing he was waiting for her to exclaim her shock, she raised her chin haughtily, but she couldn't help sneaking looks at the painted, well-endowed women with their daringly low bodices and shockingly short skirts, displaying sheer stockinged legs.

"Shall we go directly to the roulette table?" she said in what she hoped was a flat, even voice.

"That's what we came for, isn't it?" he replied, his eyes twinkling.

Suzette started laughing. Austin laughed with her and put a long arm about her. She stood on tiptoes, holding his lapel. In his ear she whispered truthfully, "I've never seen ladies so near naked in a public place."

"Darlin', I rather doubt that they're ladies." Suzette shook her head in agreement when she saw a cowboy reach out and loop a long arm around one of the women. He hauled her up against his chest and slapped her bottom soundly. Showing absolutely no outrage at his behavior, the pretty woman laughed and made no effort to escape his grasp.

Suzette was still looking over her shoulder when Austin propelled her to one of the green-felt-covered tables and bought her a tall stack of chips. She happily took a seat in front of the oblong table, carefully arranging her long blue taffeta gown about her. Austin, a well-shod foot on the lower rung of her stool, stood behind her, waving away her suggestions that he play. "I'd rather watch you." He smiled and meant it.

Above them, on the second-story landing, someone else

was watching. A tall, dark young man stood, a booted foot on the lower rung of the ornately carved banister, quietly studying the beautiful golden-haired girl at the roulette table beneath him. Suzette laughed and tossed her head about, delighted with the game and with her luck, which was good.

From his vantage point above her, the cold, handsome man was offered a tempting view of the young woman. She was all soft and feminine and curvaceous, her golden hair shining under the gaslights, the milky skin of her throat, shoulders, and bosom gleaming above the low-cut dress.

The dark man's gaze never left the unsuspecting Suzette. She continued to gamble and win. Her laughter floated above the shouts of the gamblers and the sound of the player piano. At odd moments he could hear her sweet girlish voice speaking excitedly to her husband. Though he was devoid of expression and appeared indifferent, his dark eyes didn't miss a single move she made. Occasionally the muscles in his lean, dark jaw jumped involuntarily; nothing else about him moved.

19

While Suzette was happy to be going home, it seemed her husband had been homesick for weeks, so excited was he when the stage pulled up to the sidewalk on the Jacksboro square. The long bone-jarring trip had left Suzette and the other two passengers weary and irritable, but Austin was in high spirits when he swung down from the coach and reached for Suzette.

"I swear, Austin" — Suzette stared at him — "you're behaving like a child who's been away from his mama. You must have been longing to get home and didn't tell me."

"No, darlin', that's not it." He cupped her elbow and led her across the street to the Wichita Hotel.

"Then why are you grinning so foolishly?"

"I've a surprise for you, my dear."

"I'm not sure I'm up to one of your surprises, Austin. All I want is a hot bath and a soft bed."

"Why, love, it's a long time till sundown, and it's a perfect fall day."

"I don't care what time it is. I'm tired and I want —"

"Suzette, please. Soak awhile and then let me show you my surprise." His full mouth was lifted at the corners and his gray eyes were gleaming with excitement.

At the hotel, Suzette lifted her skirts and walked up the steps. "I can't promise. I'll have a bath, and then if I'm feeling better, I'll —"

"Yes, sweetheart. You're sure to feel better after your bath. While you relax, I'll go over to the stable and get a couple of horses."

"Oh, Lord, Austin! Don't tell me we are going for a ride. No! Absolutely not, my..." — she leaned close to his ear — "...my bottom has been punished enough in that uncomfortable coach. I can't ride today."

"Very well. You're too tired." The smile left his handsome face and Suzette was immediately sorry she'd ruined his fun.

Austin stepped in front of her and opened the door to their hotel suite. Extending his hand, he motioned her inside. The plain hotel room where they'd stayed on that first chaste night of their marriage brought back sweet, tender memories to Suzette. She'd been so frightened of Austin and he'd proved to be the most understanding man on earth, never once making a move that might upset her. She smiled as she remembered and turned to her disappointed husband.

Slipping her arms around his middle, she looked up at him and said, "Austin, darling, I'll bet a bath is all I need to revive me. See about the horses. Give me half an hour and I'll go for that ride with you."

Austin's eyes lit up. "That's my girl! You won't regret it. I'll arrange for your bath right now." His head dipped to hers and his lips brushed her mouth. Then he turned and hurried from the room.

After his departure, Suzette groaned with exhaustion. She felt as though she couldn't possibly ride a horse in her condition, but she was going to try. Apparently Austin had something to show her that meant a great deal to him and she would feign interest and enthusiasm no matter what.

The hot tub did wonders for her. By the time she mounted a big bay gelding, she was feeling much better. Austin, riding knee to knee beside her, still wore a foolish grin, and Suzette was glad she'd agree to come along.

"Will you tell me where we're going, Austin?" Suzette squinted in the bright October sun.

"Home," was his one-word response.

"Home?" Suzette laughed nervously. "Darling, are you forgetting? We have no home, unless you mean my home. Are we going there? Do you want to live there, Austin?"

"No, darlin'. I mean *our* home. Yours and mine. A home that never belonged to anyone else. Ours, no one else's."

"You're being mysterious, Austin. Please explain yourself. How can we have —"

"No more questions." He cut her off. "How are you feeling?"

She shrugged. "I'm no longer tired. You've successfully aroused my curiosity."

"Good. Then let's ride." He laughed and dug his heels into his mount's belly, looking back over his shoulder at Suzette.

She shouted and raced to catch up. They galloped across the open prairie and Suzette soon realized Austin was heading toward his ranch headquarters. She figured he intended to show her the big bunkhouse he'd built for all his hands. He'd never shown it to her, though it had been there three or four years. Perhaps he meant for them to live there. She shuddered at the thought, but caught herself. If he wanted to live in the bunkhouse, he'd get no arguments from her, and it might not be so bad. In time he'd build them a home; she was certain of that.

Suzette shook her head, tossing her hair back over her shoulders. She was enjoying the ride. There was a hint of briskness in the air, enough to put color in her cheeks and renew her energy. The trees were dressed in their blazing autumn colors and the sky overhead was an indelible blue. The quiet, lonely beauty of the land was a welcome sight, and Suzette realized that she too was very happy to be home.

Austin glanced at her occasionally, and in his expressive eyes was unspoken pleasure. Wordlessly they communicated, telling each other they were glad to be riding together, happy it was such a beautiful fall day, delighted to be back in Jack County, and overjoyed that they were man and wife. Austin's heart raced at the sight of the pretty young woman riding next to him, her glorious hair flaming in the sun, her slender, perfect body sitting her mount with ease and grace.

They were on the Brand property now, but Suzette was puzzled. They were not near the burned-out ruins of Austin's home; in fact, they were miles from that site. She was about to comment when they rode over a small rise and she saw it.

Austin pulled up on his reins and his big steed stopped immediately, nervously tossing his head about. Suzette jerked her gelding's head up so quickly that the horse reared his front feet into the air. But Suzette didn't have time for the confused bay; her eyes were on the distant horizon, as were Austin's. She stared at the huge building on the crest of the rolling hill, its beautiful lines clear in the bright sun. Tearing her eyes away, Suzette looked at her husband.

Austin was grinning. He loved the look of shock on her beautiful face and sat calmly waiting for her to question him. She looked from him back to the big house. She closed her eyes and opened them; the house was still there. Again she looked at her beaming husband. "Austin..."

"Yes, my love. Our home. I built it just for you."

"But... how... I don't... Austin... when... I..."

"Come, sweet one, let's go home."

They cantered up the rise to the magnificent house. Suzette's eyes never left the shining white mansion. As Austin lifted her from her horse, she kept repeating, "It's beautiful... it's so beautiful."

Austin, chest swelling with pride, stood with his arm around his wife as they viewed their new home. It was a large, eye-pleasing, two-story dwelling with a wide gallery across the front. Small balconies graced the second-floor windows. There was a strong, solid, elegant look about the mansion — just like the man who had it built.

Austin swept his bride into his arms and started across what in time would be a lovely landscaped yard. Suzette giggled and looped her arms around his neck as he said, "I'll carry you over the threshold, my wife." He hurried up the steps onto the broad porch and with a booted foot eased the heavy double doors open. She stared in awe at the high-ceilinged, pine-paneled entry hall with its wine velvet causeuse sitting alone beneath an absolutely magnificent chandelier. A huge Palladian-style window flooded the upper hall with bright fall sunlight.

Suzette was looking at the grandeur of the chandelier when Austin whisked her into the large drawing room. A luxurious Aubusson rug in muted tones of gray and dark blue accentuated a gray marble fireplace and the gray velvet upholstered furniture.

Before she could catch her breath, Austin carried her into the spacious dining room. A polished cherrywood table was long enough to seat thirty people easily. The high-backed chairs were upholstered in blue velvet, and a Hepplewhite butler's sideboard sat under a framed mirror that stretched the length of the room and was six feet high, now reflecting the happy faces of its owners.

Austin dashed back into the foyer and up the carpeted stairs. He strode down the wide hall and into what looked like the master bedroom as Suzette planted kisses all over his smiling face, saying over and over, "Austin, I love it! I love it!" Huge and airy, the room was filled with heavy furniture and its colors were dark and rich. The walls were elaborately paneled in Circassian walnut, the fireplace was of black marble, the furniture was all mahogany, and the upholstery was a deep brown leather. An entire wall had been given over to tall bookcases of brass and leather. It was a masculine room, strictly a man's domain, and Suzette felt just a twinge of disappointment.

It soon disappeared. Austin crossed the room and opened a huge mahogany door. Beyond it was the most beautiful, feminine room Suzette had ever seen. It was clearly meant for an adored lady. As large as the other room, its walls were of sky-blue watered silk. A four-poster bed was canopied in the same lovely fabric, and on the big soft bed, a luxurious spread of blue silk had been quilted in a delicate pattern with gold thread. A blue velvet sofa faced the white marble fireplace. Two blue brocade boudoir chairs flanked the sofa. On one side of the fireplace, tall white doors gave onto a private balcony; on the other side, a Jacobean oak desk, inlaid with ivory and mother-of-pearl, invited Suzette to sit down and write notes on the blue parchment paper nested in a gold-and-pearl box.

In one corner of the room, a full-length cheval glass in a gilt frame reflected a man and woman laughing in front of the big bed. The reflection changed as the girl pulled the man's face to hers and kissed him happily and affectionately.

When Suzette lifted her head, she said breathlessly, "Austin, I cannot believe all of this! How, darling? When? It's out of this world! Is it really ours?"

Pleased with her reaction, he nodded. "All ours, love. As to how, I told you once that when you've enough money, anything is possible. I had the plans drawn up long before we got married. When you agreed to be my wife, I put all my plans in motion. You really like it?"

"Like it? I've never seen anything to compare! It's a palace, a place fit for royalty, it's —"

"To me, my sweet Suzette, you are a queen. Come, I've

lots more to show you." Austin started toward the door.

"Wait, Austin," she said.

"What is it?"

"Dear" — she lowered her voice and cast a glance at the canopied bed — "is there . . . do the beds have linens on them yet?"

Austin swung around. "Nice new blue silk sheets, honey."

Smiling, she put her lips to his ear and whispered. Austin's gray eyes widened, then closed as he kissed her. "By all means," he assured her as he picked her up and carried her to the bed.

He swept back the covers while she undressed. They got into the big bed just as the dazzling fall sun was setting. The room and its occupants were bathed in a honeyed orange light as the perfect autumn day drew to a close. Austin leaned over his beautiful wife and put a big hand into the golden hair that fanned out on the blue silk pillow.

"Darlin', do you like your new home?" he asked huskily.

Suzette raised a slender hand and caressed the thick curly hair at the nape of Austin's neck. "No. I *love* my new home, Austin! It's the most magnificent mansion I have ever seen, and I can hardly wait to throw a big party so we can show it to everyone. Can we do that soon? Oh, they'll all be envious, I know. Do you think I'm terrible? It's just that I never dreamed I'd ever live in such a grand place and I want everyone to —"

"Sweetheart," he interrupted.

"Yes?"

"Have you forgotten what you whispered to me a few minutes ago?"

Suzette smiled and sighed. "Come here," she whispered as she pulled his mouth down to hers. She wrapped her arms around her husband's back and kissed him with abandon.

The sun had long since disappeared when the couple finally roused themselves from the bed, hunger prompting their return to Jacksboro and the dining room of the Wichita Hotel.

Jacksboro had changed in the nine months the Brands had been away. Fort Richardson was at last abandoned since the Indians no longer posed any threat. All the tribes were now living on the reservation, starved off the plains they loved, as the buffalo, their livelihood, quickly became extinct.

For settlers everywhere this came as good news; they no longer feared being scalped by the bloodthirsty red men. In Jack County, the citizens were almost as glad to see the blue-coated soldiers depart as they were to be free of the Indians. But the merchants felt differently. Never again would the little town prosper as it had when the post was occupied. The generous flow of money abruptly dried up and saloon after saloon closed its doors.

The once bustling fort saw the flag hauled down, the last load of supplies roll out, moving to a fort farther west, and the last uniformed soldier disappear over the horizon. The buildings reverted back to the original owner. Never again would a rousing reveille spur young men into action. The post cemetery held the only soldiers that remained where once men marched each day on parade. All was now quiet.

The soldiers were not the only ones leaving Jacksboro. Fewer and fewer cowboys rode the range, as more cattle were shipped to the markets in the east; the railroad that had finally reached Fort Worth provided a faster, cheaper way of transporting cattle than the long, hard trail drive.

With the disappearance of the soldiers and the thinning out of the cowpokes, Jacksboro attracted fewer drifters and gamblers. The men who lived by a turn of the card and their wits moved on to greener pastures and towns more suited to their profession.

Austin Brand was delighted with the changes. Jacksboro would now be a safer place for his wife. Still, he took all precautions, refusing to let her be alone, either in their huge mansion or on the streets of Jacksboro.

"Suzette, my dear," he cautioned her shortly after they moved into the new house, "although I will no longer be away on trail drives and cow hunts, there will be times I can't be with you. I've put together an excellent staff to live at the mansion with us. You will never be alone again. When you want to go out, you will always have an escort."

"Austin, don't you think you're overdoing it just a bit?" Suzette frowned. "I know you want what's best for me, but there are times when I need privacy."

Austin smiled. "Yes, darlin', and you shall have all the privacy you desire upstairs in our suite. No one will enter without your invitation."

"That's not exactly what I mean, Austin."

"Then what?"

"If I feel like riding over to see Anna and the children, I certainly do not intend to alert half the ranch!"

They were standing in front of the gray marble fireplace in the large drawing room. Austin took a step closer and grabbed Suzette's shoulders with his big hands. A muscle was working in his strong jaw and his gray eyes were steely. "Listen to me, Suzette Brand. I'm telling you that you are not to leave this house alone. Is that clear?"

"Austin, you're hurting my shoulders," Suzette protested.

Austin tightened his grip and lifted her to her toes. "I said, do you understand that you're never to leave this house alone? Answer me!"

"Yes! Let me go!" Her eyes flashed with anger.

"That's better." Austin released her and smiled. "Darlin', it's for your own good. Don't be cross with me. Grab a wrap and come with me. I'll introduce you to some of my men."

Suzette glared at him, then mumbled, "I'm going upstairs to my room. Please excuse me." She flounced past him and out of the room. Austin made no move to stop her, but stormed from the house. Suzette jumped when he banged the heavy front door shut behind him.

In her beautiful blue bedroom, Suzette pouted and paced the floor. It was the first misunderstanding she and Austin had had and she felt miserable. She blamed him for the disagreement; after all, she was no child he could order around. He was selfish and unfair if he thought he could dictate to her. She would come and go as she pleased — and without some watchdog trailing at her heels. Austin Brand had a lot to learn!

An hour had passed since her argument with Austin and Suzette was growing bored. She wondered if he was downstairs and what he was doing. She took a deep breath and opened her bedroom door. In the hall she paused and listened, but she heard nothing. Lifting her skirts, she descended the stairs. In the paneled foyer, the housekeeper, a sweet-faced middle-aged woman whom Austin had brought from Fort Worth, was polishing the fine wood, humming tunelessly. She looked up when she saw Suzette and smiled warmly.

"Mrs. Brand, will you be wanting your lunch soon? I told Dorothy and Louise I'd only help out with the dusting until it was time to fix your meal." In the week Suzette and Austin had lived at the mansion, Kate and her two helpers, Dorothy and Louise, had needed little instruction. Intelligent and dependable, Kate knew how to run a big home efficiently, and Suzette was grateful to have her. The three servants had private quarters on the ground floor of the house and were so quiet and respectful Suzette hardly knew they were around.

"Kate, I'll wait to have my lunch with Mr. Brand." Suzette started into the drawing room.

"Oh, ma'am, Mr. Brand told me he won't be eating lunch at home today."

Suzette bit her lip. "I see. Very well, I'll have a tray in my room in an hour." Furious that he hadn't told her he would not be at home for lunch, Suzette went back up the stairs. She spent the afternoon alone, growing more contrite with each passing hour. By the time she heard Austin's deep voice downstairs, she was so glad he was home she flew down the stairs and straight into his arms. "Austin, please don't be angry with me. I'm sorry about this morning."

Austin cupped her chin in his hand. "Sweetheart, I'm not angry. I love you so very much and you must understand that if I seem overly protective, it's only because you are so precious to me."

"I know, really I do. I can be terribly bull-headed."

Laughing, Austin kissed her nose, then said, "That you are, my dear. You're also terribly cute. Could I interest you in dinner by the fire in my bedroom?"

Suzette grinned and hugged him. "Shall I dress for the occasion?"

"The decision is yours. Dressed or undressed, you're welcome at my table."

At breakfast the next morning, Austin told Suzette he wanted to take her by the stables and bunkhouse to meet some of the men. Yawning sleepily, Suzette nodded and took a sip of coffee. She pulled the lapels of her robe together and pushed her long hair out of her eyes. Slowly, she raised her eyes to her husband's.

"What's funny?" she murmured.

Austin touched her cheek. "Nothing, darlin'. It's just that you are so adorable. Eat your breakfast and I'll bring the horses around. I'll come upstairs for you in a half hour." He rose, then leaned down and kissed the top of her head.

Suzette was in her room preparing to dress when Austin knocked at her door. "Come in, Austin," she called.

He stepped inside and closed the door, then leaned against it. Suzette stood near her bed, buttoning a white blouse. A pair of buckskin trousers lay across the bed. She smiled at her husband and picked up her leather pants. Before she could put a foot into them, he moved swiftly across the room and grabbed the trousers from her hand. "My God! You don't think you're going to wear these do you?" He held up the buckskins accusingly.

"I most certainly do," she declared, reaching for them.

His gray eyes narrowed as he jerked the pants out of her reach and strode to the fireplace. He tossed the pants into the flames and turned back to look at her.

Shocked, Suzette could only stare at him. Then anger got

.the better of her and she shouted, "You had no right to do that! Damn you, Austin Brand! Damn you! Damn you!"

She trembled when he stormed across the room and grabbed her arm. "Don't swear, Suzette! I won't have it! And I won't have you going about in tight trousers either."

"I will damned well wear pants any time I choose!" she yelled at him.

"You'll wear what I tell you to wear!" he raged as he dragged her to her dressing room. His fingers pinched the flesh of her upper arm as he pinned her to his side and looked through the gowns and dresses arranged neatly by color. He chose a modest dark wool dress, then marched her back into the bedroom. Suzette, uneasy and afraid to irritate him further, looked warily at him when he sat down on her bed and pulled her to him and held her between his knees.

Suzette trembled with fury and fear; the white blouse she wore stretched tautly across her heaving breasts. Gooseflesh prickled on her arms and legs. Now Austin was unbuttoning her blouse, pulling it off. But when he looked into her hurt, frightened eyes, his rage suddenly subsided. Dropping the clothes to the floor, he sighed. "Suzette, dear, I'm sorry."

"Austin, have you not seen me in trousers many times?" she replied coldly.

"Yes, of course I have," he admitted.

"Then how could you act so... so beastly about it? What have I done? How can you be so mean to me?" Tears were starting at the corners of her eyes.

"Oh, my love, forgive me," he said and pulled her down onto his knee. "Sweetheart, let me explain. You see, I'm going to take you out to meet my men and... Suzette, those trousers show too much of you. They aren't modest. I don't want the cowboys to see my wife like that."

"If you thought the trousers immodest, why didn't you tell me long ago?" She rubbed her eyes with the back of her hand.

Austin handed her a handkerchief. "Darlin', you never wore them to town. The only time you had them on was at home. I was the only one who saw you in them, so I didn't mind. In fact, I enjoyed it."

Sniffling, she said, "Still, that was no reason to throw them in the fire. You frightened me, Austin. I thought you were going to strike me."

"Baby girl, I'd never raise a hand to you. You must know that. I'm sorry I lost my temper and burned the pants. I'll buy you new ones to wear at home. Will you forgive me?"

"I suppose, but —"

"Darlin'," he murmured against her neck, "I love you so much. You're so temptingly lovely. You've no idea what you do to a man. You don't have to wear the dress I chose. Pick any one you want and I'll wait while you change."

"This one is fine," she said as she rose. "Let me wash my face and put on some shoes."

Suzette was still upset when Austin led her into the bunkhouse near the stables, but she put on her most winning smile and the hands she met thought her charming and beautiful.

"Darlin'," Austin proudly introduced her, "this is Tom Capps, my foreman and trail boss on the drives."

"Ma'am." Tom Capps wiped his hand on his shirtfront, then extended it to Suzette. "I'm mighty pleased to make your acquaintance."

"I'm happy to meet you, Mr. Capps. My husband has spoken of you often. I understand you were quite a hero in the war."

Tom ducked his head and shuffled his feet. "Well, now, I wouldn't say —"

"He most certainly was," Austin interrupted. "But for Tom, I wouldn't be here this morning." Austin clasped Tom's shoulder and grinned. "Suzette, this man saved my life, but he's so modest he hates for me to mention it."

Tom's face reddened, but he smiled shyly. "Mr. Capps," Suzette said sincerely, "I am grateful to you. You must come up to the house soon and have dinner with us."

"Thanks, ma'am, I'll do it."

"Darlin'," Austin guided her to a square table where four men sat drinking coffee. All of them stood up as Suzette stepped up to them. "Say hello to Randy Lancaster, Bob Coleman, Red Wilson, and Zeke Worth."

Four heads bobbed and the men all smiled at Suzette, murmuring, "Mrs. Brand."

"Nice to meet you, gentlemen." Suzette looked at each man. Randy Lancaster and Bob Coleman were ill at ease and stood stiffly, hands at their sides, grinning foolishly. Zeke Worth, a man well into his sixties, bowed grandly and said, "How lovely you are, Mrs. Brand."

Before she could thank him, young Red Wilson, a lean, good-looking drover with curly red hair, eyed Suzette boldly and extended his hand. He shook her hand firmly, all the while looking directly into her eyes. "Zeke's right," Red agreed. "You're about the prettiest little thing I ever did see!"

For an awkward moment, Suzette tried to pull her hand from the man's powerful grip. "You'll turn her head," Austin said calmly and drew her away from the table. Suzette looked up at Austin and saw the possessive look in his gray eyes and hoped the young cowboy hadn't made him angry.

Near the door of the bunkhouse, old Nate sat whittling in a straight-backed chair. He rose when he saw Suzette and she rushed to him and hugged him. "Nate, how are you? It's been so long."

"Honey, I'm so glad you're married to Mr. Brand. I worried about you being over there by yourself. How was your trip up north?"

"Nate, it was wonderful." She stepped back and put her arm through Austin's. "My husband is spoiling me, I'm afraid. I never knew life could be so pleasant." She looked up affectionately at Austin.

"Well, he should spoil you." Nate winked at Austin. He looked back at Suzette and added, "He ever treats you bad, you tell old Nate. I'll set him straight."

Suzette and Austin both laughed. "I'll take good care of her, Nate." Austin assured the old man, then led Suzette out into the sunlight.

"Sweetheart, those three men over by the corral are Freddy Black, Monty Hudspeth, and Slim Hester. They're three of the best drovers in Jack County." He raised a hand and pointed. "The young kid you see currying the horse is Denis Sanders. He knows all there is to know about horses. Clyde Bonner and Jimmy Davis are my youngest cowhands, but they're already good workers."

"They all seem so nice." Suzette smiled at the men at the corral.

"They are excellent cowmen, but they are also red-blooded men with healthy appetites. Now do you understand why I didn't want you wearing those tight trousers?"

"Yes," she admitted, "you were right." She recalled the way young Red Wilson had looked at her. "Austin?"

"Yes, love?"

"Let's not fight. I can't bear to have you angry with me."

Austin cast a glance around them, then pulled her gently to him. He kissed her softly and whispered, "I could never be angry with you. I worship you, Suzette."

20

The holiday season came and Jacksboro's first couple threw a party in the new mansion. Suzette, not wanting to overlook anyone, told her husband that she wanted everyone in Jack County to attend. Ever indulgent, Austin suggested having Mr. Keach print a blanket invitation on the front page of *The Prairie Echo*.

"Austin, that's brilliant," Suzette approved. "Be sure to

add that children are welcome. And, Austin, make it clear that this party is not for couples. I want all the cowboys to come, along with as many young ladies as we can get. I think we should provide transportation for anyone who needs it. What do you think?"

Nodding appreciatively, Austin mused, "I'll get my men to help. We've several carriages, so the cowhands could pick up the young ladies or anyone who needs a ride."

Plans were put into motion and soon the town was buzzing about the party. Many people had ridden out to see the mansion being built while the couple had honeymooned. Now they could hardly wait to have a look inside.

Suzette enlisted Anna Woods's help in planning the menu and entertainment. Together the two young women busily prepared for the social event of the season. As the date drew near, farmers' and ranchers' wives sat at sewing machines and stitched new frocks. At the bunkhouse on the Brand ranch, cowhands meticulously washed and starched their best shirts, trimmed their hair, polished their boots, and looked forward to turning the pretty ladies about the dance floor.

New Year's Eve was cold and clear and by dark the mansion was aglow with lights in every room. In the big dining room, the long cherrywood table groaned under the splendid banquet. Champagne and wines were cooling in silver buckets on the sideboard, though Austin had told Suzette champagne was not the drink favored by cowboys thirsty for real liquor. He had ordered cases of good Kentucky bourbon, as eager as Suzette to cater to the wishes of the expected guests.

The expensive Aubusson rug in the drawing room had been rolled up and the oak floor was polished to a high gleam. Local fiddlers had been practicing for weeks, and Austin agreed with Suzette that although they might not be accomplished musicians, hiring an out-of-town orchestra might well hurt the feelings of the men so eager to play for the party.

Austin, handsome in a dark, vested suit, white shirt, and

silk cravat, stood at the big marble fireplace in the drawing room admiring the tasteful decorations Suzette and Anna had chosen. After taking a look at his gold pocket watch, Austin replaced it in his vest pocket and clasped his hands behind his back. He took a quiet moment to be thankful for all that he had. His home was a gracious mansion of outstanding beauty; his ranch was one of the biggest, most profitable spreads in all Texas; his health was excellent; his intellect was intact. Best of all, upstairs, fussing charmingly over her hair, Suzette Foxworth Brand was his and his alone. Of all his joys in life, she was the ultimate.

"Austin," Suzette called softly and came into the room. He looked at her and caught his breath. Her dress was of lilac velvet, the bodice tight and low, the sleeves long and fitted. Delicate lace bound her wrists and accented the low neckline. Her golden hair was parted in the middle and brushed into long curls. She was radiant. "Austin, are you feeling well?"

"You are breathtaking," he said huskily, touching the tiny gold heart at her throat.

Suzette lifted her hands to his chest, tilted her head up, and kissed his neck. "Thank you," she said against his clean skin. Then she promptly turned to rush into the big kitchen to check on the food, saying over her shoulder, "I'm so nervous I can't be still."

The party was all Suzette had hoped for. The mansion overflowed with guests and Suzette laughingly told Anna she had no idea so many people lived in Jack County. The ladies in their newly sewn frocks accepted Suzette's invitation to stroll throughout the house. The men, just as Austin had predicted, passed up the champagne for shots of bourbon. Children shouted and chased one another through the many rooms, and everyone ate and ate the delicious foods Kate and her staff had prepared.

Old Nate and Tom Capps were the first men to come up from the bunkhouse. Within the hour, all the Brand hands had arrived, bringing with them the many guests they'd ferried to the mansion. By nine o'clock the local fiddlers were warmed up and couples were taking to the floor. Suzette dragged Austin to the center of the room and everyone applauded when he put a long arm about her tiny waist and turned her gracefully around beneath the chandelier.

Out of breath at tune's end, Suzette laughed and clapped. Austin guided her to a tray of champagne Kate was passing about. They both took a long-stemmed glass. Austin touched his glass to Suzette's and said softly, "Your party is a success, my dear. I'm very proud to be your husband."

Before she could respond, Randy Lancaster and Bob Coleman were stammering their respective hellos and asking permission to dance with Suzette.

"You'll have to take turns," Austin kidded the two as Suzette handed Austin her glass and took Randy Lancaster's arm, propelling him to the floor. Bashful, yet charmed by her beauty, Randy held her stiffly and looked down into her dazzling eyes while Suzette chatted, determined to put the nice cowboy at ease. Bob Coleman was there to take Randy's place as soon as the last notes died away. Like his friend Randy, he was very nervous, but he enjoyed every minute of the lively dance.

Austin watched approvingly as the leathery drover held Suzette as though she were made of fine china. Over Bob's shoulder Suzette caught Austin's eye and blew him a kiss. Austin winked at her, then turned to Anna as she tugged on his sleeve.

Austin obligingly led Anna onto the floor and lost sight of Bob and Suzette as more and more couples began dancing. The next time he caught a glimpse of Suzette, his eyes narrowed. She was in the arms of young Red Wilson, the impudent cowboy from Montana. Red wasn't holding her the way Randy Lancaster and Bob Coleman had. Instead, he embraced her tightly, pressing her to him. The cowhand wore an expression that upset Austin as much as the way he was holding her. Red's green eyes were on Suzette's parted lips, desire plainly written in his gaze.

Austin scowled and stared at the spinning couple until he caught Suzette's eye. She was laughing at something Red had whispered and Austin felt the blood drain from his face. With a hard, flinty gleam in his eyes, he started through the crowd toward the swaying couple.

In a voice so low only Suzette and Red heard him, Austin said coldly, "Get your hands off my wife."

"Hey, Austin, old man, what's wrong with you?" Red Wilson slurred. "This here's a party. We're just dancin'."

"Release her, Red," Austin said icily.

"Austin, please," Suzette said nervously, looking about. "People are staring."

Red Wilson abruptly released Suzette and grinned at Austin. "She's all yours, Brand."

"She most certainly is, and don't you ever forget it!" Austin pulled Suzette into his arms and danced away.

At the edge of the dance floor, he took her hand and led her from the room. He closed the library door behind them. Before he could speak, Suzette said defensively, "If you're planning to scold me, Austin, I'm not going to listen. I've done nothing wrong and I won't apologize."

Austin, his back to her, poured a splash of brandy into a glass, tipped it up, and drank it. He turned to her. "I have no intention of blaming you for anything. Darlin', Red Wilson was taking advantage of my wife, and I refuse to hold still for it. Come here."

Eyeing him cautiously, Suzette went to him. Austin put his hands on her gleaming white shoulders and kissed her softly, teasingly. With his tongue, he traced the soft contours of her lips. Gently, he pulled her closer to him as stirrings of desire began deep in the pit of his stomach. His eyes dropped to her high, full breasts and he whispered, "I wish all the guests were gone." His eyes came back to her mouth as his hand moved down, sliding over the bare swell of her bosom, gently caressing it. When he reached the top of her velvet gown, his fingers traced the low neckline tenderly.

She drew a quick breath, her passions awakening. His big hand felt like a fiery brand on her flesh and she leaned to him, offering herself. "Austin," she said softly, "it's getting late. Already some of the guests are leaving. Within an hour, we'll be alone."

Austin smiled. "Yes, my love. I'll count the minutes." He brushed his mouth over hers, then straightened. "We must go back now."

But the party went on for hours. It seemed an eternity to Suzette. She was eager for her guests to depart, anxious to be alone with Austin in their bedroom. A warm, sensual woman, Suzette craved Austin's expert lovemaking. The bubbly champagne she'd drunk throughout the festive evening fanned the fire burning within her.

When the last guests said their good nights and stepped out into the cold, Suzette turned and smiled at Austin. He was exhausted; the party had lasted much longer than he'd anticipated. It was well past three A.M. and he'd graciously played the welcoming host throughout. Now he wanted nothing more than to go to sleep. But he saw the fire in Suzette's eyes and recalled their encounter in the library.

"Shall we?" He bowed gallantly. Suzette grinned, took his arm, and they climbed the carpeted stairs to her room. Inside, Austin unhooked his wife's dress while she held her long hair up out of the way.

"Austin, give me a few minutes." She giggled.

"Take as long as you need." Austin kissed the side of her neck.

Suzette, humming happily, went into her big dressing room. Austin undressed and got into bed to wait for her. Suzette's excitement grew as she stripped off her clothes and took a warm, soapy bath. Out of the tub, she hurriedly dried her gleaming body and dabbed expensive perfume behind her ears and between her breasts. She chose a daring nightgown of lilac lace. A thing of beauty she'd never worn, it left little to the imagination. Her cheeks reddened as she briskly brushed her long hair to a high sheen. Her heart pounding pleasantly, Suzette came into the bedroom, crawling eagerly into bed with Austin.

His arm under his head, the sheet at his waist, Austin was sound asleep. Suzette bit her lip, then whispered, "Darling. Austin." He didn't answer. Suzette slid closer, leaned over him, and kissed his lips. He turned his head and murmured sleepily, "Sweet, forgive me. I can't..."

Suzette touched the thick blond hair at his temple. "Sleep, Austin." She lay down quietly beside him.

Austin's broad chest rose and fell evenly. He was sleeping soundly. Suzette tossed and turned beside him. She wasn't the least bit sleepy. She wanted her husband, wanted the lovemaking he'd promised earlier in the evening. She was hurt that he didn't want her. He had fallen asleep knowing she was preparing herself for him. It had never happened before; he'd always wanted her and had tirelessly made love to her, no matter how late the hour.

Suzette turned away from Austin, punched at her pillow, and tried to go to sleep. It was a long time before she finally did.

21

Austin was busy improving his large herd of cattle. Although Tom Capps was a capable foreman and willing worker, Austin took pride in personally helping out at the huge ranch and he was consulted on any and all decisions. He continued to purchase surrounding ranches and farms, adding constantly to his vast holdings. He'd been hearing about barbed wire and told Tom Capps he'd check into it. Fencing his property would be to his advantage since he owned some of the best grassland in the state of Texas.

"Austin, my friend" — Tom Capps lit a hand-rolled cigarette as he sat on his mount in the southeast pasture of the ranch — "you know you're going to make enemies if you fence the range."

Austin squinted in the afternoon haze. "I know. That can't be helped, Tom. The land belongs to me. Why should I let men fatten their cattle on my pastures?"

"I'm not blaming you, Austin. I'm just telling you we'll have trouble, sure as I'm sitting here. You know damned well those worthless Taylor brothers won't hold still for it."

"It's high time that riffraff was driven out of this country. You and I both know they aren't cattlemen. I've overlooked the few steers they've stolen from me each year, just like the other ranchers. But I've never been fooled. Most of the mavericks they took up the trail had altered brands on their rumps. Fencing my land will solve that problem."

"Fences can be cut, Austin," Tom mused thoughtfully.

"And trespassers can be shot," Austin replied evenly and spurred his horse gently toward home.

On a lovely spring morning, Suzette was full of energy. She rushed down the stairs and into the dining room in her nightclothes, eager to catch Austin before he left the house. He sat at the head of the table, drinking coffee and reading some papers. He looked up when Suzette floated through the door.

"Morning, darlin'." He caressed her with his eyes. "You're up mighty early, aren't you?"

"Am I?" she responded cheerfully as she came to his chair. She put a hand on his shoulder and leaned down to kiss him. Austin put a big hand on her bottom, gently stroking her through the satin of her robe.

When Suzette straightened, she said hopefully, "Austin, darling, it's such a lovely day. I was thinking, wouldn't it be nice if the two of us went riding together, just you and me? I could have Kate pack a nice picnic lunch and we could ride over to Lost Creek and —"

"Sorry, Suzette. I'm afraid not today."

Disappointed, she asked, "Why not? I wanted to..."

Austin grinned and pulled her down onto his lap. Wrapping his arms around her, he nuzzled his face in the curve of her shoulder. "Sweetheart, I'd like nothing better than to spend my whole day with you. Unfortunately, I've an appointment in Jacksboro that I must keep."

Unconvinced, Suzette played with the fingers at her waist. "Couldn't it wait until tomorrow? I so wanted to spend the day with you."

"Honey, I'm flattered. I wish I could change my plans, but it's impossible. I'm to meet a man to discuss purchasing enough of that new barbed wire to fence our property. I'm doing it for us, Suzette. For you and me and our children, should we have any."

At the mention of children, Suzette's frown disappeared and she smiled. She put her arm around her husband's neck and kissed his temple. "Austin, would you like to have a family?"

Austin chuckled. "Darlin', I'm just as happy without any children. I just meant, should we have some... that sort of thing happens even if you don't plan it."

"You don't want children?"

"I didn't say that. Let me make myself clear. I love you completely; I need no one else in my world. However, if you want a child, I'll see what I can do to help you out." He grinned and kissed her neck.

"Austin, I would like a baby. I'd like that very much. Anna's children are so sweet and pretty. I want my own children. I want to be a mother. Think how it would be to have a little boy like Josh." She sounded wistful.

"Suzette, if you're planning on becoming a mother, then you'd best hop over there and eat some breakfast. I want you to be strong and healthy when you conceive."

"Yes!" she happily agreed. She got up and filled a plate from covered silver dishes on the sideboard. When she came back to the table, Austin laughed good-naturedly. Smiling, she said, "Austin, since you can't be with me today, I'm going to ride over to Anna's."

"Fine, Suzette. Tell Nate he's to go with you."

"No!" she protested. "Please, Austin. I want to ride alone, to enjoy the beauty of the day, to — "

Rising, Austin pushed back his chair. "Nate or one of the men will ride with you, Suzette, or you'll remain at home. I have to go." He kissed the top of her head and left the room.

Suzette threw down her fork and folded her arms over her chest. "No, I will not remain at home, and I refuse to have anyone tag along with me!" She pushed her plate away and left the table.

Austin and Tom Capps met with the drummer selling barbed wire. They used Austin's office at the *Echo*, and by the time the meeting had ended, they had settled on the amount, price, and delivery date. The salesman was ecstatic; though he was shocked to learn that one man owned so much land, he was delighted that Austin intended to fence it all. Hundreds of miles of the new wire would be needed, and the salesman would make a healthy commission.

After the meeting, Austin and Tom took the gentleman to lunch at the Wichita Hotel. It was afternoon when they walked across the street to the Longhorn to have a couple of drinks before returning to the ranch. They stood at the long, crowded bar, drinking quietly, when a man at one of the green-felt-covered tables called to Austin.

"Mr. Brand," Carl Taylor said in a loud voice, "can we deal you in for a hand of poker?" Carl's older brother, his left arm useless from a shooting years before, sat coolly eyeing Austin and his ranch foreman. Norman Taylor, five years older than his brother, was the quiet one; he was also the deadly one. Though his left arm hung limp, he was formidable and was feared by every law-abiding citizen in the county. Folks knew the Taylor brothers stole cattle; they also knew the Taylor brothers were a pair of the meanest men in Texas. To cross either of them was asking for real bad trouble.

Austin slowly turned to face the table of poker players. He smiled and said in a flat voice, "Thanks, Taylor, I don't gamble."

Eyes narrowing, Norman Taylor said coldly, "Fence the range and you'll be gambling with your life." His brother, Carl, laughed, as did the three card players seated at the table.

Austin's gaze was steady. "You'll find the odds are in my favor, Taylor. Any man who interferes will risk more than being left with another withered limb."

Carl Taylor rose from his chair. His older brother shoved him back into it. "Damn you, Austin Brand!" Norman Taylor said bitterly. "Do you think you own the open range?" His face was red, and his dark eyes flashed with hate.

Austin poured himself a shot of whiskey and tossed it down, then nodded to Tom Capps. Tom started for the door, while Austin sauntered to the table where the Taylor brothers sat staring at him. He placed a big hand on the backs of both their chairs and leaned over between them. "Gentlemen, I sure don't own the entire range." He smiled warmly at first one, then the other. "I just own five hundred thousand acres of it, and I damned well intend to fence it."

He straightened, turned, and strolled casually from the saloon, while behind him Norman Taylor, absently rubbing his lifeless arm, said under his breath, "That bastard can't keep us off the range. He'll leave gates or we'll cut some!"

It was mid-morning when Suzette walked to the stables. Denis Sanders was in the tack room polishing saddles. Old Nate, dozing in the sun, sat with arms crossed over his stomach, hat pulled low over his eyes. No one else was around. Suzette was delighted. Apparently Austin and Tom were in town. The other cowboys were all off doing various chores. Carefully tiptoeing past the sleeping Nate, Suzette smiled at the shy young wrangler. "Morning, Denis."

Denis's head snapped up and he got to his feet. "Ma'am." He bowed.

"Will you please saddle a horse for me, Denis?" Suzette said it matter-of-factly. "I'm going to ride over to see a friend."

Denis's slim face worked itself into a frown. "Well, ma'am, I'm terribly sorry, but I'm under orders to ... that is ... unless Nate or Tom tells me to, I'm not supposed to bring around a horse for you."

Suzette's temper flared. Her hands went to her hips. "Denis, I'm your employer, just as Mr. Brand is, and I'm asking you to saddle me a horse."

"I know, ma'am, but I can't do it. Mr. Brand, he'll have my head if I let you —"

"Never mind, Denis. I'll do it myself. I'm going for a ride and I'm going alone." She started for the barn.

Shaking his head, Denis said, "Now wait a minute. I ... I'll saddle a horse. I just hope Mr. Brand doesn't get too angry."

Suzette smiled. "Denis, don't worry. I can handle Mr. Brand. I'll ride Dancer. And, Denis, thanks."

"Yes, ma'am." The lanky boy nodded and went to carry out her wishes.

It was glorious to ride alone over the rolling prairie. Suzette galloped Dancer and loved the feel of the wind tossing her hair about her face. Wildflowers covered the hills and the air was sweet with their perfume. She felt wonderfully alive and free. And happy. She smiled to herself thinking of her conversation with Austin at the breakfast table. How delightful it would be to have a son of her own. He'd be certain to be big and healthy and blond. And handsome. With a son, perhaps Austin would stop treating her like a child.

On such a lovely day, with such pleasant things as babies to think about, it was easy for Suzette to forget that her husband had so stubbornly forbidden her to ride alone. He was over-protective, foolishly so. He'd not be angry with her since nothing was going to happen to her. She would ride straight to Anna's, spend the day, and return home in the late afternoon.

Austin would probably never know; if he did, she could easily jolly him out of his anger.

The visit with Anna was fun. The two women packed a lunch and took Josh and Sunny out into the backyard. Anna spread a quilt under a gnarled elm. Six-year-old Josh came running across the yard, expressing his desire to eat. His little sister, Sunny, a chubby four-year-old, reached for a handful of potato salad before Anna could stop her.

"Will you look at that?" Anna grabbed the pudgy little hand before Sunny could get it up to her mouth. "You know better than that, Sunny Marie!"

"Hungry, Mommy," Sunny explained, her chestnut curls dancing about her fair little face.

Josh, on his knees beside Sunny, laughed and stooped to kiss her. Catching her cheeks in both his hands, he planted a kiss on her brow while she grimaced and slapped at him.

"Josh Woods, will you leave your sister alone," Anna pleaded.

"Sure, Mother." Josh shook his dark head and picked up a piece of chocolate cake. He had it half eaten before his distracted mother noticed.

"Oh, Lord, Josh! You know you can't have dessert first." Anna cast a helpless glance at Suzette.

Suzette laughed and grabbed Josh around the waist, pulling him down beside her. She kissed his bare back and said, "How about a piece of fried chicken, Josh?"

"Okay." He nodded, trying to twist from her embrace.

Sunny was soon asleep on the quilt. She lay on her stomach, a fist jammed into her open mouth. Josh was off turning somersaults on the grass. Suzette, stretched out on her back, told Anna that she hoped to get pregnant soon.

Anna, crossed-legged beside her sleeping daughter, affectionately stroked the downy-soft chestnut hair of Sunny's head. Lazily, she replied, "That's great, Suzette. You'll make a good mother. I complain a lot about these two, but they're worth every minute of it."

"I know that." Suzette put an arm across her brow to shade

her eyes. "They're both precious and I can't wait to have one of my own."

"You should. You and Austin will have a beautiful child. I'm sure Austin's dying for you to have a baby."

Suzette moved her arm from her eyes and squinted at Anna. "I'm not so sure. Sometimes I think I've taken the place of his little Jenny."

Anna stared at her friend. "What do you mean? Has Austin said he doesn't want any more children?"

"Not exactly, but he doesn't get excited over the idea of having a child either." Suzette grimaced. "He's made me his child."

"That's not fair, Suz," Anna offered. "Austin loves you, and if he doesn't want you to have a child, I'll bet it's because he doesn't want you to go through the pregnancy and delivery. He never wants you to experience any pain. That's it, I'm sure."

Suzette sat up. "Could be. You know, Anna, sometimes he's too... Austin's so protective. He overdoes it. I'm treated like a helpless infant. I don't —"

"Listen, Suzette, you are a fool if you don't know how lucky you are. Austin Brand is one of the most handsome and remarkable men a woman could ever hope to have. If you're not in love with him, you're the only female he's ever met who isn't. Maybe that's why he's so in love with you. Every other woman he's ever come across would have given anything to find favor with him. Not you. You made him wait for years before you finally gave in."

"Anna, what are you going on about? I didn't make Austin wait, I never even —"

"I know. You never thought of him that way." Anna laughed. "Perry and I used to speculate on how long it would be before the charming Mr. Brand possessed you."

Suzette didn't think it was amusing. "Anna, no one possesses me! Austin made me his wife knowing I was not in love with him. He's a good husband. I'm very grateful to him and I try to be a good wife to him. I'm certainly aware that he's charming, handsome, and rich. I don't need you to preach to me about how lucky I am."

"Calm down, Suzette. *Possess* was a bad choice of words. And I didn't mean to preach, honest. It's just hard for me to understand that you are not wildly in love with Austin." Anna looked questioningly at her friend. "Do you love him, Suz?"

For along time Suzette was silent. "I don't know, Anna. I do know that I like living with him, and when he holds me... well, it's wonderful, but... but..."

Anna smiled and said, "But what? What more could you want?"

Suzette smiled. "Nothing more. Just a baby. Then I'd be happy. I want to be a mother."

The shadows were growing long when Suzette mounted the sorrel for the ride home. She and Anna had lost track of the time while Anna sat at her sewing maching making a pretty new frock for Sunny. Suzette, curled up in an easy chair, stitched delicate lace on the tiny yoke and gossiped with her best friend. Both women were surprised when Dr. Woods walked in to greet them.

Suzette jumped from her chair, spoke to Perry, then told Anna, "I have to get home. Austin will be worried."

She felt tense as she neck-reined her horse through the cottonwoods arched over the dry riverbed. She came out of the trees and stopped abruptly, pulling up on the reins. The sorrel danced in place while Suzette, her eyes glued to a small mesa on the near western horizon, stared transfixed. A lone rider was silhouetted against the setting sun. Motionless, he sat tall and rigid in the saddle. The coal-black horse was as still as the rider. Dressed all in black, the rider had hair as black as his mount.

Suzette felt chill bumps pop out on her arms and her heart stopped. For a time, she sat looking directly at the dark rider, and he at her; he then disappeared over the rise. Suzette blinked and looked again. There was nothing — no one there. He had vanished into thin air. Had she seen a rider? Had someone really been there, or was the sun playing tricks on her? Unease overtook her, and she was suddenly very anxious to get home.

She dug her heels into the sorrel's flanks and slapped the reins from side to side. The horse sped across the prairie, almost unseating her. Cursing the sidesaddle she had learned to endure, Suzette galloped headlong across the countryside, the sorrel's long strides eating up the miles. She topped a rolling hill and her heart rose to her throat. A horse and rider blocked her path.

Suzette sighed with relief. It was not the dark horse and rider. She immediately recognized Red Wilson from the ranch and her pulse slowed to normal. Wilson reined his horse alongside.

"Mrs. Brand," he said, his green eyes sweeping over her.

"Mr. Wilson." Suzette sat motionless in the saddle and watched the cowboy dismount.

Red Wilson walked to her and took the reins from her hand. He let them trail on the ground and reached up for Suzette. By the time she realized his intentions, he had lifted her from her horse and set her on her feet in front of him. Growing alarmed, Suzette looked up at the tall man and said, "Mr. Wilson, just what do you think you're doing? I must be getting home." She tried to pull away, but Red Wilson's hands were gripping her waist.

"Suzette, I'm not going to hurt you." One of Red's hands went up to her shiny blond hair. He stroked it as though it were spun gold. "Honey, I been thinking about you ever since that party at the mansion. I keep wondering how it would be to kiss your sweet mouth."

"No, Red, don't do this." She was pushing on his hard chest, fear making the muscles in her throat tighten.

"One kiss, honey, just one." He bent his head and sought her mouth. Suzette twisted her face to the side. His mouth was on her neck, pressing burning kisses there while she struggled violently against him. Both heard the gun cock simultaneously.

Tom Capps stood a few feet away. The Colt .44 was leveled at Red Wilson's temple. "Step slowly away from her, Red."

"Look, Tom, you got it all wrong," Red pleaded, still holding Suzette. "She begged me to meet her, said being married to an old man like Brand leaves her frustrated."

"Dear God! I never said such a thing... Tom, I..." Suzette choked.

"I'm out of patience, Red. Release her, get on your horse, and get off Brand's property."

Red stepped away from Suzette. On rubbery legs she ran to Tom Capps's side. Red, his hands in the air, was backing toward his horse. "I can explain this, Tom. Hell, nothing happened."

"Mount up, Red, and get out of my sight before I kill you." Tom Capps had the gun trained on the slender cowboy.

"Jesus, Tom, this is ridiculous. What about my pay?" Red Wilson picked up the reins of his horse.

"I'll leave it with the bartender at the Longhorn tomorrow. Don't ever let me catch you on this ranch again. Now git!"

Red Wilson threw a long leg over his horse and was spurring the animal before he was settled in the saddle. The young cowhand raced across the prairie into the setting sun.

Tom Capps reholstered his gun and turned to Suzette. "Ma'am, you'd best get on home. Austin got tied up in town. He should be back any time now."

Suzette looked the old cowboy in the eye. "Tom, I hope you haven't misunderstood what you saw here."

"Stop your worrying, ma'am. I've known for some time that Red was trouble. Ever since that party he's been going on about how beautiful you are. He's careful around me, but with some of the hands, he's said too much. We're well rid of him." He smiled and helped Suzette into the saddle.

"You're a very understanding man, Tom," Suzette complimented him.

Tom walked to his waiting horse and mounted. "I hope you'll still think so when I tell you that if you don't tell your husband about this, I will."

Suzette sighed. "Do you really think it's necessary?"

"Mrs. Brand, I've never been anything but honest with your husband. I've known Austin for a lot of years and I don't mind saying that I love him like a son. In my book he's as fine a person as ever lived, and in all my days I've never seen a man love a woman the way Austin loves you. He worries for your safety all the time, and I'd say since the tragedy that took his first wife and their child, it's understandable for him to be protective. Now I know danged well you wasn't supposed to go off by yourself. I was with Austin today, but he told old Nate to make sure he rode with you if you wanted to ride. Poor Nate's scared to death Austin will fire him."

"Oh, dear, I never thought of that. It wasn't Nate's fault. I slipped away while he slept. I'll tell Austin not to blame Nate."

"That's kind of you, Mrs. Brand. We'd better get back, sun's about gone." When the pair reached the ranch, Suzette slid from her horse and handed Tom the reins.

"Thank you, Tom. When Austin gets back, tell him about Red. I'll tell him I took advantage of old Nate." She held out her hand.

Tom clasped it in his callused one. "I'll tell him. You run on now. Everything will be all right."

Suzette was upstairs in her bath when Austin returned home. When Kate saw the look on his face, she told the other two servants to remain in their rooms until she called for them. Austin took off his gloves and slapped them angrily on his thigh as he climbed the carpeted stairs. He stormed into the blue bedroom calling for his wife.

Deep in soapy water, Suzette took a breath and answered, "I'm in my bath, Austin. I'll be with you in a minute."

Before the sentence was completed, he stood in the doorway, his feet apart, his handsome features hard. Suzette's composure crumbled and she automatically sank deeper into the tub. Wordlessly he crossed the room, his spurs clanking on the tiled floor. He reached a big hand down into the bath water and grabbed Suzette's arm, hauling her to her feet. He seemed mindless of the fact that his shirt was wet all the way up past his elbow. She stood in the tub, suds glistening on her wet body, her heart thundering.

Suzette had never seen her husband so furious. She wisely chose not to argue with him. He snatched her out of the tub, lifting her up into his arms. She was crushed against the rough fabric of his shirt, his big hands cutting into the flesh of her waist and the underside of her knees. Dripping water as he went, he carried her through her bedroom, kicking the adjoining door of his room open. Stepping through it, he announced harshly, "I'm going to spank your bottom!"

"No!" She found her tongue and began to squirm. "Austin, don't! Austin!"

He marched directly to his big bed and sat down. While she struggled and screamed her outrage, Austin turned her over his lap. Her bare bottom was turned up to him; he held her in place with a strong arm across her back and shoulders. She kicked her legs and tossed her head about, sobbing loudly. Austin raised a big hand high in the air.

It never came down. His hand poised above her wet buttocks, he came to his senses just in time. He looked down at the struggling, naked girl draped over his knees and closed his eyes. "My God, Suzette," he moaned. "What have I done?" Gently, he pulled her up, and when he saw her unhappy face, he felt a gnawing pain in the pit of his stomach. "Darlin', darlin'," he murmured and sat her on his knee. "I didn't mean it, sweetheart. Please say you forgive me."

Jerking with sobs, Suzette went limp in his arms, her pride and feelings deeply wounded. "I hate you, Austin," she sobbed.

"No, Suzette, please, don't say that, don't!" He was kissing her flushed, tear-stained face, her wet eyelids, her nose, her trembling open mouth.

"You were going to whip me!" she cried.

"No, angel, I would never have done it! Never. Don't hate me, Suzette. I'm sorry." He continued to kiss and caress her and soon she was calmer, but Austin's lips continued to brush her temples and press warm kisses to her throat. Suzette felt his lips hovering above hers and she lifted a tired hand to his face. She pressed her face against the base of his neck and felt his warmth.

Against his skin she murmured, "I'm not a child, Austin. I'm a woman."

"I know, honey," he soothed as her sweetness filled his senses and heated his blood.

Suzette's hand went to the buttons of his shirt and she flipped them open one by one while his mouth continued feathering kisses over her face, searching out her lips. She responded to his ardent kiss while her hand slid inside his shirt to explore his massive chest.

Austin lifted his head and looked into her eyes, his breath becoming labored. "I love you, Suzette."

"I'm a woman, Austin." she whispered. "*Look* at me." She raised a hand to his thick hair, pushing his head down slowly. "Look at my body, Austin. I'm a woman, a woman."

Austin's passion-filled eyes swept over her and he moaned, "You're no child. You're all woman. I apologize, my darlin'. I'll do anything to make it up to you." He raised his eyes to hers.

Suzette pulled his mouth to hers and kissed him deeply. When she took her lips from his, Austin was trembling with desire. Suzette pressed her face to his heaving chest. Open-mouthed she kissed it, whispering, "I'm your wife, Austin. I want to have your baby. Give me a child, Austin. Put a child in me, please."

"Yes, love," he whispered hoarsely and very gently put her down on his bed.

A very happy Suzette Brand went to visit Anna three weeks later. Nate escorted her and Suzette put up no argument; she was kind and talkative with Nate and excited when she ran up the steps of the Woodses' home. Stooping, she picked up a crying Sunny from the front porch and kissed the unhappy little girl. "Sunny, sweetheart, what's wrong?" Suzette cooed to the pretty child.

Anna stood at the door. "She's pitching a fit because I said she has to take a nap. Suzette, you shouldn't be holding her. She's as dirty as a pig."

Anna cleaned up her crying daughter and put her to bed. Josh played outside while Anna and Suzette traded gossip over coffee. "I've been just bursting to tell you my news!" Suzette's eyes sparkled. "I think I'm pregnant!"

"Suz, that's wonderful." Anna reached across the table and patted Suzette's hand. "Are you sure?"

"No, not really, but I think so. Isn't it exciting? I hope it's a boy. Austin would like a son, I think. I believe I'll name him Andrew, or perhaps —"

"Suz, I don't want to spoil your fun, but I think I'd wait a week or two before I started worrying about a name."

"I know." Suzette laughed. "It's just that I so want a baby. I want to feel that I can..." She looked at Anna. "Keep your fingers crossed."

"I will," Anna assured her.

While Suzette and Anna visited, Austin and his men began the fencing of the ranch. Now Austin worked every day with his men, digging postholes, stretching the menacing wire mile after mile across the plains. It was hard, backbreaking work, and Austin came home each evening exhausted but pleased with their progress.

Suzette, her happy secret inside, was waiting each day when he came in. She was so loving and sweet that Austin was elated. She always had his bath waiting and she insisted on helping him strip off his dirty work clothes. She kept him company while he bathed, happy to scrub his broad back with a long-handled brush. If he was extremely weary, she would have their dinner served in his bedroom, and she listened attentively while he told her how proud he felt when he looked out over the expanse of their land, all fenced and private, the land on which they would spend the rest of their lives, the land they would pass down through the generations if they were lucky. Suzette reddened at the mention of generations and was tempted to tell Austin her good news. Deciding to wait until she was certain, she leaned over to him and kissed him on the mouth.

Austin grinned and said, "Maybe I should threaten to paddle you more often. Ever since that day you've been all a man could ask for."

Suzette smiled. "It's because you couldn't spank me that things have been wonderful. I hope you understand that."

Austin reached for her hand. "I do, Suzette. I was teasing."

The next day it was almost sundown when Austin came home. He was calling Suzette's name as soon as he stepped inside the back door.

"Mrs. Brand is in her room." Kate looked up from the pan she was stirring.

"Thanks, Kate." Austin nodded. "Hmm. something sure smells good." He hurried through the house, tossing his hat on the velvet causeuse in the hall. He took the stairs two at a time, unbuttoning his soiled shirt as he went. "Suzette, honey, I'm home," he called as he neared her door. He paused in front of the closed door, rapping loudly on it with his knuckles, a broad grin on his dirty face.

"Come in, Austin," she called softly with no enthusiasm.

The sight that greeted him startled him. She sat on her bed, her arms wrapped around her bent knees, her chin resting on her forearms. Her lovely face was pale, her beautiful eyes sad. Austin crossed the room and sat down on the edge of the bed. Tentatively sliding a hand around her waist, he said softly, "Honey, what is it? Are you sick?"

She blinked back tears. "Austin," she murmured sadly and closed her eyes.

Terrified, he reached for her, pulling her into his embrace. He held her head to his shoulder and talked quietly to her.

"What, sweet? Tell me. Tell your old husband what's happened."

"Austin, I'm so unhappy!" she cried.

He put both arms around her and rocked her back and forth. "Have I done something, darlin'? If so, I'll —"

"No." She shook her head. "It's me."

"You? Honey, you haven't done anything. Please, Suzette, tell me what's wrong." He pulled back a little so he could look at her face.

"I was so happy. I thought for sure I was pregnant." Tears clung to her thick lashes. "I found out today that I'm not. I'm not pregnant, Austin! I thought I was going to have a baby, but I'm not." She again pressed her face against his shoulder and put her arms around his neck.

Over her head, Austin Brand smiled. Relief flooded through him and he said, "Is that all? Honey, that's nothing to cry about."

Her head jerked up and she shouted at him, "How can you say that? I want a baby, Austin. I thought you did, too."

"Ah, Suzette, sweetheart, you're my baby, you're all I need."

Suzette stiffened. Twisting from his embrace, she jumped off the bed. "I am not a baby!"

Austin rose and went to her. "Darlin', I didn't mean it like that. Don't be angry."

She was backing away from him. "I am hurt. I wanted a baby so much and I —"

Austin reached for her, pulling her to him. "Shoo! Don't cry. Listen to me, Suzette. You thought you were pregnant but you're not. I understand your disappointment, honest I do. That doesn't mean you won't get pregnant. You're a strong, healthy woman and I'm sure you'll have no trouble conceiving." He kissed her hair and whispered, "We'll just have to keep trying. I'll give you a baby if that's what you want."

Suzette slowly lifted her head. "I do, Austin."

Austin smiled down at her and traced her trembling lips

with his thumb. "I love you, Suzette. We'll have a baby."

Austin did his best to keep his word. He'd have given Suzette the moon if she'd asked for it, but the only thing she wanted was a baby. Austin made love to her as often as he could, but there were occasions when it was impossible, and then he looked at her sheepishly for letting her down. More fond of him with each passing month, Suzette assured him it didn't matter. She would cover his face with kisses and purr, telling him that to sleep in his arms was loving enough, carefully hiding her own hurt.

Suzette failed to become pregnant, and Austin, sensing her despair, sought to distract her. She loved trips and he obligingly swept her off to New Orleans aboard the Alpha. Every night they spent in the Crescent city they went out on the town, dining and dancing, gambling till dawn in the exclusive clubs. When Austin had to travel to Fort Worth on business, he took Suzette along, and there, too, he let her gamble in the wild saloons, a pistol riding the small of his back beneath his custom jacket, ever alert to any danger that might befall them.

Suzette was innocently unaware that Austin had a lot on his mind, as trouble with wire cutters kept his crew constantly mending fences and rounding up strays. A law-abiding citizen, Austin eventually had to ask for help from the sheriff. Apologizing that his hands were virtually tied, the raw-boned lawman stiffened when Austin coolly informed him that if the law couldn't handle it, he and his men would.

Austin told Tom Capps to have a hand-picked crew ready to ride when the opportunity presented itself. "Tom" — Austin ran a hand behind his neck, rubbing tense muscles — "I know damned well it's that Taylor trash. Sheriff Burnet's not about to touch them. I figure a man's got a right to protect what belongs to him."

Fishing in his breast pocket for his Bull Durham, Tom nodded solemnly. "Red Wilson's thrown in with the Taylor boys. That's how they're so well acquainted with your land."

"I'm not surprised. Keep your ear to the ground, Tom. See how many men they've got. We'll settle it one of these nights."

"Austin, are you dressed yet?" Suzette came into his bedroom wearing a soft white wrapper. Her golden hair was already dressed for the party. It had been brushed to a high gleam and wound into huge golden swirls atop her head. Strands of pearls had been worked into the mass of shiny hair. Pearl earrings dangled from her small lobes. At her throat, the gold chain with the heart and small sapphire completed her jewelry. Austin, true to his word, had never given Suzette a necklace. The locket was around her neck day and night.

"Not quite," Austin called through the open door of his dressing room. "In here, darlin'."

Suzette crossed his room and leaned against the doorframe. Austin, a huge white towel wrapped around his middle, stood shaving. Smiling at her in the mirror, he said, "What time is it? Am I running late?"

"No, but I'm afraid some of the guests might arrive early. You know how it is each time we have a party."

"Well, don't fret, I'll be dressed and downstairs in fifteen minutes at the latest." He washed the lather from his face and wiped it dry with a hot towel. Tossing the towel back over the rack, he turned and came to his wife. "You look mighty pretty. I like that fancy hairdo."

"Do you?" She patted the upswept hair and went into the bedroom with him. "I'm so nervous, Austin. I do hope I haven't forgotten anything. Let's see... the orchestra from Fort Worth will be here by eight. The champagne is cooling, the cake is on the —"

"Sweetheart, everything has been done. You and Anna have done an outstanding job, and I'm sure all will go smoothly."

Suzette sighed loudly. "I can't believe that Anna and Perry are really moving. I love parties, but I'm not happy that this party is to be their farewell. I shall miss them dreadfully."

"I know you will, honey. We'll go to Fort Worth to visit them. We can't blame Anna for wanting to move closer to her family. Then, too, with two children, she and Perry have to consider schooling and such."

"I know, but I'm selfish. I want them here close to us."

"Suzette, they'll be here for another week, so let's enjoy the time left. Now scoot out of here and let me dress. And you'd best be wiggling into something yourself. Kiss me quickly and I'll see you downstairs."

Suzette smiled and stood on tiptoes. She kissed her husband lightly on the mouth and said, "Austin, do you think I'm terribly spoiled?"

Austin laughed. "God, I hope so. I've spent the last two years doing my damnedest to spoil you."

She tilted her head. "Has it really been that long?"

"Uh-huh. You're no longer my little bride. Why, I've had you too long; it's time I got rid of you and found someone new to spoil."

Suzette tightened her arms around his neck. "You wouldn't dare. Besides, where would an old man of forty-four hope to find a sweet young thing?"

Austin's gray eyes clouded and he released her. "I have to get dressed, Suzette."

"Austin, I was teasing you." She put her hand on his arm and turned him to face her again. "Darling, surely you know I was joking."

"I know." He sighed. "But I am getting old and there must be times when I seem ancient to you."

"Austin Brand, what nonsense! You will never be old. And I'm not so young anymore myself. Why, I'll be twenty-five come spring."

He gave her a wry smile. "I must get dressed, Suzette. Please excuse me."

Anna carried a tray of glasses through the kitchen door and

returned. "Suzette, it was a wonderful party. Perry and I don't know how to thank you."

Suzette, her long gown rustling behind her, put an arm around Anna's waist. They climbed the stairs together. "I'm going to miss you and Perry and the children," Suzette said sadly.

"I'll miss you, too, Suz." Anna smiled bravely. "We'll see you often. Austin does a lot of business in Fort Worth, so you'll come with him and stay with us."

"It's not the same, Anna. I'm sorry." Suzette tried to smile. "Of course I'll see you often." They were at the door of the guest room, where Perry and the children were asleep.

Anna took both Suzette's hands in hers. "You're my best friend ever, Suzette. You always will be. Thanks for letting us stay here with you for the next week. I hope Josh and Sunny won't be too much bother."

"Never. Austin and I love them both. See you tomorrow." She leaned to Anna and hugged her tightly.

" 'Night, Suz. Say good-night to Austin."

"I imagine Austin is slumbering peacefully by now," Suzette whispered and stole on down the hall to her room.

Suzette undressed in her dressing room. Her fancy hairdo, released from its pearl restraints, tumbled down over her shoulders. Too sleepy to brush it, Suzette shook her head about and padded into the blue bedroom. Austin was not in the bed. Perhaps he'd decided they'd sleep in his room. She smiled and opened the connecting door, expecting to see his blond head on the pillow. The big bed was made up. No one was in it; no one had been in it.

"Austin?" she called softly, her eyes sweeping the room.

"Yes, darlin'." Austin's deep voice came from his dressing room.

Suzette turned down the covers of the bed and kicked off her satin slippers. She crawled into the soft bed as her husband entered the room. She sat straight up. "Austin, why are you dressed like that?"

Austin calmly buttoned up a dark gray shirt. It fit snugly

across his wide shoulders and back, and tapered around his rib cage. He had on dark trousers and black boots. "I have a minor problem to take care of, Suzette. Nothing for you to worry about."

Suzette slid out of bed and stood in front of him. "Austin, it's two in the morning. Why are you behaving so strangely?"

Avoiding her eyes, Austin went for his gunbelt. He had his back to her as he buckled the belt. She flew to him, grabbing his arm, "No, please, Austin. Whatever it is, don't do this."

"Suzette, it will be all right." He took her shoulders and looked down at her, his eyes soft. "Honey, I've not wanted to upset you, but wire cutters are plaguing the ranch. I'm going to protect the place I've worked so hard to build." He dropped his hands from her and tied the holster down to his powerful thigh.

Suzette threw herself against his chest, wrapping her arms around his waist. "Please don't do it, Austin. It's too dangerous. Let the law handle it. I won't let you go, I won't."

Austin set her back and turned to the bureau. He took out his pistol and checked it. He holstered it and went for a hat. He chose a dark one, saying to her, "Don't want my blond hair making an easy target."

Terror flooded over Suzette and all at once she was keenly aware of how much Austin meant to her. She grabbed his arm and clung to it. "Austin, darling, don't go, please don't ."

Austin touched her cheek. "I have to go. Kiss me, Suzette."

She threw her arms around his neck and kissed him wildly, fiercely, willing him to stay with her. Austin slowly lifted his head and looked down at her. His big hand came to her face, tracing the high, molded cheekbone, the pert nose, the full lips, as though memorizing each dear feature. His forefinger went to the gold heart at her throat.

Abruptly he released her and walked to the bedroom door. Suzette stood rooted to the floor, tears stinging her frightened eyes. Austin paused with his hand on the doorknob. Without turning back to look at her, he said softly, "You've made me a happy man, Suzette Brand. You cannot imagine how much I love you." He opened the door and was gone.

Suzette flew to the door and fell against it, sobbing. "Austin, don't leave me. Austin!"

When Austin got to the stables, six mounted men were waiting. His favorite horse, Captain, was saddled. Austin mounted and turned the big horse to face the men. In front of him, Tom Capps, Randy Lancaster, Bob Coleman, Zeke Worth, Freddy Black, and Slim Hester sat silently awaiting his word to depart.

"Men, you're the best there are and I'm grateful to each one of you. If anyone wants to change his mind, do it now and it will never be mentioned, either by me or the other men. I needn't remind you that I've little idea how many men the wire cutters have, how well armed they are, or how well they shoot. You're risking your life if you ride tonight. It's not too late." He sat quietly, his arm draped across the horn, studying each man's face.

"You talk too much, Austin. Let's ride," Randy Lancaster said and turned his horse, digging the big-roweled spurs into his chestnut stallion.

"Hell, Yes!" Bob Coleman echoed his pal and raced to catch up.

Smiling, Austin urged Captain into a gallop and overtook the two cowboys, circling in front of them. Tom Capps, hat low over his gray hair, raced to meet Austin. Side by side they rode in silence to the west.

The tenseness of waiting gone, Austin relaxed as he and his men thundered across the gently rising plains in the cold night air. A Colt .45 swung from a gunbelt worn low around his hips. A Winchester rifle was strapped to his saddle. The powerful beast beneath him was his third weapon. Eleven hundred pounds of sleek muscle and bone, the big gray horse was as fast as a racehorse and as sensitive to the commands of his master. Sixteen hands high, Captain was one of the tallest mustangs at the Brand ranch or any other ranch. A magnificent creature, intelligent and loyal, he was prized by Austin above all the other horses in the remuda.

Captain, his head held high, his big eyes alert, moved easily across the rolling prairie, his heavy mane and tail blowing in the cold wind. Man and horse felt the exhilaration that came from traveling fast across the dark plains — two tightly coiled bodies unwinding, muscles relaxing, powerful chests expanding with deep, cold breaths, hearts accelerating from exertion and excitement. Austin didn't realize he was smiling, but he was. Next to nights in Suzette's arms, it was in the moments spent on a good horse's back, riding fast across his vast empire, that Austin felt most alive.

Austin turned to look at Tom Capps. Tom, ramrod-straight in the saddle atop his fine-looking bay, was smiling, too. He felt Austin's eyes on him and turned his head. Shouting to be heard over the wind, he said, "You damned fool, what are you grinning about?"

Austin threw back his head and laughed. "My friend, the same thing you're smiling about."

Tom nodded in understanding. "Ain't nothing like riding over the range in Texas to make a man glad to be alive."

"I know. Texas gets in a man's blood. I'd never be happy anywhere else. Tell you something, Tom: if I live to be a tired old man, or if tonight I draw my last breath, I'm gonna spend the rest of my life right here in Jack County."

Tom hollered, "I think the good Lord's gonna watch out for a man that loves Texas as much as you. And if he won't, I will." He patted the revolver on his thigh.

Austin smiled again. "Thanks for coming, Tom. I feel better with you along."

Tom cast a quick glance at Austin, then turned to look ahead. "Son, I'd ride with you into hell."

The riders came in sight of the gleaming new barbed-wire fences of the western pastures. Austin slowed Captain to a walk and headed for a stand of cottonwoods seventy-five yards from the fence. Dipping his head under a low branch, he rode into the trees and the six men followed. Under the cloak of darkness and the protection of the trees, the horses and riders were well hidden.

The wait began.

No one could guess when the wire-cutting rustlers would appear. Or even if they would appear. Austin was almost certain that they would show up. They had brazenly cut wire all over his land. Only this southwest portion had remained untouched. Austin had told no one outside the ranch of the incidents and he'd cautioned his men to keep it to themselves. He wanted the intruders to think he intended no retaliation.

For over three weeks he'd been moving almost all his cattle into the southwest pasture and he had let it be known he was doing so. He talked it up at the Longhorn Saloon, explaining he was letting all his grass rest while his herd grazed the southwestern section. He'd made certain that he told men who could be counted on to tell every man they saw about his plans. Certain the cutters now knew of his actions, Austin felt sure they would soon strike the southwest pasture.

He longed for a smoke now but didn't dare light up. He wanted to give the criminals no edge whatever. If they did show up tonight, he wanted to be the one with the advantage of surprise.

All the men sat silently atop their mounts. The night winds picked up and howled around their cold ears. Their hands grew stiff and each man rubbed and flexed his fingers, refusing to don gloves. They had to be ready.

At a little after four in the morning, the first rider apeared on the dim horizon. Austin counted seven more. Waiting until the riders drew alongside the fence, Austin, his eyes narrowed, watched as the men galloped directly to the wire. Three men jumped from their horses and within seconds the heavy wire was cut and rolled back. While the three remounted, Austin gave the signal. He, Tom, and the rest of the Brand men rode out to meet the trespassers.

The Brand outfit formed a wedge with Austin and Tom at its point. This formation swooped down on the startled thieves.

Guns drawn, they reached the shocked intruders within seconds. When the first shot rang out, no one knew for sure which side it came from, and no one cared.

Austin shot to kill, mindless of the bullets hissing about his head. The horses snorted and reared in panic. Captain, though his big eyes were wide with terror, stood his ground, taking commands from Austin's knees. Some of the gang were down, as were two of Austin's men. Bob Coleman was hit in the face, his jawbone shattered. Still he continued to shoot until a second bullet ripped into his chest. Still firing, he fell to the ground. Randy Lancaster saw Bob fall and turned his horse to where his friend lay in the grass. He jumped from his horse and ran to help Bob. Before he could bend to him, a bullet burst into his backbone, splintering the spinal column and exiting through his heart. Randy slumped to the ground beside Bob, his eyes wide open.

Austin, spurring his horse after the retreating thieves, aimed and fired. The man he shot fell from his horse. A tall man riding beside him pulled up on his reins and his horse turned. For a split-second he was silhouetted against the night sky, his useless left arm swinging back and forth. He shouted something and rode away. Behind him galloped a younger man. Austin recognized Red Wilson.

Austin, Tom Capps, and Zeke Worth rode in hot pursuit. Austin leveled his gun at Red Wilson, then hesitated. It was a mistake. The gang's leader turned and fired. The bullet slammed into the right side of Austin's stomach. He didn't feel it enter his body, but within seconds he was gasping for air. Captain felt the big body slacken and stopped immediately.

Tom Capps motioned for Zeke and Freddy Black to continue the chase and turned his gelding back. By the time he reached Austin, the big man had fallen to the ground. Captain was nuzzling him gently.

"Gawd Almighty!" Tom Capps cried as he dismounted and dropped to the grass beside Austin. Austin, conscious and alert, was having difficulty breathing and already his bronzed face was turning pale. Tom ripped Austin's shirt collar open and said, "You'll be all right, Austin. I'll get you home."

Perspiration dotting his upper lip, Austin nodded, and with Tom's help, he rose from the ground. Knowing Austin's mustang would take him in, Tom draped Austin across Captain's saddle and before he could mount his gelding, the big gray horse was trotting across the prairie. By now the others had turned back and were heading toward Tom. Shouting to them to see to Randy and Bob, Tom rode after the big gray carrying his boss and best friend.

At the mansion, Suzette, dressed and wide awake, silently paced the floor in the drawing room, praying for her husband's safety. She vividly recalled all the love and kindness the big, gentle man had shown her. Sadly she remembered the times he'd held her in his arms and told her how much he loved her. Never had she said it to him, even when his great gray eyes held a pleading, hopeful look.

Shaken from her reveries by the sound of horses' hooves, Suzette held her breath and ran to throw open the heavy front doors. She stumbled down the steps and was halfway through the yard when she saw them — two horses, one with a man's large frame draped across the saddle. Without seeing the blond head, she knew. She said his name so quietly, Tom couldn't hear her.

Tom was lifting Austin from the saddle when Suzette turned and flew back into the house. Taking the stairs two at a time, she was shouting all the way up. "Perry, come quick! Perry!"

Lights went on in the guest room before Suzette reached their bedroom door. In seconds, Perry was descending the stairs, his nightshirt stuffed into his trousers, his feet bare, his black case in his hand.

Tom and Suzette were helping the wounded Austin up the front steps when Perry reached the hall. Handing Suzette his bag, he relieved her, shouting orders to her. "Boil water, get clean sheets, and spread them on the dining table."

Anna was coming down the stairs when Suzette called to her. "Anna! Bring clean sheets. They're in the linen closet upstairs."

"Perry," Austin managed to say, "two of my men got it. They'll be along soon if..."

Shaking his head, Tom motioned to the doctor that the other two didn't make it. Kate and her girls were awake and had swung into action, boiling water in the kitchen and making coffee for everyone. Suzette spread a clean white sheet on one end of the long dining table and Tom and Perry carefully laid the bleeding Austin on his back. Suzette, gnawing her lip, leaned over him, smoothing back his thick blond hair. Unable to speak, she gently kissed his cool lips.

"Don't cry, darlin'," Austin managed. "I'm okay."

Perry motioned for Anna to take Suzette out of the room.

"Come, Suzette," Anna coaxed, her hands on Suzette's shaking shoulders, "let's wait in the other room."

Ignoring her, Suzette said to Perry, "I am not leaving my husband. I'm going to help you."

"All right," he responded, looking only at Austin. Anna left the room. Kate came in with the boiling water and clean bandages, then made a hasty exit, her face showing her concern for the big, injured man.

As Perry began cutting away Austin's bloody clothing, he spoke quietly to Suzette. "Get the chloroform from my bag and set out a thick square of gauze."

He took the chloroformed gauze from Suzette and stepped up to Austin's face. "When I put this over your nose and mouth, breathe as deeply as you can, Austin."

Without another word, he clasped it over Austin's pale face and held it firmly in place while Austin fought it, twisting his head, his eyes rolling. Tom and Suzette held him down, amazed at how strong a wounded man could be. Suzette held her breath while Austin struggled. Finally it was over and his writhing body went limp.

Tossing the gauze aside, Perry rushed to cut away the

remainder of Austin's clothing. Tom, big-hearted but weak-stomached, quietly slipped from the room. Only Suzette remained.

Following instructions from Perry, Suzette washed away the drying blood and dirt from the wound, while Perry pulled away the pieces of flesh and blood-soaked shirt. Nervously glancing at the big clock on the sideboard, Perry worked rapidly and heard Suzette say resolutely, "I've heard Daddy say there's nothing worse than a stomach wound. If a man is hit there, he has only an hour to live with the bullet in him."

Without lifting his head, Perry said calmly, "We must hurry."

Austin lay naked under a snowy-white sheet. Perry probed until he found the poisonous lead bullet. He lifted his eyes rapidly to the clock, lowering them immediately. Suzette, at Perry's elbow, staunched the flow of blood with hands as sure and steady as those of the young doctor. In minutes it was over, the bullet extracted, the wound cleaned with a saline solution, and Austin bandaged from waist to thigh.

While Perry washed the blood from his hands, Suzette gently pulled the sheet up to Austin's chest. Leaning close to his face, she murmured, "Austin, darling, I need you so much. Please, Austin, don't leave me."

"We must pray, Suzette. It's in God's hands now." Perry put an arm around her slender shoulders. "I'm not going to move Austin for a while. Do you think you can go upstairs and sleep?"

Looking at her husband's ashen face, Suzette shook her head. "I'm staying with Austin."

Perry nodded and pulled up a chair for her. "I need coffee," he explained and left the room. Perry told Anna to go back to bed, and within five minutes he was back inside the dining room, ready to begin the long vigil with Suzette.

When the chloroform wore off, Austin Brand lay babbling deliriously. This went on for three days and nights. Suzette stayed throughout, refusing to go to bed, dozing sporadically.

Austin talked incessantly, though most of what he said was unintelligible. At times he simply said Suzette's name over and over.

On the third day, Austin's delirium ended, and he slipped into unconsciousness. Perry, though he hid it from Suzette and the others, had begun to think the big man wouldn't pull out of it.

A week passed and still Austin was unconscious. Perry and Anna were scheduled to depart for Fort Worth and their new home, but Perry wouldn't leave Austin. Perry's replacement, a gentle doctor with fiery red hair and a winning smile, arrived in Jacksboro and immediately rode out to the Brand ranch. After conferring with Perry, the older man examined Austin and smiled. "He's going to make it," he announced in a deep, booming voice. "This man is made of stern stuff. He'll be awake within twenty-four hours."

Suzette, though grateful for the reassuring words, remained unconvinced. Alone with her husband as the long winter night dragged by, she studied the handsome face and felt that if he didn't open his eyes soon, she would scream. He had to wake up, he had to get well. He had to *live*.

Rising, Suzette stood over him and her heart began to pound. She could feel tears stinging her eyes, but she didn't try to stop them. Feeling she had to touch him if only for a minute, she very gently peeled the sheet down to his waist and laid her cheek on his broad chest. Contact with his warm body brought forth a well of emotion. She let the tears flow. "Please, Austin, wake up. Wake up, Austin." She lifted her head and looked down at his face and her breath caught in her throat. He was struggling to open his eyes. "Austin," she murmured and touched his cheek.

His gray eyes opened; he had difficulty focusing. When he did, he saw a beautiful laughing and crying woman above him. A hint of a smile touched his cool lips.

"Suzette," he said softly and tried to lift an arm.

"Austin," she said again and picked up his big hand in both

of hers. "Austin. Oh, thank God!" She kissed him.

Before he could kiss her back, she was dashing from the room shouting happily, "Perry, come quick! He's awake! Austin's all right!"

22

As soon as Austin woke, he wanted to know the condition of his men. Shocked and saddened by the news that Bob Coleman and Randy Lancaster had died in the gunfight, he turned his head away and said softly, "They were good men. The best." And then he turned back to Perry. "I think I got the youngest Taylor. Did he make it?"

"No." Dr. Woods shook his head. "Carl Taylor died where he fell. One of the others was hit. He lingered two days and finally died."

"Norman Taylor got away?"

"Afraid so. The sheriff got a posse together, but he didn't have much luck."

"Maybe Taylor will stay out of this part of the country now," Austin said. "I'd hate to think I lost two of my best men for nothing."

"I'm positive Taylor and his men are far away by now, Austin. Try to put it out of your mind. You need plenty of rest. I'll be leaving you in Dr. Phillips's care. He's a competent physician and a nice man."

"You and Anna are going to be missed." Austin shook Perry's hand.

"I hate to leave Jacksboro, but it's a decision we made. You and Suzette must visit soon."

"As soon as I'm well." Austin smiled.

Austin Brand had spent two happy years coddling and pampering his pretty young wife. Now the roles were reversed and Suzette fussed over her husband from morning to night, refusing to let anyone else do anything for him. Weak from loss of blood, Austin didn't argue. Flat on his back in his big bed, he smiled lamely while Suzette moved quickly about his bedroom, pulling heavy drapes to let in the winter sun, poking at the burning logs in the black marble fireplace, standing on a chair to choose a book from a high shelf.

Grateful Austin's life had been spared, Suzette tried to make up for the times she'd taken him for granted. The days and nights he'd lain near death had made her realize how much he meant to her. Though she was not in love with him in the romantic, once-in-a-lifetime way, she wisely concluded that the closeness they shared was precious and that if she never loved him the way he loved her, the need and affection were enough — much more than most couples had.

Austin was pleased with all the attention. Spending every waking hour with Suzette by his bedside was a joy for him and it hastened his recovery. Dr. Phillips came to call and complimented Suzette.

"Mrs. Brand," he smiled as he winked at Austin. "It appears you're just about the best medicine this ailing man could have. I've never seen such rapid mending."

Beaming proudly, Suzette stood at the doctor's elbow and watched unflinchingly while he changed the dressings on Austin's tender wound. "Why, thank you, Doctor," she said, accepting his praise. "I'm the daughter of a doctor and I learned a great deal from him. In fact, although we welcome your company, I know you're a busy man, and if you say the word, I'll be more than happy to see to it Austin's bandages are changed each morning."

The doctor looked at Austin, who nodded his consent. "That will be mighty fine, Mrs. Brand. You sure you won't faint or get sick?"

"Doctor," Suzette reminded him, "I was here when they

brought my husband home that night. I stood at Dr. Woods's side throughout the operation when it looked as though Austin might bleed to death. If I didn't pass out then, I assure you that cleaning his wound won't bother me."

"She looks fragile, Doctor, but my wife is a very capable, independent woman." Austin reached for her hand.

From that day forward, Suzette took over the care of her husband. "You know, Austin," she grinned wickedly one cold morning as he lay naked on his bed while she gave him his bath, "if it weren't for your pain, this situation would almost be fun. For once, it is I in the role of protector and provider, and you in the role of helpless child, totally dependent on me." She ran a soapy cloth over his hairy chest.

Austin sighed and twisted a long, shiny blond curl around his finger as Suzette leaned over him. "Tell you a secret, sweetheart — with a girl as fetching as you taking care of me, I'm rather enjoying it."

And he was. Suzette went out of her way to be caring and tender. She insisted she feed him, though he told her that his arms were as good as ever.

"Maybe so," she retorted, brushing his hands away and spreading a white napkin over his chest, "but I don't want you tiring yourself. Dr. Phillips said you should do nothing for several weeks. I intend to see to it that you don't."

In the afternoons Suzette read to Austin in her sweet, clear voice while he lay quietly, his gray eyes locked on her. When he grew tired of the stories, Suzette would pull the curtains and turn out the lamp by his bed, leaving only the glow of the fire in the grate across from the bed.

"Don't go, sweet," he said sleepily.

"My dear, I'm not about to leave you." Suzette smiled and kissed his temple. "Do you think you'd be uncomfortable if I stretched out beside you?"

His sleepy eyes opened. "Baby, yes. I mean, no. Come on in here." He threw back the covers with a powerful arm.

Giggling, Suzette stripped to her underwear and got into

the warm bed with her husband. Carefully avoiding any contact with his injured stomach, she kissed his neck and whispered, "Sleep, love."

And then it was Christmastime. Tom Capps, Slim Hester, and the young wrangler, Denis Sanders, went up into the south pasture and chopped down a tall, full-branched cedar. Suzette clapped her hands when she saw the three red-nosed cowboys standing on the broad porch with the Christmas tree. Throwing wide the double doors, she welcomed them warmly and asked if it would be too much of a struggle to take the fragrant tree up to Austin's bedroom. Assuring her it would be no trouble at all, the cowboys climbed the stairs with the big, beautiful tree.

Suzette received a Christmas greeting from one of her Louisiana cousins. Emily Foxworth Morrison wrote saying she and her new husband were making their home in Dallas and she hoped Suzette could soon visit them. Suzette shared the message with Austin, and when she refolded the neatly penned letter she asked excitedly if they could go to Dallas for a visit once Austin was healthy again.

"Austin, I've not seen Cousin Emily since I was a little girl, and now that she's so close it would be nice to get to know her. She's my age and the daughter of Daddy's only brother, who was killed in the war. Oh, Austin, could we please visit?"

"In time we will, darlin'." Austin nodded. "Is that the newspaper?"

"Yes." She put the letter away and picked up the paper. "Shall I read it to you?"

"I'd appreciate it." He patted the bed beside him and Suzette slipped off her shoes and climbed onto the bed, facing Austin.

She spread out the newspaper and leaned over it, pushing her hair behind her ears. Her eyes immediately fell on the article with the headline: DESPERADO'S LUCK RUNS OUT

The Prairie Echo

December 23, 1880
Jacksboro, Texas

DESPERADO'S LUCK RUNS OUT

The bold bandit often called "Prince of Darkness" took one too many chances and was apprehended in the Bon Ton Saloon on Fort Worth's wild side, Hell's Half Acre. Marshall "Long Hair" Jim Courtright, acting on a tip from unknown sources, surprised the cunning outlaw in an early morning raid.

Kaytano, the copper-skinned bandit, appeared impassive and unshaken when he was led away in iron cuffs. Marshall Courtright says he doubts the elusive lawbreaker will be so calm when he goes to the gallows. Wanted for robbery of a federal bank, the half-breed is being fitted for a necktie of rope.

Suzette lowered the paper and looked at Austin. His eyes were on the ceiling, a long arm bent over them. "Do you think they'll hang him?" Suzette asked cautiously.

"Yes, I do," Austin said in a flat voice. "I think they'll hang him and I think that's what he wants."

"Austin, what a foolish remark. No one wants to die."

"When you behave like that Indian bandit, there's a good chance you'll perish. To live such a life is to constantly court death."

"Hmm, I guess so," she mused. "Why do they call the man the 'Prince of Darkness'?"

Austin lowered his arm. "Because he once robbed the Franciscan Brotherhood of their gold hoard on the way to California. After that infamous deed, he was considered a devil. Sweetheart, do you think we could change the subject? He's just another criminal. There are hundreds on the frontier. What else is in the paper?"

The new year came and with it a nice, newsy letter from Anna. It had been a wonderful Christmas and they were looking forward to a visit from the Brands. Suzette read and reread the letter.

"I miss them. Don't you, Austin?"

"Yes, baby." Austin saw the wistful look on her face. "Tell you what, the Cattlemen's Association is having its first big convention in Chicago in February. If I'm able, I've got to attend, and —"

Suzette interrupted: "May I please go with you, Austin? I would love to visit Chicago and —"

"No, darlin'," Austin quieted her. "You can't go this time. Several men from Graham, Bryson, and Jacksboro are going up as a group. None of the wives are going along."

"Austin, I don't care about the other wives. If we go in the Alpha, the other gentlemen won't even know I'm along. Let me go, please, I'm just dying to go on a trip and I —"

"Suzette, I know you're tired of being cooped up here. You've been an angel about taking care of me and I'm sure you long to go out and enjoy yourself. I'm sorry, I can't take you to Chicago. I'm not taking the Alpha this trip. I'm booking a regular fare in order to be a part of the group. We've a lot to discuss and I'll be taking my meals with them. I wouldn't have time to be with you."

Suzette, Anna's letter still in her hand, slumped into a chair beside the bed. "Sometimes I wish I were a man," she said glumly, her disappointment showing.

"Sweet," Austin laughed and put out his hand to her, "I'm sure glad you're not a man. Come here."

Suzette sighed and laid Anna's letter aside. She rose reluctantly from her chair and let Austin pull her across the bed.

"Listen to me, pretty girl. As I tried to tell you before you interrupted, I must go to Chicago in February. Why don't you travel to Fort Worth with me and visit Anna and Perry while I'm in Chicago?"

"Austin!" she squealed. "Yes!" Her eyes sparkled with

excitement and she soundly bussed her smiling husband. "Thank you, Austin. Thank you, thank you!"

Austin continued to mend rapidly. Dr. Phillips claimed that he had never seen a case like it. "Mr. Brand," the good doctor said, shaking his red head, "you have a superb body and an astonishing constitution. Most men wouldn't have lived through such a wound, and here you are, almost good as new."

"Doctor, I've a lot to live for." Austin grinned, indicating his wife.

"So you do, Mr. Brand," the doctor agreed. "You're a lucky man; she's not just beautiful, she's also resilient."

"Will you two quit speaking of me as though I weren't here," Suzette scolded. "I thank you both for the gracious compliments. Now, Doctor, I want to know if my husband will be well enough to travel in February."

"I see nothing to keep him from it. The wound is healing nicely and each day he grows stronger. You can plan on your trip if nothing goes awry."

And plan Suzette did. She was eagerly looking forward to getting away. She'd not been out of the house since the night of the shooting, and though she was happy to wait on and watch over her ailing husband, it was confining, and she and Austin agreed that a change of scenery would be good for both of them. Suzette had suggested that they visit her cousin in Dallas while they were in nearby Fort Worth, but Austin said no. Suzette was disappointed, though she didn't belabor the point.

She continued to keep Austin company. It was becoming a habit for her to read the newspaper to him as soon as one of the hands delivered it to the house. On a snowy afternoon in January, young Denis Sanders came to the back door and handed Suzette the morning edition. Suzette thanked him and walked through the house. At the bottom of the stairs, she paused, looking at the damp front page.

She didn't climb the stairs but turned and walked into the

library, dropping to the rug in front of the fire. Under a photograph of a darkly handsome man, she read the name: Kaytano. Suzette felt a chill run up her spine as she stared at the picture and at the dark, glittery eyes, the aristocratic nose, the hard mouth, the high, chiseled cheekbones, the thick black hair. Fascinated by the likeness of the renegade, Suzette trembled and let the newspaper drop to the floor. Still she could see the picture and it seemed the cold, beautiful eyes were looking at her. With shaky fingers she picked up the paper and began to read.

January 20, 1880
Fort Worth, Texas

In an unbelievable escape, the bold bandit Kaytano slipped from the clutches of the federal authorities. Like a snake slithering through the weeds, the mysterious man stole away from his cell in the city jail and out into the night. When the sun rose this morning, the jail's most prized prisoner had disappeared into thin air. Authorities say...

"He's like a cat," she murmured aloud. "He has nine lives. They'll never kill Kaytano." Slowly she lowered her head. Those compelling eyes were on her. Suzette shuddered and impulsively hurled the paper into the fire. It caught immediately, curling and blackening in a second. The last part of the paper to burn was the chilling countenance of the elusive Kaytano. Waiting until only soft gray ash remained of what had been the morning paper, Suzette rose and climbed the stairs to her husband's room.

When she entered, Austin was sitting up. His color was good, his face was fleshing out, and today he was in high spirits. "Come here and give me a kiss, sweetheart."

Suzette flew across the room, almost throwing herself into his outstretched arms. She clung to him and kissed his throat, closing her eyes, inhaling deeply of the warm, clean smell of him, loving the feel of his big powerful arms pressing her safely to him, the sound of his deep, soothing voice whispering endearments to her.

"Honey," he said against her ear, "you're trembling. Are you cold? Suzette, you're freezing."

"No, I'm not," she murmured. "I just want you to hold me a minute longer, Austin."

"Of course, darlin'," Austin assured her. He gently stroked her back through her woolen dress. His hand went up to cradle her head. "I'll hold my little baby forever," he whispered, his breath warm against her cheek.

When finally she was calm, she pulled back a little and smiled at Austin.

"Austin, is there anything I can get you? Would you like something to eat?" Her fingers traced his strong jawline.

"I thought you were going to read the paper to me. Isn't that what you went downstairs for?"

"Austin, I'm sorry, Denis brought the paper and, clumsy me, I dropped it in the snow. It was wet so I had to toss it in the fire." Suzette wondered, even as she heard the words, why she wasn't telling him the truth. She could think of only one reason. Austin seemed unduly upset any time Kaytano's name was mentioned in the papers. The Indian's escape from jail was bound to annoy him. She didn't want her husband worrying about things that had nothing to do with them. If he didn't read about it, Austin would never know the man was out of jail.

"Doesn't matter." Austin yawned. "I'm getting a little drowsy anyhow."

Austin improved daily and by the first of February he was out of bed and dressed, though Suzette warned him not to overdo. She thought that since Austin was up, he wouldn't object to her going into Jacksboro. She wanted to buy some things for their trip, and though she never said as much, she felt she would scream if she didn't get away from the ranch for an hour or two.

Austin did object. He didn't bother to explain to her that since the shooting he was more concerned than ever for her safety. He didn't tell her that it was he who shot the young Taylor brother and that he suspected Norman Taylor would not rest until he'd avenged his brother's death. Hopefully Taylor would be after only Austin, but Austin was taking no chances. He refused to let her go into town, even with an escort, and Suzette, misunderstanding his motives, was furious.

"Are you saying you forbid me to go into Jacksboro?" she cried, her heart pounding.

Her temper ignited his and he shouted at her. "Yes! I forbid you to leave this house! If there's something you need, you know damned well one of my men will be happy to get it for you. There's no reason for you to go out."

"No reason! I'll tell you a very good reason! I'm about to go insane! How's that for a reason, Austin 'God Almighty' Brand? I've been in this house for weeks. I've done nothing but nurse you and I think I shall scream if I don't —"

He rose and grabbed her wrist. "You didn't have to take care of me! Hell, I've enough money so you don't ever have to lift a finger. I thought you wanted to take care of me. If you're going to complain about it, I sure as hell wish you'd stayed away from me!"

"Oh, you do, do you?" She clawed at the strong fingers encircling her wrist. "You loved every minute of it! I know you, you wouldn't have let Kate or one of the girls do all the things I did for you! My Lord! Is your memory so short that you don't remember the things I did? Have you forgotten the morning I had to —"

"That's enough!" he bellowed. "If you ever tell anybody..."

Suddenly Suzette felt like giggling. She tried to suppress the laughter bubbling up in her because she knew Austin was livid, and if she broke up he would grow even more angry. She couldn't help it; she kept visualizing the particlar incident he was so sensitive about. While he glared down at her with a face red with rage, Suzette fell against his chest and started laughing.

"What the —" Austin snatched her back. "Look at me, Suzette!"

Fearing he might lose control when he saw her laughter, she had no choice but to raise her eyes to his. The vein in his forehead throbbed as his big hands gripped her shoulders. "Why, you little... my God, doesn't *anything* scare you!"

His anger evaporated as he looked down at his headstrong wife, tears of laughter shining in her eyes.

"Austin, I'm sorry," she said, gasping between giggles. "It's just... I..."

Austin's full lips started twitching and he was torn between shaking his stubborn wife until her head rocked on her shoulders and pulling her into an embrace. He did the latter.

"What am I going to do with you?" He laughed and buried his face in her hair.

Suzette slid her arms up around his neck and said, "I can't help it, I keep seeing you lying there with your —"

Austin silenced her with his mouth. His lips burned into hers. Suzette responded in kind, and when he dragged his mouth from hers he said raggedly, "Woman, is nothing sacred to you?" He was smiling, his gray eyes warm with love and affection.

"Yes, some things are. I'm sorry, sweetheart. If you'll come upstairs, I'll show you." Wordlessly he took her hand and led her through the corridor and up the stairs. On the way up, she clung to his arm and begged, "Austin, afterward, can't I please go into Jackboro?"

At the door of his bedroom, he handed her inside and closed it behind them. "No, Suzette, you can't."

Her hands went to his shirtfront and she plucked at the buttons, murmuring, "Austin, I would just stay for an hour and Tom or one —"

Austin put a big hand into her hair and pulled her head back. Bending, he kissed her, forcing her lips open. His hot tongue slowly descended into the dark, sweet recesses of her mouth. When he raised his head, his lips hovered just above hers. "The subject is closed."

She sighed and pulled his mouth back down to hers.

Anna and Perry were delighted to see the Brands. Young Josh and Sunny were as thrilled with all the gifts Austin and Suzette brought them as they were to have visitors. For two pleasant days, the four grown-ups visited, talked, went out to dinner, and shared nightcaps in front of the fireplace. The weekend flew by and early Monday morning Austin said good-bye and boarded the train to Chicago. Suzette and Perry saw him off at the station, Suzette waving until the train was out of sight.

"Shall we return home, Suzette? It's dreadfully cold and Anna will be waiting with breakfast for us." Dr. Woods took her elbow.

"Perry, will you give me five minutes?" She turned to the slender chestnut-haired man. "I want to make arrangements to go to Dallas on Wednesday. Austin keeps our railroad car here. While he's away I'm going to see a cousin from Louisiana who recently moved to Dallas."

Perry obligingly waited while Suzette spoke to a railroad employee.

"Mrs. Brand," the elderly man told her, "any time you or your husband want to use the Alpha, let me know. Mr. Brand gave me the names of your staff, so I can get in touch with them."

"How very efficient." Suzette nodded happily. "Very well, I wish to depart for Dallas on Wednesday afternoon."

"That's possible. Let's see." The railroad employee studied a schedule. "You can leave at straight up three o'clock. You'll arrive in Dallas before five P.M."

"That's perfect. If you'll be so kind as to notify the staff, tell them we'll only stay in Dallas for a couple of days. Will you do that Mr. . . . . ah, Mr. . . . . "

"Dunlap, ma'am, and I'll be happy to see to it."

Suzette didn't mention her plans to Anna until that night after Perry and the children were in bed. The two women had sat up talking, and when, after midnight, Anna yawned and said she could no longer hold her eyes open, Suzette nodded her agreement. "One last thing, Anna." Suzette took her friend's hand. "Wednesday I'm going to Dallas on our railroad car." Anna looked skeptical. "I'll tell Austin when he returns. He's smothering me, Anna. I can't be his little girl forever. I don't want to be. I'm a grown woman, and if I wish to go thirty miles to see a cousin, I see nothing wrong with it."

"Nor I," Anna conceded. "But why didn't you tell Austin? You didn't, did you?"

"Anna, I'm going. When Austin gets back, I'll tell him."

On Wednesday, a weak winter sun popped out as Suzette arrived at the Fort Worth train terminal. The weather had warmed considerably. Feeling free and excited, Suzette, in a traveling suit of luxurious pink wool, twirled her parasol and adjusted her pink velvet bonnet, tucking the net veil neatly under her chin. She was smiling as she boarded the Alpha. Inside she touched familiar pieces, remembering the happy times with Austin.

A polite Chinese staff member entered after knocking, and bowed, inquiring if there was anything she might want.

"Chin, if I could have a nice cup of chocolate, I'll not bother you again for the rest of the journey."

"It will be done." His eyes disappeared into slits as he smiled.

Behind steam, the Alpha made its way east. Inside Suzette removed her hat, suit jacket, and gloves. On the marble table between the brocade couches, a cup of steaming-hot cocoa and a small plate of cookies waited on a silver tray.

Suzette Brand, delighted to be alone, delighted to be traveling, delighted to be on her way to a new city, hummed as she dropped down onto one of the shiny couches. She took a quick sip of chocolate and was up again. Patting her up-swept hair, she giggled and went to the painting where Austin had shown her the wall safe. She slid the masterpiece aside and looked at the small round safe. Recalling the combination, she twisted from left to right, and back again, pulling open the tiny door. She laughed and stripped off her jewelry. She'd worn her diamond engagement ring — a big, flawless blue-white stone that Austin had bought her in New York on their honeymoon. She shoved the diamond deep into the safe along with her solid gold bracelet and earrings. She fingered the small gold heart at her throat and shook her head, then pushed the round door shut and twirled the locking mechanism.

Feeling like a very rich and important lady, Suzette twisted the gold chain and went back to her cocoa. She curled her legs beside her, the soft kid leather of her shoes resting on the fine brocade. With a dainty sugar cookie in one hand, the bone china cup in the other, Suzette felt all was right with her world.

Seconds later she heard the first gunshot. Calmly she set the cup on the marble table and took the last bite of the cookie. Rising, she started to the window. She was lifting the curtain when the car lurched violently, sending her sprawling.

"What the devil?" she said aloud. Before she could rise, the train had stopped and she heard shouting and more gunfire. The little Chinese man appeared from the galley wringing his hands, a look of terror on his sallow face.

The door of the Alpha was jerked open and a gun-toting Mexican scrambled up the steps. Behind him a bigger man, a lighter-skinned Mexican, stood in the door. Suzette was on her feet, her eyes on the stocky Mexican waving a gun. She was being robbed. Her beautiful diamond ring would be stolen. From behind her, she heard the frightened Chinese say, "Mrs. Brand, please give them all your money."

Pressing herself flat against the wall, Suzette nodded.

"Under the painting" — she inclined her head — "there's a wall safe."

The short Mexican gave her a toothy grin. "No, you do not understand, *señora*." He was coming toward her, the gun pointed to the ceiling. The taller man waited at the door, his gun trained on the Chinese. "You come with me!" the stocky Mexican exclaimed happily and grabbed Suzette's hand.

The horror of his intention sank in and Suzette began to struggle. "No!" she screamed. "No, I won't! Let me go!"

"Ah, do not make me hurt you, *señora*." The greasy little man laughed and lowered his gun to point at her chest. "You will come with me."

"I will not!" she screamed. "I'm not leaving this car!"

"You must," the Mexican said and picked her up. Still she fought him, pounding on his shoulders, pleading, "I've jewelry in the safe. Money in my purse. Take it and leave me, please."

"No, you come," he insisted and carried her to the door, the gun pressing into the small of her back.

He handed Suzette to the tall man waiting at the door and turned to warn the Chinese servant to stay put or die. The tall Mexican held Suzette high in the air as though she were no heavier than a feather. She kicked and clawed, but she was taken from the train and lifted up across the saddle of a tall, slender rider. No sooner was she mounted than the black horse was thundering across the stark, wintry countryside.

Squirming within the strong arms encircling her, Suzette twisted around to look at the face of her captor. Her heart stopped its beating. The blood in her veins congealed. Her breath caught in her tightened throat. There was no doubt in her mind. She'd know those eyes anywhere, the aristocratic nose, the hard, cruel mouth, the coal-black hair, the smooth mahogany skin.

Kaytano.

23

Too stunned to scream, Suzette gaped at the man whose very name spelled danger. Never had she seen such a cruel, cold face. His features appeared as if chiseled from stone, and his expression was one of cool indifference. His lean jaw was rigid, top lip thin, the bottom one full. His black eyes stared straight ahead, as though unaware of her closeness.

Suzette clung to the strong arms around her as the big black stallion galloped across the prairie. Behind them the train continued making its way eastward. The Alpha sat alone on the tracks, unhinged from the steaming locomotive. Suzette cast a wistful look at the sleek shiny car as it grew smaller and smaller.

"Please" — she found her tongue — "there are jewels in the railroad car. You can have them, they're worth a fortune. Turn back, turn back and they're yours." Her eyes were riveted to his smooth face, hoping to see a flicker of interest, some sign of his intentions. There was none. He didn't even look at her and he was deaf to her pleas.

Behind them rode the short, stocky Mexican and two other men. One was the tall Mexican who had lifted her on the horse. The other, a middle-aged white man with sandy hair and a shaggy beard, looked less menacing. Perhaps she could persuade him to release her. If she could only speak to him, he would understand; he was white, he might let her go.

They all rode fast. Suzette had no choice but to hold tightly to the dark man's arms. The ground rushing past made her grow dizzy. Her head spinning with fear, she felt herself grow faint. The tall rider behind her never looked at her. He sensed her weakness. Wordlessly he raised a black gloved hand to her shoulders and pulled her back against the hardness of his chest. When her cheek came in contact with the soft black fabric covering his rock-hard chest, Suzette gasped but didn't try to lift her head.

Her eyes fluttered open. Inches from her own, his smooth brown face looked shiny-clean. His lips were slightly parted and his teeth were very white against the darkness of his skin. His black eyes, still fastened on the horizon, were lined with a double row of sweeping black lashes. He wore a black hat low over his forehead; from under its wide brim, thick black hair flowed clean and luxuriant. His long lean legs were encased in tight black trousers, and rubbing uncomfortably against her side, a black gunbelt rode low around slim hips.

Unlike his men, he carried no gun in his hand. With a flicker of hope, Suzette surmised that the discomfort she felt at her back was likely his pistol. If she could somehow reach around and grab it, she could jam it into the bandit's side and demand he release her. She was in a very good position to pull it off. She was pressed against his chest; she would move her left arm around him, pretend she wanted to hold on to him to keep from falling. It would be simple.

Suzette moaned a little and squeezed her left arm between her body and his. Looking up at his impassive face, she put her hand around his slender back and fingered the soft silk shirt. Certain that he suspected nothing, she let her hand stay there for a time, then slowly moved it down. Inching toward the leather holster on his thigh, she kept her eyes trained on his dark face. She bit her lip when she felt the round bullets in the belt. Sliding her fingers forward and down, she touched the cold butt of the big gun. Her arm ached in its socket as she slid her fingers over the gun. They were touching the smooth handle; one quick jerk and she could pull the weapon clear of the restraining leather and jam it forcefully into the outlaw's ribs.

A feeling close to ecstasy filled her as she closed her cold fingers around the handle and began to ease the gun up. Suddenly, Kaytano's gloved hand rested lightly on hers. Suzette screamed. He said nothing, nor did he look at her. Instead, he very gently moved her hand back around his waist, then pulled the big Colt .44 from its resting place. Suzette trembled. Had she so infuriated the animal that he would put the deadly gun to her temple and squeeze the trigger?

Kaytano slowly eased the revolver around in front of her face, and she blinked when he held it before her frightened eyes. The fancy white pearl handle shone in the winter sun. Suzette clung desperately to his slick silk shirt while her wide eyes were riveted to the huge gun. She watched in fascinated terror as his black gloved hand slowly turned the gun's barrel up to the sky. His long arm shot up and Suzette's eyes followed; when he pulled the trigger, Suzette automatically flinched.

The gun discharged six loud shots in rapid succession before he lowered it. It was smoking and warm when he thrust it into the waistband of Suzette's pink wool skirt, where it rested against her flat midriff, the barrel against her quivering stomach, the pearl handle touching her breasts.

She studied his immobile face. What sort of game was this cold, cunning man playing with her? Hate mixed with her fear; the heartless half-breed was toying with her. He wanted her to try to pluck a bullet from his gunbelt. He was amusing himself, waiting for her to foolishly extract a bullet and struggle to load his gun.

A proud and willful nature had always been hers. Afraid though she was, she was still Suzette Foxworth Brand, a woman unwilling to surrender her free spririt to her husband or any other man, not even this callous outlaw. With a triumphant cry, Suzette yanked the gun from her skirt and threw it as far as she could.

The dark, hard face above hers changed not at all, but the rider immediately pulled up on the reins. The black horse halted. Kaytano turned the mount in the direction Suzette had thrown his gun. The other men stopped, but Kaytano motioned them to proceed. Suzette, her heart pounding, was already sorry she'd behaved so stupidly. She'd baited a killer and she was sure he must be furious, though his face and actions didn't change.

Suzette froze when he stopped the big black horse. He took off his black leather gloves, dismounted, grabbed her about the waist, and pulled her down. Dropping the reins to the ground, he started walking, pulling her along with him. He didn't try to hold her close to him, he didn't put an arm around her and crush her to his side, but held her around her wrist with his long fingers. They walked across the hard, dead grass, the ground crunching under their feet. There was no other sound save Suzette's heartbeat pounding in her ears.

He walked directly to the gun, which lay in plain sight. For the first time since he'd pulled her up into the saddle with him, he looked into her eyes.

Suzette gasped. There was a menacing familiarity about him. Where had she seen those eyes? They stood looking at each other, and though neither spoke, his flashing black eyes spoke for him. They were clearly telling her to pick up his gun.

She hated his arrogant stance, the cocksure tilt of his head, the blaze of those dark eyes telling her she *would* obey.

Stubbornly she glared at him, though her knees were weak and her bosom rose and fell. For what seemed an interminable time they faced each other, each determined to break the will of the other. Just when Suzette thought she was the victor, when Kaytano's cold gaze dropped from hers and his rigid body moved, he surprised her. He didn't stoop and pick up his gun. Slowly he stepped behind her. His fingers released her wrist. His hands went to the tops of her shoulders and he began to apply gentle pressure.

Struggling weakly, she quickly realized how helpless she was against this lean, powerful man. In seconds she was on her knees in front of him. She could feel his warmth as his hands left her shoulders and went to her head. His fingers raked through her hair and he pressed her head back against his thighs. He leaned over her and snapped her head back so suddenly she winced. She was looking up; he was looking down. Their eyes locked; narrowed black eyes met wide blue ones. She trembled visibly. Slowly he sank to his knees behind her as she lifted her head away from him, then bowed it. His breath was as labored as hers. She waited for his next move. His long arms came around her; his hands went to hers. Long, dark fingers closed over white, shaky ones. He moved her hands to rest on the gun. Then he was still.

They stayed like that for countless minutes. He meant for her to pick up the gun; he was not going to do it for her. She could feel his hot, steady breath, those intense black eyes of his impaling her.

For the first time in her life, Suzette could feel someone's power molding her, moving her. This dark, mysterious man neither shouted at her nor begged her. There was no need. His will was so forceful it enveloped her, covered her, wrapped her up with a magical mastery. Knowing she was beaten by him, her fear of him increased as she picked up the gun slowly. They held the gun together. She heard him exhale.

Kaytano returned the gun to his holster. Rising to his feet gracefully, he put his hands on Suzette's waist and eased her up. Her throat aching, her eyes stinging with unshed tears, Suzette tossed her hair from her eyes and started back toward the grazing horse. Kaytano followed, knowing he was the victor, that she would go dutifully to his horse without being led or pushed.

Kaytano picked up the reins and looped them over the horse's sleek neck. Suzette avoided his eyes as she stepped up to him and put her hands on his shoulders while he lifted her across his saddle. Effortlessly he swung up behind her and slapped the reins across the horse's flanks. The big steed went into a comfortable lope and Suzette let her tired head fall back against the tall dark rider's chest. With one hand gripping the saddlehorn, the other around Kaytano's back, Suzette began to cry.

She'd been with the dark bandit for less than an hour and she knew her life would never again be the same. What lay ahead she couldn't bear to wonder about — perhaps torture, maybe even death. Already she'd lost something, though she wasn't certain what. This mute man had taken something from her that she could never take back. Her heart drummed alarmingly as she pressed her face to the black silk shirt and wept. The bandit's strong heartbeat was slow and steady under her cheek. He was utterly calm, while her world had turned upside down. Suzette had the uneasy feeling he'd be calm and placid when he tortured and killed her.

They rode steadily to the southwest. The winter sun was setting and the unusually warm February day grew chilly. Suzette shivered. The pink frilly blouse was no protection against the numbing cold settling over the plains. She knew it was useless to complain so she remained silent, unconsciously pressing nearer to Kaytano's warmth.

His men were slowing their horses now, as though waiting for Kaytano. He reined the big stallion in between the stocky Mexican and the white man. He turned his head slowly, sweeping the horizon with his black eyes.

He said nothing, but pointed to a stand of trees a hundred yards to the right before spurring his horse away. Bolting down a gentle incline, the big beast reached the trees in seconds. Dismounting, Kaytano reached for the cold, shivering Suzette. Darkness was quickly closing in and the temperature was dropping rapidly now. The men reached them and dismounted. Speaking in Spanish, they addressed Kaytano, who shook his head in reply.

Kaytano reached for Suzette's hand and she took his obediently. He led her into the trees, ducking his head to avoid the low-hanging, bare branches. She could hear the men talking behind them as they went about unsaddling the horses and building a fire. Kaytano continued walking, leading her farther away into the privacy of the trees, and she felt new terror building. When he stopped and dropped her hand she looked at him questioningly, but he simply turned away from her and put his hand over his eyes. Sighing with relief, she realized what he meant and took advantage of it, quickly turning away from him.

Afterward, her cheeks crimson, she went to him and

touched his sleeve. Again he took her hand and led her back to where his men were laying out a meal. Kaytano motioned her to the ground near the fire and she gladly dropped down, stretching her cold hands out to warm them. He handed her a plate of beans and dried beef. When she tried to eat, she had difficulty swallowing and felt she would never be hungry again.

Kaytano sat near her and ate every bite on his plate. His men sat across the campfire from her, eating and talking in low voices. Far away a lone coyote called mournfully, its lonely cry echoing Suzette's despair.

Kaytano sprang to his feet and reached for her plate. She'd hardly touched her food. He set both plates aside for the others to clean. From his saddlebags, he pulled two heavy blankets. Tossing them over his shoulder, he extended his hand to Suzette. She took it and he pulled her to her feet easily. He led her to where his black saddle lay on a grassy spot a few feet from the fire. Suzette stood watching while he dropped the blankets and took a coiled lariat from the saddle. He tied one end of the rope around his slim waist, leaving the loop loose enough for comfort. When he drew her close to him, Suzette lifted her arms, knowing instantly his intentions. He tied her to him, leaving four or five feet of rope between them.

Suzette was utterly exhausted. She wanted warmth and rest. While she watched the dark man spread one of the blankets on the ground in front of his saddle, she stifled a yawn and hoped he meant this as her bed.

While his three companions remained seated around the fire, Kaytano indicated that Suzette was to lie down. When she did so, he covered her with the other blanket. She sighed and pulled it up to her shivering chin. Her tired eyes fluttered open to see Kaytano getting underneath the blanket with her. She tensed. He pulled the cover up to his shoulders and turned away from her. She closed her eyes.

Loneliness and need washed over Suzette with an intensity

she'd never experienced. If only she could turn back the clock. Was it possible that only Sunday night she had slept in her husband's big arms, safe and warm?

Austin, she silently prayed, *please save me.* Hot tears slid down her cheeks and onto the blanket. Her slender shoulders shook with sobs, while her eyes remained tightly shut. *Austin, Austin, help me. Oh, Austin, I want to come home to you,* she prayed.

A movement beside her made her eyes fly open. Kaytano had turned and his dark, penetrating eyes were on her face. Sniffing, she bit her lip and tried to still her cold body. She was paralyzed with fear when she saw his arm go under the blanket. Expecting to feel those long, brown fingers moving up her body at any second, she exploded into sobs when his hand came from under the cover with a clean white handkerchief he'd taken from his trouser pocket. He laid it beside her face and wordlessly turned over once again.

Suzette grabbed the handkerchief and jammed it into her mouth, trying to smother the sounds of her sobs. It was impossible, and she cried until she became too tired to weep any longer. Sleep finally claimed her with its sweet oblivion.

One of the last thoughts to run through Suzette's weary mind was that Austin was right about her. She was a helpless child and she needed her big, strong husband. She should have listened to him. She shouldn't have disobeyed Austin. She never would again.

24

Cold and uncomfortable in her fitful slumber, Suzette, in the habit of sleeping close to her husband's warm body, sleepily snuggled close to Kaytano's back. Carefully the dark man turned to face her. She was unaware of the near smile curving the hard mouth of her captor. Kaytano pulled her gently to him, wrapping a long arm about her slender body. She moaned in her sleep and nestled her face against his throat, but she didn't awaken.

Kaytano's long, brown fingers spread out on her back. He pressed her against his warm chest, trapping her hands between their bodies. While Suzette slept on, Kaytano studied her pale, pretty face. Her luminous eyes were closed, the thick long lashes curving against the flawless cheeks. Her pert nose gave her a haughty, proud look. The soft, sweet mouth, slightly parted in slumber, was as tempting as the smooth white throat and the high, full breasts touching his chest. Her golden hair had come loose from restraints and tumbled about her neck and shoulders; its sweet, clean fragrance filled his senses.

Kaytano felt his stomach muscles tighten. Suppressing a groan, he turned his face from hers to look at the cold stars high above them. He trembled. He'd had her for only a few hours and already he felt his life would never again be the same. She'd taken something from him he could never get back. For the first time in his life, Kaytano was afraid.

At sunrise, Suzette awoke stiff and confused. She saw bare trees instead of a carved ceiling. She heard men speaking in Spanish. Then it all came back to her. Before she could rise, the tall, dark man was standing over her, looking down at her with those cold, black eyes. She blinked at him and sat up, trying to scramble to her feet. He quickly crouched down beside her, stopping her with a hand on her shoulder.

He handed her a cup of steaming hot coffee and watched while she drank it down. Her mind was racing. It was time she stopped behaving like a frightened child. She had been taken by bandits and their purpose could only be money. This cruel Indian knew she was married to a very wealthy man and he intended to ransom her. Were that the case — what else could it be? — she was quite safe. Alive, she was valuable;

dead, she was worthless. She would explain to these people that it was time to send a message to Austin. They might not know he was in Chicago; she would tell them so they might proceed with the negotiations.

Holding the tin cup between her cold palms, Suzette smiled at Kaytano. "I know who you are, you're Kaytano. I've read about you, as has everyone in Texas. I'm sure you must know my husband, Austin Brand, is a rich man. You'll have no trouble with Austin; he loves me very much and will gladly pay you for my safe return. I'm afraid you are unaware that he is in Chicago now on business and is staying at the Palace Hotel. Why don't we go to some town near here and you can wire him? I guarantee you, you'll have your money with no delay." Pausing, she studied his smooth, expressionless face. If he understood a word she said, he gave no indication. He took the coffee tin from her hands, rose, and emptied the remaining brew, then put a hand to her elbow to help her up.

"Please," she tried again, "he'll pay for my return. There's no reason for us to ride farther. Take me to a town. You'll get as much as you ask for." Kaytano didn't reply, but gathered up the blankets. Within minutes she was again sitting in front of him as they thundered across the plains. Her mind kept on churning. When they stopped, she would go to the white man and plead her case. Perhaps this dark man she rode with spoke no English. She'd heard nothing but Spanish since she'd been taken. Maybe Kaytano spoke only Spanish and an Indian tongue. That had to be it. He didn't understand her. If he had understood, he'd contact Austin immediately and she'd be free soon. That was it — a simple lack of communication. When they stopped for a meal, she would speak to the white man and bring this frightening situation to an end.

Feeling better about her chances, Suzette tried to relax as much as possible. It wasn't easy. She was tired and dirty and she longed for a nice hot bath and some good food. Her hair was a tangled, frightful mess, her pink wool skirt and filmy blouse wrinkled and filthy from a night on the ground. Surprisingly enough, however, she didn't feel as bad as she should have after sleeping on the cold ground with only a blanket. It was a miracle she'd slept at all. Oddly, she couldn't remember suffering from the cold or waking in the night.

Suzette sat uncomfortably, leaning away from the hard man whose dark eyes constantly swept the horizon. Determined she would not touch him, she clung to the horn with both hands, in constant danger of falling. She felt her back would surely break before they stopped again. Balancing herself in such an awkward position already was taking its toll. She squirmed, she sighed, and she kept casting daggerlike glances at the hard-hearted Kaytano.

Suddenly Kaytano pulled his horse up. He wrapped the reins around the saddlehorn and ignored the look Suzette gave him. To her shock, his hand went to her long pink skirt; before she could protest, he'd pulled its heavy folds up over her knees. Fighting the lacy petticoats she wore, he yanked them up, too, while Suzette glared at him and shouted, "You animal! What in blazes are you doing? You harm me and my husband won't pay you a cent! Do you hear me?"

Trapped in a swirl of pink wool and lacy petticoats, Suzette reddened as her long, stockinged legs were exposed to the cold biting air and his piercing eyes. In seconds she was astride the saddle and her long skirts and petticoats were flowing about her while the hands that had arranged them were pulling her back against him. Sputtering and jerking, she was subdued and pinned within the encircling arms as her head rested on his left shoulder in the curve of his neck. "You filthy half-breed!" she cried, knowing full well he didn't understand a word she was saying. "You have the nerve to put your dirty hands on me! You'll hang from the tallest tree once I'm safe, you miserable savage!"

Though Suzette would never let on to Kaytano, she was much more comfortable now. She didn't have to worry constantly about falling, and with his chest to cushion her aching back, she could almost relax. She let her eyes flicker to his face, just above hers. She frowned. While her face felt chapped and unclean and her hair felt dirty and tangled, the half-breed's face was freshly shaven and shiny-clean. He wore no hat today and his long, thick hair gleamed in the sunlight. He'd worn a black silk shirt yesterday. Today a snowy-white shirt of soft cotton looked as clean and fresh as Austin's. Unwittingly turning her face into his throat, she inhaled deeply and her senses were assailed with a clean, masculine scent. This man's personal habits were obviously those of a refined gentleman, though he lived the life of an animal. She must not forget that he was cruel and heartless, a dangerous beast that would kill her with his bare hands. His cleanliness and dark good looks belied the power and menace of the serpent occupying his slim, brown body.

The sun had traveled all the way up and was heading in the other direction before the gang stopped to eat. Suzette had slept against Kaytano for the past hour. So sound was her slumber that he gently shook her awake to dismount.

Her first waking thought was to get near enough to the white man to speak to him. Glancing nervously at Kaytano while he unsaddled the lathered black hourse, she almost smiled at her small victory. Already the half-breed trusted her enough to turn his back on her. Quietly she lifted her skirts and hurried to where the white man was unsaddling a dun-colored stallion.

Catching his sleeve, Suzette let the words tumble out. "Please!" she begged, "you must listen to me. Your leader doesn't understand me so I have to talk to you. My husband is rich. He'll gladly pay for my safe return. Will you help me?" The tall man stared down at her, his arm across his horse. She saw little interest in his eyes, but she hurried on, anxious to make him understand. "You see, my husband is in Chicago. We'll wire him and he'll make arrangements to give you the money. There's no need to continue traveling. Take me to a rail depot. Wire my husband; I promise you'll get your money." Suzette pushed her tangled hair over her shoulder and stepped closer, her voice becoming shrill. "Don't you understand? You must help me! Dear God, you're a white man!

Do you want to see... do you..." Suzette's words trailed off. The tall white man was no longer looking at her but at something above her head. In his pale eyes was a flicker of fear. Suzette whirled about and bumped into the tall, dark Kaytano. Wordlessly he steadied her, his cold eyes on her trembling lips. "Please." She looked up at him in desperation. "I... I..." She shook her head and fell silent, knowing it was hopeless.

The long, tiring ride continued, her captors avoiding settlements and towns. Suzette felt hope slipping away. Each hour took her farther from home and safety. Time and again she attempted to make them understand her, but they refused to listen and she became increasingly alarmed. If they did intend to ransom her, it was time they made contact with Austin. If that was not their intention, what was? Kaytano was a bank robber, he stole money. He'd never been known to capture helpless women. His career had been spent in the quest for gold. Cold and evil though he was, he was surely handsome enough to have all the women he wanted. So what was she doing here? Why had he taken her, if not for money? Why was he waiting? Why were they still fleeing when no one had pursued them? She'd long since given up hope of the authorities overtaking them. They'd come too far and it had been too long. No one was coming for her; no one even knew where she was. Suzette shivered as the futility registered: unless Kaytano contacted Austin, no one would ever know where she was! She'd be this man's captive to do with as he pleased. Instinctively she leaned up away from him.

Weary, weak, her pink skirt and blouse dirty and torn, her scalp itching, her lips chapped from the wind, her hands red and dry, her body aching and sore, Suzette dozed while the big steed loped across the dry, flat desert. The February sun was warm and bright, the air dry and thin. Suzette awoke and looked around. They'd been riding in the desert all day, so she surmised they were somewhere deep in southwest Texas. She'd lost track of the days and nights, and she could hardly remember when she wasn't mounted on a galloping horse in tandem with a tall, dark half-breed. She was so tired of traveling, she felt she would willingly do anything the bandits wanted if they'd only stop this relentless race across the country.

As the day wore on, Kaytano felt her squirming in front of him. She was warm and uncomfortable and tired, so very tired. It was hot here, like June in Jack County. Suzette could feel her soiled clothing prickling her sensitive skin. She'd not had her clothes off in days and she was miserable. She hated the quiet, uncaring man behind her. He thought only of himself. He'd apparently planned the long, hard journey because he changed clothes every day! And he took a bath, she was sure of it! Each morning when she awoke, he was standing over her looking fresh and handsome.

Selfish. That was what Kaytano was. He thought of no one but himself. Oh, certainly he'd indicated that she could bathe if she chose, but she knew very well it would mean disrobing before him, and she was not about to do that. She'd die of filth before she'd let those black eyes rake her bare body.

Suzette felt Kaytano moving. She turned in the saddle and he offered her the canteen. She snatched it and drank greedily, raising it high, letting some spill down over her chin. When he thought she'd had all that was good for her, he took the canteen from her, though she begged for more. He shook his head. She glared at him for a minute, then turned away from him, pouting. She was grinding her teeth in irritation when she saw it.

His brown hand came in front of her; in it he held the canteen. Thinking he'd relented, Suzette smiled. To her surprise, Kaytano turned the canteen upside down over her hot, dry face. She blinked and jerked back against him, but he continued to pour, wetting her hair, her face, and soaking the bodice of her blouse. She objected loudly at first, but her cries rapidly turned to sighs. The cooling water felt good. She loved it and turned her eager face up to the small stream, drinking and spreading it over her face and throat with her hands.

Laughing, her dangerous ordeal for that instant forgotten, Suzette grabbed at the canteen, twisted in the saddle, and turned the rest of the water over Kaytano's dark head. She squealed as she watched the water drip from his thick, black hair over his forehead, high cheekbones, and mouth. He didn't smile, but he licked at his lips and tilted his face up. Suzette watched as it ran down his neck and chest, saturating his thin white batiste shirt. Gleefully she watched the soft material stick to his lean chest, the dark brown of his skin showing through.

With a defiant grin, she handed him the empty canteen and turned away, shaking her wet, tangled hair in his face. The impromptu shower had made her feel like a new woman and she let her eyes feast on the stark beauty of the desert. But reality rapidly returned and she bowed her damp head and sighed. She snapped it up minutes later.

The desert floor was falling away. They were heading down into a deep, seemingly bottomless canyon. Behind her she heard the three companions calling to one another in Spanish. She couldn't understand what they said, but she needed no one to tell her that the trail they were starting down was treacherous. Behind her, Kaytano made low, soothing sounds to his big horse as, slowly and carefully, the black stallion began to pick his way down the rockly incline.

The sun disappeared behind the distant mountains and Suzette silently prayed that it was only a short distance to the bottom. She was terrified by the perilous trail. Not two feet from the horse's hooves, the trail fell away into a sharp drop. Dust rose in the shafts of fading sunlight, further obscuring the threadlike path.

The damp blouse and chemise that had felt so good against her heated skin only moments earlier brought chills now. She wondered if Kaytano was as frightened as she. His dark arms were still around her as he carefully guided the horse, and though she longed to clasp those strong arms for safety, she was afraid any sudden movement might make him jerk up on the reins and spook the horse.

She pressed her back closer to his hard chest, then turned her frightened eyes up to his dark face. The black eyes were alert, but she saw no fear there.

As they descended into the dimness of the vast canyon, Suzette peered carefully into the depths, then shut her eyes as tightly as possible as she pressed her face into Kaytano's comforting throat. Almost ill with terror, she knew her life was in the hands of the renegade and his mount. When the black beast stepped on a small stone, he lurched wildly. Too terrified to scream, Suzette clung to the saddlehorn, while Kaytano masterfully reined the horse back into position.

She could no longer bear to look. She could hear the blowing and snorting of the horse underneath her and the call of the night birds from their hidden perches in the canyon. Kaytano's steady heartbeat helped reassure her.

She could finally feel the ground flatten out; only then did she open her eyes. It was twilight and in the distance she could see what looked to be a sprawling fenced-in compound. Suzette longed to ask questions, but knew she'd get no answers.

A Mexican sentinel wearing bandoliers across his chest swung the gates open. Suzette felt a cold chill when she heard the heavy gates swing shut behind her. Inside the compound, she was lifted from the horse and led inside a lighted building at the center. She looked about the long, rectangular room. A narrow table stretched almost the length of the room along one wall. Chairs lined the other walls. A doorway leading to what she assumed was a kitchen, opened off the back of the big, low-ceilinged room.

A short, pleasant Mexican woman appeared, smiling her welcome. "Kaytano." She beamed and spoke rapidly in Spanish. She disappeared as men began to appear from nowhere, filling up the room. Suzette moved nearer to Kaytano while she looked about at the strange assortment of humanity.

Suddenly realizing she was starving, Suzette willingly took Kaytano's hand and let him help her onto a long bench at the table. He took his place beside her and the other men sat down. From a door at the right, three young boys and a little girl came running to Kaytano. All were Mexican and all were adorable, especially the girl. She looked to be about three years old, and a prettier child never lived. Suzette blinked in disbelief when each child gave Kaytano a hug.

The little girl laughed and climbed up onto his lap, her small, brown hands reaching for his shirt pocket. Kaytano kissed her cheek and turned on the bench, nodding to a gray-haired man who'd just come into the room carrying Kaytano's saddlebags. The man was smiling as he came forward and shook hands with Kaytano, greeting him in Spanish. The man was a good-looking Spaniard, and when he looked at Kaytano, there was a warm light in his eyes, a look of real affection for the dark man. Suzette noticed the older man's hand gripping Kaytano's shoulder as though he were embracing him.

On Kaytano's lap, the little girl was standing, her short arm around his neck, while Kaytano opened the bag and drew out a stick of peppermint. Its red and white stripes brought a look of pure happiness to the child's face. Grabbing it greedily, she let Kaytano kiss her again before he put her down. The boys stood ramrod-straight behind Kaytano. He turned and ruffled the hair of each one, then handed them their candy. All four children ran laughing into the kitchen, shouting to the portly woman dishing up food. Suzette knew enough Spanish to discern that the woman was their mother.

The plentiful food was delicious. Suzette forgot her dilemma and enjoyed the meal. There were at least a dozen men at the long table. All were Mexican except the white man she'd tried to speak to on the trail. And, of course, Kaytano. Conversation buzzed around her, but it was beyond her understanding. She got the impression she was the subject of the discussion and she looked and listened for clues to what they planned to do with her. She found none. The men ate heartily and drank tequila. But not Kaytano. He was drinking red wine and he poured a glass for her. She tried it and found its taste pleasing. By the time the meal ended, she'd had three glasses.

While the stocky Mexican woman cleared away the dishes, the men enjoyed their cigars. Kaytano sat beside her, relaxed, a long, dark cigar between his fingers. Suzette felt safe as long as so many people were in the room. When they began to drift away, she became apprehensive.

Much too soon the men had disappeared and she and Kaytano sat alone at the table. The clatter of dishes from the kitchen ceased and the light went out. Smiling and drying her hands on her apron, the Mexican woman hurried through the big room, nodding and calling, "*Buenas noches.*" She opened the door at the right, and in a matter of minutes the lamp within was extinguished.

Kaytano rose and Suzette tensed. He lifted her over the bench and, with a hand at the small of her back, guided her across the big room to a door at the far end. She felt her chest constricting as they neared the door; when Kaytano threw it open and motioned her inside, she hesitated. He stepped past her and held the door for her. His black eyes were on hers and she shuddered, but stepped inside.

The room was small and clean. Two narrow beds were separated by only a tiny square table bearing an oil lamp. Across from the beds, a scarred bureau held a china washbowl and pitcher behind which a cracked mirror rested against the wall. A couple of simple chairs completed the sparse furnishings. When Suzette heard a clicking sound, she whirled about to find Kaytano locking the door. To her horror, he was still inside.

All at once her composure crumbled. The long days on the trail when she'd remained calm and hopeful were gone. As long as she was out in the open, she'd managed to keep from surrendering to total panic. With the locking of the door, Kaytano sealed her fate, took her freedom, doomed her to his prison.

He took a step toward her and she flew to meet him. A scream tore from her tight throat as she became hysterical and lost control. Certain he was going to rape her, Suzette pounded on his hard chest and hurled insults at him.

"You savage bastard!" she shouted. "You drag me across Texas to this God-forsaken hideout! Why didn't you save yourself the time and rape and murder me that first night!" Tears coursed down her cheeks and she tossed her head and shrieked, "I hate the sight of you, you brown-skinned, stupid animal! That's right!" she shouted into his face. "Stand there like a statue with those flat, black eyes staring at me! God, how I wish you could speak English. How I long for you to understand my disgust for you! Never have I seen such a cold, heartless snake. That's what you remind me of, you slippery son-of-a-bitch!"

Her hands continued to beat his chest, while he stood, absorbing each blow without so much as the flicker of a dark eyelash. "What would it take to get your attention? Will this do it?" she screamed and raised her hand to his face. Starting at his taut coppery cheekbone, she dragged her jagged nails down his right cheek, drawing blood. "There!" she hissed as tiny drops of blood appeared immediately. "How's that? Did you feel that?" She eyed him expectantly. From four long furrows, blood dripped down his face and onto the white collar of his shirt. Still he remained quiet, looking at her without expression.

Suzette began to sob and beat on him until she could no longer raise her tired, aching arms. Spent, she fell against him, still trying to hit him. Her knees were buckling and she felt herself going down. She clung to his white shirt, trying to stay on her feet, but he offered no help. She was on her knees when her hand could no longer clutch the smooth fabric. Slowly each fist opened and, with her palms flat, her hands slid over his stomach and down his thighs. Sobbing quietly, she was at his feet, her head pressed against his sinewy leg. In desperation, she locked her arms around his leg and clung to him, crying as though her heart were breaking.

For a long time, Kaytano stood above her. He slowly raised his arm and wiped the blood from his face on his shirtsleeve.

When Suzette finally stopped crying, Kaytano stooped and lifted her up into his arms. She put up no fight. She was wrung out, completely exhausted, subdued.

He carried her to one of the narrow beds and laid her down gently. Through puffy eyes Suzette watched him cross the room and return with a soft wet cloth. When his fingers went to the buttons at the neck of her dirty pink blouse, Suzette couldn't even move. He could do anything he pleased with her now; she could no longer fight him.

Deftly, Kaytano flipped open three buttons, stopping at the swell of her breasts. With a touch as delicate as a surgeon's, he gently washed her red eyes, her smudged cheeks, her runny nose. He turned the cloth over and pressed it to her neck and throat, carefully lifting the golden heart in his lean fingers, sliding the damp cloth underneath the chain.

Placing the heart back in the hollow of her throat, Kaytano moved the cloth up to Suzette's hairline, as, almost tenderly, he smoothed the dirty, tangled hair back from her forehead and cheeks. Suzette felt a deep weariness claiming her as he tended her.

He slipped her kid shoes from her feet and pulled a blanket up to her waist. That done, he rose and stood above her, looking down at her through heavy-lidded eyes. Her lashes fluttered sleepily, then flew wide open when his dark head bent close to hers and in a voice so soft and deep it made her shiver, Kaytano whispered, "Welcome to Robber's Roost, Suzette Brand."

25

"Dear God, I hope she's not suffering."

"Austin, don't torture yourself this way." Tom Capps poured two glasses of bourbon.

Austin came back to the desk. Fingering the dainty, soiled pink blouse, he shook his blond head in despair. "Tom, will you look at these clothes. They're torn and filthy and... and..." He dropped the blouse and banged his big fist. "The bastard sent her underwear, her shoes, stockings — everything! He stripped her naked, Tom." Austin trembled with rage and helplessness.

"Austin, have a drink and calm yourself. She's alive. That's the important thing, isn't it? I don't think he'll harm her."

"Not harm her!" Austin bellowed, his face blood-red. "How naïve you are, old friend. Why do you think he took her! Not harm her." Austin ran a hand through his blond hair. "As we speak that savage is... he's..." He fell silent and sat down heavily in the chair behind his desk.

Tom Capps pushed the jigger of whiskey to Austin. "Please, Austin, drink it." Tom looked at the big man slumped over the desk, his head in his hands. He'd seen Austin face dangers and tragedies in the past, had witnessed his hurt and grief before, but never had Austin's gray eyes held the kind of agony he saw there now. In the two weeks that had passed since Suzette's disappearance, Austin had hardly eaten, and he slept only an hour or two at a time. He paced the floor and moaned, cursing the dark bandit who was holding his wife; raging at his impotence against the elusive half-breed.

Austin had known from the minute he was notified of Suzette's capture. "Kaytano," he breathed, "damn your soul to hell! I'll kill you for this. If it's the last thing I do, I'll kill you."

After the initial shock, Austin had swung into action. Half the rangers in the state of Texas were searching for Kaytano and his blond captive. Law officers in every city and town were notified; posses were formed, rewards offered, informants sought out, bribes made. A legion of men was sent by Austin himself to search for his beloved Suzette.

Not one clue had been turned up. There was no trace of the slippery Satanic savage and the helpless young woman he'd stolen. Nothing, that is, until a crudely wrapped box arrived through the mail, postmarked San Antonio, Texas. It was addressed to Austin Brand. Denis Sanders brought it to the ranch, sweeping his hat off his head, telling Kate that he'd come to deliver a package to Mr. Brand.

From the library, Austin heard Denis and called to him, "In here, son." Denis, aware of his employer's tragedy, awkwardly walked into the big room, nodding to Austin and to Tom Capps, who stood in front of the fireplace. He quickly thrust the box into Austin's hand and fled.

Austin ripped open the box. Suzette's clothes tumbled out: the pink wool skirt, soiled silk blouse, frilly petticoats and underwear, sheer stockings, and soft leather shoes. Tom saw the big man sway and was at his side instantly. He caught Austin just as his knees buckled. Shoving him into the chair behind the oak desk, Tom tried in vain to pull a lacy petticoat from Austin's hands. For a long time Tom talked quietly to his friend. Finally he gave up and turned to leave. "If you need me, Austin, I'll be in the kitchen."

Austin gave no answer. He sat clutching the petticoat as though he would never release it. He was still there when the winter sun went down, leaving the spacious room in the shadowy light from the dying fireplace. Deaf to Kate's pleas that he should eat dinner, the despondent man remained where he was, staring into space, tenderly touching the soft, feminine belongings of the beautiful wife he wasn't sure he'd ever touch again.

Suzette stood at the stove and stirred the large pot of stew. Maria smiled at her. "Dish it up, Suzette. The men are at the table."

Nodding, Suzette ladled the hot, spicy stew into large bowls. She carried the first bowl into the dining room, glancing automatically at Kaytano. He was seated at the head of the table, and his eyes followed her as she came through the door. Suzette carried the heavy bowl the length of the table, placing it directly in front of Kaytano. Inwardly she cringed when he lifted his hand, then relaxed when his fingers went to his face. With deliberate, exaggerated strokes, he traced the long, deep scratches on his right cheek, drawing in his breath as though in pain. She longed to reach out and claw the other cheek, but she ignored him, and with a toss of her head she returned to the kitchen to bring more stew.

When all the food had been dished up and the men were eating, Suzette stood in the kitchen slicing big pieces of pie for their dessert. In the week she'd been in camp, she'd quickly adapted to the strange new way of life and there were moments when she forgot how frightened and alone she was.

She'd awakened on that first morning to find a tub of hot water waiting for her. On one of the chairs she discovered a pair of denim breeches, a plaid shirt, a pair of soft brown moccasins, a hairbrush, and a bar of soap and a towel. For her use, the smiling, friendly Mexican woman had assured her.

"I am Maria, *señora*," the chubby brown woman said by way of introducing herself. "I speak English and I will be your friend. Kaytano, he wait outside door to speak with you. When you clean, you come to kitchen, *sí*?"

Suzette nodded and rose from the bed. Maria disappeared and a cool, imperious Kaytano came into the room. He was immaculate, which made the long, red scratches all the more noticeable. Suzette's eyes flickered to his. Would she be punished for her foolish transgression?

As if reading her thoughts, Kaytano touched his face. "I'll overlook it this once. You were frightened and upset." His dark, brooding face was serious, his presence intimidating. Suzette took a step backward as he walked to her. Undaunted, he followed until the wall ended her retreat. Trapped, she stood looking at him, remembering all the terrible things she'd said the night before, sure he was remembering, too. Suzette held her breath.

"You need a bath," said Kaytano quietly. "Wash your hair, too. I've laid out fresh clothes for you. When you are cleaned up, I'll come for you." He left the room while Suzette stood plastered to the wall, trying to understand what the tall, slim bandit had in mind for her.

With a dismissive shake of her head, Suzette undressed

and climbed into the tub. She was soaping her long, tangled hair when Maria bustled in, offering help. Assuring the stocky Mexican woman that she could manage, Suzette protested when Maria picked up her soiled clothes from the floor.

"Where are you taking my things, Maria?"

Her swarthy face reddening, Maria hastily explained. "*Señora*, Kaytano say I am to bring to him everything. He say you will wear trousers and shirt."

"Yes, I will, Maria, but I must have something to wear underneath. Surely he doesn't expect me to go about in only the trousers and shirt."

The woman looked uncomfortable. "Yes, he does." She carried the soiled clothing from the room.

Suzette, dressed in the trousers that fit over her hips snugly and the man's plaid shirt, stood in front of the cracked mirror brushing the tangles from her long, clean hair. When there was a soft knock on the door, Suzette knew it was Kaytano. He entered, but left the door open behind him.

"Come," he said, "dry your hair in the sun."

Feeling naked and embarrassed without underclothes, she walked past him and lifted her chin. If he noticed, he gave no sign. He took her into the sunny courtyard and introduced her to his men, as though she were a guest.

Most of the names ran together, but a few stood out; one was the small gray-haired man she remembered from the dining room the night before. She recalled the affection he showed Kaytano.

"This is Pancho Montoya. He is my friend and he is second in command here. Should you need anything when I'm away, Pancho will see to it."

"*Señora*," Montoya bowed and smiled warmly. "I am honored to meet such a charming and beautiful lady."

Suzette nodded but remained silent. She couldn't believe what was happening. The conceit and arrogance of Kaytano were unbelievable. He acted as though she were there of her own free will and that she actually wanted to meet his gang of cutthroats and murderers! He called each one by name and presented her as though she were his woman. She wanted to scream that she considered his ragged band of outlaws repulsive and that she had no intention of associating with them *or* him.

Finally, Kaytano took her inside and turned her over to Maria, explaining that Suzette would help out with the cooking and cleaning.

"Maria is a very good cook; she will teach you." He looked at Suzette.

Taking offense, Suzette shot back, "What makes you think I can't cook?"

Kaytano shrugged. "I would imagine you're out of practice. However, you shall... " Kaytano stopped speaking and his black eyes lit up. The tiny girl Suzette had seen the evening before came into the kitchen. Her pretty brown face was dirty, as was her dress. Her bare feet were caked with mud.

Maria's hands flew to her full cheeks. "*Díos!* Connie, you are like orphan!"

To Suzette's amazement, Kaytano smiled at the dirty child and crouched down, his long arms held out to her. Giggling happily, the grimy little girl ran to him. Kaytano rose with her in his arms. When Connie's small brown hand touched his scratched cheek and she frowned and said the word "hurt," the dark man smiled and kissed her nose.

"No, sweetheart," he soothed, "I'm fine, just fine." He left the kitchen carrying the beautiful child. Suzette noticed that Connie's dirty bare feet were pressed against the crisp, clean shirt he wore, but Kaytano didn't seem to mind at all.

"Kaytano seems very fond of your Connie," Suzette said after he'd gone.

"He love her! He spoil all my children and they adore him."

As that first day came to a close, Suzette grew nervous again. After the evening meal, she helped Maria clear away the dishes and wash them. By the time they finished, the dining room was deserted.

"I am tired, *señora*," Maria said sweetly. "I will see you in the morning." With that, Maria went to her quarters, leaving Suzette alone. There was little hope of escape; men's voices came from just outside the front door. Suzette sighed and went into her small room. She was standing at the window looking out wistfully when Kaytano entered. She turned as he locked the door.

Leaning against it, he said in a conversational tone, "As you have seen, this is the room where you and I will sleep each night. When you are not helping Maria, you will stay in this room. At night the door will be locked to discourage any attempts on your part to escape. However, since there is a window in the room, further discouragement will be necessary." He looked into her eyes and drew a cigar from his breast pocket. Cupping his brown hands, he lit it, then moved closer to her. "You will undress each night and give your clothes to me. I will fold them and place them under my pillow."

Suzette stared at him. He never ceased to amaze her. Twenty-four hours ago, he'd let her hit him, claw his face, shout insults, all without lifting a hand to stop her. Then he'd tenderly washed her face and neck and covered her up. He'd been almost kind. Now he was telling her he would take all her clothes from her and lock her up at night! Was last night his way of letting her rest and clean up before he took her?

A chill ran up her spine, and she moved away from him. "Please, don't do this. If you don't harm me, you'll get a lot of money from my husband. Isn't that why you wanted all my clothes? Didn't you want to prove to Austin that you have me? If you send him those things and arrange a meeting, he'll pay you a big ransom. I won't run away, I'll wait for you to get the money."

"Your clothes will be sent to your husband," he said flatly, stepping between the two beds. He blew out the lamp on the small table, throwing the room into darkness. The glowing red tip of his cigar illuminated his dark, handsome face.

Suzette watched as he unbuttoned his shirt and removed it. She could see only the outline of his slender, long-waisted torso. She whirled around, her heart drumming in her ears. She could hear him taking off his tight black trousers. The bed squeaked when he got into it.

"Suzette," he spoke softly from his bed, "take off your clothes and give them to me."

Feeling as though the worst were finally going to happen, Suzette gritted her teeth and turned from the window. With feet of lead she crossed the room to the beds. In the dim light she could barely make out Kaytano's bare shoulders and dark head, the white sheet pulled up to his waist. Trembling, she turned away from him and started unbuttoning her shirt. Expecting him to rise at any minute and pull her down to him, she pushed the shirt apart and down her shoulders.

Suddenly it was so quiet in the room she could hear her own breathing. And Kaytano's. She was terrified, her hands shaking so badly she had trouble getting the tight denim trousers down over her hips. Hot tears slid down her cheeks when she stepped out of the pants and kicked off her moccasins. Naked, she stood with her back to him, waiting for the inevitable. A sob was tearing at her throat. Resolutely she folded her clothes and held them behind her, her arm jerking involuntarily. She felt the clothes being taken from her hand and heard his deep voice. "Thank you. Get into bed."

A cry tore from her lips as she pulled back the covers and slid into the narrow bed. Pulling the sheet up to her chin, she clutched it to her and cried. In the narrow bed next to hers, the red glow of a cigar moved back and forth. Tense and waiting, Suzette tried to draw into herself. Finally she saw him snuff out the cigar in a dish on the table. She was all too aware of his black eyes on her.

But her captor shocked her once again. "Please," he whispered, his voice warm, "don't cry. Sleep now."

26

As a cold blustery March hit the plains, the mournful sigh of the winds swirling about the Brand mansion echoed the loneliness of the big, sorrowful man within. Austin fought despair, knowing that for Suzette's sake he must remain hopeful, alert, ready to ride at any hour should news of her whereabouts come.

With the passing of each long, lonely day, he grew more despondent. His friend Tom Capps was growing as concerned for Austin's well-being as he was for the absent Suzette. Austin was losing weight, and his face grew gaunt, his eyes hollow. He neither ate nor slept properly and the effects were taking their toll.

At sundown on a long, cold Saturday, Tom Capps sat with Austin in the dining room of the mansion. Tom had come for supper and Kate had outdone herself, hoping to tempt Austin to eat. He tried, but the tasty roast beef would not go down. Pushing his plate aside, Austin reached for a decanter of brandy. Offering Tom a glass, he shrugged when Tom declined, then drank glass after glass of the fiery liquid, all the while speaking of the happy days aboard the Alpha with his angel, Suzette.

When the decanter was empty, Tom Capps pushed back his chair. "Austin, old friend, please let me help you up to bed."

Austin looked up and laughed hollowly. "Bed? Do you think I sleep anymore? I don't want to sleep. She may need me." He rose on wobbly legs. "Suzette may ... she might ..."

"Come on, I'll help you upstairs." Tom quickly lent his support to a very unstable Austin. From the open door of the kitchen where she'd been quietly observing the two men, Kate hurried in, nodding to Tom. She put an arm around Austin's waist. Together Tom and Kate were able to get the big man upstairs. While Kate turned back the covers, Tom removed Austin's boots. Austin, his lids drooping, his fingers struggling with the buttons of his shirt, was speaking softly, his words running together.

"What is it, Austin?" Tom leaned close. "What can I get you?"

"Not... here... I... " Austin sighed and clutched at Tom's shirtfront.

"I don't understand, old friend." Tom's creased face was troubled.

Austin blinked and spoke louder, his body tensing, trying to rise. "Not... not... the blue... her..."

Kate, standing nearby, nodded her head in understanding. "Tom," she said quietly, "he wants to sleep in her bed. He wants to sleep in the blue room."

"Yes... yes..." Austin bobbed his head up and down. "Blue... her..."

With effort, he was taken into the next room. Kate rushed to throw back the covers while Tom managed to get Austin's shirt off. Austin's rugged face took on an almost peaceful look when he stretched out and hugged a soft, blue pillow, murmuring thickly, "Suzette... my wife."

Kate turned and fled.

Tom Capps covered the sleeping man with the blue sheets. "Sleep, Austin. Forget for just a while." Then he put out the lamp by the bed and tiptoed from the quiet room.

Hundreds of miles away at Robber's Roost in the Big Bend country of Texas, Suzette Brand lay wide awake in her narrow bed, thinking of her husband. Knowing Austin as she did, she couldn't understand why he hadn't ransomed her yet. It made no sense. Weeks had passed since Kaytano sent her clothes to him. She was certain the half-breed had spelled out the terms of her release. What was Austin waiting for? Why didn't he come for her?

Suzette longed for her husband. The days were not so bad; she was busy helping Maria with the cooking, cleaning, and laundry. She was glad Kaytano made her work; the time passed faster when she was occupied. The nights were terrible. Unwilling to associate with Kaytano and his gang, Suzette retreated to their room each evening as soon as the supper dishes were cleared away and spent countless hours at the window. Having no diversion, nothing to do in the tiny room, she often watched the men in the courtyard. Some nights a couple of the Mexicans brought out guitars and strummed softly. The sweet, romantic music only magnified her distress and loneliness.

During those hours of gazing out the window, Suzette's eyes returned again and again to the dark, brooding Kaytano. He usually sat on the broad porch, his back against a post, his long legs stretched out in front of him, or his knees bent with his arms around them. A long, black cigar was always clenched between his white teeth. She wondered what was running through his mind as he sat there, moving little, saying nothing.

When the men began to break up for the evening, Suzette hurried to get undressed and into her bed before Kaytano came in. She'd blow out the lamp, strip, fold her clothes, and place them under Kaytano's pillow. Then she'd slip into her bed, pulling the sheet up under her chin. She always closed her eyes tightly, wanting him to think her asleep.

When he entered the room, she always held her breath. Every night she was filled with the same gnawing fear. Would he turn back the covers and crawl into bed with her? Would he rape her while she struggled helplessly, the sounds of her screams filling the quiet house? Would he become violent and beat her when she screamed?

While she lay awake in the darkness, so close to Kaytano she could reach out and touch him, she turned her head to look at him. He lay on his back, the sheet at his waist. In the dim light she studied his profile. In repose, his hard features looked softer, the tight mouth fuller. The thick black hair tumbled over his high forehead, and those incredibly long lashes hid the disturbing black eyes. His brown satiny chest rose evenly with his breathing, while a long, lightly muscled arm lay across his stomach.

Suzette gripped the sheet with one hand and raised herself on an elbow. He looked so harmless and peaceful. Almost boyish. He moaned a little in his sleep and turned over, burrowing his head under his pillow. His brown hand pushed the pillow from the bed to the floor, but still he slept.

Suzette's shirt and trousers lay at the head of his bed in plain sight. To her delight, Kaytano's head was not touching them. Suzette's heart began to pound. They lay there, tempting her to take them and dress! She knew the key to the door was in Kaytano's trousers pocket. His trousers hung on the back of a chair. Suzette twisted her head about to locate them. Smiling in the darkness, she saw them only a few feet from her. Easing up into a sitting position, she looked back at Kaytano. He was sleeping soundly, dead to the world.

If she had her clothes and the key, she could slip out quietly. Outside she could avoid the guard at the gate by climbing over the fence at the back of the building. If she could manage to get a horse from the remuda, so much the better. If not, she could walk out of the canyon. By morning she could be up on top! Excitement made her palms perspire. Suzette felt hope swelling in her breast. Perhaps with any luck she'd be back in her husband's big, comforting arms within a few days. The thought was so pleasant that Suzette had to fight back a happy sigh.

Lying down again, she carefully planned exactly what she would do. The first thing would be to get the key from Kaytano's pocket. Without the key, her clothes would do her no good. The key pressed in her palm, she'd crawl quietly to his bed and slowly pick up her clothes. If he didn't wake up, she'd dress rapidly, unlock the door, and slip from the room. In seconds she'd be outside, across the courtyard and over the fence, and on her way to freedom. She'd run as fast as her legs would carry her until she was out of sight of the compound.

Suzette wrapped the sheet loosely over her breasts. Her eyes on Kaytano, she rose and edged over to his trousers. Still looking at the sleeping man, she slid her fingers deep into a pocket. Almost laughing aloud, she gripped the cold key and brought it out, holding it up to her face. Impulsively kissing the metal that meant her escape, she clasped it tightly and went down on her knees. She crept close to Kaytano's bed, silently cursing the sheet that slowed her progress.

She was beside his bed, so close to Kaytano she could hear his steady breathing. One of his brown shoulders almost touched the trousers. For a time Suzette sat, gripping her sheet, staring at her clothes. Knowing it would never grow easier, she put a tentative hand over his head and let her fingers touch the plaid shirt. Then she screamed.

A warm brown hand touched her bare shoulder. Drawing back in horror, Suzette dropped the shirt and the sheet. Kaytano said coldly, "Sleep-walking?" His face was inches from her own and his hand lightly gripped her shoulder. Suzette looked into his eyes, terrified. His gaze held hers as he reached down and slowly pulled the sheet up over her bare breasts. "A good thing I'm a gentleman. A baser man might be tempted to... "

With a shriek she twisted away from him. Lunging back to her bed, she lay shaking with fear and rage. Kaytano, his weight supported on an elbow, watched her. "Calm down," he cautioned. "I'm not angry that you were trying to escape." He reached to the floor and picked up the key. "You'll learn you've no chance of getting away from me, but I do admire your spirit. A prisoner should try to escape. I'd do the same thing in your place." He flipped the key noisily to the table between them and lay down, his hands under his head. "Perhaps you've been cooped up too long. Tomorrow I'll take you for a walk."

Suzette didn't reply. She was furious that he'd outwitted her, and even more furious when, only minutes later, the heartless man in the bed next to her was sleeping peacefully.

The next morning dawned unusually cold in the canyon. Suzette's eyes opened to see Kaytano spreading a warm quilt over her. He wore a pair of tight buckskin breeches and a fringed shirt to match. Thinking sleepily that the man was a constant surprise, she sighed and snuggled down into the bed and went back to sleep. Later, as she helped serve the noon meal, she glanced at Kaytano and wondered if he still intended to take her for a walk. She longed to get outside for a while, even in his company, so she smiled at him, hoping he'd recall his promise.

Kaytano didn't return the smile. His dark eyes locked on her, but she saw a look of censure there, so she lowered her eyes. She didn't look at him again and sighed with relief when the meal ended and he drifted outdoors with the other men.

Her kitchen chores completed, Suzette returned to her room. The chill of the morning had disappeared and it was warm in the little room. Outside the sun shone brightly. A gentle breeze stirred the curtains. Sighing heavily, Suzette went to the window. On the long, sunny porch, several of the men sat smoking, their voices rising and falling. As she always did, Suzette looked about for her captor. When she located him, her eyes never left him.

Kaytano had taken off the heavy fringed shirt. Barechested, he sat with his back against a post, facing her. His long legs were crossed at the ankles, and his skintight breeches were laced at the fly with rawhide strips tied in a loose knot at his waist. He was lighting a cigar and his bare, brown arms rippled with delicate muscles. His dark chest was shiny and smooth. Slim yet powerful, his torso tapered gracefully to a trim, hard abdomen.

He was speaking, though she couldn't hear what he said. He took the cigar from his teeth, and for the first time ever Suzette saw Kaytano smile broadly. Amazed at how the smile softened his hard, handsome features, she stared unbelieving as his satiny chest shook with laughter. When she realized she was smiling also, she felt foolish and confused. Her smile faded, but she continued to look at Kaytano.

A fat, furry cat sidled up to him. His brown hand shot out and grabbed the cat, teasing the feline by tickling her head. The cat, which paid little attention to Kaytano's hand, seemed fascinated with the rawhide laces at his crotch. The cat pawed and pulled at the laces, all the while making growling noises deep in her throat.

When Kaytano had had enough, he brought a brown hand down to pull the cat onto his lap, stroking its fur with long fingers. Immediately the cat settled into his lap and was soon purring.

Suzette watched the pair and became inexplicably irritated. Suddenly she whirled away from the window, ground her teeth, and crossed the room to her bed. Throwing herself down onto it, she lay on her back and felt restless, unnerved, upset. She closed her eyes.

The unsettling sensual picture of the dark, handsome, half-naked Kaytano tenderly stroking the purring kitten with his long, lean, brown fingers made her eyes fly open. To her dismay her pulse was speeding and her stomach tightened, causing her hand to fly to her midsection. She lay staring up at the ceiling while perspiration popped out on her upper lip, along her hairline, and between her breasts. She felt confused. And afraid. And guilty. She turned onto her stomach and cried. "Austin," she murmured into her pillow, "please come for me. Austin, Austin."

At supper Suzette avoided Kaytano, refusing to look at him after the first sweeping glance she gave the men around the table. Kaytano wore a clean white shirt and a black leather vest, accentuating his dark hair and eyes. Assuring herself she cared not at all what he wore, Suzette served the food without making eye contact with him. Relieved when she saw him going out the front door, she went about clearing the dishes away, anxious to be finished so she could go back to the privacy of her small, airless room.

Maria, washing the last large platter, snapped the silent Suzette out of her reveries when she smiled and said, "Suzette, Kaytano tell me that if you like, he let you go for a walk in back courtyard."

Suzette looked incredulously at Maria. "When?"

"As soon as we finish." Maria beamed.

"With whom, Maria? Kaytano?"

"No, *señora*. Kaytano say you can go alone if you stay only in back courtyard."

More excited than she wanted Maria to know, Suzette kept her voice even. "There must be some mistake. You're sure Kaytano told you I can go out alone?"

Maria raised a chubby, wet hand. "Yes, yes. You see that back door? Outside there is private fenced yard, separate from others. It is nice and big, good for walk on spring night."

"Maria, I do want to go outdoors. Will you tell Kaytano I am very grateful to him?"

"Why you not tell him yourself?" Her brown face reddening, Maria giggled and whispered, "For two young pretty people who are... ah... you and Kaytano talk little. I do not understand."

"Maria, you have it wrong. Kaytano and I —"

"Please" — Maria wiggled out of her arpon — "do not disclose all your secrets. I know how it is between man and his woman. Before my husband die, we were foolish lovers too. Now, go enjoy yourself before darkness comes."

Suzette tossed the damp dish towel over a chair and went to the back door. " 'Night, Maria." She smiled and slipped outdoors. Stepping off the porch, she inhaled deeply, thinking how wonderful it was to be outside and alone. She smiled and sauntered out into the big fenced yard, her eyes on the fading pinks and lilacs of the western sky. She walked about slowly, enjoying the close of the spring day while a chill crept into the night air.

When she heard a horse whinny nearby, she stopped walking and cocked her head. Again she heard the sound, followed by hooves pounding the hard earth. Her interest aroused, she hurried in the direction of the sounds. She was in back of the buildings; it must be the stables. With a quick surge of hope, Suzette envisioned herself slipping into the stables, picking a gentle horse from the remuda, and galloping away into the night.

Looking about to be certain she was not being watched, Suzette hurried across the courtyard to the back fence. She saw a gate, and to her surprise, when she pulled the latch it swung open easily. A corral of split rails was no more than fifty yards aways. Suzette rushed toward the rising fence; through the boards she could see the horse. It was big and black. The beast Kaytano rode. The horse called Darkness.

The black stallion was the only horse in the corral. Sighing, Suzette spun around, looking for other corrals, other horses. She saw none. It was this big brute or nothing. There was little time to consider other possibilities. The black stallion was huge and powerful and Suzette cringed at the thought of riding it, especially bareback, but she had no choice. If she could manage to get on him, she'd stay on his back somehow. Twilight was closing in swiftly. Suzette searched for a gate, found it, and frowned. It was locked. Biting her lip, she wondered if Kaytano held the only key.

Undaunted, she put her hands on the split rails and began her climb. Splinters pierced her red, chapped hands, but Suzette clung to the fence, stepping up on the first rung. She looked up to the top and wondered why it was necessary for it to be so high.

Across the darkened corral, the red glow of a cigar briefly lighted the dark, unsmiling face of Kaytano. He watched Suzette through the fence as she grunted and struggled to the top. He was leaning against the corral, a knee bent, heel hooked on the bottom rung of the fence. When her golden head finally appeared over the top plank, Kaytano gently sighed and reached for a lariat looped over a nearby pole. Cigar clamped between his teeth, he slowly and surely began to swing the riata. Suzette sat astride the fence now and called to the big black steed. It pricked up its ears and studied the intruder.

"Come on, boy," Suzette whispered. "I won't hurt you. Here, Darkness," she called to the prancing horse.

Darkness, curious and playful, started across the corral, tossing his long mane, whinnying loudly. "That's right, Darkness." Suzette smiled happily. "Come here to me. Yes, boy, yes." Sensing freedom was at last within her grasp, Suzette suppressed a laugh as the big black horse cantered over to her.

Her scream shattered the stillness. Squirming, she fought to maintain her balance, gripping the roughhewn fence while a rope pinned her arms to her sides. Out of the darkness, Kaytano walked across the corral, speaking to his horse as he came.

"It's all right, Darkness." The powerful beast halted and went to meet his master. Nuzzling Kaytano's shoulder with his velvet muzzle, Darkness walked alongside him. The dark man and dark horse were bearing down on the frightened girl clinging to the fence.

When they reached her, Kaytano lifted Suzette from the fence onto Darkness's bare back. In one fluid movement, Kaytano climbed on behind her. Into her ear, he said, "I had no idea you were so anxious to ride. Had you told me, I'd have taken you before now. Perhaps it isn't too late." He gently raised the rope up over her head and tossed it over the fence.

Kaytano's hands were on her shoulders now. His right one slowly slid around to her throat, his fingers spreading, gently forcing her head back against his shoulder. His lips near her ear, his warm breath stirring wisps of her hair, he said in a soft voice, "I suggest you hold on to me or to Darkness's mane. You want to ride and we wish to oblige you."

He lowered his hands to his thighs. Gently he kicked the horse's belly. Dutifully the horse headed for the gate, turning sideways when he reached it. Kaytano unlocked it and spoke to the horse. Outside, Suzette, refusing to speak to the arrogant Kaytano, felt his long arm come around her as he reached for a handful of Darkness's mane. Knowing full well he intended to gallop at breakneck speed in the thickening darkness, Suzette leaned forward and grasped the horse's mane with both hands.

"Now, Darkness," came Kaytano's soft-spoken command. The big horse bolted.

Her tears drying, her heart pounding with fear and excitement, Suzette felt the cool wind whip her hair and sting her cheeks, invigorating her. Wondering briefly if she'd gone completely mad, Suzette threw back her head and breathed deeply. With a feeling close to gratitude, she smiled when Kaytano's dark left hand went to her waist to press her back against him. Releasing her hold on Darkness's mane, she leaned back, molding herself to Kaytano. Knowing that he'd never let her fall, Suzette clung to his strong arm and let the joy of the ride, the night, the spring, and the excitement wash over her.

Across the canyon floor they thundered under a rising moon, and Suzette forgot that she was a captive, a prisoner, a helpless white woman held by an Indian outlaw. For now she was a carefree, thrill-seeking, free woman riding in the moonlight with a daring, handsome man eager to show her a good time.

For a while they were equals, she and Kaytano — young, healthy, happy, and enjoying every minute of their moonlight adventure.

27

Days turned into weeks, weeks into months, and still Suzette was held prisoner at Robber's Roost deep inside Santa Elena Canyon in the Big Bend of the Rio Grande River. In a land with a reputation for its brutality, hardness, and violence,

Suzette was the prisoner of Kaytano, whose reputation matched that of the wild country.

Suzette had tried time and again to find out if Kaytano had contacted Austin. Each time she'd questioned him, all she got was a cool nod and his assurance that she would soon be going home. She clung to hope, but instinct told her that her captivity was strange. Her presence in this remote place with a robber band was much more than a ransom demand. And she knew her husband. If Austin had been contacted and quoted a price, he would have paid off Kaytano and taken her home by now. Still, she couldn't solve the puzzle and more than once she recalled Austin's strange reactions to the stories about Kaytano in the newspapers. Did the two men know each other? It didn't seem likely; Kaytano was no more than a couple of years older than Suzette. Where could they have met? That couldn't be it.

It was baffling to Suzette that she was as yet unharmed, though she felt no real security. Kaytano was the strangest of men. The enigmatic half-breed was beyond her understanding. To take her continued safety for granted would be foolish; the impenetrable outlaw never behaved as expected. So she remained respectfully wary of the slim, aristocratic-looking Indian.

Fear of Kaytano caused Suzette to adopt some of his traits; she was withdrawn, aloof, and uncomplaining. She still cried for Austin, but she contained those tears until Kaytano was a-sleep. Only then did she bury her face in her pillow and weep with despair and longing for her good-natured, affectionate husband.

Her days were busy; she was required to help Maria with much of the work. On a warm, still day near June's end, she sat on the back steps with Maria peeling apples. The afternoon would be spent in the hot kitchen, baking pies for the evening meal. Dreading the thought of going back inside, Suzette, her thick blond hair clinging to her clammy neck, sighed. "What I'd give to go over to that clear, cool creek. It's so hot today. Can you imagine how it would feel to strip and fall into the water?" She dropped an apple into Maria's big pan.

"Ah, *sí*," Maria bobbed her head. "That is Terlingua Creek. Is beautiful, but cold. You would freeze, Suzette."

"Umm. No matter, it's impossible." Suzette sighed heavily and picked up another apple.

"All things are possible." Kaytano's deep voice came from the doorway. Suzette jerked her head around. He stood looking down at her, his expression one of wry amusement and as unsettling as his iciness. Why should he find it comical that she longed to cool herself in the creek? He came outside and slowly dropped into a crouch next to Suzette. Taking the unpeeled apple from her hand, he took a bite, chewed slowly, and said, "You may go to the creek in exactly one hour. I will alert my men so that your privacy is assured." He took another bite of the apple and looked at her from under lowered lids.

Suzette stared at him openmouthed. Maria ducked her head and smiled; the two young people were looking into each other's eyes and she was an intruder. Maria had taken for granted the two were lovers. They slept in the same room and she assumed that Kaytano, though he'd hurt Suzette that first night, had long since wooed and won her. Maria reckoned that Kaytano and Suzette were silently communicating now; he was telling her that they would meet at the creek.

Maria rose from the steps. "I go do my baking."

Neither Suzette nor Kaytano responded. They were still looking at each other. Finally Suzette said, "You mean it? I can spend the afternoon alone?"

"Yes." He rose behind her. "Be very careful."

She jumped up from the steps. "I will, I promise. Thank you, Kaytano." She smiled at him, took the half-eaten apple from his hand, took a big bite, and hurried past him into the kitchen. Kaytano turned to look out over the courtyard. He was smiling.

Suzette hummed as she made her way across the canyon

floor. The afternoon was clear and hot and Suzette felt her spirits soar. Inhaling deeply, she felt more alive than she had since the night of their wild horseback ride in the moonlight. The memory of that night brought a flush to her cheeks, as it always did, and Suzette shook her head as if to banish it from her thoughts. Hairbrush, soap, and towel in hand, she skipped along, determined to let nothing ruin her day.

At the creek, Suzette took in the spring flowers, the grass, and the deep shade. The sparkling water rushing over the mossy rocks looked so inviting that Suzette could hardly wait to get undressed. Dropping her things on the grass, she kicked off her moccasins and hurried to the water's edge. She stopped, looked all about her, then cocked her head to one side, listening. Confident she was alone, Suzette whooped happily and yanked at the buttons of her shirt. In seconds it was on the ground. Laughing, she unbuttoned and wiggled out of the tight trousers, then tossed them aside. Wonderfully bare, she stood on a smooth rock on the banks of the creek and let the hot June sun beat down on her. Purposely delaying the plunge until she felt uncomfortably warm, Suzette waited, body arched, hands holding her thick hair up off her neck, her eyes closed.

She could wait no longer. She splashed into the water, screaming from the minute her toe hit the stream. It was so icy it took her breath away, but she doggedly pressed on, going farther into the depths, the water rising to her knees, her hips, her waist, while she trailed her fingers in the splash. Gasping, she finally sat down on the pebbled bottom, letting the cold, clear water close over her shoulders. Sitting on her heels, she let her body adapt to the water's temperature. Soon she sighed, then rose.

"Wonderful!" she called to the birds and trees and blue sky. "Perfect! Marvelous!" She scrambled to the bank to get her soap. Humming, she lathered her silky body and long golden hair. In a world all her own, Suzette sensuously rubbed the soap over her slippery flesh and addressed the strange man back in camp.

"Ah, Kaytano," she breathed aloud, working the bar of soap around her breasts, "you may be an animal, but you have something in common with me. You like being clean, thank God! Do you bathe in this creek? Do you come here each morning and wash that sleek body?" She laughed again and continued to caress her silky body with the soap.

Two hundred feet above her, atop a rocky ledge, Kaytano's black eyes were fastened on the beautiful naked girl innocently displaying her charms. His chest constricted when he heard her speak his name. Unable to tear his eyes from her bare beauty, Kaytano felt his love for her growing.

Kaytano closed his eyes. From the beginning this lovely young woman had touched him; now he was obsessed with her. She filled his head with foolish dreams. He'd told himself she was only a woman, like any other. But it did no good. Suzette was his beautiful blond dream, and to him she was at this very minute properly attired and in the proper place. The very ledge where he sat adoring her was called Mesa de los Angeles, Mesa of the Angels. That was what Suzette was. A fair angel. She was his beautiful naked angel and he longed to keep her here, alone with him, forever.

Suzette, refreshed, rested, and almost happy, dressed lazily after her bath and started back toward the camp. In no hurry to get back, she walked slowly, stopping to pick a wildflower or watch a meadowlark or white-throated canyon wren. And then something stopped her in her tracks. On a ledge of the mesa above her, a bronzed eagle perched, looking at her. A huge predator, he stood a good three feet tall. His hooked beak was a bluish color, his tail black-tipped. His wings were outstretched, ready for flight. His deadly talons were as black as night, and his plumage so dark brown it looked black. The hunter sat on the mountain, scanning the whole of the valley below him.

Suzette shuddered, unable to take her eyes off the majestic eagle. Something about the mighty bird reminded her of Kaytano. He, too, was a loner, unafraid, regal — and dangerous. Suzette shouted up at the big bird, "Hey, Kaytano! Looking for some creature to swoop down on? Searching for some unsuspecting beast to carry away in those dark talons?" She laughed and moved on, the hair on the back of her neck standing up. The eagle watched her go.

Near a dead log on the canyon's floor, a Texas diamondback rattler dozed peacefully. Suzette, her long thick hair still damp from her bath, walked toward the log, though it was unnecessary for her to step onto or over it to follow the path she'd taken to the creek.

Running her fingers through her hair, she decided she'd stay in the peaceful canyon until her hair was completely dry. As she looked about for a nice grassy spot, her eyes fell on the log.

Seconds later she sat astride it. She tossed her towel and soap down and raised her hairbrush. Rudely awakened, the disgruntled diamondback gave a warning rattle, but Suzette, singing to herself, never heard it. The rattler began to blow steam and slowly prepared to strike. If Suzette had held perfectly still, the angry snake might have slithered away. Instead, she bent her head over, tossing her hair down over her face, brushing at it with long strokes.

Suzette heard the shout, the shot, and the rattle at the same time. She screamed and raised her head as the snake struck. The bullet pierced the snake's head within a sixteenth of a second after it struck her. Stunned and confused, she looked up to see Kaytano toss his gun to the ground and run to her. She rose, forming his name on her lips, the brush still in her hand. Then it all became a blur.

When she could focus her eyes again, she was lying on her back. Kaytano was on his knees beside her. In his hand was his long hunting knife, glinting in the sun. She clung to her hairbrush, watching while he ripped her trouser leg and promptly stuck the point of the knife directly into the side of her right leg, three inches above the knee. She jerked when the steel cut her flesh, but Kaytano's knee was on her stomach, holding her down. She screamed and clung to her hairbrush as blood and poison intermingled and gushed from her leg.

Kaytano moved his knee from her and stretched out on his stomach, the knife discarded. He held her bare leg in both his hands and lowered his mouth to the new wound. He sucked at the venom, spitting it onto the ground. Immediately he was back at the snakebite, sucking vigorously while Suzette watched the blue ribbon of sky undulate. Dizzy, she closed her eyes and felt Kaytano's lips pulling on her flesh. He kept sucking out the deadly poison until he was exhausted and coughing. And then he was over her, looking into her eyes, calling her name. "Suzette, do you hear me? Are you all right? It's Kaytano, Suzette."

She looked up into his worried black eyes and smiled. "Lucky you came along. I didn't see the snake. I'm sorry."

Kaytano took the brush from her cold hand and laid it aside. "It isn't your fault, it's mine. Are you in pain? Are you sick, Suzette?"

Bile rising rapidly in her throat, she nodded with difficulty. "I... I need to..."

"Yes," he said soothingly and lifted her up. "It's all right, it's okay." He sat down and supported her weight, helping her to vomit, his heart pounding. Gently holding her damp hair off her face, he talked to her softly. "I got the poison, Suzette. I'm sure I got it all. You'll be okay, I promise." He handed her a clean handkerchief from his pocket.

"Thanks," she said weakly, wiping tears from her eyes.

"Lie down." He helped ease her to the grass. Then he stood up, whistled, and in seconds Darkness cantered to him. "I'll take you home," he said and lifted her up across the saddle. Looping the reins over Darkness's neck, he mounted behind her, holding her in the crook of his arm. "Don't be afraid. I won't let anything happen to you."

Suzette, weak, dizzy, and nauseated, looked up into the dark face. Never had she seen the renegade look so unsettled. There was real fear in those black eyes — concern for her. But there was something more. Warmth. He kept glancing down at her face, and with each look his eyes grew warmer. If she didn't know him better, she would have sworn he cared for her. Fleetingly she thought he had the most beautiful eyes she had ever seen and knew that she would never be able to forget the warm light she saw burning there.

Back at Robber's Roost, Kaytano cleaned the wound with whiskey and bandaged it with clean, white cloth strips. Throughout the night, he kept watch beside her bed. Suzette slept like a baby and was shocked when she opened her eyes at sunup to see a tired, gaunt Kaytano, his dark face covered with a stubble of beard, leaning over the bed and looking down at her.

"Kaytano," she asked softly, "why aren't you in bed?"

Kaytano looked at the rosy cheeks, the dazzling blue eyes, the soft, sweet, berry-red lips, and knew that she was going to be fine. Wanting more than anything in the world to lower his face to hers and cover that pouty mouth with his own, he said evenly, "It's time I check your bandage." He turned the covers up over her knees, while Suzette, heart speeding when he touched her, clutched the sheet to her breasts and watched him gently remove the bandage. When he saw it, he winced and murmured, "I'm sorry, Suzette."

"Why should you be sorry? You saved my life. I'm lucky you happened to be so close." As though the thought just occurred to her, she added, "Why were you there, Kaytano?"

Kaytano slowly lifted his eyes to hers. "Does it matter?"

"No," she said. "I'm just glad you were."

Three days after the snakebite, Pancho rode into camp, a packhorse behind him. Suzette saw him through the open window. She watched Kaytano go out to meet the small, gray-haired man. When Kaytano asked him a question, Pancho nodded his head and patted the large saddlebags draped over the packhorse.

Half an hour later, Kaytano knocked on the bedroom door. He came in carrying an armload of bound leather books.

Without a word he placed the stack of books beside her on the bed.

Smiling up at him, she said, "Where did these come from?"

"They were brought here for your pleasure. I didn't know what kind of books you like, so I — "

"Thank you. I love to read and it was thoughful of you." Her lips were parted, and her eyes sparkled. Kaytano nodded and left the room. It was not until he'd reached the other side of her door that he smiled. For one brief instant, he leaned his dark head back against the closed door and smiled broadly.

In late July Kaytano rode out of camp alone. Suzette was curious, but didn't dare ask where he was going. He'd stood in their room strapping his gunbelt around slim hips, and Suzette stood by the window watching him.

"I will be gone three or four days. While I'm away, Pancho will be guarding you. He will be outside your door each night."

"I wouldn't try to escape, so it's not necessary to have him guard me."

His gaze swung to her. She wore no shoes, and her shiny blond hair was pinned haphazardly on top of her head. Swallowing, Kaytano tried not to think how much he wanted to take her into his arms and press her against him. "Suzette, you don't understand. Pancho is to guard you. It is *your* safety I'm talking about."

"Guard me from whom?" She put her hands on her hips and padded across the room to stand before him.

Kaytano took a step backward. "*Adíos*. I'll see you in a few days."

"Kaytano" — Suzette took a step forward — "can I walk you to your horse?"

His heart almost stopped, but he said evenly, "Why not?"

Darkness, saddled and waiting, was hitched to a post at the compound's main entrance. Silently Kaytano and Suzette walked across the sun-blanched courtyard, Suzette's bare feet stinging and burning. Determined not to say anything, she carefully picked her way across the scorching ground. Kaytano stopped, but Suzette, the soles of her feet on fire, went determinedly on her way, suffering with every step. She turned to look at Kaytano.

He almost smiled. His eyes were smiling. Suzette laughed. He came to her, put his hands to her waist, and lifted her from the hot ground. Holding her away from his long body, he carried her back to the porch. Suzette let her hands rest on his shoulders and said, "Did I complain?"

Depositing her on the veranda, he said softly, "No. Sometimes I wish you would."

Suzette's laughter died. "What do you mean?"

He didn't answer, but walked across the courtyard. She watched as he mounted Darkness and the gates swung open to let him out. A hand at her forehead to shade her eyes, Suzette suddenly hoped very much that he would turn and look at her as he rode away. He was speaking to Pancho now. After wrapping the reins around the saddlehorn, Kaytano untied the white silk bandanna he wore at his throat. Lifting his long arms, he tied it around his forehead. He was making himself more of an Indian. She felt a chill; the man was a Kiowa, a savage, an outlaw.

She pressed her hands together. *I hate him*, she told herself. *I hate Kaytano, I hate* ... He was riding away, Darkness prancing to the gate. Suzette's eyes were locked on the dark horse and rider. *I hate him, I* ... Abruptly, he reined his horse in a semicircle and looked directly at her. Just at her. Then he turned and galloped out of sight.

"I hate him," she repeated, aloud this time. "I... I... dear God, please let me hate him." She turned and disappeared into their room. When she came into the kitchen to prepare the evening meal, Maria saw her red, puffy eyes and assumed it was because Kaytano was gone.

Suzette didn't realize it, but Maria was correct.

Bedtime came and Suzette found it hard to sleep without

Kaytano in the room. All the nights she'd longed for privacy, all the times she'd cast sideways glances at the half-breed, hating him for holding her captive, all the dark, quiet nights she'd been terrified he would violate her — these feelings had disappeared in the last few weeks.

Suzette stood pensively looking out the window. Outwardly, she was a calm young woman. Inside, the turbulence was devastating, threatening to tear her apart. Tormented with strange new feelings and unbearable guilt, she tried once again to sort out her innermost desires and wishes, to find the cause for her new dilemma and, having faced it, to eliminate it.

The facts were simple enough. Against her will, she'd been taken prisoner by a daring, dark bandit. He'd held her for months, made her share his room, made her dependent on him for her safety, forced her to live as he lived. Giving the devil his due, the renegade was rakishly handsome, surprisingly intelligent, remarkably intuitive, and capable of some kindness.

Tipping the scales heavily on the other side, Austin was completely honest, amazingly successful, ever indulgent, and constantly affectionate. Any woman in her right mind would be gloriously happy to be the pampered wife of Austin Brand. His age was an advantage: he'd lived longer, so he was wiser. If he were here, he would explain what was happening to her. He would know that the changing relationship between her and Kaytano was the natural evolution of a situation beyond her control. Austin, she was certain, would tell her that she need not be alarmed if there were moments when she felt regard for the renegade. It was a normal emotion that would evaporate as soon as she was back home where she belonged.

Suzette turned from the window, crossed the room, and stretched out on her bed. Always she'd been completely honest with herself. It was time to be honest now, no matter how painful. The truth was that the thought of going home to Austin frightened her almost as much as never going home.

She'd had a wonderful life as Austin's wife; she'd been happy, he had been happy. Would they ever be again?

Tears filled her eyes. Satan must surely be laughing if he could see into her mind. To no one on earth could she admit the shocking, horrible truth. If the very demon who laughed at her agony would give her a choice on this hot, still night, if he came out of hell and stood at the foot of her bed and told her she could have exactly what she wanted, that when another dawn bathed the earth in heavenly light she could either be lying in Austin's arms in their bed on the big Brand ranch in Jacksboro, or in Kaytano's dark arms in his narrow bed in this hot little room, what *would* her choice be?

Suzette's quiet tears turned to sobs. She'd let the appalling truth surface. Her chest felt as if it would explode with the weight of her agony. Her pain was unbearable, made more intense by the knowledge she could turn to neither Austin nor Kaytano for solace. Both men would think her insane. Austin would be disgusted, Kaytano amused. Austin's heart would be broken, Kaytano's hardened. Austin's life would be shattered, Kaytano's changed none at all. To Austin she was everything, to Kaytano nothing.

"Señora." Pancho was knocking on the door. "Please, señora, open the door."

Suzette sat up hurriedly, wiping at her eyes. She'd forgotten the kind, gray-haired man was just beyond the door. She'd failed to consider what he might think when he heard her sobs. She had no choice, so she opened the door. Pancho, his distinguished dark face creased with concern, stepped inside.

He closed the door behind him when he saw her. For a time he did nothing more than put a kind hand on her shoulder. Finally he said ever so softly, "Sweet *señora*, you cry because you cannot forget your husband."

Suzette looked into his warm, dark eyes. "No, Pancho, I cry because I *can* forget."

Suzette felt a little better after the soul-cleansing and finally she slept. She missed Kaytano and she no longer tried to pretend otherwise. Each meal when she served the food, her eyes automatically went to his empty place; at night when it was time for sleep, she lay looking at Kaytano's bed, while she lay on her own, fully clothed. Sleep eluded her and she tossed and turned, longing for the slim, handsome half-breed's return. Weary and too warm, Suzette rose, stripped, and crawled naked into Kaytano's bed. Hugging his pillow to her bare breasts, she slept.

On the third day of his absence, Suzette was in her room, awaiting his return. Pancho had told her that there was a possibility Kaytano would be arriving in the afternoon, but he didn't really expect him until the next day. Suzette did. She knew Kaytano would come home today. Excitement stirred within her and she kept a watchful eye on the window while she sat cross-legged on her bed reading.

It was the hottest, quietest part of the afternoon when Suzette, who was dozing, heard a commotion. She rose and walked to the window, reaching it in time to see the heavy front gates swing open. Her pulse began to pound.

Darkness pranced into the hot courtyard, his sleek, black coat shimmering in the brilliant sunshine. On his back, Kaytano, hat low over his eyes, sat regally in the saddle. Pancho rushed to meet him. Kaytano dismounted, tossing the reins to the guard at the gate. He spoke to Pancho, but had not yet looked toward the house. Other men were making their way to the pair, and Suzette frowned; they would all want to greet him and it would be ages before he came inside.

She was wrong. With a shake of his head, he stepped through the gathering crowd. Now he was inside the big outer room; she could hear his footsteps approaching. Her pulse pounded no longer. It had stopped.

The bedroom door opened slowly.

28

And then he stood framed in the doorway. Suzette looked at him and found it impossible to turn away. His soiled Stetson rode low on his high forehead. His shirt, blue-and-white-checked cotton, was stained with dark circles of perspiration and was open down his mahogany chest. A navy-blue silk bandanna was tied around his gleaming throat. Tight trousers fit his long, lean legs like a second skin, while around his trim hips his gunbelt rode low. His boots were caked with caliche mud.

Suzette's gaze, after slowly moving down his long frame, went again to his face. His dark, penetrating eyes were on her and there was almost a smile on his lean face — but not quite. He was dirty from head to toe; his thick hair and his long eyelashes were powdered with dust. Even the soaring cheekbones were smudged with dirt, and the stubbly growth of dark beard looked scratchy. Obviously he had ridden hard and fast to get home. For the first time since she'd known him, Kaytano was unclean, so it made little sense to Suzette that her stomach fluttered in the most unsettling manner.

What was it about him that made her long to fling herself against the dirty hardness of him and kiss his dusty face? She wanted to cast aside his sweat-stained Stetson and run her fingers through the thick black hair until there was no dust left in the luxuriant locks. How she yearned to lick the dust from that sensual mouth until she felt him weaken and kiss her as no man had ever done. She longed to nuzzle her face into the glistening brown throat, to inhale the masculine scent of him and feel the long, sinewy arms come around her, crushing her helplessly to the unwashed length of him. Guiltily she envisioned herself helping strip away the soiled clothing he wore. She would pull the sweat-stained shirt down over his muscled shoulders and long arms and cast it aside. She would stand in front of him and easily unbutton those tight dirty trousers and deftly peel them down his long legs, stooping in front of him while she took off the muddy boots and pants. On her knees, she would look up at his raw masculinity, a servant with her master. She, eager to please, wanting only to serve and satisfy the dark, dangerous man standing naked above her.

Suzette felt a chill run up her spine, but her cheeks grew hot with shame. Guilt flooded over her. She was humiliated that such wanton ideas would pop into her head, but she was powerless to fight them.

Kaytano was walking toward her. She prayed he couldn't read her mind. Unable to tear her eyes from his, she stood rigidly, her knees locked, until he was standing so close to her she could have touched him.

Softly he said, "I hope you'll forgive my appearance. I'm too dirty to be in your presence, but I was eager to return. I'm going down to Terlingua to bathe now."

His black eyes narrowing slightly, he looked down at himself, took off his hat, and tossed it onto a chair, then ran a hand through his disheveled hair. A small bead of perspiration started a path through the dust on his face. Fascinated, Suzette watched as it made its slow descent over the taut cheek and finally came to rest at the left corner of his chapped upper lip. Kaytano raised a hand to brush the droplet aside at the exact instant that Suzette put her fingers up to wipe it away. Her hand touched his face first. His closed over hers and a look came into his dark eyes that was so strangely intense it scared her.

"I'm... sorry," she stammered. She tried to snatch her hand away, but his long fingers were around her wrist. "I shouldn't have done that. I wasn't thinking." Her eyes remained on his and she began to tremble.

"You've never touched me before. Why would you pick a time when I'm so unkempt?"

"I don't know," she answered honestly. "It was impulsive."

His dark eyes holding hers captive, he said, "Suzette, lick

your fingers." As if in a trance, she obeyed. She moistened the tips of her fingers and watched as he brought her wet fingers back to his mouth. "Now," he said hoarsely, "wash my mouth." With her damp fingertips, Suzette gently traced his sculptured lips while he looked at her through thick black lashes.

When she felt herself swaying, he must have felt it, too. The hand on her wrist immediately went to her waist to steady her.

Then he abruptly released her and took a step backward. "Thank you," he said, unsmiling. "I'll leave you now." When he reached the door, he turned. "Maria and the boys are planning a celebration tonight. Will you dance with me?" And suddenly Kaytano smiled, a shy, boyish, endearing smile. Suzette felt her heart pound with delight.

"I can hardly wait to dance with you," she whispered. She watched him walk away from her, his catlike stride graceful. She rushed to the window to watch him make his way through the sun-baked courtyard, shouting to the men relaxing in the late-afternoon warmth. A streak of gun-metal gray fur shot across his path. Without breaking stride, Kaytano scooped the cat up into his arms, stroking and murmuring to the happy animal. Suzette felt an unsettling warmth spreading through her. How she envied that cat!

Suzette was glad she'd washed her clothes earlier that day. They smelled fresh and clean, and although for the first time she wished that she had a pretty, feminine dress to wear, she knew the trousers fit her well and accentuated the shapeliness of her legs. She would wear the soft white blouse Maria had given her. It was dainty and pretty, and it would make her feel more like a woman.

Suzette sat cross-legged on her narrow bed and brushed her damp, tangled hair. She'd borrowed some sweet-smelling soap from Maria and scrubbed at her head until her hair squeaked and her scalp was pink. Now she was apprehensive. Would her hair be dry in time for the party? Would she have to remain in the small room while the festivities began without her? Suzette lowered the brush and shook her head.

What has gotten into me? I'm as excited as a young girl, but I'm going to a dance with a bunch of outlaws. Have I completely lost my mind? Is it madness that I look forward to being turned about the floor in Kaytano's arms? Again a flush spread over her neck and face, a warmth caused by the prospect of dancing close to the tall, lean Kaytano. She was looking forward to it. She could hardly wait.

Suzette, in her tight pants and white peasant blouse, stood nervously twisting a rebellious lock of blond hair. She peered into the cracked mirror above the washstand to check her appearance. Relieved that the heavy hair had finally dried, she had brushed it until it danced with fiery highlights and lay about her creamy neck and shoulders in soft, lustrous waves.

Suzette's eyes went from her hair down to the white blouse. She frowned and bit her lip. The white batiste blouse, though lovely and feminine and embroidered with soft blue thread, was not opaque enough to ensure modesty. Its soft gathers accented high, firm breasts. Sighing, she decided she couldn't possibly wear the blouse with nothing underneath. She had started across the room to get the plaid shirt when the door opened and Kaytano stepped inside.

He leaned against the door and eyed her coolly. "Are you ready?"

"I... I... thought I'd change my blouse," she stammered, looking into the deep, dark eyes.

"No," he said evenly. "Wear the one you have on. You look like a woman. Come."

Without another word, Suzette walked to him and they went out into the adjoining room. Against the far wall, a wooden table groaned under a mountain of food. Maria, grinning from ear to ear, presided over the food. Kaytano took Suzette by the wrist and led her to the table. Maria's eyes lifted when the handsome young couple stepped up to the table.

"Suzette!" she exclaimed, pressing her chubby hands to

her face. "How beautiful you are! All my men will want to dance with you." She giggled, then looked up at a scowling Kaytano and quickly corrected herself. "You are lucky, you have most handsome man of all. The others will have to content themselves with me." She laughed harder and Suzette laughed with her. Kaytano didn't smile.

She ate so much she thought she'd burst the seams of the tight trousers she wore, so she pushed her plate aside and sighed. Kaytano, eating quietly beside her, asked politely, "Shall I fix you another plate?"

"No, no," she protested, holding up a hand. "I can't eat another bite. Maria is a great cook."

Kaytano nodded and pushed his plate away. "Then let's go out where it is cooler." He rose from the bench and took her elbow.

"But... " She looked up at him in surprise. "Don't you want me to help clean up? I mean, I — "

"No," was all he said as his hands went to her waist and he lifted her over the long, low bench. Suzette gave him no argument. Together they went out into the courtyard. Men, women, and children milled about in the dusty yard, carrying plates of food, talking, smoking, and drinking whiskey in the soft twilight. Suzette paused and felt a firm hand at her waist, urging her forward.

They walked past the circles of people, leaving the lighted building behind them. At the gates, Kaytano nodded to the guard and the smiling man threw back the bolts, swinging open the gates. Apprehension tickled Suzette's neck. Where were they going?

Her uneasiness vanished quickly. As soon as they were outside, Kaytano went directly to a flat, gypsum rock and sat down. Knees bent, he reached inside his breast pocket and took out a long, thin cigar. "Will you sit beside me?" He looked up at her as he placed the cigar between his teeth.

Suzette sat down near him, tucking her feet underneath her. She watched as Kaytano puffed the cigar to life, the red tip lighting his dark, handsome features. He drew in the smoke and lazily blew it out, expertly forming a perfectly round smoke ring. As if he wanted her approval, he turned his dark head to her.

She smiled. "You're very good." She paused and lowered her eyes. "I've always wanted to try, but I never — "

"Try now." He thrust the lighted cigar to her.

"Oh, I couldn't. Lord, I've never smoked in my life. I would — "

"There's nothing to it," he assured her. "Here. Put the cigar between your lips."

Suzette laughed and took the black cigar from his hand, cautiously placing it between her lips. "Now what?"

"Draw very, very slowly on it, pulling the smoke down into your lungs." His brown hand went to the middle of her chest and pressed her lightly. "Inhale until you feel the smoke come to where my hand is touching you."

Her blue eyes wide, she drew on the cigar and held in the smoke as long as she possibly could. Which wasn't very long. It exploded from her mouth and she began to cough violently. Kaytano grabbed the cigar, tossed it to the dirt, and jerked Suzette to her feet. "Raise your arms," he commanded and pushed her hands high above her head. "Better?"

Unable to speak, she nodded her head furiously as tears rolled down her cheeks. Gently Kaytano lowered her shaky arms, and with his hands on her bare shoulders, he gently pulled her back against him. All at once she was touching him from shoulders to toes and the contact made her head spin. Never before had he touched her, except to take hold of her wrist or her waist to lead her somewhere. She shivered as she stood pressed against him, amazed by the rock-hard chest and thighs and by the incredible heat his body exuded. Timidly Suzette laid her head back against his shoulder. His brown, smooth cheek was only an inch from her temple. She could feel his warm breath on her hair. His hands remained on her shoulders; they hadn't moved at all.

"Suzette?" His voice sounded thick, heavy.

"I'm fine," she whispered.

His hands dropped from her and he moved away. She turned to look up at him. "We'd better get back," he said. "The dancing will be starting." His black, glittery eyes were unreadable as always.

"Yes, let's go." She turned and realized it had grown dark. Kaytano silently took her hand and held it in his as they walked back to the stockade.

"Kaytano."

"Yes?"

"May I try again sometime? I promise I won't cough."

"You may do anything you please."

The dancing had begun. Suzette and Kaytano stood along the wall watching the merrymakers. Three or four Mexican women had come into camp with the men. Two of them were young and quite pretty and they cast long, inviting looks at the handsome Kaytano. If he noticed, he gave no indication and they had to content themselves with dancing with his men. The women were kept very busy, for they were greatly outnumbered. Men even danced with one another as they consumed great quantities of liquor. More than one lusty outlaw looked at Suzette with thinly disguised hunger, but no one dared approach her. They considered her Kaytano's woman and would have been surprised to learn the relationship was not what it appeared.

"Shall we?" Kaytano asked, his eyes on Suzette's mouth.

"Let's do." She grinned up at him and felt a tremor of excitement when he took her elbow and led her onto the floor. That excitement grew alarmingly when Kaytano pulled her into his embrace. Again she was astounded by the hardness of his long, lean body. She put her arm around his neck and shyly let her fingers slide up into the thick, dark hair flowing about his white collar. Her other hand rested on the hard wall of his chest, and under her sensitive fingertips Suzette would have sworn his heavy heartbeat changed its steady rhythm.

There was no doubt that hers did. It was beating wildly and

she wondered if he could feel it pounding against his chest. She tipped her head back to look up at him. His dark eyes were studying her and she found it impossible to breathe. Slowly the lean hand at her waist slid up over her back to the nape of her neck. Kaytano bent his head, pressing his smooth cheek to hers, holding her tighter, closer in his arms. His feet never missed a beat. An expert dancer, he glided slowly about the floor as gracefully as he did everything. Suzette easily followed his pleasingly sensuous movements.

They danced and danced. When they paused to rest, Kaytano led Suzette to a bench along the wall, insisting she let him bring wine to her. She never thought of declining. She drank the strong red wine, matching him glass for glass until she felt giddy and hot and happy. Back on the dance floor, they ignored the others in the noisy room. Suzette, both arms looped around Kaytano's neck, leaned back in the circle of his arms and looked up at him. His eyes were on her, but not on her face. He was looking down at the soft gathers of her blouse stretching over her breasts. The close, intoxicating contact with the dark sensual man had brought about the usual reaction from her pliant woman's body. Her nipples, hard and aroused, were standing out, their taut pink tips visible through the soft, thin batiste. Flushing hotly, she looked back at Kaytano. His dark eyes held an unmistakable look of desire. His mouth parted and he licked his full bottom lip.

Suzette, feeling faint, whispered, "Kaytano."

He said nothing, but gently pressed her closer to him, hiding from other eyes what he had seen. She clung to him and wondered what he was thinking as she buried her face in his shoulder and inhaled the unique masculine odor of his heated flesh.

It was well past midnight when Kaytano looked at her and said, "Are you ready for bed?"

29

Suzette slipped out of her clothes and folded them neatly, then put them under Kaytano's pillow. She got into her narrow bed and pulled the sheet up to her shoulders. The music and laughter from the outer room made sleep impossible. Suzette knew that even without the noise she could not have slept. It was stuffy and warm in the small room; the still night air stirred the sheer curtains over the one window not at all. And the bright moonlight was another distraction. The moon's silvery beams slanted in through the window across her bed.

The moonlight and heat were only partially responsible for her restlessness. She was very disappointed that Kaytano did not come to bed when she did. It was insane, she knew, but it was a fact. Exhausted from the big meal and dancing and singing, she'd gladly nodded her head yes when he'd leaned down to ask if she were ready to go to bed. He helped her to her feet and walked with her to the door of their room. He had released her elbow and then said good-night. Before she could speak, he had turned and was making his way to the back door. She had no choice but to enter their room alone. There was a time when she would have been grateful for the privacy, a time when his sleeping so close to her caused her great anguish, a time when she'd been terrified he would harm her.

But he never had. Kaytano had never touched her in all the months of sleeping in the same small room with her. All the nights of knowing she lay naked in the bed next to his. Eventually she had relaxed in his presence. It had become almost normal to come into the room with him, to undress in the darkness and hand him her clothing. More than one night she had fallen into her bed, slumber overtaking her the moment her head hit the pillow, as though Kaytano were her husband and she was safe with him beside her.

Suzette sighed and raised her arms over her head, turning her face toward the door. Instinctively she strained, trying to pick out Kaytano's deep, resonant voice above the music. It was impossible. He had headed for the door.

Where was he going? Would he come back tonight? Did he plan to meet one of the pretty Mexican girls who had looked so longingly at him all evening? Suzette winced at the thought. Two of the women were darkly pretty; did Kaytano find them attractive? Was he at this moment out in the moonlight with one of them? Were those arms that had held her closely now wrapped around another woman? Would a pretty *señorita* have the kisses she longed for? Would Kaytano spend the night with one of the girls?

Suzette shut her eyes and sighed. For the thousandth time she tried to understand the dark, dangerous Kaytano. He was most surely cold and evil; yet, with Maria's children he was as tender and gentle as a man could be. His men respected him, even loved him. Pancho told her he loved Kaytano as a son, that the dark young man was brave, that his life had been saved by the daring and honorable half-breed.

And with her? From the beginning he had been cold to her, but never cruel. Never had he hurt her. Now, after months of looking at her through those hooded eyes while she wondered what he was thinking, his eyes softened on occasion. More than once she had looked up to find him quietly observing her, his black eyes warm. And the day the snake struck her, he looked at her with tenderness. The indifference he'd displayed when she first came into camp was less evident.

And then when he returned today. The way he looked at her when he saw her after being gone for three days. And tonight, when they danced together, he had held her so close, his mouth almost touching her face. More than once he'd looked at her with passion in his eyes.

Suzette was shaken from her thoughts by the unmistakable sound of Kaytano's voice just beyond the door. "Really, my friends," Kaytano was protesting, "I am no longer able to keep my eyes open. I must have some rest. It was a wonderful celebration. There's plenty to drink and eat. Enjoy yourselves."

The door opened and his lithe frame was momentarily silhouetted against the light from the outer room. Suzette feigned sleep and watched through slitted eyes, expecting to see him hurriedly strip and get into his bed. Slowly he walked to his bed and she could feel his dark eyes moving over her. Wordlessly he sat down on the bed and pulled off his high black boots. With his back to her, he unbuttoned and discarded the white shirt. Then he sat, unmoving, for several long minutes. When he stood, Suzette, still looking at him, waited for him to pull off his black trousers.

Kaytano crossed the room to the window. His profile to her, he lit a cigarette, the flare of the sulphur match lighting his unsmiling face. He stood at the window drawing on his smoke, his bare chest and back glistening with perspiration. Fascinated, Suzette watched as he raised a hand to the back of his head. Long, brown fingers massaged the base of his skull. Suzette longed to toss the sheet aside and go to him, to put both her hands on his neck and rub away the tenseness and pain. She could almost feel the knotted muscles, could almost hear his groan of satisfaction as she tenderly manipulated the smooth brown skin of his neck.

Her eyes moved on to his lean chest and shoulders. She'd seen this man shirtless at least a hundred times, but the sight of his bare torso never failed to bring a flood of warmth to her face. He had the look of a superbly built wild animal — as if he possessed abundant power and was ever ready to attack his prey. With every tiny movement of his arm, hard muscles rippled under the sweat-slick dark skin.

His cigarette had been tossed out into the night. Kaytano turned and again looked in her direction. Without realizing it, Suzette held her breath. Suddenly feeling uncomfortable, she noted her arms were still up under her head and wished that she had lowered them while he stood staring out at the valley.

Now it was too late. His eyes were on her, and if she moved her arms he would know she was still awake. Knowing she must endure the discomfort a while longer, Suzette closed her eyes tightly as Kaytano crossed the room.

The bright moonlight seemed to shine right through her eyelids, and when abruptly it became much darker, she knew Kaytano was standing over her. Her heart began to thump against her ribs and she fought the strange sounds threatening to erupt from her tight throat. For what seemed a lifetime, he stood above her, not moving.

Suzette's eyes opened when Kaytano reached down and slowly pulled the sheet to her waist. Wordlessly he sat down on the edge of the bed beside her. He was leaning over her face, and when she looked up at him to see his dark eyes studying her so intensely, it both frightened and excited her. His mouth was a hard line and now it was very slowly descending to her lips. Panic gripped her; his mouth was so close to hers, she could feel his breath. Certain his kiss would be punishing and cruel, she closed her eyes.

Kaytano put his hand to her face and very tenderly kissed the right corner of her mouth. From there, he moved across her mouth, feathering soft, warm kisses over her trembling lips. When he reached the left corner, he let his open lips rest there, making not a sound. But his hand moved over her cheek to her throat. She tensed but didn't move. His fingers trailed downward, then up over the rounded fullness of her breast. With his thumb, he circled the hardening nipple slowly and moved on to her slim waist. His hand came to rest there and against her lips he said huskily, "I will not rape you, Suzette. If you are going to stop me, do it now while I still can."

He raised his head and looked down at her. The dark eyes were surprisingly warm and tender. The mouth had lost some of its hardness, and for a second Suzette would have sworn she saw a flicker of a smile.

He was waiting for her answer. She knew what that answer should be. She knew, too, that he meant exactly what he said.

He was not going to take her against her will. The decision was entirely hers.

Why her throat hurt so badly, she didn't know. Why she wanted desperately to cry was a mystery. How she could be so tempted to bury her face in the warmth of his smooth chest and sob made no sense at all. But that's how she felt.

The dark, beautiful eyes were on her face. The warm hand lay on her waist, unmoving. Within seconds this strange handsome man bending over her would either release her and go to his bed or he would make love to her. The choice was hers.

Not trusting her voice, Suzette slowly moved her arms from under her head. Praying he'd make it easy, she hesitantly put her fingers on his lean cheek. When he slowly turned his head and lovingly kissed her palm, Suzette's sobs broke from her aching throat.

The sound was no more than a faint, brief whimper because Kaytano's mouth swallowed her cries as his lips closed over hers and he pulled her up into his arms. The soft, feathery kisses were gone and in Kaytano's kiss were a power and passion that ignited Suzette's simmering desire. She opened her lips and gloried in the plundering, demanding mouth pressed to hers. His hands were gliding up her back, holding her close to his hard chest.

When at last his searing kiss had ended and he lifted his head, Suzette was clinging to his neck while the room spun around her. Smiling, Kaytano took hold of her slender wrists and moved her hands away. Trusting him completely, she asked no questions when he laid her back down on the bed. Pushing the sheet to her feet, he stretched out beside her and she smiled happily when his warm lips came back to hers. Never in her life had she been kissed the way Kaytano was kissing her. Wave after wave of warmth spread over her, and in the heat enveloping her she was aware that Kaytano's hard lean body was burning too. She spread her fingers on the wall of his chest and loved the feel of his slick hot skin under her hand. It was warm in the room, but not that warm. This dark irresistible lover wanted her as much as she wanted him.

His mouth continued to play with hers, plundering, invading, and tasting until Suzette could feel her lips becoming tender and swollen. Kaytano's sensitive lips could feel it too. They left hers and went to her neck. Gently he nibbled and nuzzled his way down to her breasts.

When he bent his dark head and sucked gently at first one, then the other, her breasts swelled and she moaned with pleasure. Her eyes were closed as she lay writhing against him, her fingers running through his thick black hair.

When finally he raised his head, she opened her eyes to look at him. "My God, you are magnificent," he said softly as his palm curved over her bare stomach. Gently he touched her, never taking his eyes from hers. "I have wanted to touch you this way since the first minute I saw you. I have lain in that bed night after night and cursed the day I took you off that train." His hand slowly moved down to cover the blond triangle of silky hair. There was no need for him to ask that she move her thighs apart. Eagerly they opened to him and his slender fingers slipped between her legs. Slowly, gently, Kaytano began to caress her while his smoldering eyes impaled her face.

There was fire in the tips of those fingers as he tenderly explored, probed, circled, coaxed. Suzette looked into those great dark eyes and felt that all she had ever wanted in her life was to lie in this man's arms while he intimately touched her. Nothing else on earth mattered. They were drifting in a universe where only he and she belonged. The fire inside her was growing ever hotter; it would rage out of control, but Suzette felt no urgency or apprehension. This very sensual man knew just how far to take her before he let the insistent craving subside slightly, only to begin again and take her dangerously close to the crest. She was his and his alone. When she arched her back and called his name, almost begging for all he had to give her, Kaytano rose from the bed.

Suzette's eyes flew open and she watched shamelessly as

he took off his trousers and stood naked in the moonlight, gazing down at her, possession in his heated gaze and poised body.

For one frightening second, she was terrified he would walk away from her, leave her, and get into his own bed. "Kaytano," she whispered through fevered, dry lips, and lifted her shaking hand to him. He dropped onto the bed beside her and she wrapped her arms around his back. He kissed her cheek, pushing a long strand of her hair away from her face with his mouth. His long, lean leg moved over hers, its darkness covering her pale whiteness. And then he was looking into her eyes again as he slowly pulled her underneath him.

"I won't hurt you," he whispered as he took her with a deep sure thrust of his hard body. If his hand had brought her pleasure, his body brought her ecstasy. Expertly he moved within her, his body sleek and slippery on hers. His breath was hot and ragged near her ear, and his strong heartbeat, pounding rapidly, mingled with hers as his chest pressed heavily on her tingling breasts. She clung to him and moaned. Kaytano grasped her hips and lifted her to him while he drove into her with mounting need.

When the zenith came for Suzette, it took her with terrifying swiftness and she was not capable of holding back to wait for Kaytano. Sobs of rapture burst from her throat. When finally she started to drift back to earth, she opened her eyes and saw Kaytano's passion-hardened face just above hers as his own ecstasy was attained on the heels of hers. "My darling," she murmured and held him to her.

He collasped on her, his head resting on her breasts. They lay entwined, their spent, damp bodies unmoving, their voices stilled. For the first time since Kaytano had entered the small room, Suzette noticed the music and laughter from just outside the door. Miraculously she had forgotten about the party going on in the other room. There had been no one and nothing but Kaytano. Only Kaytano. Kaytano kissing her.

Kaytano's hands on her. Kaytano's hard body on hers, in hers.

Kaytano raised himself up on an elbow. "Has that damned party been going on all this time?"

She grinned. "I have no idea. I didn't hear a thing."

He laughed, and the sound of his laughter filled her with happiness. He laughed so seldom. Never had he laughed with her. His laughter was almost as precious as his lovemaking.

"Suzette," he said and began to kiss her shoulder lightly. "It's so noisy here, and it's so hot. Know what I'd like to do?"

"I think so." She nodded and slowly slid the sole of her foot up his long leg.

"You do?"

"If it's the same thing I want, I do." She licked her finger and traced his full lower lip with it.

"I want to make love to you out in the open where the night breeze will cool us. I want to lie naked with you on some hilltop in the moonlight. I want you to shout my name to the stars overhead, and the wind, and the hills."

"When do we leave?" she asked happily.

"Let's get dressed. I'll saddle Darkness and we'll ride out of camp."

"But what about the others?"

Kaytano rose from the bed and reached for his trousers. "What about them?"

"The party is still going on. If we leave here together and stay away all night, everyone will know."

"We won't be followed, if that's what's worrying you."

"They'll think we've gone out to make love, Kaytano. They'll know you intend to take me out to rape me."

Kaytano buttoned his pants and laughed. "Suzette, they think I've been sleeping with you since that first night they heard you screaming. Remember?" He touched her cheek affectionately.

Color flooding her cheeks, she bent her head. "What do they think of me?"

"They know you're Kaytano's woman. And you are. Now, either get dressed or I'll carry you right through their party stark naked." She looked up at him and saw the impish grin. His smile softened his hard, handsome face.

She laughed and jumped from the bed. Standing on tiptoes, she kissed his smiling mouth. "Help me dress?"

"I'd be delighted."

30

Laughing like two small children, Suzette and Kaytano hurriedly dressed, anxious to be out of the close, warm room, far from the camp, free to explore their newly found passions. Kaytano, his gunbelt strapped around his hips, two blankets and his empty saddlebags slung over his shoulder, stood smiling at the excited young woman scurrying about the little room, packing personal items as though she was off on a long trip.

"Kaytano" — she looked over her shoulder at him — "should I... that is..." She held a bar of sweet-smelling soap in her hand.

"Take it, and grab your hairbrush. We'll be gone for a couple of days, so you'll need it." He said it matter-of-factly.

Suzette smiled and came to him, looking down at her tight trousers, plaid shirt, and beaded moccasins, the only clothes she owned, save the white blouse she'd worn to the dance. "Should I pack my other blouse?"

Kaytano grinned and kissed her nose. "That you won't need. Now, let's be off." His hand clasped her neck lightly and he propelled her through the door, back into the big room where the party was still in progress.

Shouts and cheers greeted the couple. The drunken men and women were eager to have the dark leader and his blond woman join them in their revelry. "Hey, Kaytano, you let me dance with pale beauty, no?" called a lusty, laughing man, whiskey clouding his judgment.

"Kaytano, *mi amigo*." Another came up to him and draped an arm over Kaytano's shoulder, bobbing his head around to gape at Suzette. "You make love to your woman. Now you hungry and thirsty, eh?"

Kaytano said nothing, but smiled easily and slipped from the drunk's grasp. Still holding lightly to Suzette's neck, he walked with her to the food table. "Suzette, wrap up that roast beef," he said as he pointed to a large, half-eaten mound of well-done meat. Suzette nodded happily. Kaytano picked up cheese, fruit, bread, and two bottles of red wine and crammed everything into his saddlebags.

"Wait, Kaytano." Suzette jerked a white cloth from the table, folding it rapidly and tossing it to him.

She was packing a silver fork when Kaytano said, "That's it, Suzette. Let's go."

Outside she rushed to keep up with his long, sure strides. His impatience was evident. At the stable, he led the large black horse out into the moonlight. He lifted the hand-tooled saddle, its silver conches glinting in the moonlight. In seconds the cinch was tightened under the horse's belly and Kaytano was strapping the blankets and saddlebags behind the saddle. That done, he stepped to the horse's head and patted his muzzle while he put the bit into his mouth. To Suzette's surprise, Kaytano began to speak to his horse as if it were a person.

"My faithful friend" — Kaytano's voice was low and resonant — "we are going out of the canyon, up to the south rim. Pick your way carefully; I have my woman with me and I will be giving her my attention. Don't let me down, Darkness." Bridle in place, Kaytano turned to Suzette.

"Do you suppose he understands you?" Suzette was amused.

Lifting her astride the big horse, he said, "I trained him myself. Darkness understands. You will see." He looped the reins over the horse's neck and was up behind her, his long arms encircling her. His weight had hardly settled on the horse's back before Darkness was prancing proudly across the courtyard. At the front gate, a sleepy Mexican came immediately alert when he saw the tall rider was Kaytano.

Rushing to swing the heavy gates open, he bowed and grinned sheepishly. "Kaytano! You go for pleasure ride, no?"

"*Sí.*" Kaytano nodded and let Darkness have his head. The horse went rapidly into an easy lope, and Suzette, laughing and happy, leaned back against Kaytano and did something she'd not done in years.

She began to whistle. Her attempts to whistle a Spanish love song she'd heard snatches of when she lay with Kaytano earlier brought a grin to his lips. He joined her. He whistled beautifully. Suzette fell silent, hugging the strong arms that were around her. Kaytano finished the lovely ballad before pulling up on the reins. Darkness halted and Kaytano kissed her temple. "Why did you stop? You were very good."

Turning to look at him, she said, "Not really, it's been ages since I whistled."

"Ah, perhaps you need a little practice. Shall I teach you my secret call?"

"Oh, Kaytano, please."

"I will have to look at you." He wrapped the reins around the saddlehorn and put his hands on her waist. "Throw your right leg over, Suzette."

"You won't let me fall, will you?"

"Never, love." She sat across the saddle, held firmly in place with his hands. "Okay, Darkness." The horse, heeding Kaytano's spoken command, walked along with his ears pricked, while the two laughing people he carried made strange sounds.

Suzette paid close attention as Kaytano gave a high, shrill whistle that seemed to make his whole mouth vibrate. Its sound was plaintive, lonely, and its volume low, yet far-reaching. It was unlike any sound she'd ever heard, and something about it made the hair stand up on her forearms. It was hauntingly beautiful and uniquely suited to Kaytano.

Kaytano licked his lips and looked at her, waiting for her to speak. "I could never do that." She shook her head.

"Eerie, isn't it?"

"Yes. Where did you learn it? I've never heard anything like it."

"It's an Indian call, Suzette. I want you to learn it. I've not shown it to anyone since I was a boy. It's special to me, and you're special. Try it, please."

Suzette looked into his eyes, puckered her lips, and gave the plaintive call with her first attempt.

Kaytano cocked his head. "Do you learn everything that rapidly?"

"For you I will." Suzette started to repeat the newly learned call, but his mouth, curving into a grin, came down on hers while he hooked a thumb into the waistband of her trousers.

"Thank you, my sweet. The day may come when you will need to summon me." Before she could reply, his warm, sensual lips were settling on hers. Kaytano kissed her softly, persuasively, and Suzette's arms slipped around his middle, her lips parted eagerly, her tongue mating with his. Too soon he raised his head and smiled. His hand went to her knee and he eased her back astride Darkness. Gently pushing her long hair to one side, he kissed her neck, letting his tongue tease at it for a second, before he released the shiny hair and said softly, "I must keep my mind on the trail and I cannot do it if you are in my arms." He took the reins from the horn and spoke to Darkness. They started their ascent, the sure-footed animal carefully picking his way up the rocky incline.

Suzette leaned back against Kaytano and recalled how frightened she'd been when they rode down into the canyon on that day so long ago. Afraid of him and the dangerous narrow trail, she'd closed her eyes and thought she would surely pass out from fear. Now she kept her eyes wide open, looking at the wondrous beauty of the canyon bathed in moonlight. She had to tip her head far, far back to see the top of the canyon's rim high above them. It was treacherous in the daylight, disastrous at night, but Suzette was not at all frightened. How could she be frightened when she was held inside the powerful arms of her dark love, Kaytano? He'd ridden this trail and others just as perilous hundreds of times. He'd roamed from the Indian territory all across the plains of Texas, down to the Rio Grande and across the mighty river into Mexico on this stallion they now rode. Man and beast were as wild and beautiful as this rugged terrain. Suzette smiled; how hard it would be to tame either.

"Are you afraid?" he asked from above her ear.

"No, darling."

"You mean your eyes are open?"

Suzette laughed. "Wide open! I don't want to miss a single rock formation. I don't want to miss anything. I want to become acquainted with this land you call home and... "

"Suzette, this is not my home."

"I don't understand. Where do... "

"I will tell you later. First there is something I must do."

"What?"

"Make love to you."

Suzette sighed, and Kaytano chuckled and kissed her hair. "Soon enough you will be in my arms."

They stood holding hands high on the flat south rim of Santa Elena Canyon. Kaytano and Suzette could barely pick out the lights of camp far below. They couldn't hear the loud accordion or the drunken voices. They could hear nothing but the soft sigh of the mountain winds.

Suzette looked at Kaytano and shivered. His hard, handsome face was held high, his dark eyes strange, his body poised, as though he were experiencing some communication with nature she couldn't understand. He dropped her hand and walked nearer to the canyon's rim. She gasped. He stood dangerously close to the edge. He closed his eyes and meditated while Suzette stared at him, awed by his behavior and his beauty.

After what seemed an eternity, he took a step back and

turned to look at her. Without speaking, he went to where they'd piled their gear and carefully rolled out the blanket, picking the softest spot he could find. Rising to his feet, he undressed while Suzette stood watching. In seconds, Kaytano stood naked in the moonlight, his tall, lithe body shimmering.

Suzette's gaze moved from the fine planes and angles of his face to his lean, satiny chest to the curve of his trim waist and to his powerful thighs and long legs. Never had she seen a man so beautiful, yet so totally masculine. She longed to have him stand statue-still while she circled him and let her hands slide down the shiny length of him. She wanted to memorize every hard curve, each muscle and sinew, to imprint on her hands the pleasing texture of his smooth warm skin. She trembled. Her brain was carefully recording his stance, his essence, his raw magnetism. Was it because she knew somehow that the day would come when he would be taken from her sight?

"No," she breathed aloud and started to him. "Kaytano, Kaytano," she murmured and wrapped her arms around his naked waist.

"Suzette," he responded and put his hands into her hair. His dark eyes were fathomless, his voice deep and ragged. "I want to make love to you very, very slowly. I want to learn about you, how to please you, what you desire. I stood on the rim of this canyon and purged my heart and soul of all thought save you. I am yours, Suzette, and before the sun rises I will make you mine." He kissed her and dropped his hands. Kneeling on the blanket, he reached for her hand. Trembling with passion, she slid to her knees in front of him.

"Kaytano" — it was almost a plea — "undress me?"

"Yes, my love." He smiled. His nimble fingers went to the buttons of her plaid shirt, then slowly pulled the blouse apart and down over her shoulders. Her arms were trapped inside. Kaytano looked at her bare, creamy breasts and sat back on his heels. As he studied her with the same intensity he did so many things, Suzette watched his eyes and held her breath.

She was trembling by the time he slowly leaned to her and tenderly kissed each shimmering breast, barely brushing his warm lips to the jutting peaks.

"You please me more than you know," said Kaytano. "Stand up, Suzette." He put his hands on her waist and raised her to her feet. Still kneeling in front of her, Kaytano pulled the blouse down her arms and to the ground. He unbuttoned her tight trousers and slowly peeled them down over her luscious hips and legs. She held to his bare back and stepped from the trousers, then lifted her feet for him to remove her moccasins.

Naked, Suzette started to drop back to her knees, but he stopped her. "No, not yet. Please." His hands were on her hips; his dark eyes caressed her stomach, thighs, and legs. She could feel the dry mountain wind stroking her bare, yearning body. She could feel those probing eyes burning into her flesh. She prayed he found her pretty, that he wanted her as much as she wanted him. Kaytano leaned to her and laid his cheek against her quivering stomach. He hugged her tightly to him and murmured hoarsely, "Oh, God, I've wanted to press my face to your naked body, Suzette. I watched you that day you bathed in Terlingua Creek, the day the snake — "

"Kaytano," she interrupted, her hand moving to his head to grasp his thick hair, "you watched me bathe?"

Kissing her lightly, he confessed, "Yes, my love. I stood atop the cliffs of Mesa de los Angeles and watched."

"My God! Who else watched?"

Kaytano slowly pulled her down to him, then wrapped her in his arms and nuzzled her neck. "Only Darkness. Do you think I'd let another man see you naked?"

"I should be angry, but I'm not." She let him gently push her over onto her back. Kaytano followed, stretching out beside her, his weight supported on an elbow.

"I'm glad. I felt bad about it, but I enjoyed it, too." He smiled down at her and his hand gently cupped her breast. She shivered when his thumb went to her nipple. While he rubbed it slowly, he lowered his lips to hers, kissing her with controlled passion and warmth. They lay in the high desert moonlight under the stars, kissing, sighing, waiting, as Kaytano, true to his word, began a night of lovemaking Suzette would never forget.

He rained soft, sweet kisses over her face while his knowing hand roamed over her eager body, fondling her with a touch so light Suzette strained to be nearer to the warm, moving fingertips. And throughout, Kaytano's deep voice spoke of the wonderful things he would do to her, the new joys they would experience together, the strong bond that would join them before the sun came up.

Suzette sighed softly when Kaytano eased onto his stomach beside her, his dark eyes on her face. His hand tangled in her long hair and he kissed her, chewing at her soft bottom lip before his mouth slid over her cheek to the side of her neck. His open lips covered the faint pulse and for a long, warm time remained there, while his hand began its slow descent over her body. His lean fingers surrounded a breast, moved up to the tip, gently plucking with all five fingers until Suzette groaned low in her throat and Kaytano lifted his head.

His mouth moved down to take the place of his hand and he lovingly licked at the taut nipple. His hand continued moving down, and where his hand touched, his mouth followed. Her eyes opening and closing, Suzette felt the blood heating in her veins when Kaytano's face paused at her navel, the tip of his tongue plunging into the small indentation. He was gently parting her silken thighs and her heartbeat raced when his fingers slipped between them. She clutched at the blanket when his hot, handsome face settled on the warm inside of her thigh and she felt his sharp teeth sink into her flesh.

Volcanic passions rose within her and she writhed and began to call his name, her body demanding release. Kaytano continued with his tormenting kisses and caresses until she was squirming and almost sobbing his name. He lifted his head and moved back up beside her.

He swept her into his arms and lay holding her, gentling

her. "Not yet, Suzette. Lie quietly for a time." He gave her wine to wet her dry throat and she nodded gratefully. They lay and drank wine while her pulses slowed, her urgency subsided. Warm from the wine, the summer night, the nearness of Kaytano, Suzette began to feel totally relaxed and in no hurry to consummate their loving.

But then Kaytano lay on his back and removed his arms from around her. She looked quizzically at him and he smiled and took one of her small hands and spread it out on his smooth chest. Holding her wrist loosely, he gently moved her hand down over his chest to his stomach. His hand dropped away and he slowly raised his arms behind his head and the look in his dark eyes challenged her to explore his body, just as he'd done with her. Having wanted to do just that for weeks, she put both hands on him and sensuously, tenderly caressed the hard wall of his chest, the well-defined ribs, the trim waist. And she watched his handsome face while she touched him. His eyes held a dreamy, lost look and he nodded his head as though to say he liked what she was doing.

With her hands at his waist, Suzette slowly lowered her face to his chest. Kaytano winced when she began to feather warm, sweet kisses over him, moving steadily down his body, from chest to abdomen. His eyes opening and closing with joy, he moaned with pleasure while he watched the beautiful golden hair spill over his body, its silken glory fanning out against the darkness of his skin, while her soft, sweet lips and tongue drove him mad with their teasing.

His body was completely aroused. Suzette lifted her head and haltingly put a small hand on him. She gasped at the throbbing power there. She felt him jerk involuntarily from her light touch and her eyes went up to his face. He looked at her pleadingly, though he spoke not one word.

"Kaytano," she breathed and clasped him. He groaned his gratitude, and when her timidity vanished and she stroked him confidently, low sounds erupted from his throat and his eyes closed. When she'd pushed him dangerously close to satisfaction and he was calling her name in desperation, she released him and moved up beside him. His eyes flew open when her soft lips came down to his.

She kissed him and said into his open mouth, "Not yet, Kaytano. Lie quietly for a time." She poured him wine and lifted it to his lips. His heart hammering in his chest, the blood pounding in his temples, he gulped from the cup and fought for breath. She took the empty mug and lay down beside him, gently holding him to her until he was calmer.

Again they lay and let the night wind stroke them with its cool fingers on their burning bodies. After a long, sweet time, Kaytano gently turned Suzette over onto her stomach and again he slowly caressed and kissed her soft body. Not one inch was left unkissed as he lovingly embraced even the soles of her feet and her toes. The backs of her knees got a lot of attention, his mouth warm and stimulating. Her soft, rounded bottom was a sweet delight for Kaytano and she purred like a contented cat while he lightly gripped her hips and trailed kisses over her. She sighed her approval when he slid astride her and leaned down to drop kisses on her back.

She moaned when she felt him pressing his chest to her back and his hands came underneath her to cup her breasts. Then his mouth was at her neck, kissing, caressing, coaxing, while his hands gently manipulated her swelling, aching breasts. His lips on her ear, he murmured huskily, "Darling, I'm going to raise up a little. When I do, turn over." She nodded and he kissed her ear.

Certain he was finally going to take her, Suzette felt him ease up. She turned under him and smiled when he very slowly descended to her. He lay lightly touching her, and he began to kiss her tenderly while his aroused body pressed hers and she wrapped her arms around his back and gloried in the feel of his flesh on hers. Still he did not enter her, and when his kisses continued and grew hotter and more demanding, Suzette's body molded itself to his and she shamelessly rubbed herself against him, the heat between her thighs dictating her every movement. She had to have him; nothing else could save her. Suzette pulled his face from hers, grasping fistfuls of hair. She was almost sobbing, and she looked at him with glazed, pleading eyes.

"Kaytano," she breathed, "I belong to you, to no one else. Please, my darling, take what is yours alone."

"My precious love," he breathed and took her with a deep, hard thrust that made her cry out in ecstacy.

The silvery moon had slipped below the horizon and disappeared. The sun had not yet risen in the east. The earth was submerged in total, absolute darkness, the thick, almost tangible blackness that occurs just before the dawn. The heavy cloak of ink wrapped Suzette and Kaytano in its stygian cover, but it failed to diminish the illumination of their lovemaking.

Eyes wide open, each saw the other with vivid clarity. Transported from the shadowy confines of earth, they were ushered into a dazzling bright nirvana, invited to bask in the warmth until the honeyed heat caused them to burn themselves in love's torrid galaxy, to collide with a million giant suns and shatter, shooting brilliant sparks out into the universe.

When at last the fiery release came, Suzette shouted Kaytano's name in wild abandon and it echoed from the giant canyon below. It carried on the winds to float through all eternity in the rugged, desolate countryside surrounding them.

"KAYTANO ! ! ! ! !"

31

For the next few glorious days, Kaytano and Suzette were Adam and Eve in their own Garden of Eden. They watched the breathtaking sunrises wrapped in each other's arms, admiring God's handiwork as if for the very first time. When finally the soft pinks had given way to bright oranges and at last to glaring white brilliance, Kaytano rose and helped Suzette to her feet.

They partially dressed. Kaytano stepped into his tight trousers and moccasins. Suzette slipped into his long-tailed shirt. They rode Darkness along the canyon rim to the west. Four miles down, they entered a giant fissure in the earth and started a slow descent. Suzette yawned and relaxed in Kaytano's arms.

Grinning boyishly, he kissed her temple and whispered, "I know you're exhausted, Suzette. I'm taking you to a remote place that will be the perfect spot for us to sleep."

She nodded, not answering. She knew Kaytano would take care of her. She didn't care where she slept, as long as it was in his arms. Darkness carefully picked his way over terrain so rugged and wild it appeared no man had ever been there. They reached the base of the canyon and the trail widened and turned into a network of hundreds of narrow crevices. Suzette was beginning to nod, her long hair falling into her face. She must have dozed, because the next thing she knew, Kaytano was lifting her from the horse's back. They were on the river and Suzette fleetingly thought about a bath. Before she could decide, Kaytano had unsaddled Darkness.

Lifting her in his arms, he said, "Suzette, let's bathe when we awaken. You need rest."

Her arms around his neck, she laid her head on his shoulder. "I can hardly keep my eyes open."

"Don't try," he whispered, and with sure strides carried her far back into a narrow canyon. She awoke when Kaytano laid her down in a river cave. It was no more than six feet high, and Kaytano had to duck to step inside. Its width was a narrow eight to ten feet. It was cool and quiet inside: the perfect place to sleep.

Suzette stretched and smiled when Kaytano, naked once again, lay down on the rich blanket and pulled her to him. Against her tangled hair he said, "Sleep, my love. When you awaken, we'll eat and then I'll take you to the most beautiful spot of all. We'll bathe and wash your golden hair."

Her face was pressed to the warmth of his throat. She opened her lips and kissed him. "Promise me that for the rest of my life I'll always sleep in your arms."

Kaytano's eyes clouded and his arms tightened around her. His warm lips sought out hers and he kissed her with exquisite tenderness and love. Against her lips he murmured, "The only thing I will promise is that I will love you for as long as I'm on this earth."

Suzette never heard the promise. She was already asleep.

Suzette's eyes opened slowly. She looked about, trying to orient herself. Beside her, Kaytano lay sleeping peacefully. She smiled, remembering the unforgettable night they had shared. She hated to wake him, but she longed to eat and clean up. Perhaps she should let him rest while she went down to the river for a cleansing dip. Or, first she could poke through the saddlebags for something to eat.

In a voice heavy with sleep, Kaytano said, "Were you considering leaving me?"

Suzette whirled to look down at him. His thick hair was unruly and falling over his forehead. His sultry dark eyes were half closed, his strong lean face covered with a stubble of beard. His lips were parted in an appealing grin. The trim, beautiful body was stretched out, feet apart, arms under his head.

"Never." She laughed and dropped to him. He nuzzled her neck and pulled her onto his warm body, holding her in place with his arms around her back. Her toes were on his ankles, her smooth naked legs pressing the hard limbs beneath her. Her hands were on his face and she was kissing his mouth, his chin, his forehead, while he closed his eyes and pretended dismay.

The barrage of eager kisses finally ended, and he opened his eyes and smiled. "My favorite fantasy is, you kiss me until I'm wet and then you dry me off with your hair."

Laughing, she raised up a little and drew her hair down over her head. She shook it out over his face, tossing her head about, trailing the long, tangled locks over his face. "That's about got it," said a pleased Kaytano. "Would you care to try the same thing on my chest and on my... "

Flipping her long hair back out of her eyes, she punched him playfully in the stomach. "I refuse to do anything until you feed me!" With that she slid off him and sat with her legs curled under her. Kaytano rolled to a sitting position.

They ate cold roast beef and hunks of bread, washing it down with river-cooled wine. Kaytano, his sharp hunting knife slicing bite-sized pieces of meat, watched the ravenous young woman roll her big blue eyes and sigh with each mouthful. Suzette appeared as much at home in this beautiful canyon as in her Jacksboro mansion. Kaytano wondered if there was a chance for the two of them. Could he ask this beautiful white woman to spend her life with him, a renegade half-breed? Would the fire between them burn out rapidly? Would she grow to hate him for robbing her of her safe, respectable life as Mrs. Austin Brand? Would she despise him eventually? If she could walk away from him today, would she go?

"Umm, Kaytano, this is delicious," she said happily. She sat on her heels, the long white shirt open down her middle, exposing her body to him. Her blond hair was a thick, tangled halo around her fragile face. Her soft lips were greasy from the meat. She licked her fingers and sighed. The sight of her unabashed pleasure filled Kaytano's heart with joy. It was easy to push aside nagging doubts.

He reached for her wrist and pulled her into his arms. "You're delicious," he growled and kissed the grease from her mouth. Cradled to his lean chest, she lay quiet and still while he kissed her face, her ear, her throat. His lips surrounded the tiny gold locket she wore; with his tongue he pressed it into the hollow of her throat.

"Kaytano," she murmured, "unhook my locket, please."

Unquestioning, he raised his head and smiled at her while

his fingers found the clasp. Suzette put her fingers to the delicate heart and drew it from her neck. She kissed it and draped it around Kaytano's dark right wrist, winding it around twice. She fastened it and said, "My mother and daddy gave me this locket when I turned sixteen. I've not had it off since that night." She lifted her eyes to his. "I love you, Kaytano, more than I've ever loved anyone on this earth. The locket is precious to me, just as you are. Will you wear it always?"

Touched deeply, Kaytano looked at the tiny gold heart resting on his dark wrist. His eyes went to hers and he said honestly, "To take the locket from me would mean cutting off my hand. Thank you, my darling, it's the most valuable gift I've ever been given." His lips met hers in a tender kiss. When his tongue parted her lips, Suzette squirmed and pulled back.

Petulantly, she said, "Kaytano, you promised me a bath. I'm not clean, so please don't love me until I am!"

Sighing, he raised his head. "Woman, are you forgetting to whom you are speaking? I'm the cruel Kaytano, the Prince of Darkness. Do you think you can boss me around?"

Suzette laughed and traced the curve of his lips with her fingertips. "I'm terrified," she said lazily. "I'm afraid you're going to love me to death!"

Laughing, he rose with her in his arms. "I may well do just that, but first I'll let you have your bath. You can use one — you smell of me."

"Umm." She snuggled to him. "And you of me. Take me to the river."

"No, put your pants on, we're going to my favorite place."

They rode Darkness around the bend of the river, heading in a westerly direction. The sun was still high overhead, though it had traveled far enough across the clear blue sky to cast long shadows in the deep canyon. Suzette looked about her and felt she could spend the rest of her days lazily exploring the corridors of these breathtaking canyons with Kaytano at her side.

She heard it before she saw it. She straightened, straining

to identify the sound. It was growing louder, and just as she turned to question Kaytano, Darkness rounded a glacial wall and she saw it. From high on the opposite side of the canyon, a mighty rush of water pounded over the rock formations, falling loudly into the river a hundred feet below them. Suzette's eyes filled with delight and she shouted to be heard. "Kaytano! It's beautiful! Can we go down to it?"

"It's Capote Falls, Suzette. I knew you'd like it. We'll leave Darkness here and walk down."

She stood in awe of the magnificent sight while Kaytano unsaddled Darkness and turned him loose. Then she was tugging on Kaytano's hand as she skipped along the sandstone boulders, drawing nearer and nearer to the water. At the edge they raced each other to strip. Kaytano won and was slicing through the cold, clear water toward the falls when Suzette splashed in, yelling and laughing. In her hand was the sweet-smelling soap. Gasping and sputtering from the cold, she was shouting to the dark, agile Kaytano to wait for her.

Kaytano turned onto his back and floated easily. "If you'll swim instead of walking, Suzette, you'll catch up with me."

She glared at him. "I don't know how."

Kaytano threw back his head and laughed, the sound of his deep laughter dueling with the deafening falls. "It's not funny!" she shouted at him. "I was never allowed to swim in the creek when I was a little girl. My mother thought it wasn't ladylike. You'll never know the times I was soundly scolded for slipping down to the water just to wade."

Kaytano's laughter softened. He swam to her and touched his feet to the bottom, putting his arms about her narrow waist. "I'm sorry I teased you. I'll teach you to swim, it's easy."

Suzette raised her hands to his shoulders and smiled. She was beginning to get warm. The water reached just to her breasts and was so crystal clear she could see the pool's bottom as though there were no water. Squeezing her lightly, Kaytano said, "Let's go play in the falls. The water's not over your head."

Holding to her waist, he eased over onto his back and pulled her with him. He paddled his way toward the falls until they were so close all sound was drowned out by the roaring water. Touching bottom, he took her hand and led her directly under the frothy, foamy falls.

The pressure of the water stung her sensitive skin, peppering her head and shoulders. It felt wonderful. Its stinging punishment brought blood to the surface, making her face glow with radiant health. Her hair was immediately plastered to her head and neck, as was Kaytano's. He stood beside her, his head back, mouth open, letting the raging, tumbling water hit him directly in the face.

All at once he shook his head and turned to her. Reaching down, he lifted her up on his shoulders as easily as if she were a small child, and she screamed and clung to his wet head as he settled her legs around his neck. Holding tightly to her wet, silky thighs, Kaytano did a water dance under the plunging falls, whooping and grunting while the naked girl dug her feet into his slippery sides and squealed with fear and delight. He walked directly under the falls, letting the rushing water wash over them. Then Kaytano plucked her feet from his sides and dumped her over backward, swiftly spinning about to catch her before she hit the water.

Gasping for breath, she clung to his neck. He lifted her to face him and she wrapped her legs around his waist. Kaytano locked his hands under her bottom and shouted, "I've had enough of you, white woman! I shall evaporate into the canyons, leaving you behind to mourn my disappearance." He grinned wickedly.

"Now, Kaytano —" she began, tightening her hold on him, but in the next second he easily tossed her over into the water. She emerged sputtering and indignant. "I shall get you for..."

Kaytano was gone. Suzette pushed her wet hair from her eyes and looked about. He was nowhere in sight. Laughing, she knew he wouldn't leave her here alone and she began to turn around and around, calling his name. Nothing. No answer. Growing irritated, Suzette continued to call, straining to be heard above the ferocious falls. Her hands paddling the water furiously, she turned away from the raging waterfall, her eyes scanning both banks of the river, and then the rocky inclines above her.

Suddenly feeling cold and apprehensive, she shouted again, praying he'd end this childish game and answer. "Kaytano, please. Please!"

A brown arm with a gold locket gleaming on its dark wrist snaked out from under the white, rushing falls and grabbed her. She screamed as she was pulled through the raging water and hauled up against a warm, slippery chest. "Miss me?" he shouted and bent to kiss her trembling lips.

They stood in a completely dry place: a tiny room behind the falls. The grotto was the perfect hiding place from the world. Glad to be safe in his arms, Suzette wrapped her arms around his neck and clung to him. "How did you know this shelf was back here?"

"When I love a place, I learn all I can about it. I seek out its secrets."

"And people?"

Kaytano's dark eyes flashed. He pressed his hard, wet body closer to hers. "I intend to learn all of yours," he said seriously and kissed her lovingly.

Back outside, they both lathered up their bodies, laughing and assisting each other. When they were clean, Kaytano shampooed Suzette's long tangled hair, his lean fingers massaging her scalp vigorously. Afterward they sat on a huge, flat boulder at the water's edge while Kaytano ran his fingers through her wet hair, shaking excess water from it. Suzette sat in front of him, hugging her kness to her chin, content to let him brush the long, wet locks until they were dry.

His pleasant task finished, Kaytano smiled when Suzette stretched her pale legs out in front of her and spread her arms beside her. Snatching the opportunity, he flung himself down on his back, laying his head in her naked lap. Wordlessly, they remained thus while the perfect summer day drew to a close, the canyon plunging into twilight while the sun still shone on the mountains above them.

With the sounds of the spray of the falls lulling them, they grew lazy and content and soon Suzette squirmed a bit. Kaytano shifted and she lay down beside him. Both now on their backs, their knees bent, feet flat on the rock, they held hands and watched a million twinkling stars fill the heavens high over their heads.

"Are you cold, Suzette?" asked Kaytano dreamily.

"No, but..."

"What, love?"

Suzette's hand went to his taut abdomen. "I was thinking what a great place this would be to make love, except I'm afraid my sensitive backside couldn't take much of a pounding on these rocks." She sighed lazily.

"My back is not so delicate," he said. Yawning, he leaned on an elbow and kissed her. His lips were warm and soft and Suzette shivered. His mouth played with hers, teasing, tasting, kissing at the corners, licking at the soft fleshy inside of her bottom lip.

Soon Suzette was lifting her head, longing for deeper, more meaningful kisses. Sensing her need, his mouth settled more firmly on hers and his tongue slowly penetrated. His bare chest was pressing down on her breasts, his hand stroking a gleaming naked thigh. His lips left hers and Kaytano lay down on his back. Gently he lifted her astride his waist. Suzette leaned to him and again he was kissing her, his hands eagerly caressing her bare, soft bottom. She gripped his dark hair and kissed him passionately. She nipped at his bottom lip nervously as her hunger grew. Kaytano raised his hands to her waist and she lifted her head, her blue eyes limpid with desire. Gently he eased her down over his aroused hard body and she gasped as she clung to his muscled arms and slid slowly over him.

"Love me, Suzette," he murmured, his dark eyes on her face.

"Yes," she breathed and did.

They ate at midnight. Kaytano caught a striped bass, built a fire, and roasted the fish on a spit. Both sat licking their fingers while they washed down the fish with cool wine. They talked most of the night and stumbled tiredly to a grassy place high up on the canyon wall to sleep when dawn broke.

When they woke they traveled again, finding another lush, private meadow inside the canyons. There were no booming falls, but they located a clear shallow stream, dotted with smooth boulders. They went farther, running into Burro Bluff and its white-water rapids. Kaytano explained to her that they were now on top of the falls where they'd been the day before. They were higher up in the mountains now, where wildflowers like Caliche Bahaia and Parralena, their huge yellow flowers dotting the landscape, fought with the beautiful red Chinos Paintbrush and the vivid pink Strawberry Pitaya for Suzette's attention.

She bent to pick some of the lovely pink flowers. Taking her hand, Kaytano pulled her up. "Wait till sundown. That's when the evening primrose opens. I'll gather a bunch for your hair." Nodding agreement, she let him lead her through the flowers and grass down to the floor of the canyon. Looking young, relaxed, and boyishly handsome, Kaytano grinned and said, "I want to love you, but not on the rocks." Around the curve in the river, a long, soft sandbar jutted out into the water.

"Don't tell me," she kidded, "you knew the sandbar was here."

Kaytano gave no reply. He shrugged his shoulders and laughed. The bright sun that had beat down on them all morning had gone behind a cloud. The warm sandbar was completely in the shade. Silently, Kaytano and Suzette undressed and stretched out on the sand. Suzette lay on her back, ready for his loving. Kaytano lay with his torso partially covering her, face above hers. The sky grew darker; black clouds seemed to boil up from out of nowhere. While Kaytano gently kissed her, the first giant drops of rain splattered on the canyon floor. Thunder rolled, clouds broke, and a deluge of water hissed against the limestone. Lightning streaked across the black sky and the wind changed abruptly, the temperature inside the canyon falling several degrees.

The rain intensified as the summer storm picked up momentum and crashed around the lovers' heads. Kaytano, oblivious to the storm, fiercely pounded into the woman he loved while the rain pounded down on him. He was mindless of anything save the sweet, pliant body clasping him, the soft, hot kisses, the dear sweet voice calling his name.

Suzette, her bare bottom twisting in the deep sand, wrapped her legs around Kaytano. Her eyes slitting open, she clung to his shoulders and moaned. Above her, his dark, handsome face was wet with rain, his thick black hair plastered to his head. The long lashes sweeping over his eyes were spikey with water.

He was godlike in his splendid wet beauty, and in his arms, Suzette was not bothered by the storm. He was the storm. His power was unmatched. The thunder was in his heavy heartbeat. The lightning was the fury in his blood. And when the deluge was released within her, she felt washed clean and new by his love.

Over her head two white doves flew into a gathering rainbow. They wet their beaks in the spray off the rocks, circled, and disappeared. The sun came out, rapidly drying the wet, sated bodies on the tiny sandbar.

At sunset Suzette was perched on a smooth boulder. She watched Kaytano gathering the little yellow flowers he called evening primrose. Their sweetness attracted hummingbirds and filled the rain-soaked canyon with their gentle fragrance. Coming to her, Kaytano crouched down on his heels and worked the flowers into a crown for her head.

Almost reverently he placed it on her shining golden hair and put his hand to her cheek. "Never wear anything but a crown of primrose."

"Thank you, darling." She turned her lips into his hand, kissing his palm. She patted the rock and he sat down beside her, pulling the last cigar from his breast pocket. Cupping his hands, he lit it, drawing in the smoke, holding it, then slowly releasing it. Suzette watched with interest and he knew she wanted to try again.

She took a puff and drew it deep inside. Holding it, she looked at him for instruction. "You're doing fine. Now slowly release the smoke." She exhaled and almost managed to keep from coughing.

"That really tastes awful, Kaytano. Maybe I'll let you handle the cigar smoking."

His lips curving into a grin, he said, "I thought you were dying to take up the habit."

She shrugged. "That was because I was always told I couldn't try it."

"Could be. Be advised you can and will try everything with me."

"I know." She smiled. "Maybe that's why I love you so much."

Kaytano didn't reply. He smoked quietly and watched her. Suzette was still naked, as she'd been all day. She had started to dress after the storm, but he'd stopped her.

"But you're dressing," she had countered, holding her clothes up in front of her.

"Only to cook your food and gather flowers for you. I'm willing to slave and work for you; the least you could do is to let me enjoy the sight of you without clothes."

So she sat beside him, comfortably naked, while he was fully clothed. She longed for the sight of him naked. "You're finished with your daily chores, aren't you?"

"I hope so." He laughed. "I feel lazy."

"Why don't you take off your clothes? I like to watch your skin change color in the setting sun."

Kaytano clamped his cigar between his teeth. Rising to his feet, he obligingly stripped. She sat looking up at him, her feet tucked under her. The blood-red sun washed over him, turning him a brick color. Awed by his masculine beauty, she reached out to touch a sinewy thigh. He looked down at her, the cigar between his teeth. She tilted her head back to look up, her eyes unashamedly registering her adoration.

Kaytano threw the cigar into the water and reached for her. He carried her to a grassy spot and wordlessly took her. The sweet, fragrant smell of primrose floated about them from her crown of flowers, now fallen from her head.

"Kaytano," she breathed against his shoulder, "let's don't go back tomorrow. Let's don't ever go back."

"Don't," he breathed. "Just love me, darling. Forget about tomorrow."

32

The lovers reluctantly returned to camp the next afternoon. Their fascination with and attraction to each other brought amused looks from Kaytano's hardened men. In all the time they'd ridden with the dark, quiet half-breed, they'd never seen him so enamored of a woman. There had been women through the years, many quite rich and beautiful, and several had thrown themselves openly at the lean, distant man. But Kaytano had never loved any of them. He'd made it clear to each that no woman would ever have his heart, that he had no heart to give.

To see him now behaving like a lovesick boy was both comical and alarming to the trusting men who took their orders from this man and looked to him for all decisions. They wondered how much the lovely pale woman would change the shrewd, quick-witted Kaytano. And they wondered why, after all the months Suzette had been in camp, had their leader only now become so smitten with her. They all knew that from that very first night she was in the camp, when Kaytano had locked her in the bedroom, he had raped her. Her screams rang throughout the quiet camp, and from that night forward, Kaytano had been sleeping with her. Why after all these months in her bed was he suddenly so captivated?

Kaytano saw the puzzled looks in the eyes of his men, but he was unruffled. The icy, heartless Kaytano was gone; a happier, hot-blooded man had taken his place. A man so bewitched by the slender, golden beauty that he cared not at all what anyone thought about the two of them. He was interested only in his beautiful mate and made no attempt to hide his infatuation.

The pair went about the camp holding hands, gazing into each other's eyes, constantly touching, silently communicating. At mealtime they sat side by side at the table, playfully feeding each other, mindless of those around them. If Kaytano was at the stables, Suzette was there with him. If he went out to cut wood for the coming winter, Suzette sat holding his shirt, her eyes gently caressing the lean, sleek torso as he swung the ax high over his head in the hot sunshine.

When Kaytano sat in the late evening, his back to a tree, knees bent, feet apart, talking quietly to his men, Suzette sat curled between his legs, her head back against his shoulder, happily listening to his low, deep voice as he discussed plans for their next venture. She was much more interested in the feel of his voice vibrating under her than in what he said.

At night when they went into their small, airless bedroom, they laughed and played, pulling eagerly at each other's clothing until both were naked. Then they wrestled among the rumpled bedcovers. The fact that they sometimes said their good-nights at eight o'clock seemed not in the least strange to them. After all, they'd spent the entire long hot day waiting to be in each other's arms.

After the evening's first urgent loving, Kaytano and Suzette enjoyed talking quietly to each other until the wee hours of the morning. Neither had ever been as close to another human being as they were to each other. Despite this closeness, Suzette had not yet demanded an explanation for his capturing her or why after all this time he still held her. She still had no idea why he'd not ransomed her back to

Austin. She didn't know what he would do with her, and she didn't want to know.

Suzette was a woman in love, totally, hopelessly, gloriously in love with the surprisingly warm and tender man, and she didn't want to think of tomorrow. She wanted nothing more than to lie in the moonlight in his strong arms, to lose herself in his beautiful black eyes, to feel the warmth of his brown satiny flesh touching hers as time after time he took her to paradise with his skillful lovemaking.

Day blended into night and back again and Suzette floated through both at the side of her handsome lover, peaceful and happy, in want of nothing. It was all there with Kaytano; there was no other life.

She was certain it was the same for Kaytano. He wanted her with him at all times, and any time they could sneak away from camp in the afternoon, he would hurriedly lead her to the cover of the dense trees, or behind a jutting bluff, or maybe just high grass, and take her, murmuring that he could not wait one minute longer to be one with her. Suzette found it hard to worry about being seen; she found it hard to worry about anything or anyone when his tall, lean body was pressing hers and his low, resonant voice was urging her to give herself to him.

And so it was that Kaytano made love to Suzette in every place in or near the camp and in every way a man can love a woman. Each new place and every new way brought delight to the eager young woman who adored him and craved his caresses with an urgency that equaled his. He had only to touch her hand or gaze into her eyes and she was his for the taking.

When on one warm night Kaytano seemed unusually quiet and pensive, Suzette grew concerned. His dark eyes held that distant look that had been absent since they had fallen into each other's arms. He'd had little to say all afternoon, though she'd tickled and teased him and tried to make him laugh. She'd asked him repeatedly if something were bothering him, and each time he'd dismissed her question. When she began to yawn and feel sleepy, she put her arm around his neck and said, "Kaytano, don't you think it's bedtime?"

Unsmiling, he looked at her. "Go on. I'll be in later."

"No." She shook her head. "I'll wait for you."

"Suzette, go to bed. I'm going to take a walk. I'll be there shortly."

"But, Kaytano, can't I go with you? I'll walk with you and..."

"No." His voice was strange. "Go to bed, Suzette. I will come soon."

That was the end of it. He took her to their room and hardly let his lips graze her cheek before he turned and was gone. Uneasy, Suzette undressed and got into bed, trying to understand what could be upsetting him. She had no intention of going to sleep before he came to their room, but when an hour had passed and he had not yet come, she fell asleep. The next thing she knew, Kaytano was gently shaking her awake. "Suzette, wake up. I want you to get dressed."

Looking up at him, she had by now forgotten about his strange mood. She smiled sleepily and murmured, "Honey, get in bed."

"No. Get dressed. We'll ride out of camp."

Suzette put her fingers to the buttons of his shirt. "Kaytano, no. I'm sleepy and tired. There's no need to leave camp. Get undressed and love me here."

Kaytano pulled her hands away and rose. He threw back the sheet covering her and yanked her to her feet. "I said get dressed."

Suzette stared up at him. Those dark intense eyes made her bite her lip to keep from speaking. Kaytano handed her clothes to her and waited impatiently while she put them on. The memory of his earlier behavior came back to her and she began to feel panicky. Something was definitely wrong with him. But what? Nothing could have happened that she didn't know about. Perhaps she was worrying needlessly. Maybe Kaytano wanted to take her once again from camp to spend some time alone with her. That was it. He wanted her to himself again the way it had been before. There was nothing to worry about. They would ride out and make love, then sleep along the river. It would be wonderful, just as before.

Yawning, Suzette let Kaytano lift her up onto Darkness's back. Her trepidation fading, she leaned back against her lover and dozed while they climbed out of the canyon. But once they reached the top, Kaytano continued to press his faithful horse farther into the desert. Suzette awoke and looked about. All around them she saw draws, streams, and grassy places. She hoped he'd soon find a place for them to sleep; she was tired of riding and longed to lie down once again.

They continued to ride, Kaytano silently neck-reining Darkness, his jaw set, his eyes narrowed. He said nothing to Suzette and she could feel the tenseness of his chest. Once again, she was uneasy. Still they rode until Suzette was exhausted and the approaching dawn began turning the western sky a gun-metal gray. They were now on open, flat desert, far away from Robber's Roost.

Kaytano pulled up on the reins and dismounted. Suzette looked at him and, without thinking, said irritably, "Good Lord, Kaytano, why here? Are you planning to spend the night here, where there's no shade or privacy, where we can be seen from miles away?"

He gave no reply. He pulled her down from the horse and unsaddled the big black beast. Wordlessly, Kaytano spread the blanket on the ground and ordered her to disrobe. Casting a wary eye about her, she looked at him and said, "No, Kaytano. Please, let's don't... "

"I want you," he said quietly and pulled off all his clothes. He stood naked in the dawn, waiting for Suzette to undress. Her fingers shaking, she nervously worried the buttons and wondered at the hair standing on the back of her neck. As soon as her clothes were off, he pulled her down and was on top of her. For the first time, there was no tenderness in his lovemaking. Like a fierce animal he took her, his flesh hard and unyielding.

Unshed tears shining in her eyes, Suzette looked at his hard, handsome face for an answer, a motive for his actions. Gone was the warm, loving man she'd come to idolize; the face above hers was the curel Kaytano. His icy expression matched the disregard his body and mouth had for hers. His loving was not loving at all; rather punishment, as though he wished to hurt her, to humiliate her.

"Kaytano," she breathed, and put a hand up into his black hair, "what is it? Why are you doing this to me?"

He refused to answer. He moved more violently within her and his mouth came down on hers, hard and insistent. He was kissing her with rage, taking from her, bruising her tender lips.

The torment continued and Suzette cried quietly while he pounded into her and his mouth plundered hers. She tried to toss her head, but his hand came to her hair, holding her still. He lifted his face to look at her, a muscle working furiously in his lean jaw. Long after her arms had fallen away from him and she lay motionless under him, he continued with his brutal thrusts. His mouth was back on hers, invading, demanding, brutalizing.

When at last Kaytano shuddered and moaned, his body spasming on hers, the sun was well up into the sky. He rolled off Suzette, gasping and perspiring. She turned onto her side, her slender body jerking with soft sobs. When finally he said her name, it was the first time he'd spoken throughout the savage coupling. "You must get dressed now."

Shakily, Suzette rose and put on her clothes. Behind her, Kaytano watched her closely as he stepped into his trousers. Remaining shirtless, he called for Darkness. The horse came immediately and Kaytano saddled him. He turned to Suzette and saw the look of hurt and bewilderment on her lovely face. Avoiding her eyes, he came to her carrying his gunbelt. He slipped it around her hips and buckled it. She said nothing. She was afraid to say anything; she had no idea what he might do next.

"Suzette," he said barely above a whisper, "I'm setting you

free. You've food and water; the canteen's full. My hunting knife is on the saddle. I've given you my gun and gunbelt. I'm letting you have Darkness." At the mention of his name, the big horse nudged Kaytano's bare shoulder. "If you ride due north, you'll be in Murphysville by tonight. When you arrive, you can wire you husband."

She shook her head as though to clear it. "Why? Kaytano, why? I thought you..."

"How can you stand there questioning me? I just got through brutally using you, degrading you. I'm bored with you, I want you to go. Go back where you belong. I don't need you and I don't want you. You've become a burden. Go, you'll be safe." His black, glittery eyes showed no emotion.

"Kaytano, please. I... I love you, I..." Suzette threw her arms around his neck. "Darling, I don't want to go. Let me stay with you."

Coldly jerking her arms away, he lifted her onto Darkness and handed her the reins. "I'm giving you your feedom, dammit! Get away from me." He stepped back and gave Darkness a whack on the rump. "Go!" he shouted as the horse thundered away.

Her heart breaking, Suzette sobbed, but she dug her heels into the horse's flanks. Her pride at last surfacing, she longed to get as far away from the cruel dark man as possible. She wanted to leave him far behind, never again to see him or think about him. She rode to the north, her hair flying about her head, tears streaming down her cheeks. Blood pounded in her throbbing temples and she told herself she hated and despised Kaytano. She opened her mouth and shouted out her anguish. "I hate you, Kaytano. I hate you!"

Kaytano stood, bare-chested and barefoot, indifferent to the crying girl speeding away on his black horse. For the past twenty-four hours he'd been planning for this moment. He had told himself that it would not be difficult. He would take her on the ground, brutalize her so that she would hate him. Then he'd put her on Darkness and send her home. She'd be elated to be free and she'd rush headlong across the northern

Chihuahuan desert, leaving him, never looking back. He would watch her disappear and it wouldn't bother him. He'd be much more upset to lose Darkness than Suzette Brand.

Why now that his plan was reality did he feel this coldness in the pit of his belly? Why was his chest aching painfully, his eyes burning? Why did he feel the sun would never again rise, that if she rode out of sight, she'd take with her the breath from his body?

Kaytano spoke her name. And he started walking. Then he was shouting her name and running as fast as he could, mindless of the stones and underbrush bruising his bare feet. He didn't feel the cuts and scrapes; he felt nothing but panic. Suzette glanced over her shoulder and saw him. Rage now dictated to her and she kicked the horse anew, determined to leave the ruthless savage far behind.

"Suzette, come back!" Kaytano shouted, his heart pounding. "I didn't mean it! Come back, please, please come back!"

Confused by his change of heart, Suzette sobbed louder and continued to kick the big horse, slapping the reins, urging him on. Behind her Kaytano was determined to catch her. He had to. He couldn't let her go. Right or wrong, foolish or fair, he had to have Suzette. She was his and he was going to keep her forever. "Darling," he called, gasping for breath, "I love you. Dear God, please. Suzette!"

"No!" she screamed over her shoulder. "No! You're mean and cruel and I hate you!" Even as she shouted, she looked back at him and knew she loved him as she'd never loved another.

Kaytano was losing ground. Fleet-footed though he was, he was no match for the big black stallion galloping across the desert. He knew it was a matter of minutes before he would fall, unable to go farther. Suzette refused to listen to his desperate pleas. There was only one thing he could do.

Kaytano stopped running. Fighting for breath, he put his fingers to his lips and whistled for Darkness. As though there was no one on his back, Darkness came to an abrupt halt, almost tossing Suzette over his neck. The horse slowly turned in a semicircle, while Suzette sobbed louder and begged the stubborn beast to run. She dug her heels into his middle and shouted commands, quickly growing hysterical.

Darkness paid her no mind. He looked at the tall, brown man whistling to him and whinnied. He began to prance toward Kaytano. Kaytano, his chest heaving, shouted to the horse. "That's right, boy, come to me! Bring her back. Come, Darkness."

When finally Suzette realized exactly what was happening, she screamed louder and jumped from the horse. She fell when she hit the ground, but was up immediately, running. In seconds Kaytano caught up with her. He grabbed her and together they fell. She struggled, screaming pitifully when he crawled atop her. Her tear-stained face was pressed against his bare shoulder. He said nothing, nor did he move until she quieted. Only then did he raise his head. Suzette looked up at him and felt her heart stop for a full minute.

His handsome face was filled with pain and his beautiful eyes were filled with tears. She raised her fingers to his face. His lips went to her palm as his eyes closed tightly and he said simply, "Please."

"Kaytano," she breathed and pulled his face to hers. She kissed him with all the love she felt for him and heard him moan into her mouth.

"Suzette" — he struggled to speak — "I love you. Don't leave me, I don't want to live without you. I can't..."

"My darling," she whispered soothingly, "I could never leave you. I love you, Kaytano, more than my own life. I didn't want to go, but you ... you hurt me and you said you didn't want me."

Kaytano put his hands to the sides of her head. "Oh, God, Suzette, are you okay? Did I hurt you, my love?" He moved a hand down over her slender body.

"No, not physically, Kaytano. But you humiliated me and I thought..."

"Darling, I'll make it up to you." He was kissing her then,

his lips warm and very tender, brushing her mouth, her nose, her cheeks, her wet eyelids. "I love you so much, that's why I decided to let you go, but I couldn't do it. I can't, Suzette. I can't."

"Shoo! Darling, don't. I'll never leave you. Oh, Kaytano, I love you."

While the sun climbed higher in the clear blue sky, the two lovers lay in the sand consoling each other. They clung desperately to each other until both had quieted. Tears had dried, sobs had become soft declarations of undying love. Darkness sniffed and nuzzled the prostrate pair until Kaytano lifted his head, smiling. Kissing Suzette's temple, he murmured, "Darkness thinks we've gone mad."

Smiling at him, Suzette traced a thick, dark eyebrow with two fingers. "Perhaps he's right. If we are mad, let's remain so. Being sane was always such a bore."

Kaytano rolled to a sitting position and smiled down at her. "It's time we had a talk, love. I've a lot to explain, to tell you. If you'll help me get back to my boots, we'll hunt for a nice, private place to spend the day."

"Kaytano," she breathed and moved to sit beside him. She put her hands on his feet and said, "Oh, Kaytano." She leaned down and began kissing his injured feet.

Nothing she'd ever done touched him so much. He pulled her up and murmured "Suzette, it's I who should be kissing your feet."

She laughed and said, "You've kissed my feet many times, my darling. Come." She rose and put out her hand. "Lean on me, Kaytano. I can take care of you."

Standing beside her, he draped an arm around her shoulder. "Know something? You look kind of cute with a gunbelt around your hips. Now, come, we'll find a stream. I've a long story to tell you."

33

Suzette and Kaytano climbed on Darkness's back and rode south. A stand of trees by a small brook of clear rippling water suited them both. Kaytano smiled at Suzette. He began to talk.

"In the spring of 1852 a young girl with blond, blue-eyed good looks celebrated her fifteenth birthday with her father and older brother at their modest cabin a few miles west of Fort Worth. The pretty girl was thrilled when a big, handsome man came to join in the celebration. The handsome man was acquainted with the girl's older brother, and when he took one look at the delicate blond beauty, he fell in love.

"It was the same for her, and soon the young man was courting the pretty girl. The young girl's father and brother were delighted because the young man was intelligent, a hard worker, and ambitious. He was also honorable and a gentleman. He told her that as soon as she was old enough, they would wed.

"One moonlight night after the sweethearts had spent a pleasant evening on her front porch, the pretty blond girl was asleep in her bed when a band of Kiowa Indians swept down from the north and carried her away. Her father was killed, her brother wounded. The girl was taken to the Kiowa camp and she was so beautiful and so different from the Indians, she was not harmed. When she'd been in camp for only a week, some of the warriors returned and saw her. The strongest and most handsome of the young braves was called Satanta."

At the mention of Satanta's name, Suzette eyes widened. She knew what Kaytano was going to tell her. Hadn't she always known? From the first time she'd looked into Kaytano's black, beautiful eyes it was as if she knew him. She started to speak, but Kaytano put his fingers to his lips, motioning her to remain silent.

Kaytano spoke. "The proud Satanta saw the pretty blond child and fell in love with her. He was a respected young chief. Brave and daring. The girl was given to him and he immediately took her for his woman. In a few months she was carrying his child. The girl didn't hate Satanta, but she never got over her love for the sweetheart she'd been taken from. In June of 1853, the girl bore Satanta a son."

Suzette looked at him. Kaytano nodded. "Yes, Suzette, I'm Satanta's son."

"But, Kaytano, he was... Satanta... " she fell silent. She was in love with the son of the savage who had killed Luke Barnes and the others. Suzette swallowed and studied the handsome face she loved so much. A hot day in June of 1871 came back to her. Satanta brought into the fort in handcuffs, his black eyes turning on her. Kaytano had the same eyes, the same aristocratic look, the same regal bearing, the same hard, handsome features.

Kaytano continued with his story. "Satanta was my father; the young blond girl was my mother. Her older brother, my uncle, never stopped trying to ransom his sister back from the Indians. The young white man who loved her was just as eager to have her returned. Finally the girl was brought back. She came home to her brother, and with her was her eighteen-month-old son. Me.

"The big, handsome man took one look at me and my mother knew it was over. He couldn't accept what had happened. He couldn't bear the thought that his sweetheart had been a brave's woman, had borne a half-breed child by him. The big, handsome man left her and never returned. My mother was brokenhearted. She believed in him, and all through the time she'd been forced to live with Satanta, she'd never given her heart to the warrior; it always belonged to the white man.

"I grew up watching my mother suffer. She was looked on as some kind of freak. She was treated as an outcast by old friends. No one stood by her but my uncle. He took care of my mother and me. My mother never married. No man would give her his name. The only man she loved turned his back on her. The big, handsome man she adored no longer came to see her. He went east and married a rich, influential woman and brought her home to Fort Worth. My mother's heart was broken. She never got over it and I never forgave him."

Suzette felt sick. She clasped her hands together and watched Kaytano's black eyes narrow. "Kaytano, who was the man?" She held her breath.

His gaze swung to her. "Austin Brand."

The color drained from Suzette's face. She felt as though he'd struck her. She shook her head. "Kaytano, no..."

"Yes, Suzette. Your rich, powerful husband was my mother's only love. Austin Brand cast her off like a dirty garment. He told her he was sorry that he couldn't marry her. He said he'd never forget her, but he couldn't accept the fact that she'd lain with an Indian, had borne his child." Kaytano smiled ruefully. "Can you imagine, Suzette? My poor innocent mother was stolen by Indians and forced to share Satanta's bed, and Austin Brand couldn't stand it! Did he consider what my mother had been through, what she'd go through for the remainder of her life?

"Did Austin Brand give a damn that an innocent young girl's life was ruined?" Kaytano took a cigar from his breast pocket and clamped it between his teeth. He lit it and laughed a hollow, sad laugh.

"When I was little boy, I remember seeing my mother cry and I felt responsible. I knew that the man whose name she called night after night was not there because of me. I learned to hate him almost as soon as I learned to walk and talk. As the years passed and I saw my mother treated like some whore not good enough for decent folks to associate with, I vowed I'd get even with Austin Brand. I've spent every day of my life planning to even the score. Nothing else mattered to me.

"When I was fourteen, I stood by my mother's bedside and

watched her die. She was frail and no longer pretty. She'd contracted a fever and couldn't fight it; she wasn't strong enough. But, then, she didn't want to live, her life had been over from the time Austin Brand left her. She was twenty-nine years old when she died." Kaytano drew on his cigar and shook his head. "Twenty-nine, Suzette, and she looked ancient. She was old before her time." He closed his eyes for a minute. Suzette knew he was reliving the past. She could picture a fourteen-year-old Kaytano tearfully watching his mother dying. Her chest ached for the boy, and for the man. She longed to make it up to him.

Kaytano opened his eyes. "I cried and begged my mother not to go. I told her I needed her and loved her. She clung to my hand and whispered she was sorry but she couldn't hang on any longer. She told me that my Uncle Curtis would watch after me, that I was to stay with him and mind him. I promised I would and kissed her cheek. In less than an hour she was dead. Do you know whose name she called when she died? Austin Brand's." Kaytano's eyes flashed with fury and he said hotly, "My God! Can you believe she loved him after what he did to her? After all those lonely, wasted years she still loved him."

"Kaytano." Suzette reached for his hand. "Darling, don't torture yourself. Sweetheart, it was a long time ago and she..."

Kaytano withdrew his hand. "I will never forget it, Suzette, never. Brand was responsible for my mother's death. I hate him, I always will."

"Kaytano, I understand. But what about Satanta? I realize that he was your father, but why didn't you hate him for raping your mother? You can't forgive Austin for letting her go. What about Satanta? He let the whites take her back home. He took money and let them have both of you. What kind of man would do that?"

Kaytano's black eyes were cold now. "No, Suzette. Satanta didn't ransom her back, and if he hadn't been on the warpath when they came for her, she would never have been brought back! The white men deliberately waited until Satanta was far away from camp before they went in after her. Satanta was a man. He'd never have let them take his woman and child."

Suzette sat quietly studying Kaytano. Her brain was racing with all the sad facts, with all the tragedies weaving their lives together. She could see everyone's side in the unhappy drama, even Austin's, though she didn't say as much to Kaytano.

"Darling," she said softly, "there's still so much that I don't understand. I can see you wanted to get even with Austin, but... Kaytano, did you... did you kill Austin's first wife and his child?"

She was immediately sorry she'd said it. Rage turned his face to a mask of fury, and for a minute he couldn't speak. Finally he said coldly, "No. Killing helpless women and children is as repulsive to me as to any man. I rob banks, Suzette, or hold up trains. While my life is not one of respectability, I'm not an animal who harms women and children. I never touched his wife and little girl. Renegade Comanches did that."

"Kaytano, why me?" Suzette studied him. "And why have you kept me all this time and never harmed me? It's confusing. Tell me everything."

Kaytano smiled for the first time and reached out to stroke a shiny lock of golden hair lying on her shoulder. "My naïve love. My sweet Suzette." He pulled her into his arms and kissed her nose. "I didn't steal Beth Brand because it wouldn't have hurt Austin Brand. He was not in love with her. He married her because her family was wealthy and he was ambitious. He loved my mother, but couldn't accept her after Satanta. So he set out to be a rich man. He married Beth, knowing that not only would she so adore him and give him charge of her pursestrings, but also that she was heir to a banking fortune. Of all eligible women, he picked Beth Applegate. He was a good husband and eventually grew fond of her, I think. But never was he in love with her. So I waited. And I tried to decide what I could do to hurt him.

"After the tragedy when his little girl was killed and his wife was raped, I almost felt sorry for him. I thought I might let him go, forget the whole thing. For a time I put it from my mind. Then Austin Brand married you and found true happiness." Kaytano's arms tightened around Suzette. He inhaled deeply and kissed her cheek. "I knew then how I'd get even. It was almost comical — the big, powerful Austin Brand had fallen so in love that he could think of nothing else. He was like a young boy again and I was as elated as he."

Suzette ran her hand over Kaytano's chest and said, "Kaytano, you aren't making sense. Why were you so happy that Austin loved me?"

"It's simple: at long last he was completely vulnerable. He worships you, Suzette. He did long before he married you. Did you know that? I did. I knew and I rubbed my hands together in anticipation of your marriage, just as he did. I kept close watch on both of you, and after you were married I decided it would be more rewarding if perhaps I waited to steal you until he was so used to having you that he'd be like an insane man when finally I did take you. So I waited and watched. I knew every move both of you made."

He fell silent, then laughed. "It was great fun; I knew enough about Austin Brand's relationship with you to know that now and then you were beginning to feel... uh... trapped, watched too closely, treated like a child." Suzette's head snapped up.

"How could you know that? I hardly knew myself. I thought... "

Kaytano pressed her head back to his shoulder. "Suzette, you took your little train ride without your husband's permission, didn't you?" Suzette nodded her head and mumbled. "You did," Kaytano repeated. "You boarded that private railroad car without asking him, just as I knew you would. You fell right into my arms. I was waiting for you that day. I'd planned that day for years."

"What did you plan to do with me?"

Kaytano kissed her hair. "I planned to steal you and rape

you on that first night, then force you to sleep with me each night. When I'd used you, I planned to release you to your husband."

"And you thought that Austin would never be able to accept me because I ... because you..."

"Because you'd slept with a half-breed. I wanted to take the most precious thing in his life and spoil it. He left my mother because she'd shared an Indian's bed. Surely you must know that if there's anything on this earth a white man hates worse than an Indian, it's a white woman who's slept with an Indian."

Suzette pushed back a little and looked Kaytano in the eye. "I suppose that's true, but you didn't do that, Kaytano. Why? Why didn't you rape me?"

"I couldn't. You see, from the beginning, I loved you, too. That first night we slept on the ground, I held you in my arms and I was sorry I'd taken you from the train. Then when we got to the Roost and you screamed and fought me, I wanted to take you in my arms and comfort you. I knew I'd made a terrible mistake. Within hours after I took you from the train, I was a prisoner, not you. You were so beautiful, and so sweet and clean. And so frightened. God, how I longed to hold you and love you. I didn't know what to do with you. I spent sleepless nights trying to figure out what to do. I decided I'd keep you long enough for Austin Brand to be hurt; then I'd release you."

Kaytano pulled her to him. "I kept putting it off. I wanted you in my life. I wanted to have you sleeping in the bed next to mine for a few more days, a few more weeks. I wanted to see your golden hair in the sunlight, to watch you play in the water, to hear your soft, sweet voice. I wanted you. I wanted you to belong to me. I was in agony and it was all I could do to keep my hands off you. I fought it, Suzette, I swear I did."

"I know, Kaytano, I fought it, too." Suzette nodded.

"Then came the time when I was gone from camp for three days. It was the longest three days of my life, and when I returned and saw you, I knew. I knew when you stood looking up at me that you were glad to see me. You cleaned the dust from my lips and I decided at that moment that I had to have you." Kaytano kissed her hair and murmured, "I suppose I've done very little right in my life."

"Darling," she said softly, "Satanta killed Luke Barnes. You didn't."

"And Austin Brand killed my mother, you didn't; I'm sorry I've made you pay."

"I love you, Kaytano. Right or wrong I shall always love you."

Kaytano hugged her tightly. "And I love you, Suzette. It is right."

34

For a time they embraced, clinging to each other. Kaytano spoke first. "If you love me, Suzette, will you go to my home and spend the rest of your life with me?" He kissed her neck.

"When do we leave?" She touched the thick hair at his temple. "And where is home?"

Kaytano raised his head. "I have a little hacienda in Mexico. You'll like it, Suzette. It's hot and desolate, but private. The solitude is restful." He added thoughtfully, "Of course, should you become bored, I will take you into the city or to the ocean."

Suzette locked her arms around his neck. "My dear Kaytano, I can't imagine being bored with you. All I want is to be with you in a private, desolate place. It sounds perfect — a small, modest place hidden somewhere in the hills. I'll cook and clean, Kaytano. I'll make my clothes."

Kissing her lightly, he whispered, "We'll see."

"Kaytano." Suzette pulled up on the reins of the palomino mare she rode. "Is it much farther?"

Kaytano reined Darkness alongside the palomino. His black eyes were dancing and he smiled impishly at Suzette. "We're almost there."

Suzette rubbed her tired neck. After days spent traveling on the high desert basin between the two giant arms of the Sierra Madre mountains, she was anxious to get to Kaytano's hacienda. They'd said their good-byes at the Texas camp and started down the old Comanche trail into Mexico. Over rough, beautiful terrain they made slow, unhurried progress, Kaytano proudly pointing out moutain peaks, caves, gypsum dunes, and a couple of small settlements.

Suzette looked about. She saw no signs of a house or hut, only the rugged desert, a slight barren ridge a hundred yards ahead. Skeptically, she looked at Kaytano. He was still smiling. "I suppose that grin means that when I top that ridge, I'll see your home."

"Clever woman. The house is on the edge of the Llano del Guaje. I can stand on my patio and see for a hundred miles, yet as you are aware, an intruder has to be right at my front door before he can see the house."

"You planned it that way because you're in constant danger?"

Kaytano laughed. "Suzette, we're in no danger here. I don't raid and rob in Mexico, only in Texas."

Suzette tilted her head. "Then the authorities here don't bother you; they don't try to send you to Texas?"

"Hardly. I'm a model citizen in this land and an accepted, sought-after guest among the aristocracy of Mexico. The *federales* and *ruralalies* consider me a friend."

"Kaytano, can I sleep beside you peacefully each night with no worry of them taking you from me?"

"As long as we're in Mexico."

"Then, darling, let's stay in Mexico forever."

"I can think of nothing I'd like better. Come, let's go home."

He spurred Darkness and Suzette's mare fell in beside him. They galloped rapidly to the gentle ridge, and when they topped it Suzette again pulled up on the reins. "Kaytano!" she shouted.

Laughing, Kaytano turned Darkness back. He loved the shocked expression on her face. She sat speechless, staring at the sprawling adobe home in the distance. Backlit by a setting sun, its salmon-colored walls were bathed in pinks and purples. The enormous dwelling was brightly lit; each tall window glowed. Majestic, the hacienda sat alone on the desert floor, a glorious mirage come alive. Soft, sweet guitar music floated on the quiet desert air.

When Suzette found her voice, she turned to Kaytano. "This . . . ?"

"Yes, Suzette, our home, Cielo Vista."

"It's huge . . . and beautiful."

"And solid," he stated proudly. "I designed the house myself and I assure you it will be standing long after you and I are gone. Our children's children will grow old in that house and still it will be as it is today."

"I love you, Kaytano," she said happily. She kicked her horse and bolted across the desert. Kaytano sat watching her, her laughter mixing with the sound of guitar music. He inhaled deeply of the clean desert air and took a minute to remind himself this was not a dream. It was real. He was home at last. The beautiful blond girl whose laughter filled his heart with joy belonged to him. This was her home, too. Kaytano rode to join her.

A bowing Mexican boy was there to take their horses. Suzette clung to Kaytano's hand as he led her across a wide stone gallery to a huge set of heavy carved double doors. Inside the cool entry, a red-tiled floor made their footsteps echo. Suzette was looking about at the gracious home, eager to explore its many rooms. Kaytano had other ideas.

"Suzette, you've plenty of time to see the house. Tonight we are going to have our meal and go to bed. You look tired."

"Fine, but I can hardly wait till morning."

They entered a huge, high-ceilinged dining room of such unique beauty that Suzette was awestruck. The walls were of tooled leather and burgundy marble. The three-part inlaid table could seat fifty. Heavy, carved high-backed chairs upholstered in burgundy velvet were pulled up to the long, imposing table. Place settings for two in gold-rimmed china and crystal were laid out at one end of the table. As soon as they were seated, a smiling man entered to pour cold water into heavy goblets. The pleasant man was soon joined by two other servants, as a meal fit for a king was served. Kaytano proudly introduced Suzette to his servants. When the quiet, respectful Mexicans had left them alone, Suzette grabbed Kaytano's hand and whispered, "Kaytano, I'm so embarrassed. What must your servants think of me? Here I am wearing an old pair of pants and dirty shirt. And my hair! I'm so ashamed. I should have cleaned up before dinner."

Lifting his wineglass, Kaytano took a drink. His lips twitched with amusement when he brought Suzette's hand up to his mouth. He kissed it and said against her palm, "Suzette, they aren't my servants, they're *our* servants. As to what they will think of you, if they've eyes in their heads they'll think you the most beautiful woman they've ever seen. This is your home, darling, and you may dress any way you choose." He released her hand, adding, "Now enjoy your food and stop worrying about the staff."

Suzette picked up a gold-plated fork. "Kaytano," she mused thoughtfully, "You're rich."

"Very," was his one-word reply.

"Maria and Pancho told me you give gold to the poor. They said you are a generous man, a kind one. A Robin Hood."

"I've given money to poor people, but I like my comfort as well as the next man," he said. "I don't deny my selfishness; it seems I'm something different in everyone's eyes. Pancho and Maria think me a kind man, but most people consider me a dangerous animal. Neither is true." Kaytano smiled and put a hand to her face. "And you, darling, how do you see me?"

"I see you only as the man I love, Kaytano. I don't care

about your past. I pray you'll not continue your dangerous profession because I cannot bear the thought of you being killed or imprisoned."

"Rest easy, love. I've no intention of risking my life again. I've made investments, so we've enough money to live comfortably for the rest of our lives. I've spent the last twenty-eight years running; I'll spend the next twenty-eight in one place: here, with you."

In their bedroom after the meal, Suzette rushed about looking at the luxurious private suite. The windows at the front of the big room gave on to the barren desert. Suzette stood before them, her eyes sweeping the horizon. She could see mountaintops a hundred miles away.

The sheets on the oversized bed with its carved headboard were turned down, ready for the night. Suzette turned about in the room, her eyes touching and admiring the beautiful furnishings, the gorgeous woven rug. "Kaytano, you know we... Kaytano?"

She crossed the room looking for him. The doors at the back of the bedroom were wide open. Suzette smiled and hurried to them. She gasped when she looked out at the walled courtyard. Blooming cactus and yucca plants made a colorful border around a gigantic tiled pond. Statues spewing water high into the air filled the pool. Suzette edged closer to the steps leading into the water. Never had she seen such opulence in a private residence. At the far end of the marble pool, one of the statues moved.

"Kaytano!" she screamed with delight. Naked, Kaytano dove into the water and sliced gracefully across the long pond to meet her. She crouched down at the pool's edge, shaking her head.

He neared her and stood, reaching for her. She didn't bother to fight him. In the water he stripped off her clothes and threw them over the side. Together they played, shouting and laughing under the rising moon. "Is this where you bathe?" she sputtered, pushing wet hair back off her face.

"Darling, we're civilized down here. There's a marble tub

indoors, and there's another place I bathe. I'll show it to you. You've never seen anything like it."

"So, show me," she challenged and threw her arms about his neck.

Kaytano carried her from the pond and into the bedroom. Dripping water on the rug, he crossed the room and went up three steps. He took her to the strangest-looking structure she'd ever seen. The tall, square enclosure was tiled from top to bottom. Kaytano stepped inside. Suzette slid down Kaytano's body and he released her.

"Are you ready for your bath?"

"Kaytano, what is this... this room?"

"A shower, love." He twirled gold faucets, and from over their heads needles of water sprayed them.

Suzette's head tipped up to the water. It rained down on her and she began to laugh. She was still laughing when Kaytano began to soap her gleaming body. Suzette put her hands on his chest and slid them up around his neck. "This is indecent!" she exclaimed happily.

"But sanitary," he countered and lowered his head for her kiss.

When morning came, Suzette, rested and happy, kissed Kaytano awake. "I would like to get into that contraption you call a shower again," she whispered, pressing kisses into his throat.

"I'll ring for breakfast and join you there," he said.

After their shower Suzette remained in the dressing room, brushing her long, damp hair. She took a white silk robe of Kaytano's and slipped it on. She rolled the sleeves up over her hands, tied the sash, and padded barefoot into the bedroom.

At a square table beneath the front windows, Kaytano, in a black silk robe, sat drinking coffee. He looked up when she entered and Suzette felt her stomach turn over. She walked directly to him, bent, and kissed his mouth. She started to straighten, but Kaytano pulled her down onto his lap. She put up no argument. She put an arm around his neck and looked at the tempting foods laid out on the table. A silver bowl filled with plump, red strawberries caught her eye. She reached for one, dipping it into thick, rich cream, then into a bowl of sugar. She popped it into her mouth, sighing and rolling her eyes.

Kaytano grinned and pressed his lips to her neck. Suzette giggled and reached for another fat berry. Hungrily she plopped it into her mouth, but not before some of the loose sugar dropped from the berry.

"Whoops," she laughed after consuming the delicacy. "I've sugar on my chin." Promptly sticking out her tongue, she began to lick. "That got it?" she asked of Kaytano.

Dark eyes lowering, he said, "Not quite." Sprinkled down the swell of her breasts, the sugar dusted the lapel of her robe and the bare skin where the robe gaped open. When Suzette looked at herself and raised a hand to brush it away, Kaytano's fingers encircled her wrist. "No, Suzette." He placed her hand on his shoulder. "Allow me."

"But, Kaytano," she began as he shifted her weight a little, her head on his shoulder.

Brushing her lips lightly, he murmured, "I'll kiss you clean."

His lips left hers and moved to her throat. Suzette sighed. "Kaytano, what if someone should see us?" she wondered aloud, as his mouth, warm and moist, was pressing her throat, moving lower, making it impossible to think clearly.

Without lifting his dark head, Kaytano reached a long arm out and drew the drapes together. The curtains remained open at the back of the room; the big courtyard was walled to ensure privacy. Kaytano slowly licked the sugar from her clean, soft skin.

"Kaytano" — she sounded breathless — "I think it's all gone."

"Umm," he murmured, continuing to press his lips to her flesh as his blood began to heat. With his face he pushed the white silk robe farther and farther apart, until finally a full, pale breast spilled out. Kaytano's hungry mouth moved over the creamy flesh while Suzette's hand nervously caught at his thick, dark hair, her heart beating wildly. When finally his hot lips closed over the pink crest and he slid his hand under her to lift her to him, she closed her eyes and let her head fall against his shoulder. Nipping gently with his teeth, he murmured, "You're much sweeter than the sugar." Deftly, his lips never leaving her breast, Kaytano untied her robe, sliding the soft material apart so that she was naked to him.

His mouth slid up over her body to claim her lips. His kiss was fiery, urgent, burning her mouth, igniting her passions. When, breathless, Suzette pulled back, she whispered, "Darling... the bed."

His warm lips at her throat, he said thickly, "I want you here, now." Smoothly, as he handled all things, Kaytano, his kisses continuing their fiery assaults on her parted lips, her sensitive neck, her trembling throat, her jutting breasts, pushed the high-backed chair away from the table. With his hands on Suzette's waist, he lifted her astride him, her creamy thighs and legs draped over his, her white robe still on her arms.

"Kaytano," she murmured breathlessly, clinging to his shoulders.

"Yes," he whispered, claiming her mouth with his while he opened his black silk robe. Suzette lifted her head and in a frenzy of desire, she jerked at his robe, as anxious as he for fulfillment. Both moaned when she lowered herself onto him, taking him inside her. His hands clasped her firm bottom while she moved her hips in slow circles. In a mating as unorthodox as Suzette could have imagined, she sat atop her lover in the sunny bedroom at the breakfast table and sensuously ground her eager body on his, while, from the moment of penetration to glorious earth-shattering release, she looked directly into his hot, black eyes as their souls mated too.

Collapsing, she buried her face in his brown shoulder. She felt his lips sprinkling soft kisses on her neck. Smiling, she lifted her head and said shakily, "Guess that will teach me to drop the sugar."

Kaytano laughed heartily and raised a hand to her face. He trailed his knuckles down her warm cheek and said, "I was thinking I should ask for sugar at every meal. I don't know when I've enjoyed breakfast more."

Suzette put her hands into his hair and pushed his head back. Kissing him soundly, she said into his mouth, "I love you madly. I'm foolishly, totally in love with you, my darling. Please forbid me ever to leave you."

"My sweet Suzette, I knew from the first hour I had you that I'd forbid you ever to leave me." He ran his hands down her sides, gently pushing her away from him. Bending, he lowered his head to her left breast. Pressing his lips to her rapidly beating heart, he whispered, "Promise me that this precious heart I kiss will always beat only for me."

"Yes," she sighed, "only for you."

Kaytano lifted his head. She smiled and placed her hand over his chest. "Yes," he assured her, "it beats only for you."

Kaytano was certain Suzette would need clothes, so he'd sent for three tailors from Mexico City. They traveled by train, bringing with them fabrics and patterns.

When the rich satins, silks, taffetas, and laces were spread out in the big dining room, Suzette called to Kaytano. "Darling" — she took his hand — "which ones do you like?"

Puzzled, Kaytano looked at the array of colors and textures, then at Suzette. "I'm sure you'll make the right decisions, Suzette. If you have difficulty deciding, take them all."

"You are not going to tell me what colors to choose, which cuts to..."

Kaytano laughed and started from the room. "You're a grown woman, Suzette. Pick what suits you."

Suzette stood looking after him, chewing her lip. Then she smiled. Kaytano was treating her like an intelligent, capable woman. She squared her shoulders and walked to the big dining table. "I'll take this, and this, the blue one over there, this, this..."

Kaytano told Suzette he threw a party each year to help his friends celebrate the sixteenth of September, the anniversary of Mexico's independence from Spain. It would be the perfect occasion for all his Spanish friends to meet the beautiful mistress of Cielo Vista. The elite of Mexico were invited to his desert paradise. Those from far away were invited to be houseguests.

At dusk on September 16 in the ballroom at Cielo Vista, glittering chandeliers illuminated the brightly tiled floors. The mariachi band from Mexico City, their clothes a Mexican fruit basket of color, were in place on a raised dias. Champagne cooled in silver buckets on a long table covered in white linen. Mountains of exotic foods filled the dining room. Suzette put the finishing touches on her upswept hairdo while Kaytano waited in the ballroom.

He was elegantly handsome, his snowy-white shirt set off with a brilliant red scarf knotted at his throat. His black suit fit him perfectly, tapering to his slim waist, the trousers snug over his lean legs. Kaytano was every inch the successful, respected grandee.

He turned when Suzette softly spoke his name. Startlingly beautiful, she came to him in a gown of black lace. A mantilla adorned her golden hair. Diamonds sparkled at her ears. Her slender waist only served to accent her high, full bosom swelling gloriously above her daring, low bodice. The dainty rustle of her long sweeping skirts was music to Kaytano's ears. Before she reached him, he turned to the orchestra leader and spoke. Soft strains of romantic music filled the room. Bowing grandly from the waist, Kaytano kissed Suzette's lace-covered hand and asked if she would favor him with a dance.

Overwhelmed by his magnetic, dark beauty, she nodded her head and he took her into his arms. Alone they turned about the polished floor, lost in each other, unaware that their guests were watching. At song's end, applause rewarded the embarrassed couple, so much in love they'd not noticed that they were no longer alone.

The dance was the only one Kaytano was to have. Carriages began arriving, and elegantly dressed couples swept into the ballroom. Kaytano, with Suzette at his side, shook hands, welcomed friends to his home, and proudly introduced his beautiful mistress. Politicians, generals, socialites, aristocrats, and friends both old and new filled the big ballroom and overflowed into the dining room, drawing room, and outside into the manicured courtyards.

A standout in any gathering, Suzette, with her pale blond beauty, was a visual delight for the appreciative males in attendance, and her sweet, friendly nature rapidly won over the ladies. No man there could wait for a dance with her, and she good-naturedly let them spin her about the floor. Wondering if Kaytano was jealous, she looked about for him; catching his eye, she smiled at him. Never had Suzette seen such a sense of authority and cool assurance in any man's eyes. Such confidence was terribly appealing. Kaytano looked at her as though he was positive she belonged to him and that no other man was capable of taking her from him. Smiling to herself, she reasoned he had every reason to look that way; no other man existed for her but the cool arrogant Kaytano.

It was a wonderful party, lasting until the sun's first pink haze spread like a rosy cover over the desert. All the visiting guests had gone to their rooms. All the others had departed, the last carriage leaving powdered dust rising in its wake. Kaytano and Suzette went down the long corridor to their suite, Kaytano unknotting his red scarf as Suzette pulled the mantilla from her blond curls.

"It was a lovely party." She yawned.

"The best," he assured her. "They all loved you and they're envious of me."

Pleased, she said sleepily, "I'm glad."

At their bedroom door, Kaytano whispered, "Know what I want to do?"

"Sleep, I hope," she replied. He swung the door open and followed her inside.

Taking her hand, Kaytano led her across the room and out

the back doors. He dropped her hand, smiled, and started unbuttoning his white shirt. "Let's play in the pond."

Her hands on her hips, Suzette said, "Kaytano, the sun is rising."

"Let it," he said and threw off his dark jacket and white shirt.

Weakening rapidly, Suzette stepped out of her shoes and began peeling off her silk stockings. "We have guests in all the bedrooms, Kaytano."

Kaytano kicked off his black leather shoes. "They aren't invited to this party."

Suzette unhooked her black lace dress. "You won't push me under, will you?"

Kaytano stepped out of his trousers. "I'm a gentleman, Suzette."

She turned her back to him, indicating she needed his assistance. "A gentleman? Why, you're the Prince of Darkness." She held her arms up so he could lift her dress over her head.

Unlacing her tight corset, he said, "The devil was a gentleman."

"Shakespeare?" She stepped out of her petticoats.

"Lear." He pulled her satin underwear down and she stepped out of it.

Naked they stood by the pool. Kaytano lifted her in his arms and walked down the steps into the water. She clung to him and wondered if this might be the perfect time to tell Kaytano she was carrying his child.

He splashed into the water and sat down on the bottom, holding her on his lap. "You know, Suzette, you look very sophisticated."

"I don't understand."

Laughing, he kissed her nose. "You're wearing your diamond earrings."

Her hands flew to her ears. "I forgot! What if I lost them?"

"I'd get you more." He lifted his dark arm. On his wrist the gold chain with its tiny heart glittered in the rising sun. "This is the only piece of jewelry it would be a tragedy to lose."

"Kaytano," she breathed as his mouth closed over hers. He kissed her softly, teasingly, his warm, wet lips playing with hers. He meant it to go no further. He knew she was tired; it had been a long, arduous evening and she'd played the hostess with grace and charm. He meant only to relax with her in the water for a time, then carry her to their bed.

The playful kisses continued and his hunger for her grew. He was kissing her longer, nipping at her soft bottom lip, holding her closer. She was molding her sweet, wet body to his. He rose, pulling her to her feet. She raised herself on tiptoes and put her arms around his neck, leaning to him for more kisses. Her eagerness ignited him anew and her sweet, parted lips opened wider to him. His tongue slid into her mouth, tasting, questing, mating with hers.

Their slippery bodies were rapidly heating. Her hand was gripping the thick hair at the back of his neck as she moved her mouth under his and pressed herself to him. Kaytano felt the blood pounding in his temples and he knew he couldn't wait. They stumbled toward the edge of the pool, still kissing, sighing, saying each other's name.

Kaytano, wondering if he could make it all the way into the bedroom and their bed, was crawling up the steps out of the water, bringing her with him. When his outstretched hand touched something soft, he sighed and pulled her with him. On the new black-lace dress, Kaytano made love to Suzette, their wet bodies sliding sensuously on each other. When they lay sated and spent, Suzette, her arms around his back, again considered telling him of her pregnancy. She was too sleepy and he was, too. She'd tell him when they woke.

A pounding on their heavy bedroom door made the sleepy couple jump to their feet. They hurried inside, donning robes. Kaytano, running a hand through his wet hair, opened the door a crack.

"I am sorry to distrub you, Kaytano," the servant said

apologetically. Pancho Montoya is in the drawing room. He say Curtis Baird is very sick. He say if you are to see your uncle ever again, you must travel to Texas at once."

35

Austin Brand leaned on his elbows at the table, face in his hands. His bloodshot eyes were burning, his head ached. He ran a hand behind his head to knead the tight, tense muscles. He sighed and lowered his hand.

He reached for the whiskey bottle and poured himself a stiff drink. Tossing it down in one swallow, he made a face and slammed the empty jigger to the polished surface of the table. Slowly he turned to look out the long glass windows at the east end of the room. The first faint pink haze of dawn was appearing on the horizon. Soon the September heat would be oppressive, as another long, hot, anxious day began. Another day without his beloved Suzette.

Austin again put his head in his hands. He moaned aloud. Where in God's name could he be hiding her? How could a band of murderers and one helpless woman disappear from the face of the earth? How could they continue to elude him and all the men he'd hired to find her?

Austin lifted his blond head and reached for the worn map near his elbow. He bent over it and squinted, as though if he studied it long enough, the hideout would be revealed to him. In the months she'd been gone, he'd traveled hundreds of miles throughout Texas, doggedly pursuing the smallest leads, the thinnest threads of hope. He'd hired the best trackers he could find, dozens of them, all working a different section of the vast state.

Nothing. Not one sound clue to Suzette's whereabouts. After all this time he was no closer to finding her than he'd been the day she was taken from the Alpha. Austin squeezed his eyes shut and once again berated himself for leaving her behind when he went to Chicago. He should never have gone, or he should have taken her along. She'd wanted to go with him, she'd asked that he take her. He should have done so; had he, she would be upstairs in their bed right now, safe, secure, and his.

Where was she now? Was she in bed someplace? Was she forced to sleep in the same bed with that animal Kaytano? Was she, even now as he sat here, being raped by the cruel, vindictive half-breed?

Animal sounds erupted from Austin's throat and he shook his head to clear the agonizing visions from his mind. He must not think about it, for to do so would make him crazed. He needed to keep his wits about him if he were ever to find her. And he'd find her. He had to find her. Without her, life held no meaning. Without her this big mansion was a cold and empty place. There was no sunshine here, no laughter, no happiness. There would be none until his precious wife was once again safely inside the walls of her home.

"Mr. Brand," Kate said softly from the hall. "Sir, did you call me? I thought I heard someone speaking."

Austin slowly turned to look at the stocky, good-natured woman. "I'm sorry, Kate. I didn't call, but maybe I was making noises; I'm not sure."

Smiling kindly at the big man, Kate came closer. "That's all right, Mr. Brand. Can I fix you something to eat? Some breakfast?"

"Nothing, thanks. I'm not hungry." Austin poured another glass of whiskey.

Kate wrung her hands and nodded. "I know, but you should eat. When did you get back? Have you been to bed yet?"

Austin coughed. "We got in about an hour ago. I'll sleep soon."

"I... did you have any luck?" Kate asked hopefully.

"No," Austin said flatly. "No, we didn't. It was another false lead. Another wild-goose chase. I don't know what to do, I don't know where to turn. I feel like a..." Austin fell silent and bowed his head. "Sorry, Kate. Forgive me."

"Oh, Mr. Brand, don't you be asking my forgiveness. Goodness knows you've been through more than the good Lord should put anyone through. Why, you've been a tower of strength. Don't you be worrying about what I think." She was fond of him and longed to comfort him.

"Kate, I don't feel very strong right now." He smiled sadly at her.

"You just need some sleep. Won't you go upstairs and lie down for a while?"

Austin sighed. "Perhaps you're right. I'm tired, maybe I can sleep."

"Why, sure you can. Come on with me. I'll turn down your nice clean bed and you can stretch out and rest your tired eyes."

Austin rose. Every muscle in his body was tense and aching. His head was pounding now and he wondered if he could make it up the stairs. A plump arm came around his waist and the kindly woman fussing over him said firmly, "I'm going to help you upstairs and I don't want any back talk from you."

Austin looked down at the short, stocky woman so intent on helping him. "Yes, ma'am," he said, and together they made their slow, sure way up the stairs.

Austin stood yawning in the blue bedroom while the busy little woman turned back the covers and smoothed the clean, blue sheets. "There." She stepped back. "A bed fit for a king. Now you just tumble in there."

Scratching his head, he apologized. "Kate, I'm awfully dirty. I'll soil that nice clean bed."

Kate frowned and grabbed his arm, dragging him to the bed. "Don't worry about such foolishness," she chided. "You can clean up when you waken."

Suddenly too weary to argue, Austin sat down on the edge of the bed and unbuttoned his shirt. Kate was tugging on his boots when he fell over onto his back, sound asleep. The woman rose and looked down at the bare-chested man sound asleep across the bed. Tenderness and worry filled her breast. "Bless you, darlin'," she whispered. "You'll find her, Austin. You don't deserve to suffer so. You'll find that sweet child."

Kate knew she wasn't capable of lifting Austin into a better position for sleep. It didn't matter; the poor man was so exhausted he'd sleep just fine lying across the bed. Kate took his boots and put them away. She pulled the heavy blue drapes against the morning sun and tiptoed from his room.

Austin Brand, his bare feet on the floor, arms across his chest, slept as peacefully as a baby. Throughout the long, hot September day, Kate peeked in on him. Each time she found Austin in the same position. His bare chest rose and fell with his even breathing. His feet remained on the floor. He was still there at sundown when Tom Capps came to the back door of the mansion.

"Kate" — Tom removed his Stetson — "is Austin awake? We've gotten word on Suzette."

"Come in, Tom." She took the hat and led him into the library. "Austin is asleep, but he . . . "

Before the words were out of her mouth, Austin came down the stairs, buttoning his shirt. His gray eyes were alert. "Where is she? Have they found her, Tom? Can we go get her?" He was trembling.

Tom walked to him. "One of your paid informants has finally hit pay dirt. Suzette and Kaytano are on a small ranch in the mountains eight miles east of Murphysville, Texas. It seems the half-breed's uncle is dying of consumption, and Kaytano was determined to be with him when he goes. He's got Mrs. Brand with him. Looks like the Indian is finally getting careless."

Austin never heard the last sentence. He was climbing the stairs to his room. Over his shoulder he said, "Have the men ready to go within the hour, Tom."

"Shall we telegraph the sheriff at Murphysville?" Tom called to Austin.

Austin paused on the stairs and turned to look down. "To hell with the authorities. I don't want them in on this. I'll take care of Kaytano. You'll tell no one of this, Tom. Pay the informer and tell him to forget about it. I don't even want the men to know where we're headed. Understand?"

"Yes, boss." Tom nodded knowingly.

An hour later, a dozen mounted men rode into the sunset. They began the long journey into southwest Texas behind their big, blond leader. Austin Brand's handsome face had lost some of its tenseness. He looked much younger than his forty-five years. There was a light dancing in his big gray eyes. His wide shoulders no longer sagged; he sat his horse straight and proud. His bonzed skin looked remarkably healthy and unlined. A hint of a smile played at his full, sensual mouth.

He was going to get her. He knew it. This time it was not false hope, no sketchy lead. It was almost over. Within days Suzette would be at his side, in his arms, crying her heart out to him while he held and comforted her. He'd bring her home and together they'd forget the terrible ordeal. Time would pass and the nightmare would dim. They'd be just as they'd been before. She'd be his beautiful, young, passionate wife, just as before. Never again would she be away from him. Never again would she be out of his sight.

36

Suzette and Kaytano climbed higher, the horses carefully picking their way through the dense, fog-shrouded forest. High up on the slopes of Cathedral Peak, they entered a clearing. Directly above them about a hundred yards away, Curtis

Baird's spacious mountain home nestled amid lush vegetation and towering trees. Pines, cedars, pinions, poplar, ash, and Douglas firs dueled for their share of space and sun. Uniquely beautiful trees, but none could outshine the gigantic old cypress shading the east patio of the house from a towering height of seventy-five feet. Its trunk, as big around as a wagon wheel, was the natural core of a circular picnic table built around it by the talented, industrious man who called Cathedral Peak his home.

The sprawling house was built entirely of ponderosa pine. The home of Curtis Baird was a luxurious alpine paradise — natural wonders made grander still by a caring, nature-loving man. Curtis's fondness for his rich surroundings was evident, and Suzette admired him even before they met.

The beauty and grace of his hidden home was a surprise to Suzette, but Curtis Baird proved a greater one. Expecting to find a pale man with sad, watery eyes and frail hands, Suzette grinned foolishly when a big, lanky Texan with sandy hair and clear Irish blue eyes lifted her from the saddle. Taller by inches than Kaytano, the big man had a booming, whiskey-deepened voice, a ruddy, sun-creased face, and a thick, bushy moustache that tickled Suzette's cheek when he kissed her hello.

Holding her up to his face, her feet dangling as though she were a doll, he held her tenderly in his huge hands and looked directly into her eyes. "Honey," he said, beaming, "you're the prettiest woman I've ever seen." He inclined his head toward Kaytano. "That scamp doesn't deserve you."

Curtis carefully lowered Suzette to her feet and released her. Deep laughter issued from his broad chest as he whirled and grabbed Kaytano. He clasped his nephew in a bear hug so tight that Suzette was half afraid he'd crush the life from her beloved. To her delight, she saw that Kaytano was gripping his uncle's back as though he never wanted to let him go. She knew of no one, save her, that Kaytano would allow to embrace him this way.

When the two men broke apart, they punched each other,

laughed, and cuffed each other on the chin, like adorable children. It was a heart-warming scene, and when finally they stopped their horseplay and pulled her in between them for the walk up to the cabin, Suzette put her arm around each and felt wonderfully happy that she was carrying a descendant of these two remarkable men.

Sweeping her inside the living room, Curtis said, "You made it just in time. The rain is beginning; it rains here every day, Suzette." The sky darkened as the first big drops peppered the porch and lightning cracked uncomfortably close. Suzette's eyes moved about the big, cheery room, admiring the gleaming oak floors, the colorful rugs, the massive furniture.

With a hand cupping Suzette's elbow, Curtis quickly steered her into a side hall and to a door at its end. The bedroom awaiting Kaytano and Suzette was large and comfortable. A huge bed, its counterpane of soft, red fox, sported a headboard that reached almost to the ceiling. It was carved from Mexican black walnut and was unlike any Suzette had ever seen.

Her eyes wide, she ran her hand over its dark, gleaming surface, remarking on its beauty. Kaytano slid his hand around Curtis's back. "Suzette, this big mountain man here made every stick of furniture you see. He's been dying to show you, he's so proud."

His ruddy face growing redder still, Curtis swiftly crooked an arm backward, encircling Kaytano's dark head in the bend of his arm. "Damn it all, Tano, I wasn't going to say anything. You know how modest I am." Both men laughed.

Kaytano twisted free of his uncle's arm while Suzette said honestly, "Curtis, it's the most beautiful furniture I've ever seen. You are truly talented and you *should* be proud."

Kaytano came to her, slipping his arms about her waist. He stood in back of her. "See how sweet she is, Uncle Curtis? I told her if she flattered you, you might show her your workshop."

"Kaytano, why do you tell such monstrous falsehoods!"

She plucked at his lean fingers, trying to get loose. Paying her no attention, Kaytano winked at his uncle and kissed Suzette's neck. "Curtis," Suzette assured the big man, "he said nothing of the kind. He didn't even tell me you build furniture."

"I believe you, dear." Curtis smiled at her. "I do want to show you my workshop while you're here. I could never interest my nephew in my work."

From the moment they had arrived at the Cathedral Peak ranch house, Suzette had felt right at home. On that first evening, after an excellent dinner in the candlelit dining room, Curtis had asked Suzette if she would make the coffee while he and Kaytano went into the library. Cheerfully complying, she stood in the kitchen taking china cups from the handmade cabinet while the two men sat in front of the fireplace in a room located in front of the kitchen. They talked in low voices, but Suzette easily heard what was said.

"Tano" — Curtis's gravelly voice, punctuated by racking coughs, was serious — "I suppose you'll tell me to mind my own business, but that sweet, pretty little girl in there loves you. When are you going to marry her?"

"Come on, Uncle Curtis, if you've something on your mind, don't hem and haw about it. Come right out with it." Kaytano's laughter floated to her.

"Hell, I know I'm too direct, son, but I've not forgotten a big-eyed brown-skinned little lad suffering because he was illegitimate."

"Your memory is impressive, Uncle, but your concern is misplaced. I don't live in the past. I didn't know you did. The fact that I was shunned as a child doesn't keep me awake nights." Kaytano drew a cigar from his pocket and lit it.

Curtis, his home-rolled cigarette between his fingers, waved it about and coughed. "Damn it all, sometimes I think my only blood relative is thick-headed. I'm not talking about the past, I'm referring to the future. Do you want that baby Suzette's carrying to face the same cruel childhood you had?" He thrust a finger toward the kitchen and coughed loudly.

For a time, Kaytano sat silently, clamping tightly on his cigar. Suzette, a china cup in her hand, strained to hear his reply to Curtis's last sentence. Kaytano slowly took the cigar from his lips and crushed it out. "Uncle, you mean my Suzette is pregnant?"

Grinning, Curtis teased, "Why, Kaytano, you're the Indian. You're the one who can see all things."

"Suzette blinds me with love," said an awed Kaytano. "I have lost the sight of my third eye." He rose from his chair.

In the kitchen, Suzette, her heart beating wildly, turned when Kaytano stepped through the doorway. Catlike, he crossed the room to her, his dark eyes studying her flushed face. "Suzette." His voice was deceptively calm. "Suzette?" His hands went to her stomach, touching, stroking, trembling.

"Yes, Kaytano," she whispered and slipped her arms about his neck, "I'm carrying your child."

"When? How long?" A muscle jumped in his jaw.

"I only found out for sure a week ago. I was going to tell you the night of the grand party." Growing increasingly nervous, she laughed shrilly. "Kaytano, I think I might have conceived that morning I spilled the sugar."

Kaytano wasn't smiling. He lifted a hand up to her hair. He studied her face. "Suzette, are you sorry?"

Suzette would have died laughing if not for the serious expression on his handsome face. Smiling sweetly, she lifted her fingers to the taut line of his mouth, smoothing away its tightness. "That's the first foolish statement you've ever made, Kaytano. I'm gloriously happy to be carrying your child. Should you tire of me tomorrow, I shall always have a part of you." She softly kissed his closed lips.

Pulling her closer, Kaytano said, "I'll never tire of you. And I'll never let you go. Only death can release you and our child from me."

A slight shiver claimed Suzette. "Don't speak of death. We'll grow old together in Mexico." She smiled and drew his hand back to her stomach. "This child will come to visit us there, along with his brothers and sisters."

Kaytano smiled and nodded. "I love you, I love our child." he breathed as his mouth descended to hers.

Curtis Baird was so full of life it was hard to imagine he wouldn't live for many more years. When he felt ill, he never let it be known, and when Kaytano asked how he was feeling, the nephew's concern was waved away with no reply.

Curtis had a new project and it was one in which he took great joy. On the long worktable in his shed, Curtis, singing loudly, worked tirelessly on a baby cradle of cedar. He'd given Suzette her choice of woods and she picked cedar, explaining that there were no cedars at the hacienda and she loved its clean, fresh smell.

"Then cedar it shall be." Curtis had winked at her and stripped the shirt from his big, powerful chest. He began work, promising Suzette and Kaytano that he wouldn't over-tire himself. Each morning after breakfast he worked lovingly on the cradle while Suzette kept him company. She enjoyed their time together in the workshop. They were comfortable with each other, as though they'd known each other all their lives. The big man had a wonderful sense of humor and kept her amused with his anecdotes and comical stories about Kaytano and himself. Curtis had a magical way of making the most poignant of tales take on a lighthearted cheerful side, so that touching stories about a young Kaytano brought smiles instead of tears. The way Curtis told it, it seemed like great fun and high adventure that a fifteen-year-old half-breed, a loner, friendless and cunning, should drift to Hell's Half Acre in Fort Worth to become a faro dealer. It was there that he met men on the wrong side of the law and began to ride with them; it was a natural evolution that the intelligent young Kaytano would soon be the leader of his own gang.

Curtis was a bubbling spring of information about the man she loved, and Suzette was hungry for every word. Kaytano let the two enjoy each other. He spent his time riding Darkness about in the rain forest.

On one such morning Curtis was making steady progress on the fine cradle, Suzette at his side. Kaytano, his hair growing long, his hard features relaxed, was out in the forest on Darkness. Lunchtime came and Suzette and Curtis shared a light meal on the east patio at the circular table under the cypress. The sun had disappeared and ground fog was drifting in. Curtis took his last drink of coffee and yawned.

"Hon," he said to Suzette, "why don't we leave the dishes and take a nap? I'm about to fall asleep. We'll get up when my wandering nephew gets back."

"A great idea," Suzette agreed.

An hour later, unable to sleep, Suzette in her batiste nightgown padded barefoot out onto the front porch. At the corner of the house, a weeping juniper's clustered green leaves hung downward, covered with dew. All about, the earth was quiet and still; the fog engulfed the house. She could see no more than a few yards away.

Suzette was stretching, wishing Kaytano would return, when she heard it. At first she was sure it was nothing more than a nighthawk, trilling to its mate. She tilted her head and looked around. Again she heard it and she began to smile, her heart speeding. She stepped off the porch and hurried through the yard. Kaytano, out of the magical mist, was signaling her with their secret call, the one he'd taught her the first night they'd made love.

Mindless of the fact that she wore no moccasins and nothing at all under her thin nightgown, Suzette hurried out of the manicured yard. Stopping once again, she listened, determining the direction of the sound. Grinning, she rushed through the thick, lush undergrowth, unbothered by the leaves and vines under her bare feet. As if hypnotized, she walked through the cloud forest, blindly heading in a westerly direction. She'd gone only a few steps when the house was no longer visible. Still she'd not reached the source of the sound. She kept going, her heart beating fast, apprehension beginning to nag at her. She drew farther and farther away from the safety of the house and still she hadn't found the whistling Kaytano. Now she no longer heard the sound. Doggedly she walked in the direction of the last call, her breathing growing ragged.

From out of the fog he rode into view. Suzette stopped, started to scream, and found she was mute. Directly in front of her, a naked savage wearing only a breechcloth, moccasins, and a headband sat atop his pony. The horse walked to the trembling girl and she stared transfixed at the hard, hairless chest of his rider, satiny-smooth, a sheen of moisture covering him, residue of the fog. She couldn't take her eyes from the dark, sinewy thighs hugging the horse.

He was beautiful. A savage. A wild animal. Graceful, catlike, cunning. He reined the horse to her side. A strong pair of hands reached for her, lifting her up in front of him. Long, strong arms of burnished copper held her against his naked chest. He said nothing, nor did she. She looked at his classic profile, his solemn, steady gaze, his sensual lips.

Kaytano wheeled Darkness and galloped away while an adoring Suzette smiled and pressed her face to his shoulder, inhaling deeply of his woodsy scent. They thundered through the forest, but Suzette was unafraid. Impatient, but not afraid. Impatient to once again be in his embrace, to feel those lean fingers touching her, to have that hard mouth plunder hers, to have those beautiful dark eyes raking over her.

Kaytano pulled up Darkness. He slid from the horse's back and reached for Suzette. Darkness, his reins trailing on the ground, lazily lowered his head to graze. Not six feet from the powerful beast, the lovers stretched out side by side. Suzette, feeling the powerful magnetism of the naked Indian, trembled while nimble fingers unbuttoned her soft nightgown. Kaytano pulled the batiste apart while Suzette looked into his beautiful eyes. Kaytano laid a hand on her pale stomach and

tenderly explored with sensitive fingertips for any changes.
Suzette, her heart fluttering in her breast, bit her lower lip and
watched those black eyes study her belly with an intensity
that was almost frightening. His hand went about gently probing, sliding, pressing.

Slowly Kaytano lowered his face to her, his flowing black
hair tickling her trembling flesh. His warm lips began feathering kisses over her stomach. She quivered at his touch. His
open lips pressed soft, light kisses to her warm, sweet body.

When they were both breathing faster, Kaytano lifted his
head and looked into her eyes. "My God, you're more beautiful than ever."

A moan escaped her lips. "I should be," she whispered,
"I'm full of you." Her hand went to the rawhide strip tied at
his waist. With a decisive jerk, the chamois breechcloth fell
away, freeing his beautiful brown body to her worshipping
gaze. When she touched him, it was he who moaned and
pulled her to him.

On a clear, sunny day in late September, Kaytano kissed
Suzette good-bye and rode up Cathedral Peak to hunt. It was
afternoon and Curtis had worked most of the morning on the
almost-finished cradle for the baby. Suzette and he sat on the
long porch, talking lazily, drinking homemade wine. The
maguey plant's leaves had been trimmed, toasted, pressed,
and the juice allowed to ferment. It was then distilled into the
delicious wine they sipped.

"This batch is good, Curtis." Suzette licked her lips.

"Some of the best," he agreed and promptly began enter-
taining her with a story about the first time Kaytano had ever
had a drink. "He was no more than five years old. The mis-
chievous little devil sneaked into my bedroom and found my
bottle of rotgut. By the time we got to him, he'd swilled down
three healthy slugs."

"That's terrible." She shook her head, smiling.

"Well, maybe not so terrible. Do you know that's the first

and last time I've ever seen Kaytano drunk?"

Curtis told her his favorite stories about the dark young man they both loved. "Honey, that reminds me," Curtis said while they sipped their wine and laughed. "Run in there to my bedroom and look in the top drawer of my bureau. There's a tin box of old pictures you'll be interested in seeing."

Back with the box, Suzette eagerly waited while Curtis handed her yellowing photographs of Kaytano. Kaytano at four, a beautiful, smiling little boy with the biggest, blackest eyes in the world. Kaytano and Curtis, a small fish on a line dangling from Kaytano's proud hand. Kaytano at thirteen, not yet a man, no longer a little boy. The pictures were priceless to Suzette and she laughed and oohed and aahed.

Curtis handed her another photograph, explaining, "And this is my dear sister, Virginia, Kaytano's mother, and that young man with her is Austin Brand, the boy Virginia loved till she died." He continued to rummage through the box for more pictures of interest to show her.

Suzette, the small, faded photograph clutched in her hand, felt a terrible heaviness pressing down on her chest. She looked at the two young people and felt a lump in her throat. Virginia Baird was a breathtakingly lovely, small, angelic blonde. She was smiling prettily into the camera. A tall, handsome, young Austin Brand stood with his arm around her, looking only at her. It was obvious he was madly in love with her. Suzette felt her insides twisting painfully. So many times Austin had looked at her just the way he was looking at Virginia.

Suzette lowered the photograph, while beside her Curtis innocently continued telling her about the man in the picture. "That was taken when Virginia was just fifteen. Austin... Austin Brand ... was my friend. I brought him home one day, and when he and Virginia saw each other, it was love at first sight. Austin was nineteen, but of course he knew Virginia was too young to marry. He was willing to wait. But, well, fate stepped in. You know the rest, I'm sure."

I ... yes, yes." Suzette felt her head spinning and closed her eyes.

"Hon, are you feeling all right?" Curtis clasped her shoulder, coughing loudly.

She opened her eyes and looked at him. "I'm fine, it's the wine, I suppose. You're getting me tipsy the way you did poor little Kaytano." She touched his cheek affectionately. "If you don't mind, I think I'll lie down for a while before Kaytano gets back."

"Sure thing, sweetheart." He helped her up. "Let's get you to bed."

When the bedroom door closed behind her, Suzette clasped her hand over her mouth and ran to the bed. Throwing herself face-down across the mattress, she fought the waves of nausea claiming her body. Agony clawed at her; guilt oozed like some deadly poison from every pore; pain bent her double.

How could she ever be happy knowing Austin must spend every waking hour worrying about her? What had Austin ever been to her but the kindest, most caring, loving husband a woman could have? And what had she given him in return? From the beginning she'd never returned his love. She'd taken all he had to give — his love, his money, his name, and she'd never returned anything to him. She'd been a faithful wife, but even when he made love to her she'd never once felt the way she did when Kaytano loved her.

Too heartsick even to cry, Suzette lay on the bed and felt her happiness slipping away. How could she be happy when her happiness was built on another's pain? Would God in His heaven allow her ecstasy with no payment. She thought not. She'd been raised on the Bible and, try as she might, she couldn't forget those teachings. An eye for an eye. That's what the Bible said. She'd pay; there was no doubt in her mind. But how? What would be required of her?

Instinctively Suzette turned to her side and protectively wrapped her arms around her stomach. As though an Angel of the Lord stood over her nodding, Suzette had the horrible premonition that the beautiful cradle Uncle Curtis had almost finished would never be filled.

A week later, Curtis Baird was dead. Kaytano, holding tightly to Suzette's hand, stood dry-eyed before the newly turned mound of earth. Suzette cried quietly for the dear man she'd grown to love and for the delicate new life inside her.

As they stood in the rain, the padre committing the soul of Curtis Baird back to the soft earth of his beloved Cathedral Mountain, a posse of mounted men rode ever closer to the secluded alpine retreat.

Austin Brand, his gray eyes probing the horizon, rode across the hot desert. To the south, the jutting Chisos mountains shimmered bluish-gray through the thermals of heat rising from the desert floor. Austin, his lips chapped from the sun, his custom shirt stained with sweat, felt no discomfort.

Those mountains were his destination and the long hard journey was nearly behind him. By night he'd be high up in those inviting blue peaks. There in the cool beauty of the high desert, he'd find her. His beloved wife would be there waiting. His beautiful little Suzette was in those mountains, and when he reached them and her, she'd kiss his dry, cracked lips with her soft, cool ones. With a silken touch she'd stroke all the heat and tiredness from him. In only a matter of hours she'd never again be away from him.

The rain grew heavier as Suzette and Kaytano reached the ranch house. Quietly they ate their evening meal and went into their bedroom. Suzette, though she'd not mentioned it to Kaytano, was in pain. Her back had been bothering her throughout the day, but she didn't want to worry Kaytano. She was sure she'd be better by morning.

They lay in their bed while the rain lashed the windows. A small lamp burned on a bedside table. She'd asked if she might leave it burning through the night. Kaytano shrugged and nodded. His arm about her shoulders, Kaytano said softly, "I'm taking you home on the train tomorrow."

"No, Kaytano. It's not safe for you to be on a train in Texas. Besides, what about the horses?"

"I'll put them on a railcar. You can't ride in your condition."

For a time they lay in silence, the sound of the rain and wind growing steadily heavier. Suzette said in a whisper, "Kaytano, will you make love to me?"

Kaytano turned his head. "You're sad. Don't be, Suzette. Uncle Curtis was a happy man. He made the most of the time he had."

She nodded, tears filling her eyes. Kaytano softly kissed her mouth. Warmly his lips moved on hers while he unbuttoned her nightgown. When he moved over her, she cried and clung to him. She made love to him as though they would never make love again.

The moon had gone down and the rain had stopped when the bedroom door flew open. Kaytano sprang from the bed. He was going for his gun when the bullet slammed into his chest. Suzette screamed and started to him. A bright blossom of blood appeared and his gun slipped from his hand and to the floor. Kaytano sagged against the wall.

"No!" Suzette screamed and threw her body in front of him. "No!" she screamed and whirled around, her back against Kaytano. While his blood saturated her nightgown, Suzette looked across the room into Austin's fierce gray eyes. He stood with the gun still raised. While she stared in disbelief and horror, a scalding, agonizing pain knifed through her stomach, taking away her breath, her hearing, and finally her feeling.

Blackness engulfed her.

37

Suzette could hear voices. She struggled to open her eyes.

"She's coming around, doctor." A woman's voice sounded close. Suzette fought the darkness. The bright lights blinded her so she quickly closed her eyes again.

"Nurse, move the lamp away," a man's deep voice said just above her. Strong hands were on her face, patting it. "Mrs. Brand, wake up. Open your eyes, my dear."

Suzette's eyes opened. Leaning directly over her face, his hand on her cheek, a graying man dressed in white smiled at her. Suzette licked her dry lips and tried to speak. A faint, croaking sound came from her tight, aching throat.

"Listen to me, Mrs. Brand." The man in white moved his hands to pick up one of hers. "You are in the hospital in Murphysville in Presido County. I'm Dr. Daniel Flores."

"Where is..."

"Shh! Don't tire yourself further, Mrs. Brand. Your husband is just outside. I know of your terrible long ordeal, my dear. It's over; you're safe and soon you'll be going home." The kindly doctor smiled at Suzette and leaned closer. "Before I let your worried husband in, I wanted to tell you that you lost the baby you were carrying. Since you were held prisoner for several months, I'm aware the child was by the outlaw. I've no intention of telling your husband you were pregnant. He doesn't know and I see no earthly reason for him ever to know."

Suzette watched the doctor's lips moving as he whispered conspiratorially to her; he smiled as though she'd be pleased to learn a worrisome burden had been lifted from her. Hot tears slid down her pale cheeks and she clutched the doctor's hand. "No," she said, unbelieving, "no, it can't be."

Misunderstanding, the doctor reassured her. "Yes, my dear. The good Lord has been kind. The animal who held you is dead and so is his child. You'll have no living reminder of him.

She wanted to scream. She had to scream. This well-meaning man was calmly telling her that Kaytano and his child were dead. He smiled as he assured her that Austin had shot the man she loved more than life and that she had obligingly lost Kaytano's child.

Suzette looked through her tears at him and wondered if it were he or she who had gone insane. Could this man who called himself a healer actually be standing over her smiling because a man had been shot to death and a life not yet formed had been shed? It was he, not she, who was crazy.

Weakly, Suzette pulled her hand from his and whispered, "I want to die." She tried to lift her head as her voice rose a little. "I want to die, Doctor. Help me. Help me die." She watched as his smile disappeared and a concerned look crept over his face.

"Now, Mrs. Brand, don't you... "

"I want to die!" Her voice grew louder, spiraling into a scream. "Let me die, dear God, let me die!" she screamed hysterically, rising from the bed. "Kaytano!" she cried at the top of her lungs while bitter tears wet her cheeks. "Kaytano, Kaytano!" she continued to scream, while the doctor, his face now stern, and the nurse, who'd hurried back to the bedside, tried to force her back down to the bed.

The door flew open and Austin Brand, his face contorted with pain and grief, hurried into the room. Through her tears, Suzette saw him and screamed louder. "No, no," she sobbed while Austin, his eyes full of tears, was instructed by the doctor to help subdue his distraught wife.

"Darlin', my Suzette," Austin pleaded, weeping, "please be quiet."

Suzette was looking into Austin's gray, sad eyes while his big hands forced her down and the doctor put the needle into a vein inside her elbow. By the time the needle was removed, Suzette felt the blessed blackness closing over her. It was a wonderful, peaceful feeling. So very tranquil. Suzette's tears stopped and she smiled, as the last thought this side of consciousness was that she never intended to wake up again; it was a thought that brought warmth and wonderful well-being.

Austin, watching her grow calm, stood quietly crying, his big shoulders shaking with his sobs. His hand went up to her tangled blond hair, then to her wet cheek. Tenderly he wiped away her tears while the doctor said, "Don't worry, Mr. Brand. She's going to be fine. She's been through a lot so she's distressed, but she's young and healthy, she'll snap out of it. Why, in a few weeks, she'll forget any of this ever happened, and you will also."

Austin never looked at the doctor. He continued to look at his frail, sleeping wife. Over his shoulder, he said, "Please, leave us for a while."

"As you wish." The doctor nodded and motioned the nurse to accompany him from the room.

After they'd gone, Austin continued to stand looking down at Suzette. He said softly, "My precious Suzette, can you ever forget what has happened? Can I make you forget, my love? I'll try so very hard; I know you've suffered so much; I know you've... I know Kaytano used you." Austin paused and lifted her hand to his lips. Kissing it over and over, he murmured into her cold palm, "I'm sorry, so sorry. I can forget if you can. I'll be patient and understanding. I know the animal hurt you, but he never will again, darlin'. I shot him. He'll never touch you again. Never. Never, never." The hot sun set and still Austin stood over his wife. His tears now dry, he whispered repeatedly, "Suzette, everything will be just as it was before." Even as he said the words, Austin had the feeling nothing would ever be just as it was before.

A pale, silent Suzette was handed aboard the Alpha at the railroad station in the small mountain town. Austin, fussing over her, was understanding of her silence. He asked if she'd like Madge to come in and help her into bed. She stared at him blankly and he smiled and said, "I'll bet you'd like to sit up for a time, wouldn't you?" He led her to one of the brocade couches and eased her down. Determined not to push or upset her, Austin let her sit quietly staring out the window as the train pulled away.

Hours later Suzette was still staring out the window. Austin, worried and nervous, looked at the untouched tray of food on the marble table in front of her and shook his head. He wouldn't force her to eat; she'd eat when she was hungry. He poured himself a bourbon and lit a cigar. Quietly, he paced the floor while the train made its slow, steady way homeward.

Suzette sat looking out over the Chihuahuan desert. The mountains had been left behind; they were only a distant bluish haze on the far horizon. Suzette's eyes stayed on those mountains. She felt as long as she could still see the Chisnos mountains where her joyous time with Kaytano had been spent, the link between them would not be severed. It was up there in the cool, high wilderness where Kaytano had first made love to her; and then later, he'd taken her to the Punta de la Sierra and away to his home in Mexico. Good times, wonderful times. It was up on Cathedral Peak that last she'd seen him, last held him, lost him.

Suzette's eyes stung from not blinking. She was too intent on looking at the mountain peaks. When those peaks were left behind, Kaytano would be left behind, and their unborn child would be left behind. She'd not see either of them until she followed them to the grave. When the hot desert sun reluctantly slid out of sight, it took with it those distant mountains. And Kaytano. Suzette, crying quietly, jumped when Austin touched her shoulder.

"Darlin'," he said softly, "will you let Madge help you into bed now?"

There was no longer a reason to remain awake. There was no longer a reason to remain alive. Sleep was the nearest thing to death. Suzette nodded her head. Austin sighed with relief and hurriedly rang for Madge.

Austin and Suzette talked little on the long journey home to Jacksboro. Austin was not foolish enough to think her the cheerful, fun-loving girl she'd been before the outlaw had taken her. He'd long ago prepared himself for the worst and he had every intention of making her homecoming as painless as possible.

After Madge helped Suzette get undressed and bathed and into bed, Austin came back into the room. She looked up at him with dead eyes that broke his heart. Hiding his hurt, he sat down on the bed beside her.

"Listen to me, Suzette," he said soothingly. "It's impossible for me to know what you have been through. I can't know how you feel; no one could. I want to say to you that I love you very much and I'd give everything I have to make your pain disappear. I've no intention of questioning you about any of it, but I'm here, should you need me, and my arms are waiting to hold you. I'm here for you, I shall be whatever you want me to be — father, husband, lover, or friend." He gently kissed her temple.

"Thank you," she managed lamely.

It was the first time she'd spoken to him. Feeling almost buoyant, Austin smiled. "I'll be in the next room. Good night, darlin'."

South of the border, Kaytano, gravely injured, lay in a tiny room at the edge of the sleepy village of San Carlos. The last red rays of the dying Mexican sun streamed in through the open window. From the distance, a bell chimed in the town square.

The door opened and Pancho Montoya, dusty sombrero in hand, came into the room. Twisting the brim of his soiled hat nervously, he edged closer to the dark man in the bed.

Tears filling his eyes, the small man gripped Kaytano's shoulder. He tried to speak, but couldn't. Kaytano raised a hand to Pancho and spoke. "Please, my friend. Don't grieve."

Sniffing, Pancho said, "I am so thankful you lived. Is a

miracle you got away. Is a miracle you lived after white man shot you."

Kaytano said, "I am hard to kill. Brand thought I was dead. I owe my life to Darkness. When I came to, I was so weak from loss of blood, I could do nothing more than put on my pants. I called to Darkness; he carried me down the mountain. I don't remember the ride. Enough about me." Kaytano's dark eyes held a questioning look.

"*Jefe*," Pancho spoke in a whisper, "she's on her way home to Jacksboro. She was in hospital in Murphysville." He bowed his head before continuing. "She lose the baby, Kaytano. I am sorry." He lifted his eyes and again patted Kaytano's shoulder.

Kaytano said nothing. With a wave of his good arm, he quietly dismissed the old man. Pancho backed away, longing to comfort the young man whom he loved. Wise to the ways of Kaytano, he knew he was suffering, that he loved the beautiful blond woman as he loved no other person on earth. Kaytano was different with her, very different. Losing her and his child was the most painful thing that had ever happened to him. Pancho shook his gray head and left.

Kaytano shut his eyes tightly. From his window, the laughter of children pierced the quiet evening. A dog barked far away. A lone guitar strummed by a sweetheart outside a young girl's window floated on the sweet breezes.

Try as he might, he couldn't get rid of the lump in his throat. He couldn't blink back the burning tears that kept filling his dark, sad eyes. Kaytano hadn't cried since the day he was fourteen and his beautiful mother died. Since that time so long ago he'd lived a hard, fast life; he'd seen men die, he'd killed men, he'd been near death himself. None of it had touched him. No one had been close enough to hurt him. He'd lived a life of uncertainty and danger and never given his heart to anyone. Then he'd captured Suzette.

Kaytano lay alone in the dusk and let the hot tears slide over his high brown cheekbones. He clutched at the sheet and his slender, wounded body shook with his sobs. He turned his face into the pillow and cried. He cried as he'd never cried in his life. Long after the last traces of pink had left the night sky, Kaytano wept.

The cruel, indifferent man they called the "Prince of Darkness" sobbed like a frightened, brokenhearted little boy.

Back home in Jacksboro, an understanding Kate greeted Suzette, wisely acting as though Suzette had been away on a short pleasure trip. She took the young woman's arm and said sweetly, "My goodness, honey, I'll bet you're all worn out from your trip. Isn't this October heat stifling? Tell you what, I'll open up the double doors in your bedroom so you can catch what little breeze there is." She put her arm about Suzette's slender waist and urged her up the stairs. "I'll bet a warm bath would put you right. Then it's into that nice, clean bed and supper on a tray."

Suzette nodded weakly and let the helpful woman take her to the blue bedroom. Austin remained downstairs, looking after them, his hat in his hand, his gray eyes tortured. Tom Capps came up to the house just as Austin took off his suit coat.

"I can come back later if you'd rather," Tom apologized, when Austin, rolling up his shirtsleeves, answered the front door.

"Come on in." Austin tried to smile. "Have a drink with me. We just got home." He turned and headed for the library, Tom following.

Tom respectfully waited for Austin to speak. The two men sat drinking in the late-afternoon heat. Austin, running a big hand through his hair, at last turned to his old friend. He sighed heavily.

"Tom, he had her for seven months and I guess I'll never know what happened between them. I do know that it will take much longer than seven months before she is once again the girl she was. If ever." He took a swallow of whiskey. "I must be patient. I must wait. I must... " He fell silent, shaking his head.

Tom reached out and gripped his friend's knee. "Listen to me, Austin, you have her back and that's what matters. It's been a nightmare, but it's ended. Kaytano's dead and Suzette's home. I'm not going to sit here and say it is going to be easy. I'm sure it won't, not for you, not for Suzette. But time will take care of everything. Wounds heal, fears fade, grief disappears." Tom rose. "I'll leave you now. Get some rest, my friend." He smiled and added, "Why, Austin, by Christmas you'll both have forgotten it ever happend."

Suzette jumped when Austin knocked on her bedroom door. Pulling the blue sheets up over her, she told Madge she could open the door. When Austin entered, Madge said her good-nights and departed. Austin crossed the room. Suzette held her breath as she watched him take a chair and pull it close to the bed.

"May I?" he asked.

"Sit down, Austin," she said, avoiding his eyes.

He was seated and she waited. The talk that had been avoided on the long trip home could no longer be put off; she knew it, he knew it.

"Suzette," he began, "I think it's time some things were cleared up, brought out in the open."

"Austin, please, I..." She didn't feel she could stand his questioning on this first night back.

"No, Suzette, I have to speak to you. Please just listen for a time." Austin rose abruptly and crossed the room to the double doors. He stood, thumbs hitched in his pockets, facing away from her. "Suzette" — he pivoted — "I have always known about Kaytano. Unfortunately, I had no idea he despised me so much that he would take you from me." Austin came back to the chair and dropped into it heavily. "I'm certain he told you that I was once in love with his mother. She was a lovely, sweet girl, very much like you." Austin pulled a cigar from his shirt pocket and lit it.

"I met Virginia Baird and felt my life complete. Within months, Kiowas took her from me. When she was returned home, she was no longer the innocent fifteen-year-old child.

She had been Satanta's woman. She'd borne his child, Kaytano. I should have taken her back; it would have been the decent, kind thing to do. I've spent many an unhappy hour in my life knowing I did the wrong thing. She was good, sweet, and she loved me. I loved her, but I was young and foolish. I couldn't bear the shame that an Indian had taken what I felt should have been mine alone." Austin smiled ruefully and drew on his cigar. "The arrogance of youth would be humorous if it were not so destructive. I was unbending. I turned my back on the girl I loved. I broke her heart, ruined her life." He glanced at Suzette. "I'll say this for her bastard son — he made me pay. I deserved it; you did not. It was not your fault I deserted his mother; he shouldn't have made you suffer for my sins."

"Austin, he..."

"Let me finish, please." Austin wanted to tell her everything now. "I left the poor girl and her half-breed child and I decided that since I could not have love, I would have wealth and power. While the memory of the sweet Virgina Baird remained in my heart, I sought out the young ladies whose backgrounds were power and money. Beth Applegate won the dubious honor of becoming my wife. I didn't love Beth, but her family was powerful and monied and I thought I could have the best of both worlds."

Austin again rose and crushed out his cigar, then put his hands in his pockets and paced. "I'd have Beth Applegate for my wife, and I'd make secret visits to my soiled angel, Virginia, for my baser needs." Austin laughed hollowly while Suzette stared at him. "Virginia would have no part of me after I married, so I was left with Beth and her money. She was a sweet and remarkable woman and I grew fond of her. I worshipped the child she gave me. When they were killed I thought that finally I'd been fully punished for my sins. I was wrong." He came back to the chair. "I know you're tired, so I'll end this depressing little turn and let you rest." He looked at her. "After I lost Beth and Jenny, I fell in love with you. I couldn't believe what was happening to me. I was twenty years old again and so in love I was consumed with passion for you. In all my life, I've never loved anyone, not even the young, sweet Virginia, the way that I love you. Kaytano must have known it. He was cunning enough to know that taking you would kill me." Austin again rose and stood near the bed, tentatively reaching for her hand. He looked down at her and said in a breaking voice, "Suzette, he was right. I love you more than life and I will not make the same mistake twice. You slept with Kaytano because he made you and it doesn't make any difference to me. I'm sorry you had to endure the degradation, pain, and shame, but to me you're just as pure as you were the day he took you from the Alpha."

Her hand icy, she longed to jerk it away. Slowly she pulled it free and said, "You don't understand, Austin. You don't know what... "

"Please"—he cut her off—"you don't need to explain. None of it matters. That's what I've been trying to tell you. I don't care. I love you more than ever. He's dead, I shot him, and you're back where you belong. I want us to put it behind us and be as we were."

Suzette began to cry. "Oh, dear God, what have I done?" she said miserably.

"Nothing!" he insisted. "Nothing at all. You're still my precious little Suzette. Now, I'll leave you and let you rest. I'll be in my room. I'll leave the door open in case you need me. Good night, my love." He leaned over her and kissed her temple. Suzette's eyes closed and she remained silent.

Austin crossed the room to his door. Pausing there, he turned back to look at the pale, frightened girl in the big blue bed.

"Suzette," he whispered.

She turned her head to look at him. "Yes?" she asked tearfully.

"Welcome home."

38

Late Indian summer turned to autumn. Suzette, hollow-eyed, pale, and thin, spent hour upon hour alone on the balcony outside her bedroom. She constantly scanned the horizon, as though she expected Kaytano to ride over a distant ridge and back into her life. She couldn't face the fact of his death; it was too painful. How could he be dead — a man who had cheated the Angel of Death so often, had laughed in the face of danger, had been so vitally alive?

Kaytano never came. He would never come. Her only love was dead and she watched the countryside dying too, as the leaves fell from the trees and the rolling prairie turned a burnt brown. The sky began to take on that strange wintry look, as the sun now shone from a different, more northern angle. The winter of her despair was beginning and Suzette wished more than once that she had been allowed to perish with Kaytano and his child.

Austin's heart was as heavy as Suzette's. The sad truth was becoming evident: Suzette was never going to be as she had been before her capture. Austin would never know what had happened in those months Kaytano held her, but he knew she was no longer his playful, trusting, affectionate young wife. Determined to give her all the time she needed to recuperate, Austin fought his impulses to take her in his arms and hold her. He was not certain how she would react and he would do nothing to widen the chasm between them.

He wondered about Suzette's relationship with Kaytano. What had it really been? Did he rape Suzette repeatedly until, afraid for her life and her sanity, she had given in to him, stopped fighting him, offered herself to him? Austin cringed. A bitter taste rose to choke him when he recalled the night in the mountain cabin. Kaytano and his beautiful Suzette sharing a bed; Kaytano stark-naked, his copper arms around

Suzette, her soft, white body clad only in a filmy nightgown, pressed to the length of Kaytano, her limbs entwined with the Indian's. Try as he might, Austin couldn't blink away the vision; it was stamped upon his brain with vivid clarity and it rose before his eyes time and again to mock him.

The entire scene played itself out before his tormented eyes many a night while he lay awake in his room, unable to sleep, his chest aching with unhappiness. Again he could feel the door swinging inward as his booted foot kicked it. He stood in the doorway, his gun raised, his eyes rapidly sweeping the room. Kaytano going for his gun. A flash of fire as he, Austin, pulled the trigger; a stunned look on the Indian's dark face; bright red blood exploding from his chest. Suzette screaming. Suzette placing her body in front of Kaytano's. Suzette pressed against the half-breed, looking at Austin with hate as though he were the intruder!

The cold north wind swept down over the prairie, its sound mournful, its bite punishing, forcing Suzette from the balcony and into her room. There she spent most of her time, seated in front of the closed double doors, her hands clasped together in her lap, her eyes still tiredly sweeping over the bleak horizon. Her pain, no longer the intense agony of those first weeks, remained with her but became bearable in the same way one grows accustomed to an old wound.

Suzette knew Austin suffered too, and she was compassionate enough to have sympathy for him. She was grateful that he didn't force himself on her, that he was kind and thoughtful, as he had always been. Unfortunately, Austin refused to let her tell him the truth about what had happened in her absence. Suzette had no desire to lie and hide the facts, but Austin stubbornly turned a deaf ear when she tried to bare her soul to him. Since the day he'd taken her from the Cathedral Peak cabin, Austin had successfully kept himself from hearing about her real relationship with Kaytano. It was as though if he refused to let her form the words and say them to him, he could continue to tell himself nothing had happened between her and her dark captor.

Suzette had long since tired of trying to tell Austin the truth. He didn't want to listen. He was, as he had always been, determined to mold and shape her into his dream of perfection, his golden madonna, his innocent little girl. Clinging obstinately to his idealized, romanticized conception of her, he demanded she remain on the pedestal where he'd so carefully placed her. A silken, blond young angel would never cavort willingly with a dark, dirty, degenerate devil! His precious Suzette would never cavort with the renegade Kaytano!

On a cold, dark Sunday in December, Austin knocked lightly on Suzette's door. He stepped inside and walked directly to the fireplace. "Suzette, I'm afraid you'll catch a cold," he said, looking at the dying embers in the grate. He took several big pinion logs from the box and placed them in the fire. With a silver-handled poker, he stirred the smoldering ashes and watched as flames leaped upward, sending out warmth. "There," he said, smiling. "That's better, isn't it?"

Suzette, sitting in a chair with a book on her lap, nodded. "Thank you, Austin."

"You're most welcome." He dropped into the matching chair beside her, his big hands nervously smoothing the brocade pattern on the chair's arms. "I've been thinking, what you and I need is to have a party."

Suzette opened her mouth to object, but when she saw the hopeful, pleading look in his gray eyes, she remained silent. "Do you remember the New Year's party we had here the winter we first moved in?" Austin continued eagerly.

He was looking at her, expecting an answer. Twisting her book in her hands, she nodded. "Yes, Austin, I remember."

"Now, that was a party!" He leaned toward her, a broad smile on his face. "I'll never forget, you wore the prettiest lilac velvet dress. You looked like some sweet confection and all evening long I was tempted to ... I wanted to ... ah, remember how the whole town turned out? I'll bet they'd do the same thing this New Year's." He rose from the chair and walked to the double doors. His hands clamped behind him, he continued to speak enthusiastically of throwing a party. Suzette felt dread creeping over her as he spoke. The last thing on earth she wanted was to be around other people, especially the people of Jacksboro, people she'd known all of her life, had attended church with every Sunday since she was a little girl. The thought of facing them made Suzette ill; she'd not been out since returning. She'd been allowed to remain safely isolated from the outside world, seeing no one but Austin and Kate. Now Austin was speaking of bringing the whole town to her sanctuary.

Austin had turned to her, an expectant look on his face. She knew he was waiting for her answer, but she didn't know what the question was. "I ... I'm sorry, Austin, I ... "

"No, Suzette," he pleaded, "don't say no. It'll do you good, dear. Tell me to go ahead with the plans. Let's have our New Year's party. Say yes, Suzette."

"All right, Austin," she said flatly.

"Oh, sweetheart!" He beamed and rushed to her chair. "You won't regret it. It will be a grand party. You and Kate can plan the menu and I'll see about an orchestra. We'll see the new year in properly!"

Time passed and day of the party drew near. Austin was hopeful and excited. He felt that a gala party would help signal a return to happier days. He was pleased to see that Suzette was helping Kate plan what foods would be served; he was sure it was a step in the right direction.

Feeling cautiously optimistic, Austin stopped by Suzette's room one cold evening to say good-night. She opened the door and watched nervously as he strolled inside. "I was wondering," he said warmly, "what you plan to wear to the party."

Suzette didn't tell him that she hadn't considered what

gown she would wear because she didn't care. The thought had never entered her mind; to her the party was a chore to be gotten through. What difference did it make what she wore? "I... no, Austin, I'm not sure yet."

"Good." He grinned. "I was just thinking, if you still have that lovely lilac gown you wore to the..."

"That will be fine, Austin." She nodded her head. "I'll wear the lilac velvet dress."

Pleased she had so quickly agreed, he said, "Suzette, I... there's something else I wanted to talk to you about."

"All right. Would you like to sit down?"

"No, I'll stay only a minute. I know you're tired and need your sleep." He walked to the door and turned to face her. Needlessly clearing his throat, he said, "Suzette, I've missed being a husband to you. You've been through a lot, so I haven't pressed you." He looked at the floor for a moment, then raised his head. Looking directly into her eyes, he said, "On New Year's I thought perhaps we could start all over. We'll have our party and then afterward... afterward I want to come to you, Suzette. I want to make love to you that night."

"Austin, I..." she began.

"You're my wife, Suzette."

"Yes, Austin, but you must let me tell you..."

"No, darlin'," he interrupted. "You're my wife. I'll come to you New Year's Eve." He left the room.

When the night of the party came, Suzette, wearing the lilac velvet dress, stood in front of the cheval glass in her bedroom. Studying herself disinterestedly, she noted how loose the gown was. She'd lost weight since she'd last worn it; she could recall on that occasion it was so tight in the waist and bodice, she had been uncomfortable. Now she needed no corset with it. Suzette tried to jerk the low bodice up to cover more of her bare bosom. She was futilely tugging when Austin's loud knock startled her.

"Suzette," he called, "the first guests are arriving."

By nine o'clock it was apparent even to Austin that less than half the expected guests had shown up. The rest never came. Suzette knew the reason; so did Austin. Some gentlemen came without their wives, staying only a short time, making flimsy excuses about how the cold weather or illness had prevented their attendance. The Brands were not fooled. The unmistakable truth was that Mrs. Austin Brand had lived for months with an Indian. Whether her fault or not, the unalterable facts were that she was no longer considered fit company for the decent ladies.

Of the guests who did call, Suzette suspected many came out of curiosity. There was an accusing look in their eyes when they greeted her, and throughout the evening she could feel their eyes upon her, stripping her bare, branding her with their disgust. Clumps of whispering men brazenly eyed her behind Austin's back, and Suzette, feeling she could bear it no more, fled to the kitchen.

Suzette was horrified to find a twittering bunch of ladies in the kitchen, giggling and bobbing their heads up and down. All eyes turned to her and they fell silent. One of the bolder ladies, the respected wife of a banker, stepped away from the others. She came directly to Suzette and slipped her arm through Suzette's trembling one. Looking at Suzette with false pity, she said sweetly, "Suzette, dear, perhaps if you spoke of it, you'd feel better. Get it off your chest, so to speak." She looked hopefully at Suzette while the other ladies crowded around, all eager to hear firsthand what Suzette's confinement had been like. "We're your friends, you can tell us. Was it terrible? Did the beast... did he... well, you know?"

Suzette's trembling ceased. She looked about at the eager faces turned to her, all dying to hear in detail what a dirty savage had done. Suzette felt more disgust for them than they could ever have felt for her. It would be with great pleasure that she shocked their delicate sensibilities.

"Oh, thank you," she began, making her voice sound purposely grateful and relieved. "I do want to tell you all about it." The women grew wide-eyed and moved closer to Suzette. They became very quiet, dying to hear what vile things the Indian had done to her.

Suzette began to talk, whispering low, making them strain to catch her provocative words. She made up the wildest, worst stories she could think of, shocking them with her confessions that the filthy savage had made her do such despicable things that she was no longer fit to be in the same room with the gentry of Jacksboro. Spellbound, the ladies listened as she told them that the Indian's exotic tortures were so debased and loathsome that she wasn't sure they would want to hear more.

"Oh, please, we do," one woman pleaded. "That is ... it would do you a world of good to share it." The others hastily agreed.

Suzette looked from one plain, questioning face to another. Coldly she announced, "You all make me want to retch. Each of you wants to live vicariously by hearing how the infamous Kaytano repeatedly raped me. You can each imagine yourself the one being ravished and brutalized by the handsome half-breed." Suzette laughed when they began to protest, shaking their heads, declaring Suzette wrong. "If you knew the truth," Suzette announced, "you'd be envious. I'll tell you something else... Kaytano never raped a woman in his life." Suzette turned to go.

The banker's wife said, "You mean you made it all up? He never did those things to you, he never... he never even..."

Suzette pivoted. "Made love to me? Oh, yes, he did that every night and it was wonderful." She laughed and left the room. She was still laughing when she climbed the stairs to her room, not bothering to say good-night to her guests.

It was much later, when the guests had all departed, that Austin came into her bedroom. She stood in front of the double doors wearing a sheer blue nightgown. She took a deep breath and turned to face him.

He was looking at her and in his gray eyes was an expression that chilled her blood. She'd seen that look in the eyes of many of the guests at the party. It was a faint look of disapproval, of censure, of disgust. He started toward her and she stiffened. She'd not expected this night to be easy, but it would be even worse than she thought. The look in Austin's eyes made it unbearable.

Silently he put his hands on her shoulders and stepped close. "It was a nice party," he said without conviction.

"Was it?" She looked up at him. "Half the people didn't come."

"Doesn't matter," he said and lowered his face to hers. He hesitated, his mouth inches from hers. A muscle worked furiously in his jaw. And in his eyes was that look. He closed his eyes and started to kiss her.

"No," she said, pulling back. "Wait. Wait, Austin." Suzette took a step backward and jerked the bodice of her gown down to her waist, all the while looking into Austin's eyes.

"Don't, Suzette," he said. "Wait. I'll put out the lights."

She grabbed his arm. "No. Leave the lights on." She shoved the pale blue nightgown over her hips, and wiggling out of it, she let it drop to the floor at her feet. She stood naked in front of him.

"Suzette, my God, don't... "

"Look at me, Austin!" she shouted. "Look at me." She watched his gray eyes slowly slide over her body. "You look ill, Austin. Are you sick? Does my body make you sick?!"

His face tortured, Austin said, "Please... put on your —"

"No. Take a good look at me. Don't you think I see the disgust in your eyes? I disgust you, you can't bear to look at me." She was trembling now. "Well, let me really disgust you! Kaytano didn't rape me, he didn't have to rape me. I gave myself to him and I slept in his arms every night." Suzette's eyes were wild as she finally poured out the truth. Her hands went to her bare belly. "Look at my stomach; I carried Kaytano's child, Austin. Did you know that? I was pregnant by

Kaytano. I lost it and it broke my heart! I wanted his baby!"

"God, don't... no more, please." Austin pleaded, the color draining from his face.

"There is no more. That's all, Austin. That's what I've been trying to tell you since the day I got back, but you wouldn't listen."

Austin inhaled and stooped to pick up the discarded nightgown. Rising, he handed it to her, his eyes filled with a mixture of hurt and contempt. Suzette took the gown and held it in front of her.

Calmly, she said, "I am going to Fort Worth tomorrow. I'll stay with Anna for a while. It will be better for both of us to be apart for a time."

Austin turned to leave, his big shoulders drooping wearily. At the door he turned and looked at her. The distaste was gone from his eyes; now there remained only sad resignation. "Yes," he said tiredly, "perhaps it would be best."

39

Suzette felt an alarming surge of excitement as she leaned over the roulette table and pushed three shiny yellow chips onto the black square with number eleven painted boldly in white. Her palms felt moist and it was difficult to suppress the hysterical laughter threatening to burst from her parted lips. It was foolish, she knew, to feel such an overwhelming thrill over a game of chance. But the sensation was there, just as it always was when she placed a bet in a casino or watched a sleek Thoroughbred flash across the finish line. Since the first time Suzette had gambled at the casino in Saratoga, she'd been hooked. Now, when there was little left in life that brought her pleasure, gambling could still lift her spirits and make her heart beat just a little faster.

Tonight, for reasons she couldn't fathom, she felt more excitement than usual. It was as though she was certain that her lucky number eleven would come up, and with it would not only come money, but fulfillment, joy, happiness. So sure was she that number eleven was the number to pick, she idly wondered why, of all the people crowding around the table, laughing and placing their bets, not one was wise enough to bet with her. Anna, standing beside her, was happily dropping chips up and down the felt layout, passing over eleven, leaving only Suzette's chips riding there. Perry was just as blind to the number.

After allowing everyone ample time to deposit chips on their favorite numbers, the croupier smiled and said, "Last call, ladies and gentlemen. Place your bets, please." His manicured right hand went to the tiny white ball to spin it furiously around and around the turning varnished wheel. While the ball flew rapidly about the circle, a long arm reached out from behind Suzette. A man's black-jacketed, white-cuffed hand dropped a single red chip atop Suzette's three yellow chips. She alone was watching as the lean, brown fingers gently caressed the three yellow chips before letting his drop. She was hypnotized by the graceful long-fingered hand; she stared unbelieving when a slight flick of the wrist sent a gold chain from under the white stiff shirt cuff. The tiny chain shimmered against the dark brown of the skin. A gold locket, one lone sapphire at its center, lay on the slender wrist.

The hand moved slowly away. Suzette's heart began to pound wildly and her hand flew to her bosom. She could feel the heat of his trim body though they were not touching. *Kaytano!* Her heart screamed the name tearing at her aching throat. *Dear God, you're alive!* She swayed slightly, but was helpless to right herself. From just behind, he moved, steadying her immediately. His hard chest was gently pressing her bare back and shoulders; his thigh and knee gave sure support to her hips and rubbery legs.

Her face flushed, her cheeks crimson, she swallowed and

closed her eyes briefly. Knowing she had to look at him, if only for a second, she opened her eyes and slowly turned her head. All eyes were on the spinning white ball, save hers. And Kaytano's. Her eyes lifted to his and she moaned softly. His dark beautiful eyes were on her. His handsome dark face wore a look of love, a look she'd seen so many times when he'd made love to her throughout the hot, desert nights. His mouth was parted in a hint of a smile. A shock of black hair fell over his high forehead, thick and shiny with health. His face was smoothly shaven, his breath warm on her cheek.

The dear hand that placed the red chip atop hers unobtrusively touched her forearm, then slid down her gloved wrist to her hand. Still looking only into her eyes, Kaytano pressed a key into her palm, and closed her shaking fingers tightly around it. His hand left hers and just as the white ball came to rest in a slot on the slowing roulette wheel, he slipped away into the crowd.

"Number eleven, folks," the smiling croupier announced. "It's lucky number eleven for the lovely lady and the handsome gentleman." He looked up at Suzette and pushed a tall shiny stack of chips across the table to her. His eyes darted above her head, then came back to rest on her. "The gentleman?" he said questioningly.

Unable to speak, Suzette shrugged her shoulders. "That's strange" — the man was insistent — "I saw a well-dressed gentleman place that red chip on eleven. Now he's gone." He looked around, shook his head, and paid off the red chip at thirty-five to one, setting the stack to the side.

Suzette, her throat dry, her left hand gripping the key tightly, didn't stop to question whether she would go to Kaytano. She knew as soon as she'd seen his hand that she had to be with him. It didn't matter that it was wrong, that Austin would be terribly hurt, that Anna and Perry would be shocked by her shameless behavior. It made no difference; nothing in all the world made any difference except Kaytano. She was his and his alone. They were one; nothing and no one could change that.

"Anna," Suzette tapped her friend's white shoulder. "I've the most frightful headache."

"Oh, Suz, I'm sorry. And just when you were getting lucky. Shall we go home, then?"

"No, no. Tell you what. You and Perry stay and enjoy yourselves. I'll just stay here at the Mansion tonight. I'll spend the night in our suite and come over to your house in the morning when I'm feeling better."

"Are you sure, Suzette? I hate to think about you alone in a hotel room."

"What's the discussion, ladies?" Perry Woods leaned close to be heard above the crowd.

"Perry, Suzette has a headache and she wants to spend the night in town. I told her I don't think she should." She looked to her husband for a decision.

Perry looked at Suzette. To her surprise, he said, "Suzette will be safe here."

"Thank you, Perry. I'll see you two tomorrow. Good night." Smiling nervously, she backed away, turned, and hurried toward the front door. In the wine-carpeted lobby, she at last raised the door key. And she smiled. The key was to suite 213 right here in the Mansion. The suite just next door to suite 211, the Brand suite, where she had told Anna and Perry she would spend the night.

Suzette lowered her hand and looked around. She went up the winding staircase on her right to the upper floor, her long skirts rustling. At the top of the stairs, Suzette took a deep breath. The wide hall was deserted. Kaytano's room was at the far end of the hall. Feeling the urge to lift her skirts to her knees and run all the way down the long, dimly lit corridor, Suzette smiled happily and took the long walk into the arms of the man she loved.

Suzette stood outside suite 213. With a calm that surprised her, she raised the shiny key and slowly inserted it into the lock. It turned easily and the heavy wooden door swung open. She removed the key and stepped inside, closing the door behind her.

He was silhouetted in the open window. A gaslight hissed above the bed, casting shadows over the big room. He stood completely still and looked at her. She leaned back against the door and studied him. Lord he was beautiful. Tall and trim, he wore a fine custom suit of black Chinese silk, a white starched shirt and white tie. He looked cool, sophisticated, and successful. He was all of those things and he was none of those things. First and foremost he was her Kaytano, her beautiful half-breed, who looked better out of clothes than in them. Kaytano of the dark, sultry eyes and long, lean limbs. Kaytano, the sleek satin-skinned savage who taught her about love. Kaytano, the lost little boy who resided inside the powerful, mahogany body of a man.

"Kaytano!" she cried and started to him. He met her half-way and she felt tears stinging her eyes when his warm, sensual lips closed over hers. Too long denied the pleasures of her body, Kaytano found it impossible to be tender. His kiss was at once deep and demanding, his embrace almost punishing as he crushed her to him. If he seemed callous and uncaring, Suzette never noticed. She, too, demanded immediate fulfillment from this man who knew her more intimately than any other.

When finally Kaytano lifted his mouth from hers, she sobbed his name and tore at the studs of his shirt, anxious to have him naked. Kaytano was just as determined to have her free of her gown. His hands, surer than hers, were under the fine white brocade dress, swiftly peeling down the satin underpants, pausing to caress her bare bottom. Holding the long worrisome skirt high in one brown hand, his other went to her back, trying in vain to unhook the dress. No match for the stubborn hooks, Kaytano wisely abandoned them and moved around in front to the top of her dress. He slid the shiny material down over her shoulder just as Suzette succeeded in pushing his white shirt apart, exposing his bare, smooth chest.

Her tiny hands went to the waistband of his trousers just as he managed to free a creamy breast from the bodice of her gown. "Oh, God, Suzette," he moaned. Still struggling, they fell across the bed. Her dress was pushed up around her bare hips. His trousers were unbuttoned, his aroused body freed. "I can't wait, darling," he murmured apologetically as he moved into position.

"Nor I," she responded and pulled him to her. They mated violently, both moaning and breathing hard. And it was wonderful, wildly erotic. They rocked the bed, half dressed, half undressed. His fine black jacket was touching her heaving breast. His stiff white shirt was rubbing her shoulders. His bare, hot chest was touching the brocade of her dress. Her silk-stockinged knees rubbed against his trouser-encased legs. His slick brown stomach was pressed against her gown where the rumpled satin bunched up around her waist.

Suzette's hands frantically ran up and down Kaytano's heaving chest. Kaytano's hands were on the soft, bare bottom she lifted to him, as he took her with sure, fast thrusts that rapidly brought them both to a blinding climax.

"Kaytano!" She gripped his shoulders as the first explosions began.

"Baby," he groaned and dipped his dark head to her breast. His tongue flicked at it briefly before he surrounded the jutting peak with his lips and drew her into his mouth.

"Kaytano," she screamed and he raised his head. She bit into his shoulder, through his jacket, while her body writhed and bucked against him.

"Suzette," he soothed and put a hand into her blond hair, pulling her face from his shoulder. He was holding her head against the pillow and she watched as his climax reached the apex and he exploded within her. While small, involuntary tremors buffeted him, his mouth came down on hers and he kissed her with lips so hot she felt her own would surely be seared by the heat.

Then he was still. His lips left hers and went to her neck. "I'm sorry," he murmured and rolled off her.

Suzette began to laugh. "You're sorry?" She turned to him. "What in heaven's name for?"

"For being such an animal that I couldn't wait until we were undressed." He looked down at himself, then at her. And he laughed, too. "Come to think of it, you didn't exactly discourage me."

Suzette lowered her crumpled skirt. "I'd have killed you if you'd made me wait." She laughed harder and put her hand on his stomach. "You were really comical, darling. Making love in a tuxedo. Really, Kaytano."

"And what about you?" He lifted her hand to his lips. "That satin skirt was everywhere I looked or touched. Every time I tried to put my lips on something, all I got was a mouthful of rumpled brocade. Shall we, Suzette?"

"Let's do." She smiled and they both rose from the bed. Minutes later they crawled in between the sheets, their clothes discarded in a heap on the floor. Wonderfully naked and free, they lay facing each other, the lower part of their bodies touching, legs entwined.

Kaytano's hand was at her waist, his dark eyes probing hers. Tears were shining in her eyes. "Kaytano, they told me you were dead. I didn't know you... "

"Don't, sweetheart. I'm very much alive. Don't cry."

"Kaytano, I lost our child. I'm sorry, darling."

"I know, love," Kaytano said softly.

"But how, Kaytano? I... "

"I had Pancho find out for me. While I was recovering, he came and told me."

"I wanted him so much, Kaytano. I wanted your child. It broke my heart, especially since I thought you were... "

"Sweetheart," he soothed and kissed her tenderly. "Don't be sad. We're here together, we'll forget the past. There's only now; there's only the two of us." He kissed her again, gently pulling her closer. "I love you, Suzette," he whispered into her mouth. "I've lived to hold you like this again. I knew I would."

"Kaytano, I didn't know you were alive but still I prayed for you. I told myself you couldn't be dead, you couldn't... "

"Shhh! Sweet baby, that's all behind us. I'm alive; I was

determined to live to see you again." His fingers lightly stroked her velvety cheek, then moved to her shoulder.

"Kaytano, are you safe here? Why did you come to Fort Worth? Why aren't you at Cielo Vista?"

Kaytano smiled and his dark eyes flashed. His eyes moved down to the swell of her breast and tenderly caressed her. "I'm here to see you, love."

"To see me? How did you know I'd be here? Kaytano, you knew I was visiting in Fort Worth and you thought there'd be a chance you'd run into me?"

He wore a satisfied grin. "I knew I'd see you, Suzette. You see, I've carefully kept up with your every move long before I met you. You have one weakness besides me. Gambling. I knew you'd be in the casino during your visit to Fort Worth." His thumb began to brush over her nipple, teasing at it until it stood erect, a hard little berry, tempting him to taste.

Suzette wrapped a silky leg around his and smiled. "Guess you think you're very clever? Think you know just about everything, don't you, half-breed?" Her eyes were filling with desire once again.

"I know everything about you, Suzette. I spent the happiest hours of my life learning your secrets." He brushed his lips over her aching breast, lifted his head and smiled.

A soft white hand slid down over Kaytano's chest to his flat abdomen. Muscles tightened under her gentle touch and she said teasingly, "If you know everything about me, Indian, then you must know that at this minute I think I shall scream if you don't make love to me again." She leaned to him and began to kiss his chest, opening her mouth to tickle him with her tongue.

A lean brown hand pulled her head away and hard, burning lips came down on hers, kissing her passionately.

Suzette's lips were just as heated. Her mouth opened to his, eager to feel his plundering tongue deep inside. She didn't have long to wait. He was kissing her with searing urgency and his hands were sweeping over her naked body, arousing, stroking, stimulating, as only he knew how. Animal sounds came from deep in Suzette's throat as she abandoned herself to carnal pleasure, caring not at all if their loving was right or wrong.

As with the first time Kaytano had taken her on that warm night so long ago, Suzette wanted nothing more from life than to lie in Kaytano's arms while he brought her exquisite joy. To be held and touched while his beautiful dark eyes watched her was ecstasy beyond compare.

Kaytano began to whisper words of love while he gently eased her onto her back and shifted his weight. His dark eyes were intense with passion and Suzette closed hers and felt his mouth come down on her breasts, his sharp teeth raking over the nipples before he began gently to suck, drawing tenderly on her while she clutched his dark head and pressed him to her.

He felt her wince as his hard, determined flesh entered her. His thrusts were insistent, but slow. Kaytano wanted to prolong her pleasure. Murmuring to each other, they moved together, and try as he might to keep the pace slow, his hunger for her was too great, her nearness too new, the sweetness of her soft, warm body too intoxicating. Soon he was thrusting fiercely into her, unable to stem the tide of raging passion sweeping over them both. Together they rushed headlong into a red-hot release that left them shaken and clinging to each other, terms of endearment spilling from their lips.

"Was that better?" He nuzzled her ear, his breathing still rapid.

Suzette, her blond hair fanned out on the pillow, lay on her back licking her dry lips. "It was wonderful, darling," she whispered, her eyes closing.

He leaned up on an elbow to study her beautiful, flushed face. "Stay with me forever?"

She didn't open her eyes. Nodding her head yes, she smiled lazily. They lay together then, quietly talking, saying little. The conversation was mostly the talk of two lovers. Finally, spent and happy, they fell asleep.

With the first loud rap at the door, Kaytano's dark head

raised from the pillow and instinctively his hand clamped firmly over Suzette's trembling mouth just as she opened her eyes in shock and fear.

40

The Prairie Echo
January 17, 1881
Jacksboro, Texas

PRINCE OF DARKNESS SEIZED

The infamous Kaytano was arrested last night in his opulent hotel suite at the Mansion in Fort Worth, Texas. The half-breed was sought for a number of outstanding crimes.

Sources say a beautiful blond companion was with the outlaw when he was apprehended, but Kaytano gallantly kept her identity secret, saying she was innocent of any crime and unaware he was a bandit. He warned Tarrant County authorities that if they wanted him confined without trouble, the lady must be allowed to leave.

Under heavy guard the Prince of Darkness was taken to the Fort Worth city jail. U.S. marshals will soon relieve the local lawmen of their famed guest, for Kaytano will be incarcerated in a federal facility.

Austin lowered the newspaper to his lap, then sighed and closed his eyes. When he opened them, he lifted the paper and again read the article. Rising, he walked to the fireplace and tossed the paper into the flames. He stood watching as the paper quickly ignited and within seconds was nothing more than gray ash. But Austin could still see every word clearly: "... sources say a beautiful blond companion was with the outlaw..."

Austin lifted his palms to his throbbing temples and pressed. It did little good; he couldn't drive the torturous thoughts out of his mind. Perhaps whiskey could. The cut-crystal decanter was half full when Austin poured himself a drink and sat down in his easy chair by the fire. Suzette was to return tomorrow. Would she come? Did he want her to come? Had she been in the Mansion Hotel with Kaytano? Why in hell didn't he make sure the half-breed was dead when he left him wounded at the Cathedral Peak cabin?

Suzette hugged Anna good-bye. In Anna's eyes was a look Suzette could not deny. Her best friend did not approve of her. Suzette had told Anna and Perry the truth about her relationship with Kaytano. She'd told them she loved the half-breed, had spent the night with him at the Mansion, was there when the authorities came for him, and that she was going home to tell Austin she could no longer live with him.

Anna had said she understood, but Suzette knew that she didn't. Anna and Perry had always been fond of Austin, and the couple found it impossible to understand how Suzette could betray a man so kind and good. There was no way she could explain.

She waved good-bye and boarded the Butterfield stage. As it pulled away, she saw that Anna, her husband's arm around her, was crying. Suzette wasn't sure if Anna cried for Austin or for her, or for them both, but Suzette had a feeling that she'd not be seeing Anna and Perry and their two children again.

Suzette swallowed and leaned her head back against the hard leather seat. She was tired from the sleepless night she'd spent and she was very sad. She'd found her love only to lose him again. Even now while she began the journey to Jacksboro, Kaytano was locked up, never to be released, and it was all because of her. He had come to Fort Worth to see her. She was responsible for his capture.

Suzette sighed. If she never saw Kaytano again, she could no longer live with Austin. She loved Kaytano and would until her life ended. It was not fair to stay with Austin, to live a lie. She'd tell him as soon as she got back. She'd confess everything and then she'd pack a few things and leave. She'd give Austin a divorce. He was rich and handsome, and many women would love to be his wife; he was still young enough to find happiness. She wanted him to be happy; she hoped he would be someday. And she hoped that someday he would forgive her.

After a long afternoon of drinking alone, Austin looked up and smiled when Tom Capps came up to the house at dusk. Austin told Tom he wanted to go into Jacksboro and have a drink at the Longhorn Saloon. Tom quickly agreed, though he thought Austin was in no condition to leave the ranch. Tom knew Austin was drunk and would be drunker before the evening was over, but if Austin was determined to go to town, Tom wanted to be there to look after him.

It was nearing midnight as Austin and Tom sat at a corner table in the Longhorn. Both were drunk. Austin talked, Tom listened.

Lifting a shot glass of whiskey to his lips, Austin said thoughtfully, "You know, Tom, I should never have brought her back. I should have left her with Kaytano."

"Austin, what the hell do you mean? The bastard captured her, held her against her will. Have you lost your mind?"

Austin smiled sadly. "Yes, I believe I have. And I'll tell you why. Suzette loves Kaytano." He took a drink and wiped his mouth on the back of his hand.

Tom leaned across the table. "Listen to me, Austin. I'm sure there was some attraction between the two. He had her quite a while and he's notorious with the ladies. But she's back now and she'll forget all about him. Remember this, old friend, it took you a long time to get her to marry you, but finally she fell into your arms and you two were happy till that outlaw grabbed her."

"Yes, I guess we were," Austin said tonelessly.

"And you'll be happy again, mark my words. Give her some time, she's young, she'll..."

"No, Tom," Austin said sadly. "It's different now." He poured another drink. "When I married Suzette, she didn't love me, but she had never loved any other man. Now that she's lived with Kaytano, loved Kaytano, she'll never again be happy with me."

"Now, Austin, I'm not sure..."

"I am. I should know. I was happy enough living with Beth, but I could never be happy with someone like her now, not after Suzette. Once you've lived with someone you're in love with... well... and, too, Kaytano is alive. They took him from a hotel room..."

"I saw the paper. Austin, I wish to hell there was something I could do." Tom frowned.

Austin said, "You are doing something. You're sitting here listening to the pathetic babbling of a rejected old man."

A loud voice cut across the room, followed by a man's derisive laugh. Austin rose from his chair. His gun cleared his holster and the man who'd said Suzette Brand was a whore who slept with Indians lay dead on the barroom floor. Red Wilson, intending to bait the drunken Austin, had gotten more than he expected. Austin's gray eyes swept the room, his gun still raised.

"Anybody else think my wife is less than a lady?" he said, slurring his words.

There wasn't a sound. The man with the withered arm standing at the end of the bar waited for Austin to turn his back. His judgment sorely impaired, Austin did just that.

Tom shouted at him, but it was too late. Norman Taylor put a bullet in the center of Austin Brand's back. Before Austin slumped to the floor, Tom killed Taylor. Austin, his eyes already glazed, crumpled. "Did you get him?" Austin asked Tom when his old friend bent over him.

"Yeah, Austin, they're both dead. You killed Red Wilson. Norman Taylor plugged you, I killed Taylor."

Austin lay on his back. "Tom, you laid me in a puddle of water. My back's wet."

"I did," Tom said, fighting back tears, "I'm sorry Austin."

Austin grabbed Tom's shoulder with what little strength he had left. "Promise me you'll watch after Suzette for me, Tom. You know she's just... she's only a... she's my little girl and I... "

Tom nodded, the tears running freely down his weather-beaten face now. Austin Brand never finished the sentence.

The cold winter rains continued throughout the funeral. Austin's big coffin, draped with a Confederate flag, lay under a huge tarp. Suzette, seated in front of the casket, could hear the big drops of rain pelting the canvas above her head. She was sure it would turn to sleet by nightfall.

That thought triggered her tears. She'd not yet cried. Now as she sat saying good-bye, she remembered the cold January day that Austin had driven her through the sleet into town to make her his wife.

A lone tear slid down her cheek, but it was quickly followed by others. She bowed her head and wept. When the dreary service had ended and the huge crowd was departing, Suzette noticed Anna and Perry standing under the tarp. They came forward, but it was obvious they'd come out of their high regard for Austin; after no more than a handshake, they made their way to their buggy.

Suzette gripped the Confederate flag in both hands and walked to the coffin, oblivious to the stragglers watching her. When a strong hand grasped her shoulder, she looked up into Tom's creased, sympathetic face. She blinked her eyes in acknowledgment. Then she knelt before the big bronze coffin and put a gloved hand out to it.

"I'm sorry, Austin," she whispered as she leaned forward and kissed the cold metal.

"Are you certain you want to do this, Suzette?" Tom Capps stood in the library, warming his hands in front of the fire.

"Yes, Tom." Suzette opened the heavy drapes to let the bright March sun stream into the room. "You're to immediately start the search for a buyer. Let's try to find a syndicate or individual that will leave all the men in place. I don't want to see anyone out of work. If it takes some time, that's fine. I've no real plans, so there's no rush."

"Ma'am, I wish I could change your mind. Austin left it all to you because it's your home. It's where you belong."

Suzette walked over to Tom and looked up at him. "Tom, you were his best friend. You two talked so you must know about Kaytano." She lowered her eyes briefly, then took a deep breath, lifted her head, and continued. "I just don't feel right about living here. It's not my home. I don't deserve to live here. You see, I wasn't a fit wife to Austin and I . . . "

Tom threw up his hand. "Don't, Suzette. That's not true. The whole terrible ordeal is in the past. You couldn't help what happened."

"Tom Capps, you're a fine, understanding man. No wonder Austin thought so much of you." She smiled and touched his shoulder. "Sell the ranch for me, Tom. I'll see you get a healthy commission and retain your place here with the new owners." She hesitated before she said quietly, "I don't want to live here, Tom. I'll move to Fort Worth or Dallas. People look down on me here. I want to get away."

"I understand." Tom nodded sadly.

Suzette took one last look around the blue bedroom. "That about does it, Kate," she said to the helpful woman closing the big trunk.

"Don't go, Mrs. Brand," Kate tried.

Suzette smiled. "Oh, Kate, I must. The new owners will be arriving next week." She went over to the woman and slipped an arm around her thick waist. "Now, you're going to love the Morrisons. Mrs. Morrison is a lovely woman, and with three little girls she'll sure need your help."

"I suppose," Kate conceded. When Suzette turned to leave

the room, Kate stopped her. "Won't you let me cook you a birthday supper?"

"Kate, you're thoughtful, but thanks, no. I'd just as soon forget today is my birthday."

Suzette hurried down the stairs and into the library. *The Prairie Echo* was on the desk where Denis Sanders had left it. Holding her breath, Suzette snatched it up, hoping against hope that she would read of another daring escape by her beloved Kaytano. She was sure he'd slip from their clutches again.

But this time the front page bore his fate — and her own: KAYTANO TO HANG TODAY! She didn't bother to read the article.

A week ago, under heavy guard, Kaytano had been transported back to Fort Worth from the federal prison in El Paso. There, on this seventeenth day of May 1881, he was to go to the gallows.

In the early afternoon, Suzette rode over to the old Foxworth ranch. A family named Bates occupied the house; the man was an employee of the Brand ranch. Suzette was greeted by Mrs. Bates, who was busy making lye soap in the backyard. She assured Suzette that she was more than welcome to visit the small enclosed plot where Blake and Lydia Foxworth were buried.

Suzette looked down at the identical headstones, then began to speak. She was dry-eyed as she told her parents how much she loved them and how she had made arrangements to have their resting place tended. She knelt and gently laid a rosebud across each grave.

When she neared her horse, she saw a pretty young girl run out of the house to meet a young cowboy. The rider swung down from his mount and rushed to the blond girl, wrapping his long arms about her slim waist. Suzette smiled. Sixteen-year-old Betty Bates was shyly embracing her beau, an eighteen-year-old horse wrangler named Denis Sanders. The youngsters never noticed Suzette's presence. She mounted and rode away.

She rode directly to the small graveyard on the Brand ranch. Beneath a giant oak tree, three graves had been placed side by side. One had new dirt on it, but already the spring grass was claiming it for its own. Austin lay buried beside Beth and his beloved daughter, Jenny. Suzette stood under the big tree, the breeze lifting wisps of hair about her face, then bent down to touch the smooth, cool marble headstone marking the newest grave.

"Austin," she whispered, "dear Austin."

At sundown Suzette sat alone on the long gallery, rocking in Austin's favorite chair. Her fingers held the wooden arms as she laid her head against the high caned back, her eyes moving restlessly over the rolling prairie.

A decade ago this very day she had turned sixteen. Suzette sighed wistfully. It had all been in front of her on that sweet spring night. Now it was all behind her. At twenty-six, her life was over.

Suzette lifted her head and shook it soundly. No! Life was not over. She was alive and she'd keep pressing on. And if nothing wonderful ever happened to her again, didn't she have more glorious memories than one woman deserved?

Her handsome daddy and beautiful mother handing her the tiny gold locket on her sixteenth birthday as she vowed to wear it forever.

Luke Barnes, so young, so full of life, proudly tying the red bandanna about his neck.

Austin Brand, elegant and handsome in dark evening clothes, sweeping her up the steps to Delmonico's on a cold New York night.

Romantic midnight suppers aboard the Alpha.

Kaytano holding her on his shoulders beneath Capote Falls.

Kaytano splashing through the fountains outside their Cielo Vista bedroom. Kaytano prowling through the cloud forest in breechcloth and moccasins, his dark hair tied back with a headband. Kaytano's dark, lean fingers dropping a red chip on top of hers at the roulette table. Kaytano. Kaytano. Kaytano.

The sun had slipped below the horizon, but an orange glow still lit the sky. All was quiet except for the occasional lonely call of a whippoorwill. Suddenly the cry of the whippoorwill sounded like... like... Suzette strained to listen. The call was louder. The bird flew away and all was quiet again. Suzette relaxed.

Again she heard it, but she saw no whippoorwill. The sound was nearer and Suzette's heart began to pound. Clear and distinct, the eerie call she remembered so well drifted toward her on the still evening air. Suzette began to smile. And she began to eagerly scan the horizon.

Over a ridge to the west a lone rider loped into sight. The horse he rode was coal-black, his sleek, powerful body shiny. The tall, slim rider was dressed all in black. Hatless, his blue-black hair was as shiny as the horse's coat. The rider was urging his steed toward the mansion. And he was whistling — a spine-tingling call that brought happy laughter to Suzette's lips.

Lifting her skirts, Suzette fairly tumbled down the porch steps. Across the big yard she ran, trying in vain to pucker her lips and answer his call. It was impossible: she was laughing too hard and her lips refused to obey her.

She was out of the yard now, running swiftly across the rolling green plains. The rider galloped to meet her. In seconds he reached her and a pair of strong hands reached down and lifted Suzette easily up into the saddle in front of him. His arms surrounded her and pressed her close to his hard chest as they thundered across the prairie, heading southwest. Laughing and crying, Suzette clung to the rider and covered his dark, smiling face with kisses, joyfully shouting his name.

"Kaytano!"

RECKLESS LOVE

MADELINE BAKER

"Madeline Baker's Indian romances should not be missed!"
—*Romantic Times*

Joshua Berdeen is the cavalry soldier who has traveled the country in search of lovely Hannah Kincaid. Josh offers her a life of ease in New York City and all the finer things.

Two Hawks Flying is the Cheyenne warrior who has branded Hannah's body with his searing desire. Outlawed by the civilized world, he can offer her only the burning ecstasy of his love. But she wants no soft words of courtship when his hard lips take her to the edge of rapture...and beyond.

_3869-2 $5.99 US/$7.99 CAN

LEIGH GREENWOOD

The Cowboys BUCK

Golden-haired and blue-eyed, Hannah is lovely enough to make any man forget the past. Any man except Buck Hogan. For though she has more than fulfilled the promise of beauty in the fourteen-year-old girl he once knew, Buck will always remember that back then he was her father's whipping boy. Now he will have his revenge by taking the old man's ranch and making it his own. But he is falling in love with Hannah, whose gentle sweetness can heal his battered heart if he will only let her.

___4360-2 $5.99 US/$6.99 CAN

Dorchester Publishing Co., Inc.
P.O. Box 6640
Wayne, PA 19087-8640

Please add $1.75 for shipping and handling for the first book and $.50 for each book thereafter. NY, NYC, and PA residents, please add appropriate sales tax. No cash, stamps, or C.O.D.s. All orders shipped within 6 weeks via postal service book rate. Canadian orders require $2.00 extra postage and must be paid in U.S. dollars through a U.S. banking facility.

Name_____
Address_____
City_____ State_____ Zip_____
I have enclosed $_____ in payment for the checked book(s).
Payment <u>must</u> accompany all orders. ☐ Please send a free catalog.

ATTENTION ROMANCE CUSTOMERS!

SPECIAL TOLL-FREE NUMBER
1-800-481-9191

Call Monday through Friday
**10 a.m. to 9 p.m.
Eastern Time**
*Get a free catalogue,
join the Romance Book Club,
and order books using your
Visa, MasterCard,
or Discover*®

Leisure
Books

GO ONLINE WITH US AT DORCHESTERPUB.COM